The author's first attempt at fiction was on a train, visiting his brother and his wife, shortly after his own wife for thirty years had died. On that long journey from Penzance to Ipswich, he wrote 'The Banquet': a light hearted tale of a Georgian squire trying to marry off his three daughters. He found that writing was therapeutic and he then became addicted to it.

'A Pair of Dolphins' came to him much later when his grandson became a teenager. Comparing the privileged life of a teenager today with his fifty years previously, he remembered the austerity of those times and knew there was a good story in the offing!

A PAIR OF DOLPHINS

Peter Edgemoores

A Pair Of Dolphins

Vanguard Press

VANGUARD PAPERBACK

© Copyright 2003
Peter Edgemoores

The right of Peter Edgemoores to be identified as author of
this work has been asserted by him in accordance with the
Copyright, Designs and Patents Act 1988

A CIP catalogue record for this title is
available from the British Library
ISBN 1 843860 17 1

Vanguard Press is an imprint of
Pegasus Elliot MacKenzie Publishers Ltd.
www.pegasuspublishers.com

First Published in 2003

Vanguard Press
Sheraton House Castle Park
Cambridge England

Printed & Bound in Great Britain

Dedication

With thanks to my wife, Lorraine and her friend,
Jackie, who did all the work on the computer for me.

Tribute

In remembrance of all those friends I grew up with, and to those of my parents' generation who helped and befriended me; many of whom have now passed on; and all those sea-faring voyagers, fishermen, boat and ship builders who give Appledore and Bideford the special place in history that it deserves

CHAPTER ONE

The piercing, staccato, drumming din of the rivet gun clattered off the steel plates of the small coaster laid up in Richmond dry-dock. It reverberated up the steep hill to the substantial Manse on the corner of Odun Road and terraced onto the more imposing Odun Hall. The clatter penetrated the open bedroom window as Paul awoke to another day of his school summer holidays, only recently started.

He was used to the noise but not the present humid weather during this unusually warm summer. As he got out of bed he looked out of the window to check the weather situation. He knew that his friend, Barry, would still be suffering from asthma on this windless, muggy August morning during the austere days of 1954.

Paul decided he would cycle out to Greysands Point. He could hear the strains of an orchestral work of Bach, coming up the stairs from the radio in the dining room, where his father, the Reverend Stephen Baxter, Congregational Minister, was having his breakfast. Paul quickly washed, dressed and went down to have his breakfast.

"What are you going to do today now Barry is poorly?" asked his mother, after Paul had finished his boiled egg and got up from the breakfast table.

"Oh, I think I will just go for a cycle ride Mum," said Paul, feeling claustrophobic and keen to get off. He opened the back door and walked out into the quaint semi-circular courtyard which housed the coal bunker where he kept his bike. The humming-bird hawk-moths were already hovering over the lavender in the border atop the high wall, which looked down on the exterior of the kitchen with the meat safe on the wall. Steep steps led up to the cottage garden which had a summer house in the corner with yellow climbing roses growing up the sides, over the roof and top of the wall.

Paul pulled out his Raleigh Sports bike opened the yard door and was off down the hill, cycling past the hammering and banging noises in the dry dock and along Marine Parade. He turned the corner which came out onto the quayside. He stopped his bike and looked at the ketch '*Irene*' and the three-masted schooner '*Kathleen and May*', the remaining sailing vessels trading out of Appledore, the last seaport in Britain to have a fleet of merchant sailing ships. Paul never tired of looking at these old vessels, moored up alongside the quay, in their evocative dignity.

Paul was brought back to the present by the sound of Frankie Laine singing 'I Believe', wafting over from a nearby café. Paul liked the modern pop music of the fifties and was irritated by his father's refusal to have it on the radio. Paul used to tune in to 'Radio Luxembourg' sometimes when his father was at a meeting in the evening. He would spend time frequently adjusting the set, as the tuner searched for the evasive signal, continuously going off station.

An old fisherman sat on a public bench mending his net. With his navy cap and his pipe he looked as if he belonged to this place, like a part of the scenery. Paul envied him secretly, and wondered if he would ever belong anywhere. It was school holidays now, thankfully, but all too soon he would be back in that horrid place with those horrid, pointless lessons; filing along those endless corridors to enter a stuffy classroom and be intimidated into learning some old clap-trap or other. Paul looked across the mud flats and listened to the gulls' mournful cries. There seemed to be something depressing about tidal estuaries when the tide was out, he thought. It made quite a difference when the tide was in, with the boats bobbing up and down on their mooring ropes. The paddle-steamer made a fine sight coming in from Lundy Island; also the other cargo boats with timber aboard, sometimes listing slightly if the cargo was not stacked evenly. He enjoyed the long summer holidays but Paul also liked the wintertime and the darker evenings. It was better for him and Barry to meet a couple of girl friends then. They could 'snog' away and not be seen, whereas in summer they had to be home by dark. Paul was just going to pedal off on his bike when he saw a pretty young girl, roughly his age, walking towards him. There was a tingle of hormonal chemistry that brought a flush to his cheeks and drew out beads of perspiration on his forehead. She had short black hair and was wearing a white blouse with a short navy skirt, similar to many of her peers at that time. She was carrying a shopping bag. Paul smiled at her and as she came nearer and said "Hello," whilst fearing she would ignore him and walk on by. His heart leapt when she smiled back and said in a Scottish accent, "Hello! Are you enjoying the view?"

Paul wondered momentarily if she was teasing him, but felt quite excited as she stopped,and was obviously not in a hurry to move on. Nervously Paul said, "I haven't seen you before, are you here on holiday?"

"Oh, yes. I'm staying with my Auntie. My name's Maureen. What's yours?" she said, sending him off balance with her forthrightness.

"Pleased to meet you Maureen," said Paul awkwardly, but smiling. "My name's Paul, my father is the Congregational Minister here."

"Oh really?" said Maureen, and Paul noticed a look of interest on her face, and thought that being a minister's son had some advantages as well as disadvantages. Maureen frowned and said, "My aunt is a Baptist, I expect I will be going to the Baptist Church on Sunday."

Paul took in Maureen's youthful curves straining through her tight blouse and said, "That's a pity. Well I won't hold it against you anyway." Just after he said it Paul realised the double entendre and blushed fiercely.

Maureen laughed enigmatically and said, "I suppose you are on your holidays now. Haven't you got any friends to go out with then?"

"Well, my best friend is poorly with asthma today. I was going to cycle out to the Point." Paul paused momentarily before asking, "Do you have a bike here?"

"No," laughed Maureen again "but my Auntie does."

"Were you going anywhere special this morning Maureen?"

"Only to do some shopping for auntie."

"I tell you what we could do. If I help you with your shopping and we take it back to your aunt's house, you could ask her if you could borrow her bike, either today or tomorrow, and then we could go out for a short ride, just to get used to it. What do you think about that?" asked Paul nervously.

Maureen felt in a bit of a panic. She was not used to being propositioned by boys in her holiday location, although there should not be any harm in a cycle ride, and Paul's father was a minister of religion after all.

"Oh I don't know," smiled Maureen, showing her white even teeth in her pretty, open face.

"It's not very far to the Point. You can ride a bike can't you?" said Paul, as he made a silent prayer saying, "Please God, yes!"

"Yes I can ride. Well after a fashion anyhow. I was just worried what my auntie would say," said Maureen, laughing a little nervously now. "All right then," she said shyly as Paul walked beside her pushing his bike.

"Do you have any friends of your own age here?" asked Paul, and was quite pleased when Maureen said she hadn't.

"I came down here a few years ago. I think I was about nine years old. You wouldn't have known me then," said Maureen smiling.

"I suppose not," said Paul, thinking what a difference a few years had made to them. Maureen did the shopping whilst Paul did his best to help, but he got a bit embarrassed when the proprietor of the grocery shop started asking questions about his 'friend'.

"I hope your friend goes back to Scotland nice and brown, Master Paul," said the grocer, grinning at him. Paul beat a hasty retreat from the shop carrying the shopping bag, which he placed over the handlebars. They made their way back to the house of Maureen's auntie, heading west up Irsha Street

"Hang on while I ask auntie if it will be all right," said Maureen. She went inside the terraced cottage and soon came out again with Auntie Florence, who looked at Paul sternly as if she would beat him with the broom that was against a wall.

"Well, you are the minister's son right enough," said Auntie with a hint of a Scot's accent under her mainly West Country brogue.

"Paul wanted to know if it would be all right if I cycled a short way with him tomorrow?" Maureen enquired.

"What! You using my bike? Oh I don't know about that. I'll have to think about it. I haven't been using it much lately, and it will need some attention," said Florence, a bit flummoxed.

"I could have a look at it for you if you like. I do my own bike: oiling and adjusting brakes. I expect I shall have to pump up the tyres," said Paul eagerly.

"How do you know so much about bikes then?" asked Florence suspiciously.

"My father makes sure my brother and I keep the bikes in good order, so that we don't have an accident," said Paul, trying to get Maureen's aunt on his side.

"Mmm…You had better come inside then and have a look at it," said Florence, prepared to give the boy a chance, especially if he might maintain her bicycle for free.

Paul's heart leapt as he opened up his saddlebag and brought out a cloth folder with spanners and small tools wrapped inside along with a small can of oil. He left his bicycle propped up against the wall as he went through the house into the small backyard. Florence brought out her bicycle from an outhouse, which also had a toilet with a high cistern and chain. Paul tried the brakes first, tightening up a little nut on a long thread on both the front and the back brake. He gave the bell some oil after he had taken it apart and cleaned it. Next he turned the bicycle upside down as he oiled the chain and wheels, spinning and cleaning at the same time, also lubricating some special spots on the wheel hubs and three-speed gear lever. Paul then pumped up the tyres and then turned the bicycle back on to its wheels, running a slightly oily cloth over the frame and the saddle to shine it up. He presented it as a fait accompli. Florence was duly impressed and said so.

"M…m…m…. It looks a different bike I must say, and if you have checked the brakes and tightened 'em up a bit, I suppose 'tis ready for a trial. Perhaps you had better try it out Maureen."

"It's all right to take it for a spin then Auntie?" she asked, surprised.

"Well, you will have to be back for lunch, won't you, so don't go too far. You are only giving it a trial today, mind," said Florence sternly, though relieved in her own mind that the boy seemed to know what he was doing, mechanically speaking. Paul knew more than herself as she used to have to take her bicycle along to a friend's house for her friend's husband to look at it, when there had been a problem in the past.

"Right you are Auntie," said Maureen, picking up a cloth left outside to wipe any sooty grime off the clothesline before pegging. Now she used it to wipe the saddle of any remaining grease and grime.

Paul followed Maureen until he realised it would be better to go ahead and open the doors for her. Once out on the street Paul set off slowly, looking back to observe how Maureen was coming along. He could see she was having difficulty with the gears, so he stopped his machine, lent it against someone's wall and went over to Maureen. He glanced back to see Florence still looking at them, her hands on her hips. He twiddled the small round nut on the end of the gear cable, tightening it up around a threaded metal stem. He back-pedalled and then engaged the gears until they clicked individually. Convinced that they were working correctly he handed the machine over to Maureen, who pedalled away successfully. He looked back to see that Florence had gone inside and he felt exhilarated at the prospects ahead.

Paul cycled alongside Maureen to suggest his plan, "We can carry on around the docks and then up the hill to join the main road going back to Appledore, down the steep hill. That would give you a good chance to see how the gears and brakes are working, all right Maureen?"

Maureen nodded, smiling nervously as she strove to keep her balance, as well as negotiating the ancient three-speed gears. They carried on along the quayside, then along Marine Parade until they turned the corner by Richmond dry dock, along the road, shaded by the dense growth of elms, coming down the steep bank that separated the Council house estate from the old docklands and wharves. The cyclists now passed the main dockyard at the New Quay dry dock with its busy noises. Soon, on their right, they passed Chanter's Folly, a tower at the top of a quarry, supposedly built by a merchant to view his boats coming in. Now they were cycling up a gradient going away from the River Torridge, that could be viewed through gateways, until they reached the road junction at Marshford where they turned right. Maureen was grateful to be on the level again after the up-hill pull on the ancient bicycle.

They passed the football club ground, one of the few recreational facilities of the town. Just before they started the wide sweep of the bend that took them down the steep hill, Paul said, "We could go up to Lookout and rest on the seat up there, to get our breath back and check your brakes again before you go down the steep hill, if you like."

Maureen pictured herself sitting on a bench with Paul, and for a moment, thought that it might not be a good idea. Then she thought that if the brakes proved faulty she would feel rather foolish, so she acquiesced.

They turned off the main road, carrying on up the hill past the Folly on the right hand side of the road. It was a tower, presumably built for the wonderful view of Bideford Bay, but now derelict with broken window panes. They cycled up to the bend of the road where the seat on a concrete plinth was next to the path that led up to a coastguard property. There was a public pathway at its side going on down to West Appledore. Paul parked his bicycle against the hedge, near a gateway, and looked out over the top of the gate at the view of the Burrows and the sea. Maureen parked her bicycle on the other side of the gateway against the hedge.

"It's a lovely view isn't it Paul?" she said, feeling awkward at mentioning his name.

Paul swung around to look at her and said, smiling, "I think it's my favourite view, and even when it's dark you can usually hear the sea."

Maureen was disturbed by the romantic connotations, but did not say anything. Paul pointed out the pylons that looked like flimsy Meccano ladders, but were several hundred feet high and used by the military for gathering radio signals.

"My brother and I climbed up to the first platform once," he said, remembering how frightening the experience had been. Maureen looked at him, wondering if he had made it up.

"I'll check your brakes while you have a rest," said Paul, taking Maureen's machine away from the hedge and pressing down on the brake levers, individually, to test them. Satisfied that they were working normally, he joined Maureen on the seat.

Maureen looked at him nervously as he said, "So what do you think of your new passport to freedom?"

Maureen looked blank for a moment, then she said, "Oh, you mean auntie's bike?"

"Yes, of course. What did you think I meant?" said Paul, grinning.

"It's not exactly the latest model," she said, at which Paul laughed loudly. "Beggars can't be choosers, I suppose," she added ruefully.

"Will you come for a cycle ride tomorrow then? We can cycle out onto the Burrows and over to Greysands Point," he said excitedly, moving nearer to her.

"I don't know yet. I shall have to ask Auntie Florence if it's all right," she said, looking around to see if anyone was near.

"You're not afraid of me, are you Maureen," said Paul. He was close enough to put his arm around her waist, which he longed to do, but did not yet have the courage, or the confidence that it would be welcomed.

"Afraid of you?" she gave a nervous laugh and jerkily moved her head sideways to look at him, but there was no real humour in her smile.

"It's not been unknown for a boy and girl to hold hands and kiss, you know Maureen," said Paul hopefully, but not very prudently, as his hand reached out to touch hers. Maureen pulled her hand away from him and rested the other on the arm of the bench. "You said your father was a parson," she said, trying to create some sort of diversion from her feelings. A part of her wanted him to touch her but the other part of her was frightened, especially as they were on view to anyone passing near by.

"Yes, we could drop in to our house and see my Dad and my Mum if you like. That is if they are in, of course," said Paul, knowing that it might be a good move to pacify Maureen and his parents in one move, so to speak. Something to keep him in good stead, by reassuring Maureen of his own background, even if his intentions were not completely honourable. His parents would in turn see that he was befriending a personable and respectable girl. The latter was important so far as the reputation of his father was concerned. Paul had made his own observations and made an intuitive judgement about Maureen in the very short time he had spent in her company. He hoped that her outward respectability would not interfere with any romantic intentions of his. He now sat in an awkward silence and looked across at the old stone wall opposite that guarded the extensive grounds of The Holt, the big house. Paul remembered the kiss-chase games that he and his peers had been involved in when they climbed over a gate just down the road. They had played in the field bordered by numerous trees, giving it the name of The Plantation. This had happened in their pre-teenage years, but Paul thought it a good idea to pass this on to Maureen, to gauge her reaction.

"Kiss chase! My! You Devonshire children must be more," she paused, "forward than us in Scotland. I dinnae think that would be approved of back home," she laughed.

Paul was encouraged by her new found warmth and moved closer to her. "Come on Maureen, I don't suppose you can say that you have never been kissed by a boy, not a pretty girl such as yourself."

"I didnae - didn't– say I hadnae– had never kissed a boy," she now said, embarrassed and flustered into using her broad dialect which she tried to control now she was in England; she knew that the local people sometimes had difficulty in understanding her.

Paul thought it a good opportunity to try his luck, so he grabbed hold of Maureen's arms as he leaned forward and kissed her long and hard on her mouth. He did not notice that her eyes registered alarm and astonishment; her momentary immobility through shock was taken for acceptance as his hand went to her thigh. The latter action brought her back to earth and she pushed him away forcefully. "I think we had better cycle on to your parent's house, don't you?" she said, trying not to smile, in case that encouraged him to start again.

Paul was content to notch the kiss to his belt with the knowledge that at least she was not going off home in flight. Paul copied her actions by retrieving his machine from the hedge and started to cycle along Staddon Road heading eastwards past the allotments, bordering the ruins of the Civil War hill fort. When they came to the road junction opposite the vicarage, Paul stopped, pointed down hill, and said, "My father's church is on the corner of the next road junction, and the Baptist church is a bit further down on the left, as you know."

Maureen nodded, and said, with a twinkle in her eye, "Do they have kiss-chase games in your church then?"

Paul laughed and said, "We do have social evenings for young people when we play postman's knock and other kissing games."

Maureen did not know whether to believe him and Paul could see this by the quizzical look in her eyes.

"It's true. Perhaps you will be able to come one evening. I can always call for you," said Paul, glad of another excuse to see her again. Maureen smiled but said nothing They cycled along the road known as Green Lane which bordered Odun Farm, with it's large old house and farm buildings.

"We'll take our bikes around to the side," said Paul as he pushed the handlebars around to the side entrance, lifted the bicycle up the step and opened the door set in the high wall. He quickly leaned his machine against the courtyard wall and helped Maureen in with hers, stacking it next to his. He walked under the high garden wall to open the back door. He beckoned to Maureen to come inside.

"Is that you Paul?" shouted Ruth Baxter from the kitchen. Paul opened the kitchen door to see his mother with an apron round her waist and her hands full of pastry. His younger sister, Deborah, was helping Ruth make jam tarts out of shared pastry. Ruth Baxter looked at her son and then at the other figure standing behind him and realised it was quite an attractive looking young girl, about the same age as her son.

"I've brought a friend in to see you Mum."

"Well, you could have picked a better opportunity. My hands are all covered in pastry," she said, cleaning them off with her fingers and then a cloth.

"Oh, this is Maureen, Mum. Maureen this is my mother, and my young sister Deborah," Paul hastily made the introductions, realising his mother did not have the faintest idea who his friend was.

"I'm very pleased to meet you Maureen," said Ruth, shaking Maureen's hand, but giving her a peck on the cheek as well.

"Nice to see you Mrs Baxter, and you, Deborah," said Maureen, going a little puce with embarrassment.

"Where's Dad?" Asked Paul suddenly.

"He's out visiting. Would you like a cup of tea, or a cold drink, Maureen?" said Ruth, automatically when a guest entered the house.

"A cold drink please," said Maureen shyly.

"Orange squash all right?" asked Ruth, knowing that there was not much alternative except for lemon barley, which she kept more for winter time when the family succumbed to coughs and colds.

"That's fine," said Maureen nodding deferentially. Ruth poured out three glasses of orange squash, giving the first to Maureen and the others to her son and daughter.

"You seem to have a Scottish accent Maureen, in which case you are a long way from home," said Ruth smiling.

"Aye, that's right," said Maureen, feeling it her duty now to accentuate it. "I'm staying here with my aunt, in Irsha Street, whilst I am here on holiday," she added.

"Well, I hope you enjoy your holiday here Maureen," Ruth said, and turned towards her son. "So how did you meet Maureen then, Paul?"

"Maureen was just coming along the quay to do some shopping in town, so I offered to give her a hand," said Paul, a slight flush going up his cheeks.

"That was very good of you Paul. You aren't usually that forthcoming and eager to do shopping for me," she teased.

"Well I don't usually refuse to do any, do I?" said Paul

grumpily.

"That's true. He's not too bad that way. I just wish he would have a better attitude towards his school work that's all," said Ruth sighing.

Maureen looked across to Paul who looked uneasy and drank the rest of his orange squash down in one gulp.

"We'd better get on. I'm giving Maureen's bike a bit of a road test Mum," he said, trying to make it sound something quite involved.

"Oh really? Well you two had better be off then. I've got baking to do in any case. Nice to see you Maureen," said Ruth, going back to her pastry.

"Yes, well, let's go then Maureen," said Paul, not wanting to be drawn into the school-thing at that moment.

"Cheerio Mrs Baxter, I hope to see you again," said Maureen, and immediately realized that she was involving herself in a friendship with Paul by implication. Both Maureen and Ruth realised it at the same time, making Maureen blush again; Ruth smiled with genuine warmth and with a twinkle in her eye. She saw them out, envying the young couple their youth and not realising that she was a handsome woman herself, just more mature.

Little Deborah watched the couple depart with innocent curiosity. Paul and Maureen were manoeuvring their bicycles in the courtyard when Ruth remembered something. She dashed out and said to Paul, "I suppose you have invited Maureen to come to the social tonight."

"Tonight?" he said genuinely puzzled.

"You must have been day dreaming again when the notices were read out in church," said Ruth, leaving them with another smile across her face.

As the young couple watched Ruth go back into the house, Paul said to Maureen, "How about the social tonight then Maureen?"

"I don't know, I'm sure. I feel I'm being asked by your mother more than you. At least she likes me enough to ask me. I don't know if I want to be at a social gathering kissing a boy with his mother looking on though, do I?" she said, tongue-in-cheek.

"You and my mother are a good pair. Well, you are both a tease," said Paul with a wry grin. "Neither mother nor father will be there tonight, and I really did not know there was a meeting tonight, but I would be really pleased if you could come Maureen," said Paul, pleading. "I'll see you home and then I'll ask your aunt if it's alright for you to come to the social tonight."

"What makes you think I want to come to the meeting tonight anyway. You are taking a lot for granted Paul," said Maureen, not really knowing herself whether she ought to go, or give Paul the idea that she was keen on him.

Paul was not really sure that he wanted other people to see how much he was intrigued by this girl. Suddenly everything seemed so complicated.

"I really would like to see you again, and I should be very pleased if you wanted to see me again tonight," he said truthfully.

This statement put Maureen in a quandry, but she said, "Well if it's a social evening and I am expected to mix with other people as well as you, I'm going to be safe for sure," she said grinning.

Paul looked at her and the truth of what she had just said did nothing for his self-confidence. "Let's see what Auntie has to say," he said, easing the brake lever of his bicycle and letting it start off slowly down the steep hill named Myrtle Street, but known locally as Post Office Hill.

They soon got back to Auntie's house and Florence was relieved that the bicycle was behaving itself. Paul thought this a good time to mention the social evening and asked if it would be all right for Maureen to come. When Auntie agreed to the proposal he thought it a good opportunity to say, "Would it also be all right for Maureen to come out for a cycle ride tomorrow?"

"Where have you got in mind, Master Baxter?" said Auntie gravely, and Paul had difficulty in keeping a straight face, as he could see Maureen trying to stifle her giggles behind Auntie's back.

Oh, just across the Burrows and ending up at Greysands

Point," he said, nonchalantly, trying not to look at Maureen.

"Greysands Point? Don't you go getting in the water there. There's dangerous currents there you know," said Florence, looking sternly across at Paul, who nodded.

"Is that all right for tomorrow then Auntie?" Asked Paul insistently.

"It depends how I feel in the morning," said Maureen, feeling left out of the conversation, and both Paul and Florence looked at Maureen as one.

"I'll see you tonight then," Paul said, as Maureen took her bicycle through the house and disappeared. Florence looked at Paul, looked in the direction Maureen had gone, muttered something under her breath and went indoors as well.

CHAPTER TWO

Paul held his hand up to attract Maureen's attention as she turned up at the social evening, just before it officially started. She sat down with Paul on the long benches which were lined up facing a raised staging. Fifteen young people were there, seven girls and eight boys, ranging from thirteen years old to seventeen. The voices of Gracie Fields and Vera Lynn rose up from an ancient wind up gramophone on a table in the corner, with a pile of 78rpm records keeping it company.

Richard and his fiancée, Felicity, pretty and intense, were lay workers for the small church, sometimes helping out with the services, but helping just about every week with the young people. They were doing a final briefing of what they wanted to do for the evening, given time. Richard then turned off the gramophone and came to the front of the staging.

"Right everyone! I thought we would start off in our usual way with a hymn from the Sankey Hymn Books. Paul! Perhaps you would like to hand them out," instructed Richard, and the obedient Paul did as he was bid, handing the faded and tattered small hymnals around the gathering. An old favourite, 'Will Your Anchor Hold in the Storms of Life?' was then lustily sung, to the accompaniment on the battered, but lovingly tuned, piano by the lovely Felicity, her deft long fingers never missing a note. Her slender legs worked the pedals animatedly within the confines of her tight skirt, modestly tailored below the knees. After this hymn, sung with spirit by the youthful, standing congregation, they sang another belter 'Jesus Lover of my Soul,' in the same stormy vein, was rendered appreciatively by all. There seemed to be a certain amount of emotional outpouring that relieved the tensions brewing up amongst the boiling hormones of the teenagers. Richard then said general prayers them they all joined in the Lord's Prayer.

Duty done, the rows of benches were removed except for

two, facing each other. The girls were made to sit next to each other on the two forms whilst the boys stood behind the benches. The boy without a partner sitting in front of him had to wink at a girl on the bench opposite, whereupon that girl was to get up, walk across to the boy, kiss him and then sit on the bench in front of him. The boy left without a girl in front of him continued in the same way, ad infinitum, or until Richard decided to move on. Richard and Felicity joined in, and much merriment was had when Felicity had to kiss a boy; for some reason a most common occurrence. The chosen boy would end up with indelible lipstick marks on his cheek.

Benches were cleared to skirt the walls, and everyone was given a number to remember. Then a large metal plate was left spinning in the middle of the floor. A number was just called and the corresponding person had to pick the plate up before it landed flat on the floorboards. The favourite trick was to wait until the plate had started to wobble before shouting a number, then if the person was not quick enough, he or she had to do a forfeit. If the person who spun the plate was judged to have not given reasonable or possible time for it to be picked up, then that person had to do a forfeit. Most forfeits involved a certain amount of ritual good natured humiliation, centred around such things as reading aloud tongue twisters. These were provided by Felicity who was also the final judge of fairness. One of the forfeits did have it's compensation. The loser (or butter-fingers) had to pick a partner and do an impromptu Romeo and Juliet sketch, whereby he or she had to say 'Oh Romeo!' or 'Oh Juliet!' This would be done three paces away from each other and after the third pose, the couple had to embrace and kiss each other. Some of the less romantic wags added their own unkind names, such as 'fish-face', 'pumpkin features.' When Maureen was caught out, she chose Paul to be her Romeo and, embarrassed, played it straight, with more 'oohs' and 'aaahs' from the audience, after they embraced.

The last game of the evening was Postman's Knock. Here again everyone was given a number. Four young people were posted to the four small rooms in the corners of the Sunday School building. There was a front porch around from the front of the main church building. A back entrance down a lane provided a smaller access area to the toilets; this tended to interrupt the proceedings because of legitimate weak bladders, and also by those less attractive, or unco-operative enough, not to be picked, who pretended that they needed to go. Another room was used, which was more of an office. It was next door to the most suitable room which was really a large store cupboard with shelves, pitch black without the light on as it had no windows. This was the most popular room for snogging and quick furtive gropes of burgeoning bosoms and tempting rumps. Anything more exciting would not have been advisable in the small time slot available.

Paul became jealous when Maureen called out a number which was not his, and a boy he did not like too much knocked and entered the dark room. Maureen came out later, more dishevelled than Paul would have expected. He had remembered Maureen's number but, smarting a bit, chose another girl a couple of years older than himself, but about the same height. Angela was wearing lipstick and a little eye shadow and although he had thought of her as unattainable in the past, because of the important difference in their ages at their time of life, she now seemed to enjoy a good snog, using her tongue, whilst Paul clasped her buttocks in a sensual embrace and fingered the outline of her suspenders under her skirt. To tease him, perhaps for being too raunchy, or else not enough, she placed distinct lipstick marks on both cheeks. Later on Paul did call out Maureen's number and tried to do the same with Maureen as Angela had been doing with him. Maureen did not seem to want to co-operate with that form of oral tradition and seemed awkward and ill at ease. He hugged her until he could see she was getting embarrassed, and left her in the darkened room. Maureen then deliberately picked the youngest boy in the room, a couple of years younger than her, and came out shortly after a big kiss had been placed on the youngster's cheek.

The social evening came to an end with benediction. The forms, were replaced in the same manner as when they arrived.

Paul walked out with Maureen, and as they skirted around the building to go down the steep hill, He said, "What did you

27

think of our social evening then?" knowing that something had disturbed her.

"I'm not used to kissing games in a chapel. I thought you were joking when you mentioned it earlier. I believe they do something similar in the Orkneys or some other islands off the south west coast of Scotland," she said still subdued.

"Perhaps it's something that goes back to a pagan or Norse past. There were a lot of Norse settlements around here. Lundy is a Norse name," said Paul, trying to cheer Maureen up.

"Is it all right to walk home with you now. It's starting to get dark. Nice to have a bit of company, eh?"

"You'll have to clean that lipstick off, if you're walking with me. I don't want people to think I have placed it there like that," she said, with a hint of a smile.

"Am I so bad, that you are ashamed to be with me?" he asked, pretending to be hurt. She looked at him sideways, wondering if he was serious or not. She took a small handkerchief out of her cardigan pocket and then, licking it, stopped him and rubbed it hard over the offending marks, succeeding in erasing most of the lipstick but leaving the cheeks inflamed, even redder.

"Oow!" said Paul smarting with pain. "Oh, sorry!" giggled Maureen, somehow finding it easy to laugh at someone else's discomfort.

"Were you getting your own back or something?" asked Paul irritably.

"My own back? No not really. I'm sorry. I forgot your number in that silly kissing game, but I didn't know if you wanted everyone to think we were serious about dating, or something," she said uncomfortably.

"Well I'm pretty shy really, but I would like to see you again this holiday. In fact, quite a lot. Is it going to be possible to see you in the morning, about nine?"

"Well now, let me see. Is there going to be any likelihood of any more kissing games?" she teased.

"Well, I can't guarantee that. But I can guarantee that there will not be as big an audience to watch us," said Paul grinning.

"I shall have to see if Auntie Florence says it's all right, I suppose," said Maureen, as they moved along the lane between the Baptist Church and the cemetery grounds. They never have kissing games in that church, she thought to herself, before they crossed over the road that veered around from the coast on it's way westwards.

As they walked up Irsha Street, Paul started to feel tense. "If you ask Auntie about tomorrow, I'll wait outside so that you can tell me, OK?" he said nervously.

Maureen looked at him, thoughtfully and it was not until she stopped outside the front door that she said anything. "I'll see what she says then," and she disappeared inside, leaving Paul with his heart thumping, feeling slightly sick with anxiety.

It seemed an age before she came out again, but was in fact only a few minutes: time for Maureen to relate a censored version of the events of the evening.

"Auntie says it will be all right providing the weather is kind. She says the weather pattern might be breaking up shortly. I think that your stint as a mechanic has done the trick. She probably would not have been too keen otherwise, my going off with a stranger," said Maureen, with a hint of a smile.

"I'm not a strange person. I'm the Reverend Baxter's son," he parried jokingly, although he was very relieved with this outcome.

"See you in the morning then," said Maureen, and was gone, slamming the door, leaving him in a euphoric mood nonetheless.

CHAPTER THREE

Paul turned up at Auntie's house at just gone nine in the morning, with apprehension. Would there be a change of mind and a sour attitude towards Paul from either of the females in the house? They could have fallen out with each other, prejudicing Paul's chances of another meeting. He pressed the doorbell and could hear it ringing indoors. Auntie's face appeared at the doorway, frowning. Paul's heart skipped a beat.

"Er, will it be all right if Maureen has a bike ride again this morning?" he asked nervously.

"Well, I have more or less promised that she can go now, I suppose," Auntie said grudgingly "Maureen says you are thinking of going to Greysands Point. I don't know why you want to go there. It's a bit smelly from the Council dump, where they are reclaiming the land. It's not very far though, which I suppose is a good thing. Nothing to spend your money on either, which is another good thing when you haven't got much I suppose," Florence gave a quick laugh, which was really more of a grunt.

Paul had his own reasons for having Greysands Point as their destination. He knew that there were reasonably secluded sand-hills to be traversed to get there.

Maureen appeared in the doorway having heard what her Aunt had said. She smiled knowingly at Paul as she bounced her bicycle over the step. The rather ancient machine was cherished, nonetheless by Florence, who was getting a little old for using it herself nowadays.

"I'll let you have a couple of pasties that I baked yesterday," said Florence, turning to go into the house. She came back holding a couple of pasties, wrapped in a linen towel, in one hand and a bottle of Corona in the other.

"Go inside and get a couple of tin mugs, Maureen," instructed Florence, and Maureen dutifully obeyed, whilst

Auntie put the food and drink in the saddlebag. Florence looked at the bicycle. Gone were the days when she had used it regularly to cycle into Bideford, up and down the steep hills, to visit a good friend. The two ladies would go shopping, or visit the cinema of a summer's evening. Florence was a Scot who had long ago married an Appledore seaman, whom she had met in her home town of Aberdeen, she had then moved to Appledore to live with him, but was now widowed.

"Be careful now!" she warned, as she watched the young couple slowly cycle up the street. Florence was left with her thoughts and memories as she sighed silently before going indoors.

Paul cycled ahead to show the way, leaving Auntie's little terraced cottage with its hard scrubbed step and freshly painted walls and windows. Up through the narrow cobbled street with other freshly painted houses until they came to the corner; they passed the lifeboat house and slipway, then on into the countryside. Looking back, Paul saw Maureen cycling as fast as she could on her Auntie's low-geared machine. Maureen's youthful breasts swayed slightly as her slender hips moved in co-ordination with the laboured exertion of her pedalling. Paul looked to the front quickly as his front wheel started to wobble and he accelerated out of his difficulty. They had a good view of the sea now, with the Point in the distance.

"That's it over there," gestured Paul.

"It looks great, and not too far," said Maureen, catching her breath.

They came to a crossroads and soon were going down a high-banked lane with hawthorn trees lining it. They came to a gate, Paul opened it and they were out on the common land that had mostly been taken over by cows and sheep. The gate was mainly there to stop the animals from getting on the road. A small humped bridge crossed a stream and allowed the cyclists to skirt the landfill site where the town's rubbish was buried. The gulls were screaming as if the could not bear to part with any of the treasure they were feasting on. Paul and Maureen were on the Burrows now, a vast expanse of sandy turf, reclaimed from the sea centuries ago by the action of wind blown sand. Now it's main purpose was to act as host to an army of golfers; it had been a golf course for over a hundred years, with patronage from royalty. The sun was hot, making Paul and Maureen sweat as they crossed the sheep-cropped turf of the Burrows and headed for the sand dunes to the north. They cycled along a rough road that separated one half of the golf course from the other. Paul slowed down now, so he could cycle alongside Maureen and take in her beauty more readily.

Skylarks soared ever upwards, singing their varied musical compositions, encouraged by the black and white crested-plovers who gave vent to their cry of 'pee-wit' as if in appreciation of the skylarks' efforts. Before the flat plain of the Burrows merged into the wind blown sand dunes, Paul thought a satisfactory diversion might be to watch the golfers from the top of a grassy bank which formed a mini-ravine between another grassy bank and was favoured by recreationalists wanting shelter from a cold wind. It was also an ideal spot for a small hearth, made up from displaced stones from the pebble ridge a short way ahead.

"Shall we have a rest here, and watch the golfers and the scenery?" he said, mouthing his thoughts.

"All right! It's a nice enough spot, with the skylarks singing so joyfully," said Maureen, lifting up Paul's spirits, until a black cloud suddenly spread its ominous shade over his mind.

Although it was the last thing he wanted to think about, Paul found himself asking Maureen, "Do you like school then Maureen?"

"It's not bad I suppose. Do you like it?"

"I hate it," said Paul, "I don't want to go back."

"Oh come on! You've got to go back now, haven't you?" said Maureen frowning.

"I know, but wouldn't it be great if we just cycled off somewhere and forgot about school."

"You're a dreamer Paul. That's what you are," said Maureen.

They stopped, laid their bicycles on the turf, moved to the top of the ridge and lay down. Paul remained quiet and was unmoved by the unending musical compositions of the skylarks, each aria different from the last; he lay with his morose thoughts.

Maureen, though, was content. She was glad to be on holiday in this beautiful part of England. She was pleased with the lovely sunshine and the cool breeze that rarely stopped sweeping this exposed coast. She lay on her back a few yards from him, squinting into the brilliant blue sky with the alto-cumulus clouds moving quite quickly up above. Maureen looked over furtively to where Paul lay and could see he was watching the golfers sullenly. She felt sorry for him if he did not like school, but surely he was old enough to realise that it was important for him to do his best at this time of life. She imagined him being moody and petulant. She had seen a little of that the evening before. He seemed quite sensitive – and moody; what a combination. A chill thrill tingled up her spine. Another sly look revealed him to be quite handsome but thin. She had already noticed that yesterday but hadn't studied him like she was studying him at this moment. He might turn towards her at any time, and she would look away quickly before he noticed. Suddenly he took his blue cotton shirt off to expose his skinny torso.

"It's just as well to let the sun get to your body," he said, looking across to her and grinning.

"Well I shall no' be taking my top off. I can assure you of that Paul," said Maureen, but effected a small compromise by pulling her skirt up a few inches to give her a chance to get her legs brown.

"Shall we stop for a while and sunbathe?" he asked, and she replied in the affirmative with a nod. Paul knew that it would not take that long to cycle and walk across the sand dunes to Greysands Point. He was not the sort to lie still doing nothing for long, even when it was a lovely day. However the longer he could be with a beautiful girl like Maureen, the happier he would be. It would also mean that she would become more relaxed, and what then? After what seemed to be a long time Paul's torso was becoming angry looking; he put his shirt back on and suggested they move off. Maureen would have been content to stay a while longer, but agreed nonetheless. They moved off on their bicycles and went on a short way through the gullies. Instead of heading eastwards, as Maureen knew to be the direction of Greysands Point, Paul was definitely heading westwards. Maureen had confirmation a moment later when Paul said, "I thought we would just pop over to have a look at Sandy Mere."

"What's that then?" asked Maureen.

"It's a small lake formed by an underground leak the other side of the pebble ridge somewhere. There is a thick layer of boulder clay under the sand here, and I suppose it traps sea water and also the run-off from the drainage channels criss-crossing the Burrows," said Paul knowingly. Soon they stopped at dunes surrounding the lake and looked down on it.

"Those children look as if they are having a whale of a time," said Maureen, pointing to a group of pre-teen children on and around a raft made up of old oil drums roped together and decked with weathered driftwood planking.

"Well they are certainly splashing around like whales," agreed Paul with a laugh. Soon the antics of the children had both of them in stitches, until things got a bit out of hand on board *HMS Enterprise*, and blows were struck.

"Looks a bit like a mutiny, but it could be piracy," said Maureen giggling, as concerned parents waded out to separate the feuding parties. The last blow was struck by a girl of ten who whacked an older boy with the flat of her wooden spade as hard as she could against his backside. The father of the girl shouted at her to desist and struggled up to his thighs, losing his footing at times on the slippery clay floor. Two more fathers were struggling out, with the plump mother of one of the older boys, in a one piece bathing costume, struggling on behind. The children stopped their bickering to laugh at their parents struggles as they slipped and fell into the luke warm water. The three fellows seemed to take it in better humour than the plump lady, who on catching up with her recalcitrant son, gave him a hefty slap to the back of his head then pointed in the direction of the sandy beach under the cliff where Maureen and Paul were standing.

"Look's like a bit of piracy on the part of the older boys," said Paul.

"I hope you didn't do that sort of thing when you were younger," said Maureen, with a hint of a tease in her voice.

"I think there's been disputes of ownership for donkeys years. Old car tyres have been brought out here, and big logs and planks, ever since I have been coming. As they don't really belong to anyone, everybody seems to think they should have temporary possession I suppose," said Paul philosophically.

"Yes, they need an adult referee or something to keep them in order," said Maureen smiling. "Is that a job for us for the summer then?" queried Paul tongue-in-cheek.

Maureen looked at Paul sideways and gave him a little push with her hand against his shoulder.

Paul enjoyed the physical contact and said, "Do I take that as a no?" giving a little chuckle.

"You do!" said Maureen with a hint of a smile at the corners of her mouth. They stayed for a while enjoying the water sports and chatting. Paul was pleased that Maureen seemed to be warming to him and much of the reserve she had previously shown had vanished.

"Perhaps we had better be making a move," said Paul, looking across at Maureen to gauge her reaction.

"Right-ho! Off we go!" sang Maureen happily.

Paul picked up his bicycle which was resting against a clump of marram grass, pushing it along until there was a mat of the coarse grass-like plants that favoured this sandy wasteland, and then he pedalled off, keeping to the back of the dunes. Maureen did her best to keep up with him but had to stop sometimes and walk out of a difficult gully, whilst Paul waited patiently ahead. As they skirted the controlled turf of the golf course, the cycling became easier. Paul headed for a natural break in the dunes.

"Over there, is a place to leave our bikes and then we can walk to Greysands Point," said Paul, pointing. They dismounted in the gap and then Paul manoeuvred his machine around to a gentle slope. "We can leave our bikes tucked in under some dune grass and walk from here. I wonder what time it is? Are you hungry Maureen?"

"Yes. I expect it's the fresh air and the cycling."

"I think it must be around noon," said Paul, squinting up at the sun and pretending to be able to tell the time by it's position in the sky. "It would be just as well to have our lunch here and then we won't have to lug it any further, right?" he said. Maureen nodded and they leaned their bicycles against the start of an overhang of the marram grass where it was not yet starting to tumble down. The wind had been cutting into the back of the cliff where there had been no grass to bind the sand together. "We can sit in the sand pit and have our lunch if you like, with our backs against the cliff," said Paul, with an ulterior motive in mind. Maureen paused for a moment as if reading Paul's mind and then pulled out the pasties wrapped up in the linen towel. "You bring over the bottle of Corona and the tin mugs, then," Maureen demanded. She moved out onto the soft clinging sand and made her way slowly until she stopped and sat down with her back against tufts of marram grass that had fallen into the sand pit. Paul followed her along and slumped down beside her. Maureen glanced sideways at him warily, and handed him a pasty. Thinking about what happened the last time he sat next to her she decided to pour a drink of Corona for both of them. Making a flat base for the mugs in the sand she placed them together and flicked the ceramic stopper back using the metal spring As the Corona had been bouncing around in the saddlebag it should not have surprised either of them that it now exploded as the pressure was released. Maureen jumped, then screamed with laughter as the foamy liquid continued to leak out until she snapped the stopper back into the neck of the bottle. "We'll have to leave that to settle for a bit," she laughed.

Paul loved the way Maureen laughed, throwing her head back and gurgling in a very feminine way, although earthy and extrovert. They sat in the dry sandpit eating their pasties, and then Maureen filled the tin mugs with the Corona, not so fizzy as it had been, but succeeding in quenching their thirst. Paul sat wolfing down his pasty contentedly. He looked across at Maureen trying to nibble hers in a more genteel manner, self-consciously, knowing that Paul could not seem to take his eyes off her. She was torn between two modes of thought: on one hand she felt flattered, and on the other hand, here she was out in the wilds with a stranger, even though her Aunt knew him to be the son of a preacher. Her thoughts were interrupted when almost half her pasty collapsed on itself, probably being weakened by the banging about in the saddlebag. She tried to save it as it slid down her front, but only succeeded in pushing it into the sand. "Oh! damn!" said Maureen crossly as she looked hungrily at the now soiled piece of pasty lying on the sand. Paul was just going to laugh when the mature part of his brains clicked into gear and something told him that it was not the thing to do– to laugh at a young lady's misfortune.

Paul moved closer to Maureen and breaking his pasty into two pieces, offered a half to her whilst he picked up the soiled piece and said, "Here you are Maureen, you have the clean piece. I can have the sandy bit and clean it off. It's dry so it should brush off."

Maureen felt a little embarrassed but to save a fuss agreed, smiling shyly as she received the piece from Paul who was rubbing the sand off against his cream cotton shirt, gently using his fingers to get the final bits off. He bit into it not really appreciating the grittiness and discovering how sand can easily penetrate every little nook and cranny.

"So you don't like school much then Paul?" asked Maureen, as much to break the silence, as from curiosity.

"Oh God, no!" stated Paul vehemently, then almost apologetically, as he realised he had taken the Lord's name in vain. "Well you see, I didn't want to go to the school where I am going now, which is the Grammar School at Bideford. I wanted to go to the Technical School at Barnstaple," said Paul, pointing in the general direction across the estuary of the Taw.

"Isn't the Grammar School a better school than the Technical School?" asked Maureen, a surprised note in her voice.

"Don't you start as well. I was hoping I had found a friend," said Paul in a mocking tone of voice, but not wishing to offend his new friend, said quickly. "You see Maureen, I don't think I am cut out for all that type of learning. I can't seem to relate to the stuff we are being taught at that damned school."

He pulled roughly down on a handful of marram grass

breaking it off from the stems and then threw them up into the air, as if to throw his problems to the winds.

"Umm, surely your parents can see you are not happy where you are. Why did they send you to a different school from your choice? They must have known that you wanted to go to the Tech?" asked Maureen, now generally sympathetic to Paul's plight.

"Well, my brother was already going there but I suppose it's because they think that the Grammar school is a better choice. Well academically it is. But that's the point, I don't want to be an academic," said Paul ruefully, starting to flush a little.

"What is it you would like to do when you leave school then Paul? I presume you will not be wanting to stay on and study for university then?" said Maureen, teasing.

Paul noticed the mischievous look in her eyes and let a smile cross his freckled face as he said, "No! I don't think so. I think I would like a job that keeps me out of doors most of the time, like farming or gardening. I help my Dad with the gardening at times, and I have made a bit of pocket money doing weeding for friends of my parents. I've also done potato picking – but that's jolly hard work."

Paul had finished his pasty and was just about to ask Maureen if he could top their mugs up with more Corona, when Maureen's eyes sparkled as she said, "All that potato picking would make your muscles bigger, Paul, even if it made your back ache."

"You're teasing me again, aren't you?" he said, going across to her and grabbing her sides just above her slim waist; he tickled her roughly, his arms brushing against her feminine curves pleasurably and inciting screams of mirth from Maureen. Whilst they were close together, almost in an embrace, Paul's heart thumped wildly as he looked into Maureen's eyes and viewed her kissable lips hungrily.

"Time for the Corona," he croaked huskily, as his nerve failed him and he pulled away, sitting back in his former position.

"Uh, yes. I suppose it is. It shouldn't explode too violently now. It ought to have settled down by now, hadn't it Paul?"

Maureen eyed him with an almost insolent smile on her face that tantalised Paul, but also gave him more boldness and confidence. It seemed to him that there was no real sign of rejection of or disinterest in him. He wondered whether she was goading him on to do something. To kiss her? He poured out the fizzy pop and they both gulped it gratefully down, enjoying the tingling sensation on their upper lips and laughing at each other's burps.

"What do you want to do when you leave school then, Maureen?" quizzed Paul.

Maureen thought for a bit and said, "I don't think it will have anything to do with animals or plants, but maybe with other people – like nursing of some kind or other. I wouldn't mind being in an office as a secretary I suppose." She paused and then said, "We don't have much in common for prospective jobs, do we?" Paul laughed.

"No. You're an insider and I'm an outsider by the looks of it. Never mind, perhaps there are other things you like that I both like."

"Do you like the music that comes on Radio Luxembourg?" asked Maureen unexpectedly.

Paul's face lit up, "Wow! Yes, but I have to wait until my dad goes out in the evening before I can play it on the wireless."

Maureen giggled and then said, "Well my mother likes the modern music, but also she likes stuff by Gracie Fields and Arthur Askey, people like that. But when dad goes out in the evening to go to the pub, we both listen to Radio Luxembourg. Mother does her ironing, and I do my homework, or try to." she giggled again,

Paul said, "There's not usually anything interesting on the Light Programme is there? Pearl Carr and Teddy Johnstone? Anne Ziegler and Webster Booth? Oh, and Donald Peers and his blasted 'Babbling Brook!"

They both had a fit of hysterical laughter, which burst out again after Paul said, 'My dad calls modern music, 'Scat music' and says it is the 'music of the devil'." They had drained their mugs and decided to leave the remaining Corona in the bottle in case they got thirsty later. A rumble in the sky above made them both look up.

"It's a Canberra, from Chiverton Airfield. It does a lot of photographic reconnaissance work, although it was designed to be a bomber. Our first jet bomber I suppose. It keeps an eye out for any Russian shipping," said Paul knowingly.

"You seem to know a lot about planes," said an impressed Maureen.

"I thought about training to be a pilot when I leave school, but I know that maths is something that you have to be good at, and I hate maths anyway."

"All the more reason to try harder at school isn't it?" said Maureen smugly.

This off-hand statement was like a smack in the face for Paul, and smarting, he retorted back, "I've told you that I am just not cut out for studying. I'd sooner study you," and with that he grabbed at Maureen's waist and pressed himself down upon her trying to press his face against hers. Maureen struggled, doing the ladylike thing and not making herself too available. Paul was motivated, by his natural maleness, to discover more about this attractive female, and also felt that Maureen was challenging him to a confrontation. Gradually Maureen's struggles subsided, until Paul's mouth engaged hers and they embraced each other tenderly.

Maureen pulled back, pressing him away.

"That's enough for the moment, preacher's son," said Maureen, a flush on her cheeks, but a half smile on her face.

Paul was content to sit back and admire this new treasure that had come into his life, but knew that he had to take it further as soon as he could. Maureen was not so at ease with herself – or Paul for that matter. She was torn between two choices. She could put a stop to any more kissing and cuddling and play the part of the prude, which was not her really – and she knew it– or she could just play it by ear and enjoy being a teenager. After all, this parson's son did not seem boring. She had known a couple of boy's back home who seemed more interested in football and cricket than herself. In her time in Appledore she had not yet been able to meet friends of her own age. Although she was a bit worried by what Paul might do next, she felt he was sensitive enough not to want to hurt her or do anything against her will.

Maureen moved up to the top of the sand dune and shouted to Paul, "Show me where Barnstaple is Paul. Come up here!" Paul dutifully clambered up and stood beside her, pointing.

"You can't actually see it. It's behind a bend in the Taw estuary."

"It's quite a long way to go to school from Appledore, isn't it?" she enquired

"Not as the crow flies, and I suppose I could have got a ferry across to Instow and a bus from there to Barnstaple. It would have been cheaper for my father to buy season tickets from the Western National Bus Company for the whole distance. Perhaps that's the reason he pushed me to go to Bideford Grammar School. It's a lot cheaper on the bus," said Paul with bitterness.

"Oh come on, Paul! I'm sure it's not that, now," said Maureen, putting a hand on Paul's shoulder. Paul's momentary bitterness left him as he felt her touch him. Her presence was a salve to the general depression that had been building up since he had been packed off to the Grammar School.

The hot sunshine was suddenly curtailed as voluminous charcoal grey clouds started to cover the sky.

"Drat! It looks like a thunderstorm's coming," said Maureen, annoyed.

"Maybe it will go over fairly quickly," said Paul watching the clouds race overhead. There was a flash of lightning out to sea, followed by a distant rumble of thunder. "Famous last words," giggled Maureen, as a few spots of rain dropped on them, and intensified.

"Oh dear, we are going to get soaking wet!" moaned Maureen, as it started to come down in a torrent.

"Let's get in under the bank over there," said Paul running as fast as he could in the difficult soft sand to get to a place where there was a good overhang of turf – a limited protection from the driving rain. Paul dived in underneath and Maureen followed him. Paul pulled Maureen closer and said, "We need to get as tight as possible, or the rain will start to get down the back of your neck, and that's the worst part of it."

Maureen looked at Paul shyly and said, "Well, we can't get any closer can we?" The rain teemed down and soon both of them were soaking wet. Paul noticed that Maureen's blouse was showing the outline of a thin vest underneath, and she was obviously not wearing a brassiere as the outline of her nipples was plain to see under her cold wet garments.

"Are you feeling cold?" asked Paul.

"Well I'm not as warm as when the sun was out," said Maureen frowning a little.

"I'm afraid I haven't got anything dry or warm to put around you. only my arms, they're warm," said Paul shyly but boldly, as he put one arm behind Maureen's back and clasped her shoulder with his hand. Then he was uncertain what to do with his other arm, so he brought it across Maureen's stomach and clasped her hip. Paul was in pure heaven, and the rain did not bother him one little bit. He could feel a stirring inside him that seemed urgent and demanding, but he controlled the urge for the moment.

Maureen was secretly enjoying the situation. She was enjoying the chance of being with a boy from a different background than she was used to. She liked the look of Paul, his sensitive eyes and mouth. Maureen could see he was pretty skinny, but fairly tall and good-looking. She liked his fair skin and tawny hair, quite long, which he continued to brush out of his hazel-grey eyes when the wind took it. Now Paul had his arms around her; what was he going to do next? What would she do? What should she do? She shivered.

"I'm sorry I brought you out here now it's raining," said Paul caressing Maureen's side and underneath her breast.

Maureen drew in her breath but did not move away; said, "Well it's not your fault. The weather I mean." Paul noticed a little smile in the corner of Maureen's mouth.

"What are you smiling about Maureen?" Asked Paul raising the hand underneath Maureen's breast to gently massage the whole of it.

"I'm not smiling," said Maureen, but could not stop a fit of giggling.

"Well, perhaps I ought to stop you from giggling at me," said Paul, and he moved himself around to the front of Maureen on his knees.

"Are you going to propose to me, Paul?" said Maureen giggling again.

"No, I'm going to kiss you," said a determined Paul. He placed his hands on the top of Maureen's shoulders and kissed her gently on the mouth. Maureen put her arms around Paul's back and the kiss got more passionate until Paul lost his balance and they both fell on the wet sand, with Maureen laughing hysterically.

Paul straddled Maureen and started kissing her again. Maureen responded by running her fingers through Paul's hair, the way they did it in the movies. However, being wet, it clung close to his scalp. They stopped for a breather and both were quite excited, especially Paul. It had stopped raining, but they were wet through; their clothes, now having acquired a liberal coating of sand, clinging to them.

"Do I look as strange a sight to you, as you do to me?" laughed Paul.

"Worse I expect," giggled Maureen. Paul stripped off his shirt and started to shake the wet sand off it.

"We'll have to get our wet things off, Maureen," said Paul, taking his grey flannel trousers off and exposing his skinny frame as he stood in only his Y-fronts. Maureen started to get worried now, as kissing was one thing, but a respectable girl had to stop somewhere. She watched Paul laying his wet clothes out on the tussocks of marram grass. Paul looked around at Maureen, who was looking at him shyly.

"Come on, Maureen, you'll never dry out like that," said Paul, trying to convince her.

"Oh, I don't know about that, really," said Maureen, still indecisive.

Paul went up close to Maureen, "You don't want to go home wringing wet do you?" he said, and started to undo the buttons of Maureen's blouse.

Maureen felt a little uncomfortable but didn't stop Paul, who removed the blouse. After shaking the worst of the sand off, he placed it by his clothes on the marram grass. Maureen felt quite exposed as her nipples strained against her thin vest.

Paul walked back to her saying, "Now the skirt," as he looked for the buttons.

"All right I'll do it," said Maureen, trying to keep her dignity as Paul stepped back and watched her. Maureen stepped out of her bedraggled skirt and with a flourish threw it at Paul. Paul grinned, looking at Maureen admiringly, standing there in her white panties and vest which, wet as the blouse, clung to her female curves. He used her skirt to cover his now throbbing erection.

"I wish you wouldn't gawp at me like that," said Maureen, feigning indignation. Paul turned around to spread her skirt beside the rest of the clothes.

"I hope nobody else is around to see me like this," she said frowning again as Paul jumped back into the sand pit and sat down in front of her.

"Don't worry. There's no one around. If there is, they'll be in the same predicament as us," laughed Paul.

"We're stuck here until our clothes dry. What are we going to do?" said Maureen anxiously.

"We were doing very well after the rain started," smiled Paul.

"Well, I thought that the rain would have cooled you down a bit, but obviously it hasn't," said Maureen shyly.

"I know. Let's have a quick swim, then the sun will have dried our clothes enough to put them back on," said Paul.

"It'll take longer than that, but I haven't had a swim yet this year. Maybe I'm safer in the water than out of it," giggled Maureen.

"Right. Come on then. Last one in is a cissy," said Paul, climbing out of the sandpit and starting to run through the gap between the clumps of marram grass out onto a narrow plain of sandy turf, before reaching the pebble ridge.

Walking over the pebbles in bare feet cannot be done speedily and Maureen caught up with Paul only to curse the stubbing of her toes as her feet slid off the loose rocky pebbles.

"Ow! Hey, why don't you give me a hand Paul? This is hard going," said Maureen stopping. Paul stopped and looked around. He came back to where Maureen was and took her hand.

"Thanks," said Maureen quietly as they stumbled over the ridge until they were down on the open sandy beach.

CHAPTER FOUR

The tide was not too far out, and coming in. There were quite a few bathers and surfers in the water near the Westward Ho! side, but not near them. Suddenly Maureen let go of Paul's hand and ran down to the water. Paul ran after her and as they reached the water together Maureen shrieked as the cold water splashed up around her body. Paul felt the shock of the cold water but tried not to make too much of it. They both jumped the surf until they were deep enough in the water to swim properly.

"It's not too bad once your in, is it?" said Maureen, enjoying the exhilarating surf which broke over them at regular intervals.

Paul was trying to stop his teeth from chattering with the cold, but said, "No, not too bad at all. You're not afraid of the water are you?"

"No. We've got an indoor pool back home in our town. That's where I learned to swim," said Maureen, showing off a bit by doing a competent backstroke until a breaker caught her off guard and broke over her, making her cough and splutter.

"Are you all right?" asked Paul going nearer to Maureen. "Yes. I just wasn't expecting that one," said Maureen ruefully. Then she turned to Paul and quickly putting both her hands on top of his head, plunged him under the water.

"You treacherous little madam you," said Paul, and retaliated by wrestling with Maureen while they were standing up to their waists in water. Paul enjoyed his contact with Maureen's body and forgot the cold as they continued their horse-play until Maureen said, "We had better get back to our picnic spot and see if the clothes are dry yet."

"I doubt if they'll be dry yet, but we have got to dry our underclothes now, haven't we?" he grinned.

"While the sun is still shining we can get dried off, especially as there's a bit of wind blowing now," said Maureen, as they moved out of the surf and up the beach.

"Come on then, I'll help you over the pebbles again," said Paul and, holding Maureen's hand, did not worry when his toes got stubbed pulling the extra weight of Maureen behind him. He continued to hold her hand until they reached the spot where their clothes were spread out drying on the grass.

"Right. We can lay down on the sand and dry our underclothes, or we can take them off and dry them better," said Paul, looking at Maureen to see how she would take this suggestion.

"I'm not going to take mine off, anyway," said Maureen, who had enough of a traditional upbringing to know that decent girls just did not do that sort of thing.

"All right," said Paul, secretly relieved as the thought of his own nakedness made him feel nervous in Maureen's company, the chill of the water reducing his manhood. "Let's sunbathe anyway," said Paul dropping down into the sand pit and scooping the top couple of inches of wet sand away with his hands to reveal the dry sand underneath.

"See! The sand is dry here now. Come and lie down here Maureen," said Paul.

"I wish we had brought costumes and towels," said Maureen, the water still dripping off her.

"The sun will soon dry us off," said Paul, as he lay with his stomach facing the sun and his head on one side. He waited in a tense expectancy until his heart leapt as he heard Maureen's gentle footsteps and a soft crunch as her body lay down beside him on the sand.

"This is the life. Better than school any day. Right Maureen?" asked Paul, trying to get Maureen in a good mood.

"We can't be on holiday all the time, now can we?"

"No, but school work is so boring. Look, hadn't you better take that vest off and dry it out in the sun?"

"Stop changing the subject Paul. You might be right about the vest though." Maureen got up quickly and stripped her vest off and squeezed the salt water out of it, throwing it on a tuft of grass.

"Satisfied now?" she said after she dropped face down onto

46

the sand, but not before Paul had had a quick look at her whole torso.

"Yes, I'm very satisfied now," said Paul, as he let his hand gently caress Maureen's back. Maureen shivered slightly.

"Are you still cold?" asked Paul.

"Well, a little I suppose," said Maureen quietly.

"Maybe I should warm you up," said Paul, and he gently kissed the back of Maureen's neck. He continued rubbing her back until Maureen turned over and Paul kissed her gently on the mouth. His left hand supported her neck and his right hand explored her breasts, gently brushing off the clinging sand from her skin.

Soon their passion became more urgent until Maureen said, "Stop, Paul. We're getting carried away. It's no good like this is it?"

"Oh, Maureen, I've never felt this way about a girl before," he said huskily.

Maureen sat up and said, "Oh, really Master Paul, and how many young girls have you brought out here in the sand dunes?" she said, trying to look stern.

"You're the first, Maureen. I've been friendly with a few local girls but, they are a little silly really. You're a bit more grown up I suppose."

"I don't know how to take that. Is that a compliment or does it mean that you think I'm a girl who has had plenty of experience?" said Maureen not sure of herself at all.

Paul put his hand around her waist and said, "I like you Maureen. I like you a lot. I just think you're a super girl. I just want to be with you that's all," ended Paul, feeling frustrated and unfulfilled.

Maureen looked at his face and seeing that it looked sad suddenly felt protective. She put a hand on Paul's shoulder gently and said, "Look, Paul, we can still be friends, well for a while anyway. But you mustn't get too serious now. You understand?"

"Yes I understand," said Paul and gently traced a finger over her breast, ending up teasing a nipple.

"What are your folks doing today?" asked Maureen trying

to get down to more mundane subjects.

"Father will be in his study writing a sermon or visiting some sick folk. Mother will be doing cooking or washing, or out taking part in some women's meeting. My brother will be out with his friends somewhere and my young sister will be with Mother."

"What's it like being a parson's son?" asked Maureen, lying down again in the sand and looking up at Paul.

"I think the majority of people think that a parson's son should be better behaved than other children," said Paul.

"Oh, that's a laugh!" said Maureen grinning.

"You're worse than most. Well, when it comes to girls you are."

"What do you mean Maureen? Do you mean I'm a fast worker or something?" said Paul, not quite sure that there was a compliment in Maureen's last statement.

"You know what I mean." She smiled.

"What is your family like, Maureen?"

Maureen looked sad and said, "My Mother's all right, but my Father sometimes gets drunk and beats my Mother pretty badly."

"Gosh. I'm sorry to hear that," said Paul, who did not know anybody who beat their wife. "Any brothers or sisters?"

"I've got an older sister who works in a shop, and a brother hoping to go to university."

"I wish I had started work," said Paul.

"Well you're silly then. My Mother says you should enjoy life whilst you're young."

"I don't call going to school enjoying yourself."

"You aren't tied down to a dead-end of a job, which is what you will be, if you flunk school," said Maureen. "That's what happened to my Dad. He does a lot of labouring jobs which didn't give him any satisfaction, then he comes home from work and takes it out on my Mum." Maureen's eyes filled with tears.

"I'm sorry Maureen," said Paul, putting his arm around her shoulders and looking down into her sad eyes. "Perhaps I can be a father to you and care for you," said Paul, He realised the absurdity of what he had said as soon as he had said it.

"You? Be a father to me? How old are you Paul?"

"Sixteen and a half!" said Paul dejectedly.

"Well I'm not sixteen until next month, and I don't want you for a father. I need you just as a boyfriend," said Maureen, pinning Paul down on the sand, to give him a forceful kiss on his mouth.

As the realisation hit him, Paul succumbed to this heavenly embrace, putting his arms around her, holding her tightly. This was the first time that Paul had felt a real buzz for a girl who seemed to reciprocate his feelings. He felt an urgent need for Maureen to be his lover, his companion and confidant. Maureen wanted Paul for a companion and someone her own age to talk to, and to experiment in the ways of love with, but in an age when family values were mainstream there were boundaries. Unwanted pregnancies left a stain on families and it was assumed, in most families, that the bride would be a virgin on her wedding day. Maureen was a normal if spirited teenage girl, and hoped that she could control her emotions when it truly mattered.

The young couple writhed in the sand pit, exploring each other's mouths and bodies, until Maureen clamped Paul's hands to his sides and said, "You were supposed to be taking me to see Greysands Point, remember?"

"I think you have already seen the point, haven't you Maureen? I think I have, anyway," said Paul shyly. They smiled at each other until Paul squeezed Maureen's hand and said, "Actually, it's called Greysands Point because of the grinding down of the pebble ridge, to make grey sand over there on the Point."

"I think we had better dress more respectably now. Auntie would have a fit if she saw us here like this," said Maureen, climbing back up to the top of the dune where their clothes lay. Maureen quickly picked up her skirt and stepped into it, buttoning it up as Paul picked up his trousers and put them on, watching the more visible charms of Maureen disappear under the white blouse. Then, fit to be seen by the public, they walked off the sand dunes and across the strip of turf before the pebble ridge. Slowly, stumbling occasionally, they came down onto the beach with the surf nearly coming up to the pebble ridge.

"We shall have to hurry now, or otherwise we are going to be forced back by the tide. Come on, I'll race you, Paul," said Maureen, starting to run along the dwindling foreshore. Paul gave chase as their clothes flapped in the strong breeze, drying out any damp patches. Only the white plimsolls on their feet showed the grey signs of wetness as they splashed in and out of the odd shallows. They reached the end of the peninsula that had curved back on itself, vulnerable to strong tides. An occasional waft of putrefying rubbish anointed their nostrils when the wind blew towards them from the direction of the reclaimed land. This caused Maureen to put a hand over her nose in disgust.

"A nice view. Pity about the smell though," she said.

"It will be a nice, place all along the mouth of the estuary here, when the land-fill is finished. I wouldn't be a bit surprised if they put a road over the top of where the rubbish is now," said Paul, trying not to let the afternoon be spoiled by anything.

"Yes, that would be nice. No need to go scrabbling over sand dunes then," said Maureen, in what was to become a familiar mocking tone. Paul grinned, looking around the vista.

"I hope I can be here with you many years from now when we have both finished school."

Maureen frowned and said, "Neither of us know what the future holds for us. Especially at our age, Paul."

"We had better start walking back to our bikes I suppose," said Paul, a little crestfallen, finding the path behind the pebble ridge. They walked back mostly in silence, although Paul was still buoyant with optimism now he had found someone special. Paul was thinking of the immediate future now. What were they going to do tomorrow? Breaking the silence, he said brightly, "I've got a good idea of somewhere to go tomorrow. We could go through the copse to Bideford."

"Do we need our bikes, or is it just walking?" Maureen asked, wondering if she should slow things down, and tell him she had planned something for the morning.

"We can't really go very far on our bikes. Better to walk it. We can see the river from most of the pathway. It's great scenery," said Paul with enthusiasm.

"I hope Auntie hasn't got anything planned for tomorrow. If she has, I won't be able to come, will I?" said Maureen, scrutinising Paul's face for his reaction. Paul's face looked as if a ravine had opened up in front of him.

"Oh! I hadn't thought of that," he said dejectedly.

Maureen's heart warmed to the fact that Paul seemed genuinely in need of her. "Well, I suppose I could tell Auntie that it's about time the Baptists and the Congregationalists got together for a bit of Church unity," said Maureen giggling. Paul's face quickly changed as his jaw tightened into a broad smile.

"You could say that there is an organised er... treasure hunt, couldn't you," said Paul beaming.

"Oh, naughty, naughty. Telling fibs? No I can't do that, I shall say 'We are two young people who are lonely, bored and without anything to do. You are going to tell me about the local and natural history of the area and show me some interesting places.' Oh! that's naturalism, not naturism, we've had enough of that already!" said Maureen, starting to giggle.

Paul's spirit lifted at the memory of the brief semi-naked vision. He put his arm around her waist and pressed his face against hers. They made their way back to the bikes, finished off the Corona, which reminded Paul that they would need to have a picnic lunch ready to take with them in the morning. They cycled back to Auntie Florrie's house on a wave of euphoria. Their clothes did not show any obvious signs of rain, although close observation would reveal telltale creases. They explained to Auntie that they were able to shelter from the worst of the weather and Auntie did not ask any awkward questions, pleased to see her niece looking happy.

Maureen was a little self-conscious about bringing up the planned excursion through the copse to Auntie Florrie, but the latter surprised Maureen by her acquiescence. Auntie's main worries being that Maureen would be wearing a clean white blouse and underwear. Also, to carry a lightweight mac and woollie in case the weather turned 'funny' again.

When Paul told his mother, on returning home, who he had met, where they had been, plus his plans for the following day, she was surprised, but not displeased. She was not unaware of Paul's unhappiness, although she did not realise his depression was in any way serious. She had assumed Paul had been with Barry, having lunch at his place.

CHAPTER FIVE

The next morning the weather was fine again, and Paul called for Maureen. They set off, their haversacks on their backs; old army ones, purchased cheaply from the Army/Navy surplus stores. They both felt self-conscious as they passed the stares of the residents of Irsha Street. Although they were greeted with cheery enough 'good mornings', they did not realise that eyes were boring into their backs until they were out of sight. Soon they left Irsha Street and walked onto the start of Appledore Quay, approaching from the west, past the boating pool, set in a rocky shelf, where bathing was discouraged after a child was believed to have contracted polio there. A fisherman was sitting on one of the public benches mending his fishing net. As Paul espied him, he noted with satisfaction that he felt a lot happier than the day before, when he had come along the Quayside from the opposite direction, before he had met Maureen. They both slowed down to look into the interiors of the *Kathleen and May* and the *Irene*, the sailing boats resting propped up on their sides against the quay wall.

"They really are fantastic aren't they Paul?" said Maureen. Paul beamed proudly, as though they belonged to him. They had become so much a part of his life, his environment.

"Yes. It would be great to see them in full sail going through the bar, wouldn't it?" said Paul, his eyes sparkling. Maureen picked up his enthusiasm saying, "What about sailing on one to Lundy Island then Paul?"

Paul laughed and said, "If only we could. That would really be something, wouldn't it?" Soon they were passing the bus shelter and alongside Richmond dry dock, sounding as busy as usual with its industrial noises. They then walked along a twisting narrow road, approaching Harris' main shipyard and the new Quay Dock where more industrial noise interrupted the morning air. They peered through a gateway to see the massive hanger-like structure, which housed a new tug being built. The wartime vessels, such as motor torpedo boats and landing craft, had been built for the war effort in this yard. They still built military vessels, such as wooden minesweepers, occasionally.

As the road turned inland, they went through a gateway that gave way to a causeway. The ground around was damp and marshy but there were also lush meadows for cows to graze in. The pathway led onwards to join up with the old narrow-gauge railway track that skirted the bank of the Torridge. This was a struggling branch-line between West Appledore, Bideford and back via a circular route, going through the Kenwith Valley and underneath Kenwith Castle, one of King Alfred's strongholds. From there Alfred is thought to have routed the Danes.

The track then led across to the cliffside near Abbotsham and thence to Westward Ho! where the railway station was now used as a bus station. Where the station waiting room had been, there was now a chip shop and restaurant. Owing to the co-operation between the railways and the emerging autobus in the early years of the twentieth century, it was with probable relief, that the whole locomotive stock was sold to the government during the First World War and, in a quirk of fate, was sent to the bottom of the sea by a German U-Boat. Now the only thing to remember the railway by was atop a built-up causeway, separating the river from the marshy ground, the occasional iron rail, apparently too difficult to remove. Where the small station platform in West Appledore was situated, a bizarre reminder was the near-intact fireplace of the waiting room. Some local wags would tell a tale of the ghostly whistle of the steam train and the silhouette of a Victorian lady waiting at this spot for the 'last train'.

Paul was amusing Maureen about the 'ghost train' when the causeway came to a halt as it confronted a small beach in front of a cottage. They took the path behind the cottage and after a while approached a creek with the large hulk of an old sailing barge, left slowly rotting where beached. With most of the keel part intact, but nothing left on top; the deck planking was in a sorry state. A short way off behind it, was one of the few remaining landing craft from the Second World War, its invasion markings still on it. The pair stopped and looked silently at the old and the comparative new vessels.

"What is going to happen to them then, Paul?" asked Maureen, whilst Paul was thinking on similar lines.

"I expect the old barge will stay just there until she rots away completely, and the landing craft will be towed away for scrap shortly; I wouldn't be a bit surprised. I can't see them being used again in a war. Russia is a big place to invade, but not many beaches as in Normandy, I shouldn't think. What's your geography like, Maureen?"

"Oh, not that good. I don't know very much about Russia. Nobody knows much about Russia. But there's an idea!" Maureen smiled across at Paul until he said, "What do you mean, there's an idea?"

"You could join the forces. You could join the Army. That's an outdoor life," said Maureen still smiling.

"The Army? You must be joking. I am not volunteering to be shouted at worse than school," said Paul, knowing that Maureen was in one of her teasing moods again.

"It's more exciting than farming or doing weeding in somebody's garden," she said. Paul felt a flush of resentment coming up from his collar.

"Well, I heard that Army life is really more about polishing boots and brasses and things in reality, in peacetime. I want to do something meaningful in my life. Something – sort of – creative. Getting things to grow is creative," said Paul, his face flushed and eyes blazing.

Maureen was a bit sorry to have goaded Paul into this last outburst, and said, "Aye, perhaps you're right Paul. How about the building trade? That's creative work too, isn't it?"

"You fancy me as a navvy or something do you?" he said laughing, back to his former self. Maureen was pleased, and held his hand to walk on. Paul felt awkward but pleased to walk hand in hand with Maureen, but too young and immature to want to be seen by anyone else, holding a girl's hand, especially by his peers. They moved onto some shingle and then up a rough, steep woodland path, coming out into a glade at the top, separated from a field by a hedge on one side with woodlands on the other, sloping down to the water. The sun was high in the sky and shining down onto the grassy bank dotted with clumps of the thistle-like florets of the purple knapweed.

"Let's sit down on the grass and have a bite to eat; I have got some tea in a Thermos," said Paul enthusiastically.

"It's a bit early isn't it? Mind you I could do with a cup of tea. I have only got some lemon barley in a bottle. Auntie says it's good for you. All right, let's find a comfortable spot to sit." said Maureen, looking for a clean patch, whilst Paul was looking for somewhere that would be the most private. He opted for the farthest corner, which at least gave a fair amount of privacy from people approaching from the Bideford end.

"Ah yes! This is nice and sheltered over here, Maureen," he said, sitting down, patting the grass beside him.

Maureen had thought that she had found the best spot and was about to tell Paul, but he had beaten her to it. Now she glowered at him, hands on hips,"Sheltered ye say? I thought ye would be looking for somewhere that caught a bit of breeze this hot weather." She walked slowly over to the spot where Paul was sitting and remembered the lightweight mac in her haversack. She took it out and spread it on the ground. Paul looked at her and grinned enigmatically, saying nothing. He poured the tea into the mugs and brought out a couple of cheese and pickle sandwiches from a tin lunch box. They munched away silently, looking through a gap in the trees down to the tidal river, the water gently flowing upstream, lazily reflecting the sun like a silver serpent.

"You weren't serious about running away when you mentioned it yesterday, were you, Paul?" murmured Maureen thoughtfully.

"Well, I would like to in one way. But I think I would be too scared to. After all, I haven't got any money. Nobody would give me a job because of my age, either. Where would I live? I probably would if I felt desperate, though," said Paul morosely.

"Poor Paul!" said Maureen, putting her cup down and clasping his hand. Paul's frustration was leavened by the close proximity of his desirable friend and he grabbed Maureen by her shoulders, pinned her down against the mac, bringing his head down towards hers and finding her mouth. They exchanged kisses, passionately at first, and then more gently, as Paul discovered that Maureen seemed to like having her ears and neck caressed lightly with his lips. Maureen shivered slightly and her breathing grew more laboured. She did not stop him as he moved his hand to unbutton her blouse, to slide his hand under her thin vest, to caress her breasts. It was only when his hand went under her skirt and was sliding under her knickers that she realised, that it was possible for them to be seen, so she sat up quickly.

"I think that's enough for today, Paul. Anyway, you haven't finished your tea. Have you?"

"Ah yes. My tea," said Paul sighing. They packed their haversacks and moved off. Maureen at peace with herself and Paul with an ache in his groin. After a short time Paul stopped by a huge oak tree.

"The path downhill to the right of the tree goes down to King Alfred's cave," he said.

"Is that where he burnt the cakes?" asked Maureen flippantly.

"Could be, but more likely to be a good vantage point to keep an eye out for Viking raiders coming up the river. It's a historical fact that there was a battle between the Saxons and the Viking Danes nearby. Traditionally it was at Bloody Corner at Northam. There is a plaque on the wall there in memory of it," said Paul knowingly.

"Did the Viking Danes get a 'Viking' good hiding then?" quizzed Maureen with a straight face. Paul looked around at her blankly for a moment until the penny dropped. Then they both laughed hysterically at the same time.

"I do believe they did," said Paul, chuckling as he led the way down the steep path, stumbling and grabbing saplings to slow himself down. Maureen screamed as she also found it difficult to stop until they landed in a ditch just before the cliff edge. There on the right was the cave. Sure enough it had a very good view of the river in both directions. They stopped to enjoy the view, picking out the arches of the ancient medieval bridge spanning the river.

"Some people think the Danes came up the river and landed in the creek that we have just passed through. It could have been a waterway going a mile or two inland a thousand years ago, and would have brought them near Kenwith Castle, where Alfred's men had a stronghold. They found that the Saxon forces were more numerous and more organised than they had bargained for and fought a running battle back to where the main party of Vikings were, at West Appledore, their longboats pulled up on shore."

"So you believe the Viking Danes turned tail and fled. That's not the usual picture we have of them, now is it?" said Maureen unconvinced.

"Well if, you think about it, they would have been very vulnerable to an attack by a small army of determined trained soldiers. The Vikings were raiders. Their policy was to pick on undefended villages, take what they wanted and move on quickly. Not to fight a prolonged battle, like the Norman's were prepared to do, later on. Perhaps the Danes got a little too cocky. No! If the Saxons got to the longboats they would have stove in the keels as quickly as they could. I imagine the Danes would have..." Paul broke off as Maureen had a fit of giggling.

"I think you should be a history teacher, Paul. You certainly know a lot about history." Then Maureen started giggling again until Paul saw the funny side and guffawed himself.

"History eh? I know a little about local history. Our Sunday School Superintendent knows a lot more about it. That's probably who I got most of my information from. I don't like history lessons at school. They are really boring. I mean who wants to know about Bismark's foreign policy. I wouldn't mind knowing how the Royal Navy sank the German battleship Bismark, but they don't teach us interesting things like that. We haven't got a television at home, but a friend of mine has one, and I go over to his house to watch 'The War at Sea' programme when it is on. That's history, but it seems alive somehow when it's on film." As Maureen's eyes seemed to be glazing over slightly, Paul asked, "I don't suppose history is your favourite subject either?"

"No. Not really."

"What is your favourite subject then?"

"English and Maths, I think."

"Maths?" said Paul in disgust. "You've got to be joking!" He started forward to leave the cave, almost as if a blasphemy or something unspeakable had been perpetrated in the cave.

"We might as well move on," he said, starting to climb back up the steep path.

"Hey wait for me!" exclaimed Maureen, slipping and sliding back, as she tried to followed Paul up. He came down and gave her a hand. They both reached the main pathway and walked on until they came alongside a garden wall. They started passing whitewashed cottages, quiet havens for retired people trying to get away from the rat race. Soon they came to a junction, where a metalled road converged with the walkway. The riverbank was reinforced with stone and concrete to prevent erosion and flooding. There were jetties and a small beach with small boats moored up to buoys and wall rings. A small boy was fishing with a rod from the end of a jetty wall. They stopped to watch him for a while.

"Do you ever do any fishing Paul?"

"Oh, I don't think I have the patience to stand all day in one spot and then go home with nothing."

"That's your main trouble, I suspect. You haven't the patience for anything," said Maureen keeping up her teasing habit.

This statement stung the sensitive Paul, who replied, "That may be true up to a point. Especially if I am not interested in something. But if I am interested in something, then I do stick to it."

"Well if you can stick with boring things like weeding the garden for instance, then you should be willing to study more at school," said Maureen, knowing that she was treading on thin ice as far as Paul was concerned. Although she was worried about his rebellious attitude towards his education, she had just discovered that he was interested in local history, and he was definitely not anti-social in any way. She was starting to feel a little sorry for him, over-riding the conflict and tensions that tend to keep male and female apart until the biological urges declared otherwise. Maureen noticed that Paul had gone quiet, sulking a little, his mouth setting into a definite pout, which she found strangely comical, though endearing.

They were now on the wide expanse of Bideford's esplanade, with a road separating pavements, and the gently sloping embankment used by the Rowing Clubs – the Reds and Blues. On the right side of the road the large expanse of the playing fields, rugby, cricket and soccer pitches, were now in good use during the school holiday, with the usual noise of excited children spilling out through the mesh of the high metal fencing which stopped all but the unlikeliest of heftily kicked footballs or spooned 'sixers'. In a gateway some boys about Paul's age were loafing, discussing the inane irrelevancies that schoolboys throughout the ages have discussed; they are of course very important to schoolboys. One of them recognised Paul, and seeing Maureen walking alongside, shouted out, "Hi! Paul. Who's your friend?"

Paul was not in the mood to talk much and gruffly shouted back, "She's called Maureen and she's from Aberdeen in Scotland," then walked on quickly, giving a half-hearted wave, whilst Maureen beamed widely as she waved in a friendly manner. The schoolfriend looked enviously after the retreating couple, wishing he was accompanying the attractive, nubile young woman.

"A school-friend of yours, Paul?" said Maureen, tiring of Paul's sulk.

"Yes. Well, he's in the same form as me. He's a bit of a know-all though." Maureen was thinking of saying that at least he did not want to be a know-nothing, but she bottled it up as they approached an entrance into the park gardens.

"Let's sit over there on that seat and have our lunch, shall we Paul?" said Maureen pointing.

"Yes all right," he agreed, brightening up with the thought that his school friend would be speculating with the others, about what they no doubt would look on as a conquest. Something to raise his image, which he knew instinctively was waning because of his lack of competitiveness. They sat and ate the rest of their packed lunch, Maureen sharing her lemon barley with

Paul. They could hear the gentle taps of the woods colliding on the bowling green over the hedge. The murmuring and gentle laughter contrasting with the squeals and shouts from much younger participants further up.

"Got any plans for tomorrow then Paul?" asked Maureen shyly.

"I was thinking of staying in and do some studying," said Paul, trying to keep a straight face, until he got a thump in the shoulder from a well-aimed punch from Maureen.

"How about cycling to Landcross? It's about a mile from Bideford, off a little from the Torrington road. We, my friends and I, used to go cycling around there. It was great for birds-nesting, and there's a stream that runs into the Torridge; the sea water comes just about up to a little bridge. You can usually see a kingfisher or two from there," said Paul, brightening up again.

"Did you used to take the eggs out of the nests," enquired Maureen in an accusatory tone.

"Oh, only if it was a rare species, and we did not have it," said Paul apologetically.

"But the rare ones are the ones that should be left alone, aren't they?"

The logic of this remark made Paul think for a moment; he said, "We only used to take one egg from a nest. There were usually three or more eggs left in a nest."

"What about sea birds? A lot of them only lay two eggs," said Maureen indignantly.

"Oh! er, didn't usually bother with sea birds. A bit dangerous dangling from cliffs, and all that sort of thing," said Paul unconvincingly.

"Hm. Well I hope that is all in the past. I shan't let you go birds-nesting if I am with you," said Maureen firmly.

"No, we are just going to look and enjoy the views. That's if you want to go out with me again," said Paul ruefully.

"I thought it was you that was cooling off. It was you that had the sulks," said Maureen in a matter of fact way.

"I wasn't sulking," lied Paul, "I was just sad that you were nagging me about school."

Maureen put her arm around Paul and said, "Come on, kiss

and make up."

The fact that they could be seen by the public was not too much of a deterrent to Paul, who was glad to get back on the same footing with his sweetheart, and they kissed and cuddled for an hour or so, basking in the warm sunshine. They talked about the cinema, what they would like to do and where they would like to live. They started back eventually, walking most of the way home holding hands or with their arms around each other, until they arrived home for their tea.

Maureen had decided to stay in for the evening with her Auntie Florrie, now that she was going out in the daytime with Paul.

After the brief goodbye kiss, Paul said, "You know my surname Maureen, but you have not told me yours yet."

Maureen smiled coyly, and said, "Actually it's McKenna," and spelt it out for him.

"Well goodbye Maureen McKenna. I'll see you in the morning," said Paul, kissing Maureen quickly on her cheek, in case other people were watching them. They were standing outside the gates of the British Legion, opposite the Richmond Dry Dock, where the paths to their respective homes parted. "Goodbye Master Baxter. Oh! I must be careful how I say that mustn't I?" said Maureen, giggling as she walked around the corner to Marine Parade, before taking a short cut through an alleyway known locally as the 'drang', reputedly a hangout for members of the press-gang about two hundred years previously. Paul walked up the steep Post Office Hill towards home, wondering why he had not asked Maureen for her surname before. He was not always good with names, but he did not think he would forget Miss McKenna.

CHAPTER SIX

They set out for Landcross, bright and early by school children's standards, and Maureen was to test the steep Devonshire hills for the first time on her auntie's bycycle. Paul decided it would be better to start off on the same road that they had walked the previous day, but instead of following the river all the way, they would keep on up the hill and past the football field before turning left to join the main Bideford road. This cut out a killer of a hill. Maureen would find out later that it was an easier ride going into Bideford than coming home, as far as hills went. It was exhilarating riding downhill and she used her brakes until they protested. Paul, who had sped on, stopped at the bottom of each hill to wait for her. He pointed out the memorial stone at 'Bloody Corner', the supposed battle site where King Hubba the Dane was slain; they stopped to read the inscription. Then on and mainly downhill before coming onto the flat wide road that led to Bideford Quay, continuing along the river road passing the bus stop where Paul's school bus parked.

On the left and in the water were various small vessels: loading, unloading or waiting for the right tide to take them anywhere in Europe including Scandinavia. Ahead, the old bridge, with each arch a differing width, according to the funding of the time, straddling the Torridge, with its club feet parting the water. Joining up with the bridge the High Street lived up to its name with a painful climb to the top. Their road followed the river for a couple of miles after which they turned off right, by a chapel on the left. Then, following a tributary of the Torridge, the River Yeo, skirted the district known as Landcross. The river came meandering alongside the road, the tide in a gentle surge covering the unsightly mud, meandering out of sight of them with only the tall Devonshire hedges to look at.

A break in the hedge on their nearside revealed a narrow road to a bridge and Paul signalled to turn left towards it. They stopped, parking their bikes against the low wall of the bridge. Paul leaned on the parapet and looked back in the rough direction from whence they had come.

"You see that bank over there, a sort of low sandy cliff going into the water?" Paul said, pointing.

"Yes," said Maureen, wondering what he was looking at.

"That's where the Kingfishers nest. If you look closely you can see nesting holes in the bank. Most of them will be old nesting holes I expect, but I wouldn't be surprised if one of them was used last spring. I've seen sand martins going in and out of them in the past as well," said Paul, almost proudly.

Maureen was looking at the meadowland and the sweep of the river, without too much enthusiasm, when her eyes were attracted by darting flashes of light beneath her. Looking down she saw that the flashes were quite large silvery fish.

"Look Paul! she said excitedly, pointing downwards. "Look at those huge fish, are they salmon?"

Paul dropped his distant gaze and was immediately aware of them, darting forward quickly up to the bridge where the water was getting shallow.

"They look as if they might be salmon, but it's a bit late for salmon to come up river for spawning. They could be sea-trout. They would be about the right size for them. It's maybe a bit early for them as they are supposed to migrate and spawn in the autumn. But that's not far away now, is it?" said Paul, getting quite excited about their sighting, as well as Maureen.

Maureen rushed over to the other side of the bridge to see if there were any fish there. "There isn't any fish over this side. It's a lot shallower, but they could probably make it through if they were determined," said Maureen. The fish sensed the lack of depth and were broadsiding themselves to turn back into comparatively deeper water, only to try again.

"I think it will be better for them in about an hours time, when the tide is higher. They should get through without any trouble then," said Paul, "Shall we go and explore the woods over there to the right. We found a buzzard's nest in there; my brother climbed up but got 'buzzed' by the buzzards so much, that he was frightened to go right up to the nest."

"Do you mean he was attacked by them?"

"Oh yes. They just swoop down as close as they can to frighten you off. Mind you, seagulls are probably worse, if you get near their nests," said Paul smiling.

"I thought you didn't interfere with them," said Maureen indignantly.

Paul paused, frowned, and then said, "Seagulls can be a real pest. One of my friends had them nesting on his flat roof last spring. Every time anyone went in or out of doors, they were swooped on by the gulls. His dad is going to put wire netting or something at the back, near the chimney, to stop them nesting there next year. We'll just push our bikes up the track and leave them somewhere out of sight. All right?"

Maureen nodded, and they left the bridge behind. On entering the woods they left their bikes stacked against the back of a large elm tree and walked on along the rough track. The quiet solitude, with occasional birdsong, had a calming effect on them as they walked hand in hand.

"Look! A squirrel, and another," whispered Paul. As they watched, two red squirrels undulated over the forest floor, their red bushy tails flicking with indignation as they scampered up the bark of a large beech tree to hide. Paul looked up the tree and said, "I wonder if there is anything much inside the beech nuts? This can be a hard time for squirrels until the nut harvest."

"You like the countryside and the wildlife, don't you Paul?" said Maureen with a warm squeeze of the hand. "You could be a nature warden, but I imagine you would have to have some educational qualifications though."

"That lets me out then, doesn't it?" said Paul wryly.

"There's still time. I bet if I could be with you in your spare time, we could do our homework and study together. Then perhaps you could concentrate better and get stuck into it," said Maureen earnestly and innocently.

Paul said, "I think I know what you mean. I would be more content and have more 'peace of mind,' as they say, but I might be tempted to get stuck into something a little more personal," he said grinning.

"Oh! You are naughty Master Baxter. You have a one track

mind," scolded Maureen. "I don't suppose I think any differently from any other boy of my age. There aren't many of what you would call real 'swots' now, are there?" rationalised Paul.

"Well, I thought you would be more afraid of being a failure at school, than going your own way. You are not stupid, Paul. You know a lot about all sorts of things, but to get on in life you will have to..."

"Knuckle down? Is that what you were going to say? You are sounding just like my parents. I know you mean well, and so do they, but you must realise that I have to do something I'm interested in doing, something with more practical implications, like I would have learned if I had gone to the Tech," said Paul, a redness spreading up from his neck to his cheeks.

"You mustn't keep a chip on your shoulder about that you know. Anyhow, I'm not going to nag you any more about that: well, not today anyway," said Maureen, turning to Paul and smiling.

They found a clearing and made towards a huge felled tree. Maureen had found the old mac, useful for a picnic, so she had brought it along again and they spread out their picnic resting their backs against the log. The silence was broken by a woodpecker drumming the bark of a tree, looking for grubs.

"There are some spotted woodpeckers in this wood. I saw one myself once," said Paul, after Maureen had enquired what it was. "Usually you just hear them, and not see them, unless you are very still for a long time, like we are now."

They munched away at their sandwiches until a large spotted bird flew overhead making a sort of high-pitched laughing noise.

"That was a greater spotted woodpecker," said Paul, a smug grin on his face.

"All right, clever clogs. What is that beautiful bird song in the distance we have been hearing for some time?" quizzed Maureen.

"It's the Common Blackbird. Beautiful song though, I must admit. The song thrush is quite similar, but a bit scratchier. The blackbird's song is a bit more melodic. The thrush's nest is similar to the blackbird, but lined with mud and looks like a coconut shell cracked in half," said Paul, as Maureen made movements with her hands to indicate his head growing bigger.

They sat there enjoying the midday sunshine and the buzz of the bees and hover flies flitting from flower to flower. Having finished the packed lunch, Paul felt another hunger as Maureen stretched out to lay on her back. As she slid down to clear her head from the log, her skirt rode back up, exposing her white panties, her legs splayed apart. This was not lost on Paul, who quickly eased himself down beside her. He gazed longingly at the soft white flesh of her inner thighs and sent tentative fingers to caress the inviting area. Maureen stayed still as if asleep, so Paul placed the palm of his hand to slide over the top of her panties, then under the vest to the smooth round of her belly. A few rotary movements brought his fingers underneath the elastic top of her panties. His finger tips tingled as he encountered the small bush of her pubic hair; he pressed his middle finger along the lips of the labia. He was not to know that the place that gave Maureen the best sensations of pleasure when caressed, was in the other direction. Now Maureen felt that an opportunity had been missed, but could not bring herself to tell Paul that.

Getting back up on her elbows she said, "Perhaps we should be moving on." Disappointed, and deflated, Paul pulled his hand away and stood up.

"Spoil sport," he muttered, getting his haversack together as Maureen did the same. "We could go to Greencliff via Littleham, then look out for the signpost to Abbotsham Cross. There should be a more direct road to Greencliff if we bear left after Littleham. We'll find it somehow," he said confidently. They back-tracked to their bicycles and free-wheeled down the track to the road, stopping at the bridge.

"Let's have a last look here, shall we Paul?" said Maureen.

Paul agreed, smiling and looked for the fish but there were none where there were plenty before. Only a couple of minnow-like brown trout sheltering in the shadows under the bridge.

"The tide's come in a bit more. Enough to let those fish up river I would say. Wouldn't you?"

"Yes, I hope so. I hope they successfully do their business, so to speak," said Maureen giggling.

"What do you mean, their business?" teased Paul.

"You know, their spawning. That's what you call it, isn't it?" said Maureen giggling again.

"I wouldn't know about anything so... Hey! There's a kingfisher on that rotten tree stump. See him?" Maureen looked to where Paul was pointing and saw the flash of rainbow colours as it dipped down into the water and came up with a small fish in it's beak, returning to the same perch to quickly swallow it, head first.

"Oh! Isn't it gorgeous? The colours! They are so vivid," said Maureen in awe.

"Yes. I'm glad you have seen it. There is usually a few around somewhere on this stretch of the river. A good fishing place I expect. I wouldn't mind fishing here if there were as many fish here all the time. It would be illegal though. Especially if fish were spawning. Have you seen enough now, Maureen?"

"Let's stay a little longer and look at the Kingfisher. I've never seen one before you know," said Maureen wistfully.

Paul acquiesced until Maureen said, "All right, let's go."

They mounted their machines and turned left, cycling in the direction of the north Cornish coast. They had to turn off the main road on the right, to go through the outskirts of the pretty village of Littleham. Following the signpost to Abbotsham Cross, they came out onto the main road from Bideford to Bude. Crossing over they continued into the large, picturesque village of Abbotsham where they soon found the turning for Greencliff.

The narrow road meandered down between the high hedges until they came to the path – fields that led down to the cliffs. They were glad to get off their bikes, they were sweating profusely in the hot sunshine. There had been a lot of hill work and they were both tired, especially Maureen, because of her ancient bike and also not being used to negotiating very many hills. Paul related the hackneyed joke of the time – that it must have been a 'Rolls Canardly', because it rolled down the hill, but can hardly get up the other side.

"That's what we could do with!" said Paul, pointing at a shiny new Norton 750cc motorcycle, upright on it's stand before them.

"Whew! That's a powerful looking bike. Do you think you could handle that?" laughed Maureen.

"I doubt it," grinned Paul ruefully, laying his bike down on the grassy bank and walking over to the motocycle.

Maureen did the same and then said, "Nice view from up here, very rocky though. Not very good for bathing." Maureen pointed at the rock pools slowly being covered by the incoming tide.

"It's a good place for finding things with your shrimping net, in the shallow rock pools when the tide is out," said Paul grinning, and remembering an occasion a few years back.

"Drat! I didn't bring my shrimping net, or my swimming cossie," said Maureen with exaggerated disappointment.

Paul was mulling over in his mind the prospect of exploring rock pools – boys and girls never really grow out of this relaxing recreation – when his long-sighted eyes picked out movements in the bumpy hillside below him. He noticed a man and a woman partly hidden from view in a hollow. There was something animated about them, and in a trice he realised that they were making love. He looked across at Maureen, but she had already started to walk down the stoney pathway. He could see that she hadn't noticed anyone and that she was probably short-sighted, the opposite to him. Paul followed behind her, watching the couple writhing on the bank. As they got closer Paul noticed the woman was wearing a gingham-type dress with a wide-low front, with the top buttons seemingly undone. The fellow was wearing the traditional sailor uniform, with bell-bottomed trousers but no hat.

As they approached the woman rolled over on top of the man and now Paul could see the woman's dress was up over her hips, the man's hands were clasping her bare buttocks; her strong but shapely legs clad in black stockings. Suddenly Maureen noticed them and stopped dead, with a surprised "Oh!" On seeing and hearing the grunts and sighs of the engrossed pair, who had not noticed anyone else, Maureen hurried on down the hill. Paul could not move now, mesmerised by the scene, now only about ten yards away. The man had rolled on top of the woman again and was thrusting vigorously, ending with a cry as if he was in great pain. The woman was moaning in a quiet way, until the man stood up with his back to Paul and seemed to be fiddling with something. Paul stared at the woman who had rather coarse features under heavy make-up. As the man had got up from her, she noticed Paul staring at her, and instead of closing her splayed legs and exposed raw nakedness, she let out a cackling laugh which pierced Paul's heart. The shame that might have been hers, was deflected to Paul as he fled after Maureen.

"Piss off you little bugger!" shouted the man, having followed the direction of the woman's eyes. Paul ran down the path with the woman's cackling laugh still following him. He caught up with Maureen who was sulky and quiet.

"Why did you stop and look at those awful people," she said, confused.

"I, I don't know, I suppose, I was curious. That's all," said Paul, flustered.

"You were being a peeping Tom weren't you?" Accused Maureen.

"Um. A peeping Paul, really," grinned Paul, embarrassed but also feeling a mixture of excitement and guilt.

"It looked a bit ugly to me," said Maureen quietly, after a while.

Paul looked at Maureen's sullen face and then said, "I'm sure two people making love is quite natural, and should be a beautiful thing shouldn't it?"

"Well, if they are husband and wife, yes. I would have thought if they were husband and wife they could have done that sort of thing at home. Not out here in public," said Maureen crossly.

"Um, they probably weren't married. You know what sailors are, don't you?" teased Paul, on the defensive. Maureen trembled with suppressed fury, although she did not really know why.

"I'm beginning to be a bit sick of this whole sex thing. I feel like going home," she said defiantly.

Paul pondered her statement dejectedly, thinking of the

temptations of the woman's open flesh just up the hill.

"If you go back home now, you will have to walk back and confront them again. You don't know what they will be up to now, do you?" said Paul, trying to be logical and selfish at the same time. Maureen looked at Paul, realising that there was some truth in what he was saying, and then a thought came to her.

"What about our bikes? What if the man does something to our bikes?" she said with a worried look on her face. "How would I explain that to Auntie Florrie?"

"Why would they do anything to our bikes? We haven't been doing anything wrong," said Paul exasperatedly.

"You have been a peeping Tom, haven't you?" accused Maureen again.

"That's not a crime. No need for them to do anything criminal. Anyhow, didn't you hear that woman laughing. She thought it was a big joke. She seemed to enjoy it. I'm the one that was made a fool of," pouted Paul.

"Oh! So you are the poor victim of a female flasher are you. I thought it was only dirty old men in raincoats that terrorised women, not women terrorising men," said Maureen sarcastically.

Paul was stumped temporarily, and thought that it was a good thing that Maureen had not seen the last thing he had seen. Paul was curious about sex, the same as all his peers. He had never bought any magazines himself because he did not have much pocket money, but he had at every opportunity thumbed through his friend's girlie magazines. These were mainly note book sized magazines, with black and white photographs of young women in various stages of undress, but never without any pants on. *Men Only* and *Liliput* were more respectable, being general magazines, with stories and articles in them, besides the pin-ups. *Spick and Span*, it's sister, was devoted entirely to titillating men's imagination, however.

"Do you want to have a quick look around the rock pools before we go home, Maureen? By that time, I expect it will be, er, safe to go back to our bikes. We could take the bikes all the way along the cliff path to Westward Ho! if you like. That would be an easier ride without any steep hills. We would have to push the bikes to start with, but then we would have a nice easy ride home." Paul looked at Maureen, hoping to lighten the mood.

"Do you mean that we will have to walk back up that hill only to come down again, with the bikes?" she scolded, keeping Paul in his place: on the defensive.

"Well, er, yes," he gulped, smiling weakly.

Maureen watched Paul squirming and explaining how it would save all the extra effort later on, and that they could pick up an ice cream in Westward Ho! Her bad temper simmered down to a sullen frown as they walked down the last part of the steep hill to join up with the path at the bottom. They soon found a cutting down onto the rocks where a few people were already poking around in the pools: as many adults as children. They clambered over rocks, keeping their plimsolls on, whilst wading through some of the deeper parts, with the tide coming in fast near the top of the rocks. In the end it became a duel between them and the tide, with them losing to the encroaching fingers of foam as they surged ever forward. This necessitated a rearguard action, and a scream from Maureen, every time a larger wave than usual pounded the rocks to produce an ariel spray to drench them. They made their way back up the hill towards their bikes keeping a sharp lookout as they neared the spot where the 'incident' had taken place. Relieved that the couple were not in evidence they returned to the bikes. Paul and Maureen inspected the machines to see if they were, indeed, intact. Paul noticed that his machine did not seem to have anything missing, or any tyres let down and, in fact, seemed to have acquired another object for it's inventory.

"What's that, hanging from the crossbar?" enquired Maureen, who had picked up her bike, ready to move off, when she noticed Paul staring at something.

A whitish balloon-like appendage, tied with a simple knot to the crossbar confronted Paul, who was momentarily puzzled until it dawned on him. He remembered a get-together with some of his brother's older acquaintances on the sand dunes at Westward Ho! on a previous occasion. Then a youngster in his late teens had been handing around a packet of protective sheaths, or 'Johnnies' as he was informed. The individual was boasting of his familiarity with the rubber apparatus and how it was used. Paul untied the knot and threw it into the hedge, rubbing his fingers on the legs of his trousers.

"Well, what was it?" enquired the innocent voice of Maureen.

"Well, it was what the fellow used on his, doo-dah. You know!" said Paul, unsure of whether he should make a joke of it. Maureen's face screwed up in disgust.

"Oh! The beastly thing. Come on Paul, let's get away from this horrible place.

"They free-wheeled slowly down the hill with one foot on the pedal, both hands on the brakes and the other foot just touching the ground, to steady themselves, as they slowly got to the coastal path at the bottom of the hill. They were both thinking about the rubber contraption as they were making their way along the cliff path, but pretending to look at the sea view. Maureen was not so innocent as she had claimed to be, having once found a packet in her parent's medicine cabinet when she was looking for some Elastoplast. She had examined a rubber thoroughly and deduced what it was used for, before putting it back with its comrades. Paul was plodding along wondering when he would have the nerve, or the money, or both, to procure a packet for himself. That would be the ultimate joy now he thought. To make love to his sweetheart and be able to relax, knowing that he would not make her pregnant. He felt the uncomfortable tightness in his trousers and thought how unfair it was, growing up.

Maureen was still thinking about the sailor and his partner with the mixed feelings of distaste and curiosity. At the back of her mind were the dire warnings about fornication and the damnation of Hell, that were preached from the Baptist pulpit of a Sunday. She was a normal intelligent girl and although aware of the dangers of unprotected sex, whenever that should turn out to be, she was still interested how mature people of different sexes behaved. She was vaguely aware of how attitudes change, and of the hypocrisies of the Victorian age. She felt she instinctively knew what was natural and what was unnatural.

Her mother had touched briefly on 'the facts of life', but had not explained, in any great depth, the emotional and physical effects of hormonal activity during puberty and the years after. Unlike Paul, she could not wait to become an adult and embrace the responsibilities of having a decent job, getting married and raising a family. She did not mention any of these things to Paul but said, "The heather and gorse are a picture, aren't they Paul?"

"Yes. Have you noticed these vine like plants growing over the gorse?" Paul said, fingering some.

"Yes, what are they called then?"

"Dodder. They are parasitic plants."

"Really? It's fascinating how they climb over the other plants, like pink wire with little bits of white cotton stuck to them where the little white flowers are," said Maureen, fingering them gently in case she pricked her finger on the gorse.

"We should be joining up with the place where the old railway came from Bideford shortly. There are still a few rails visible."

"I would have loved to travel on that railway. Maybe they will open it up again one day. There is some lovely scenery to look out on. – from a railway carriage I mean. It would be lovely for people down here on holiday," said Maureen, caught up with a new vision.

"I can't see anyone finding that sort of money, to build a railway, for tourists," scoffed Paul, with a chuckle.

"Well maybe one day you will be proved wrong," said Maureen, pouting.

"I hope you are right," said Paul, putting his arm around her waist and kissing her on the cheek; a difficult manoeuvre as they were pushing their bicycles at the time. Needless to say, Paul overbalanced his bicycle; its front wheel turned in on him, forcing him over to one side, consequently bearing across Maureen who was pushed over on top of her bicycle. They both landed on the pathway in a tangled heap, laughing heartily.

When they joined up with the railway track the way became much wider and more suitable for cycling, which they did, making good progress into Westward Ho! Paul kept his word, spending some of his meagre pocket money on ice creams for them. They stopped for a while, enjoying them and watching the people in the sea from the top of the slipway. They had a good view right across the beach. Families were sitting in deck chairs the whole length of the concrete slipway, which was really built to enable people, and the odd vehicle, to go down on the beach, instead of crossing the pebble ridge, the natural barrier from the sea. The tide was not all that far from it's limit. The beach had a very shallow incline, which meant it came in very quickly. Bathers with curved plywood surf-boards were enjoying body surfing in the exhilarating 'combers'.

"Let's stay a while to watch people getting caught out by the tide," murmured Paul. "It's always the same. People never seem to realise how quickly the tide is coming in. They seem to think that the big sea wall on the side and around the corner is going to stop the water coming up the slipway," he said grinning.

"I think you should go down and warn them, Paul," said Maureen, a twinkle in her eyes.

"You can if you like. I'm going to enjoy the fun," said Paul, trying unsuccessfully to dodge a hefty slap on his bottom from Maureen. Paul was soon proved to be right: the sea came in a surge travelling right up to the pebble ridge and also travelling uphill for about a quarter of the length of the slipway. There were squeals of delighted surprise from the children, but curses from the adults as they gathered their sodden flotsam from the tide that had terminated their lazy sojourn. They hastily beat a retreat up the not so crowded slipway, as it began to dawn on everyone that the force of the tide was stronger than they imagined.

Paul's stomach told him that it was time for tea. But he waited until the aromas of fish and chips, and the other culinary delights wafted out onto the seafront from the surrounding restaurants and kitchens, titillating Maureen's nostrils until she exclaimed that it was time to go home. They cycled up the road from the slipway, turning left on the corner at the cricket pitch, and took the flat road to West Appledore that they had cycled on their first day together. Paul was impressed by his recent memories of the surf coming in at Westward Ho! and asked

Maureen if she would like to go swimming there the following morning. Maureen thought that it might be a good idea if the weather was reasonable. They parted at Auntie's house in Irsha Street. Paul cycled home going along the quayside but pushing his bike up the steep Post Office Hill, through the courtyard door to home.

CHAPTER SEVEN

Ruth Baxter heard the strident sounds of Beethoven coming out of her husband's study and suspected that Stephen, or part of him, was reliving the past, and in particular, ten years previously. Around the time that he was an Army Chaplain somewhere in the Naga Hills of Burma between Imphal and Kohima, and the bitter fighting between the British Commonwealth troops and the Japanese. She had been irritated before when the volume had been turned up on the gramophone, and she had entered his study to get him to turn it down; froze in the doorway as she saw him looking at photographs of his comrades, many of them blown to pieces by mortar bombs, or else stopped in their tracks, victims of a snipers bullet. The hand that held the photograph shook slightly and his face seemed to register a mixture of sadness and grief. That was the only way she could describe it.

Ruth now wanted to talk to him about Paul and Maureen and whether they might be getting too friendly, as they were seeing each other everyday now. They had both thought it good when their friendship had started, but Ruth had not forseen how close they would become. Ruth knew that Stephen was not the same man that had left to go to war: His patience was not long-lived any more. Very often he was on a very short fuse. Perhaps she would leave him alone with his music and his memories.

Paul and Maureen enjoyed the continuing good weather and the use of their bicycles, usually ending up in the sand dunes or on the beach at Westward Ho! Occasionally they took a ferry across to Instow for a change, but that cost money, something in short supply.

Regatta Day was a real treat though, with most of the population turning out for it. Maureen and Paul got down on to the quay-side early, so that they could be at the front of what was going on during the day. They chose a spot by the slipway which they thought would give them a good view. Traditionally the main events were the rowing, with varying classes differentiated by the number of rowers in a boat. The only female contestants in those days of the Regatta, were impersonated by good sports in the flour and soot fights, when burly males put on long dresses and bonnets and pelted each other with flour and soot bombs, whilst trying to keep afloat in small dinghies. Sailing races went on at different times, but were not particularly relevant to the spectators, unless they had a relative in a boat.

The racers had to be clear of the main channel between Bideford Bridge and Appledore Pool, where the deep water was set aside for boat mooring. A running commentary was amplified by a radio van, with a well known charismatic clergyman, who was kept up to date by strategically placed military-type walkie-talkies from Bideford Bridge down to Appledore Quay. The colour of the rowers' vests determined their place of origin, with many clubs from South Devon. Local folk would be cheering for Bideford Reds or Blues, as Appledore did not have a rowing club itself. There were gig races and sculling races, but the favourite event was probably the 'greasey pole;' not a race, but a competition for the competitor to balance on a suitably greased up pole lashed to the deck of one of the sailing vessels, usually the *Kathleen and May*. The person who managed to traverse the farthest without falling off was the winner. Most fell off at the start however, causing great hilarity for the onlookers. Paul and Maureen did not feel confident enough to try it, but enjoyed the spectacle just the same.

Florence wandered over in the afternoon, but she did not like crowds too much so she did not stay too long. Maureen found it all very exciting and great fun; she went home to tell Florence about the things she had missed, and Florence was content to see the flush of youth in her niece's cheeks.

The next day dawned with a sullen blanket of fog enveloping the port and the surrounding district. Unbeknown to Paul, Auntie Florence had noted that the weather was not suitable for bathing in the sea; Maureen had informed her of their intention to do so the previous evening. Florence had decided that it would be a good day to go into Bideford on her own to do some shopping. She would get Maureen to look for the Monopoly game, thinking that at least there would be some wholesome hours of fun to play it with her friend, if they could not go out. She thought that she should be able to trust the young couple not to do anything foolish; she had to trust them at other times in any case. Florence caught the early bus so that any bargains would not be missed in the market place, and to take advantage of community-based stalls that had flourished for over an hundred years. It was a covered market similar to Appledore's market in the narrow Market Street, but much bigger. There were other shops that she wanted to look around and it would be nice and cool even if it was damp. She preferred that to the hot humid weather and would take advantage whilst she had the opportunity. There was one nagging thing that she needed to sort out whilst she was in Bideford, but she would deal with that when she came to it.

Maureen remembered other damp and gloomy times when recreation for herself and Auntie Florence had been needed. Maureen had dreaded these sessions in the past, but had politely acquiesced on the odd evening that Auntie Florrie suggested it. Now Auntie murmured that it might indeed be a good idea if Paul and Maureen whiled away the morning playing Monopoly. Maureen knew that Auntie usually had her lunch in Bideford as a special treat, her visits now being less frequent in spite of the distance being only a few miles.

Paul turned up at the doorstep as usual and rattled the old brass knocker with gusto. This always made Maureen jump, but also made her heart flutter a little at the prospect of something a little different each time Paul came to the house.

"Come in Paul," said Maureen, opening the door to a slightly nervous youth, who was expecting Auntie to open it.

"We are going to play Monopoly this morning on Auntie's instructions."

Paul looked at Maureen blankly, standing in the narrow hallway.

"Monopoly?" he gasped in disbelief and disappointment.

"Yes, Monopoly. That's me having you all to myself. That's what Monopoly is all about, isn't it? Auntie's gone away for the day," said Maureen with a teasing smile.

Paul looked at Maureen still confused, until a wide grin stretched his freckled face.

"Well, what do you know about that then?" he chuckled.

"What I do know Reverend Baxter's son is that you have get to get the Monopoly board out of that box under the sideboard in the front room and set the game up, while I do the dishes and make the beds," said Maureen, trying to look serious.

As Paul looked at her protestingly, Maureen disappeared upstairs leaving a disgruntled Paul to set up the table for Monopoly. A few minutes later the door opened; as Paul casually looked around he dropped some of the little red hotels he had in his hand onto the floor; he gazed at Maureen in disbelief.

"Well come on, upstairs. It's Monopoly time. I want you all to myself." Maureen was standing there, in the doorway, in her knickers and nothing else! Paul needed no second bidding. He hurried towards Maureen, who ran quickly upstairs to her bedroom, with Paul in hot pursuit. Maureen jumped into her bed and pulled the sheets up, trying to look innocent and demure. Paul looked in through the open doorway at her smiling coyly back at him.

"You had better undress and get in beside me, hadn't you?" she said, surprising herself as well as Paul.

Paul was conscious of Maureen's gaze as he shyly stripped off to his underpants and joined her in the single bed.

"We'll have to cuddle up as there is not really enough room for two, is there Maureen?"

Maureen laughed, but then said quietly, "Hold me close Paul."

As Paul cuddled into her, his arms around her waist, Maureen was conscious that they had to make the best of the limited amount of time available to them. She knew that she had to steer Paul in the right direction; to spend their time making each other happy, without doing anything that would lead to ugly recriminations.

"I don't want to leave this place, but we will have to make the best use of our time before I go home. Then we shall just have to forget each other," Maureen said, her moist eyes crestfallen. With his arms around Maureen's waist, a gloom came over Paul, to match the sound of the foghorn booming around Bideford Bay. Maureen used the sheet to dab at her tear sodden cheeks as she continued to cry.

"No we can't forget each other. Don't be silly Maureen," said Paul, trying to console her, but knowing that there might be an ominous truth in her statement.

"We will be seeing each other for several days yet and there will be other times. The summer holiday next year if we cannot see each other before," said Paul, not knowing if he could bear to wait that long. He consoled himself by kissing Maureen's neck and nuzzling around to her delightful mouth, in which he inserted his tongue and searched for hers. She responded warmly and soon they were both writhing around each other, caressing each other in an almost desperate manner as if to make up for lost time – past, present, and future. It was obvious that they were too restricted by the bed clothes.

Paul threw the coverings to the floor, stripped off his Y-fronts and pulled Maureen's panties off. She watched him, her eyes wide and the pupils growing large, but she did not stop him. She knew that she had initiated this and would have to see how far he would go. Before he could embrace her again, she moved him off the bed and then pulled out a large beach towel from the bedside cupboard and spread it over the sheet. She then lay down on top of it and held out her hands for him to come on top of her. He did this willingly; a warm sensation throbbed through his groin as his sex laid on top of hers.

"Don't move for a while. Let's just hold each other like this," she whispered.

He granted her wish regarding his body from the waist down, but carried on nuzzling her neck and brushing his mouth against her's, nibbling at her sensuous lips. A peace fell over them as drizzling rain tapped the window glass and the foghorn moaned intermittently. Paul brought his hands up to caress her facial features with his forefingers. He wanted to remember how she was at this moment forever. Supporting himself with his left elbow, arm resting on the pillow, he carried on tracing his forefinger over her features. She smiled up at him, her elbows and hands around his waist to help take the weight of his upper body. He ran his fingers through her short black curly hair making her scalp tingle. His right index finger gently traced around her left ear registering how the top flap of her ear flared slightly outwards. He pressed his forefinger along each eyebrow noticing each sweep and curve. They were soft, black and luxuriant. She arched them in fun to give them a quizzical expression. He stared into her eyes and tried to register the exact colour of brown in the iris. She counteracted his stare by going cross-eyed and giggling. He traced his forefinger from the bridge of her nose along the slightly upturned end; generous in proportion to match her wide mouth. Her lips were naturally full with a small pout on the lower lip. He was entranced by those beautiful lips, running a finger tip over them very gently round and round until tingling.

Maureen opened her lips wide to smile at him, showing her natural ivory teeth: strong and healthy but not prominent. Next he traced her jaw line: fairly square and strong with a chin to match. He realised if he was going to venerate the rest of her body, then he would have to change his position and move down the bed slightly. This he did with difficulty, co-ordinating his elbows with his knees. His penis moved down from contact with her pubic bush but he was compensated by a better access to her delightful breasts, whose erect nipples dragged against his chest. He moved down just enough to be able to trace the outline of her slender but fairly short neck, which he nuzzled with his mouth and along to her shoulders: strong and athletic looking.

Moving down the bed again he lay his head between her breasts and kissed the crease between them. He used his tongue to trace the outline of her left breast and enjoyed the yielding nature of this soft tissue, which quivered gently as she breathed. With the palm of his hand he gently touched the left nipple, enjoying its hardness, moving to the pink aureola with its bumpy texture. He could not resist nibbling at her nipples alternately, using his pursed lips to start with and then his teeth resting on top of a nipple and his tongue underneath. Maureen started to sigh, which encouraged him to bite a little harder with his lower teeth as well. He continued to suckle and knead her breasts until Maureen sounded very excited, and moaned, whispering his name at intervals. He lowered himself again kissing the navel briefly before the palms of his hands slid down her sides to her waist and then flared out over her hips.

Paul was kneeling by now, not far from the bottom of the bed. Maureen had to open and raise her legs to make room for him to stay on the bed. His heart pounded as his eyes viewed her open charms. He put forward his right hand and gently caressed her dark delta, which he had felt before at Landcross, but from a different direction. He looked up at Maureen's face to see that her eyes were closed: her breathing was heavy. He let his hands run up and down her thighs and up over her hips and then he lay down on his left side with his head against Maureen's right thigh and started to caress the lips of her labia. For a moment he had a flashback of the memory of the woman on the cliffs which unnerved him slightly. He was reassured by Maureen's hands on the back of his head, so he continued to explore her vagina running his middle finger up and down to caress her; he noticed that the further his fingers moved gently up the channel, the more excited Maureen got. He was starting to get a little cramped and stopped, to work out his next plan of campaign.

Maureen whispered, "Don't stop now, Paul. Kiss me down there. Use your tongue again if you like."

This was breaking into new ground for Paul, but if that was what Maureen wanted he would be only too pleased to oblige. He put his hands under her buttocks to lift her up slightly, and then used his mouth and tongue to caress her inner thighs with his lips brushing gently over her pubic hairs, until he bit into the bone at the top of the vulva. Then he used his tongue to explore her labia, marvelling at the different folds of lips and the seemingly different apertures.

As his tongue rubbed around the top of the labia, Maureen held his head up and said, "That's it at the top. Can you feel it?"

Paul extricated himself slightly and said, "There's a little, sort of, like the thing in the back of our throats, er, uvula, I think its called. Is that it?"

"Yes. It's the clitoris you silly. That's what gives us girls pleasure."

"Oh, really? I never knew that!" said Paul in amazement.

"Well you don't know as much about girls as you think you do then. Anyhow, carry on and then I'll help you," said Maureen mystifyingly.

Paul used his tongue to massage this new organ he had discovered. As he worked away he noticed that things were getting a lot more moist, and there was definitely something oozing out of the orifice besides his saliva. The more excited Maureen became, the more it oozed around him. Maureen was pressing his head further inside herself now and also using her legs to wrap around his shoulders and back. He did his best to simulate the rhythm to match her, forthcoming orgasm– released with a loud sigh. She relaxed her grip on him and he let her rest while he looked back and marvelled how slippery the area had become, it had started to seep down to the towelling on the bed. His tongue tasted quite salty, although not unpleasant as Maureen had prepared herself by bathing before Paul arrived. Maureen might have been sated, but Paul was in a high state of excitement. He moved back up the bed, to lie facing her. She smiled at him drowsily.

"That was nice. I'll attend to your needs now," she whispered mysteriously.

"There must be something to be urgently got rid of, I should imagine," she chuckled. Maureen sat up and said, "Turn on your left side with your back facing me!

Paul needed no encouragement; as Maureen's breasts pressed into his back she reached out for his proud manhood. She had never been as intimate with a boy as she was now, and she ran her fingers gently along the erect shaft with interest and felt the increased girth at the head. Running back down again, she gently reached under his testicles, playing with them, and curious about how they were made.

"That's nice," he murmured in approval. She then alternated these movements with a massage of his member.

"I think you're pulling it over to one side a bit. Perhaps a change of position is in order," said Paul shyly.

"I know! If you lie on your back with your head on the pillow, I'll come and sit in front of you." Paul pushed himself back and pulled his knees up as Maureen came and sat in front of him, her feet crossed and locked, with her left hand on his shoulder. With the other hand she grasped the shaft of his penis and began to massage it. Paul lay back and watched her naked body in front of him and was soon in a state of high arousal. He came quickly and forcefully; the semen spurting across to hit her left breast and trickled down to her lap. She jumped and marvelled at how far it had reached. She used the bottom corner of the towel to wipe herself clean. It looked a bit like the flour and water paste her father used to make up for hanging wallpaper. She sniffed it and funnily enough it also had a starchy smell.

"I think we both could do with a bath. I'll go and run the water," she said, getting up off the bed and heading for the bathroom.

"Come back and lie with me as soon as you have turned the taps on," said Paul. Maureen turned around smiling, and nodded. She turned on the hot water tap to fill the cast iron bath with clawed feet and put the plug in. She quickly had a pee, sitting on the wooden seat of the high cisterned toilet which required the chain to be pulled to flush it. She washed her hands and then went back to the bedroom and jumped on the bed to cuddle into Paul. Paul pulled her over on top of him, enjoying the feel of her naked body and her face next to his.

"If only we could stop the clock. Stop time from going on!" said Paul desperately. Maureen put a finger on Paul's lips as a gesture of the inevitability of time.

"We have just got to make the best of things," she said simply. "Now there's a thought. Is the best still to come?" asked Paul, tongue-in-cheek.

"I think that's about as far as I can go, don't you Paul?" said Maureen, trying to convince herself, as well as Paul.

Paul sighed and said, "Perhaps you're right. Maybe I could get hold of some of those er, 'Johnnies' though."

Maureen pushed away from him and said, "Don't spoil it by

thinking about those two – animals – yesterday. Don't start to get greedy now, Paul. You should be satisfied with what you've got."

She glowered at him until he said, "I am satisfied with what I've got. More than satisfied. It's just that if we are growing up to be adults, why shouldn't we do the same things that adults do?" He put his arm around her to comfort both of them.

"You know why we shouldn't do it. You are a parson's son. What would your parents say if they found out what we were doing. My father would probably would want to kill me if he knew that I was lying here naked with you."

"We don't know what our parents did when they were young, or even what they get up to now. We have to be discreet just like them," said Paul, forcefully venting his feelings. Maureen lay quietly for a while thinking that, for once, Paul might have said something logical.

"Fancy you saying those things about your father and mother. I haven't met your father, but I am sure your parents are very respectable people. I think you should just be grateful for our time together, especially here this morning." She gave him a peck on the cheek and said," It's getting chilly now, let's get in under the bed covers and cuddle up."

They pulled the bed clothes up around themselves; these had got thrown back during their previous excitement. They lay there quietly for a while, listening to the drizzly rain beating gently against the bedroom window, and the distant sound of the foghorn warning ships off the bar. Time had lost its meaning until Maureen's thoughts turned to the tap water running into the bath. She looked across at the clock on the mantelpiece of the small open fireplace of black ironwork. It was not far off noon and she suspected that Auntie would be heading for an early lunch in the market place, where they served good wholesome food at a reasonable price. Maureen was conscious of her stickiness, and said to Paul while sitting up and lifting the bedclothes from her side, "I'm going to take my bath now, Paul!"

Leaving a bewildered Paul alone in the bed, she quickly entered the small bathroom and tried the temperature of the water that was half way up the bath. It was quite hot, but the tank that fed the gas geyser, fixed to the wall above the bath, had emptied of hot water and so the water coming out now was only tepid. However, she decided that the water in the bath was too hot without a top-up of cold water, so turned the cold tap on. Paul heard the sound of running water and realised that he needed to urinate. He got out of the bed and went across to the bathroom, tried the door handle and found that the door was locked.

"I am seeing to the taps," giggled Maureen.

"Hurry up! I've got to go to the toilet," said Paul urgently. Paul noted the silence as the taps were turned off. A shy face peeped around the door.

"You can come in now," said Maureen.

Paul relieved himself and then looked across to Maureen who was now sitting in the bath, swirling and mixing the hot water with the cold, using a hand as a paddle.

"It's a pity letting all that hot water go to waste. I think I had better jump in with you," he said, striding over.

"What do you mean going to waste? It's not going to waste if I'm having a bath in the hot water, is it?" she scolded.

Paul was not deterred and slid into the bath, keeping his back away from the taps.

"Be careful you don't bang yourself against the tap," said Maureen, conscious of the awkwardness of each other's legs and toes in the cramped confines of the bath. Paul met that statement with his own logic and thrust himself forward on top of Maureen making a wave flip dangerously near the top of the bath.

"Oh Paul! Don't be stupid! If the water goes all over the floor and makes the bath mat sopping wet, Auntie will know something strange has been going on, won't she?"

Paul recognised the logic and looked around for something to wash himself with. Maureen sat back frowning, pretending she was cross; Paul sat opposite her beaming with pleasure, enjoying the somewhat tepid water.

"Well? Where's my flannel?" he enquired, as Maureen washed her arms, her neck and shoulders.

"You'll have to use Auntie's sponge," she giggled, picking

it up from the flat shelf that had been built to the side of the ancient bath, throwing it towards him. It bounced off his head and dropped to the floor making Paul struggle to reach it, while Maureen continued to giggle hysterically. After retrieving the sponge Paul worked soap and water to make a froth into a lather, which he proceeded to sponge over her breasts vigorously, causing Maureen to protest.

"Careful Paul. Girls are delicate things. That's the trouble with boys. They are so rough. You have got to be gentle, if you are going to woo a young lady," she said, only half teasing.

"Like this you mean?" said Paul, grabbing her flannel and trying to tease her nipples while his other hand reached for her body below the water.

"That's not going to be a very good idea," she snapped, startling Paul.

"Look. You can wash my back, and I'll do the rest," she said, turning over in the narrow confines and kneeling, her back towards him. Paul, chastened, did her bidding, gently soaping her back with the sponge.

"There, that's better. You can do things properly, if you try," she murmured, enjoying the sensual tingle as the sponge skated up and down her back, ending with a gentle sweep around her hips and half exposed rump.

"That was nice," she whispered appreciatively, turning around to face him again.

"You bathe yourself whilst I finish my ablutions," she said, turning and sliding her back down into the water to rinse herself of the soap.

Paul stood up to give them both some room.

When Maureen had finished, she said, "Sit down in front of me and I'll wash your back."

Paul did as he was told; Maureen's legs straddled his slim waist as she soaped his back with a flannel. She thought that she would help him clean his genitals as he might be embarrassed to do that with her watching. Boys were not so matter of fact when it came to bodily functions and hygiene; she knew that from living with her brother. She soaped the flannel and proceeded to cleanse Paul's now throbbing member, squeezing the slippery flannel up and down the shaft until Paul's body stiffened and he reached back to hold the underside of her thighs as he lay back on her breast until the bath water started to turn slightly milky, under the soap bubbles. Maureen gave a little laugh after Paul's body went limp and he gave an audible sigh.

Maureen eased herself out of the bath. Grabbing a large towel she wrapped it round herself and said, "I'm going to get dried off, so you finish off your ablutions and join me in the bedroom." She left Paul and went to the bedroom to dry herself thoroughly. As she was doing this she remembered some things that were said at her school, by friends mostly older than herself. These were what things a boy and a girl could do with each other, at the same time, that were pleasurable but not in any way dangerous; just one step forwards from what they had already done. She decided that she would ascertain if Paul was up to it and waited for him in anticipation, lying on the white linen sheets.

CHAPTER EIGHT

Paul and Maureen had decided that if the following day was fine they would cycle to Clovelly, quite a distance by bicycle, with many of the usual West Country hills. Day dawned and the weather was fair, so Paul got his mother to make some sandwiches and a packed lunch for two.

"Where is it you are planning to go?" quizzed his mother, cutting slices off the fresh loaf on the bread board.

"We thought we would try to cycle to Clovelly, Maureen has only been there once before," said Paul, washing a couple of apples under the tap.

"Clovelly? That's a long way to cycle. Are you sure that girl's bike is good enough to go that far?" asked his mother, a worried look on her face.

"Yes, Mum. We can take our time, even if it takes the best part of the morning to get there. I always take a puncture outfit and a pump. We shall be all right."

"I know you are quite fond of that girl, and she seems nice, but I don't want you to be wearing her out with that ancient bike of her Auntie's."

"Oh, stop worrying, Mum. As I said, we will be taking it easy and enjoying ourselves."

"Mmm. Yes, I am a bit worried about that as well," said his mother, looking directly at her younger son.

Paul flushed a little and said, "Look Mum, we are not doing any harm. Anybody would think it was a crime to go off riding on a bike."

"Well, like I say, be careful you do not overdo things, all right?" she said pointedly.

Paul felt both a little sheepish and cross at his mother's nagging, and left hurriedly. Ruth sighed and contemplated the pain and frustrations of growing up. She really wanted to go after her son and hug him and tell him she knew how difficult it was for him. She cleared away the breakfast table while a piano solo from Mozart tinkled its way out of her husband's wireless in his study.

Paul called for Maureen and received from Florence much the same as from his mother; his obvious irritation gave Maureen a touch of the giggles. The fact that Paul was a parson's son was probably the deciding factor for Auntie's decision to allow Maureen to undertake such a 'hazardous' journey, as everyone knew that a parson was someone to look up to. They cycled on the now familiar road to Bideford, but turning right at Northam to carry on over the top of Westward Ho!, turning left to come into Abbotsham and Abbotsham Cross where they left the Bideford road for the north coast going westwards to Cornwall.

They were both conscious of time pressing down on them – time that robbed them of a future together –and also because each had never experienced so intense a relationship before. The significance was now becoming unbearable. In a few days time Maureen would be on the train going home. Then what? When would they see each other again? It was a grim future that beckoned Paul, now that he had found someone special; someone that was really interested in him and who shared intimate secrets. Someone who had given new meaning to his life but was going away from him. How could he cope with that? How could he carry on with his schoolwork as if nothing had happened, as if Maureen had never existed; or worse perhaps, someone just passing through his life like a fleeting memory. That was how his parents and teachers would see it.

"It's all part of growing up, Paul." He knew he could never settle for that; but what could he do? He was just a sixteen year old boy. He wished he had the same competitive spirit that some boys of his age had for sports. He quite enjoyed sports as part of the school curriculum – they were better than double maths any day, but apart from a kick around Pitt Court and the risk breaking someone's window with a tennis ball, there was not a lot of scope for sport unless you were good enough, or keen enough, to get into the organised competitive sports played outside school hours. Cricket and football on the wireless left him cold, although his friend Barry, seemed, like a lot of other boys, including his brother Graham, to be obsessed by it. Paul felt a bit guilty about deserting the companionship of Barry, although Paul had on occasion been in the same position when Barry was out with a girlfriend, even though they had often gone around as a foursome. Paul knew that he had to make the best use of the short time left of the holiday. It was a good day for an excursion, a bit hot for cycling, but a lot better than the average summer holiday weather.

Paul looked back to see how Maureen was coming along. He could see it was not easy for her using Auntie's bike. It seemed literally to creak along as if to protest at being used for anything other than the most basic of requirements: a bike suitable for a priest or a district nurse.

"It is not very far from Hoop's Inn now. We can stop there for a cool drink and a rest if you like, Maureen," said Paul, taking pity on her valiant efforts

"Oh, good," gasped Maureen, "I've got some money that Auntie gave me."

"That's all right. I have brought enough to cover that," said Paul, wishing he received regular pocket money like his friend Barry, whose father was a skipper on a tanker.

"You can save your money and buy me something nice in Clovelly," laughed Maureen.

Paul smiled back at her but doubted if the five shillings and nine pence, all the money he could lay claim to; resting in his trouser pocket right now, would buy much.

On reaching the Inn, they leaned their bikes against the wall and went inside. They were both unused to public houses and looked for the off-licence or quiet bar, as they knew they were under age for the partaking of alcohol.

"Hello there young Sir and Miss," boomed a voice behind them. "What can I do for you then?" said a smiling portly middle aged publican, the sweat gleaming on the top of his bald head.

"We would like a cold drink please," said Paul nervously but trying to sound grown up.

"I think I may have just the thing for you. A large bottle of Whiteways Cydrax straight from the fridge. Would 'ee like to come out back in the garden and drink it in the fresh air? 'Tis 'ansome weather in't it?" The publican led the way as Paul nodded his head towards Maureen to ask for a quick acknowledgement; she affirmed with a quick smile as they hurried along the passageways and out into the garden, which was really more of a yard, where a table and chairs awaited them.

"You sit there my 'ansomes and 'I'll be right back," said the publican, hurrying off. He returned shortly with a tray and a bottle with two glasses.

"There you are my dears," he said beaming. "That'll be one shilling and thruppence please."

"That's fine, thank you," said Paul, automatically putting his hand in his pocket, but Maureen quickly produced her purse to pay the man.

He looked around to Paul saying, "You are a lucky young fellow and no mistake, having a pretty young lady buying you a drink."

Maureen giggled as Paul smiled sheepishly and the landlord entreated them to enjoy their drinks. They were busy gulping the fizzy, ice-cool refreshment down, when he returned holding a euphonium.

"I would like an opinion from you about a piece of music. Here goes!" he said abruptly, and proceeded to blow the music out of the large horn. It was a piece entitled 'Oh My Papa' that the trumpet player Eddie Calvert made famous in the nineteen fifties'. The euphonium player was struggling along now, purple faced, sweat dripping off the bottom of his chin. When he had finished, Paul and Maureen clapped furiously, though there were times when it was difficult to keep a straight face.

The landlord gave a quick bow and said, "I'm glad you enjoyed that, twas more of a young person's music really. My regular customers are a bit old for modern music. I had better get back inside now. 'Twill be a busy time shortly. You can go out that side gate when you have finished my dears. I hope to see 'ee again one day. Cheerio for now then." A quick wave and he disappeared.

Paul and Maureen finished the bottle, making them both

burp-up the gas in the drink They made their way to the gate and found their bikes had been brought inside for safety, so they went out on the road again refreshed to finish their journey.

"I know who I shall think of every time I hear 'Oh My Papa'," said Paul, starting to get into his cycling rhythm again.

"Don't make me laugh too much or I shall fall off!" said Maureen, with a fit of giggles coming on.

"Well I must admit I don't usually have a cabaret laid on when I take young ladies out for a drink," said Paul giggling.

"Don't forget you owe me, young man," said Maureen jestingly.

Paul wished he had the money to buy something nice and was brooding over this on the last stretch before Clovelly. He knew how tiring the cycling must be for Maureen and he wished he could give her a new bike. They arrived at the top of the little fishing port after cycling down a tree lined lane and propped the bikes up against a hedge just inside a gateway. They started to walk down the steep hill but paused to admire the view of the sweep of the bay. Maureen was grateful to be able to get her breath back. They found a suitable corner of a step to sit on and rest while they enjoyed the prettiness of the little whitewashed cottages with the brightly coloured flowers in the tiny flower beds.

They slowly made their way down the steep gradient of cobbles and watched a donkey with a pack on his back being slowly coaxed up the hill by an old man wearing a straw hat that matched the donkey's, which made Maureen squeal with delight when she noticed it. There were quite a lot of people on holiday taking photographs and enjoying the atmosphere of the place. Muted squeals of delight came wafting up from the little shingly beach where children splashed about uninhibitedly in the warm sunshine.

Maureen wanted to look around a gift shop halfway down. Peering in through the window at all the trinkets displayed on cards, she fell in love with a silver ring that had two dolphins entwined on it. They walked inside and smiled at the proprietor, dusting some shelves. As Maureen looked longingly at the ring, Paul fished out the silver he had in his pocket surreptitiously and looked at it sadly. The proprietor was watching them closely, but discreetly, fascinated by the apparent unity of a couple so young.

"Isn't it marvellous?" said Maureen.

Paul affirmed with a nod. When he asked how much the ring was, the man told him that it was five shillings, much to Paul's surprise; although he did not know about prices, he felt that the ring should have cost him a lot more.

"I'll take it!" said Paul, in a daze, Maureen laughed with excitement, jiggling from one foot to the other. They both thanked the proprietor and went out of the shop smiling. The proprietor watched them until they went out of sight further down the hill, smiling to himself, glancing down at a ring on his finger, given to him by his late wife.

When they reached the little harbour at the bottom of the hill they sat on the edge of the harbour wall and ate their lunch, which Paul had carried in a small haversack. While they were eating Maureen kept holding up the hand with her ring on

"I will treasure this ring, Paul. Thank you for buying it for me." Maureen leaned over and kissed Paul on his cheek.

"I hope I shall get more than a peck on the cheek later on," said Paul with a glint in his eye.

Maureen brought her hand around behind Paul's back and gave him a hearty slap, making him momentarily lose his balance, until he over compensated and lay back on the granite slab. Maureen had a fit of giggling, so Paul pulled her down on the slab bringing his mouth close to hers as she complied with his forceful kiss. After the prolonged embrace with which they were both unaware of the interest and amusement from a few onlookers, Paul said, "That's a proper kiss, isn't it, Maureen?"

"Yes," sighed Maureen.

"That was nice. Perhaps I may remember that kiss – when I'm old and grey." Paul looked across to her and smiled.

"I didn't think it was that good."

"Maybe it's because it's such a nice setting here and the weather is so nice. The sun is shining, but there's a cool breeze coming off the water. I feel at peace just at this moment, but I know only too well what's around the corner. We must enjoy what we have at this moment, Paul," said Maureen, sighing.

Paul looked at Maureen's youthful body longingly and could not feel peace of mind. He watched the boats bobbing about in the harbour, the water looked clear and tempting.

"Time for a swim," he said, breaking into Maureen's reverie.

"Can't we just enjoy the sunshine for a bit? It's so nice just sitting here on the wall, enjoying the day. I'm still tired from the bike ride, Paul," said Maureen, although she knew how restless Paul got, just sitting there, doing nothing.

"Just a wee while longer. We have'nae given our stomachs a chance to digest our lunch yet. They say it is'nae good to go swimming just after ye have eaten," she said, lapsing into the brogue she usually tried to control.

"Oh, that's an old wives tale, but I can understand that you might want to rest a bit longer. I've got my fishing line in my haversack. You never know, I might be lucky and catch a mackerel or herring," said Paul hopefully.

"I thought you didn't have the patience for fishing?" said Maureen, quickly adding, "You might be lucky and catch – what is it? – A sea bass or something."

"Huh! – Fat chance of that. Anyhow, let's see what we can do," Paul said, rummaging in his haversack and bringing out a fishing line with a piece of bacon rind on the hook.

"I see you came prepared," laughed Maureen.

"Well, Dad usually has bacon for breakfast and I know that mackerel are not all that fussy what they take. That's why the fishermen only need feathers to hook them when there's a shoal around." Maureen shuddered.

"I don't like the idea of fish on a hook. It seems so cruel."

"Ah! That's because you're a townie. My Mother thinks nothing of gutting a fish, or skinning a rabbit come to that."

"Oh how horrible! I hope you don't catch any fish, Paul. I couldn't bear to see one jumping around on the end of a line," said Maureen, screwing up her face in distaste.

"Well, you do eat fish don't you? Somebody has to catch them for you," said Paul teasing.

"I don't mind once they are dead I suppose. I just don't like to see them dying," said Maureen sadly, as Paul threw the line out enough to clear the jetty.

After a while he thought the line was pulling a bit, although it was rigged to catch bottom feeders like flatfish, usually a dab or a fluke. Paul hoped it was not an eel, as none in his house liked eating eels and they were an awful job to get off the hook. Paul started drawing the line up, winding the cord around the square wooden frame. On clearing the water an orangey-red under-belly revealed what was known locally as a 'howler' crab. It was prized by young boys, who dipped short string lines, anchored by a single knot around a heavy stone, with another knot around an ejected limpet, hacked off a seaweedy rock and the flesh dug out with a penknife, or a hefty bash with a rock. 'Howlers' were not considered to be big enough for consumption so they were always thrown back into the water, to perpetuate the sport for others. Paul duly dispatched the crab with disgust and then, as Maureen was laughing at his obvious disappointment with the crab, said, "I think that's enough fishing for the moment. Have you rested enough to have a swim yet Maureen?"

"So you have lost patience with the fishing then Master Paul? Oh well, I suppose our lunch has gone down now. Right then, let's change into our cossies and no peeping." Maureen drew up her large towel round her neck for modesty's sake, although there were not too many folk around; Paul donned a towel around his waist and in no time had his swimming trunks on.

"Why are we waiting?" he sang, as Maureen struggled under her tent.

"It's all right for you. We girls have got more to cover up," she moaned.

"Don't worry too much. I've seen it all before," said Paul laughing.

"Shush!" said Maureen, looking around anxiously to see if anyone had heard, or was looking at them.

"It's not you I am worried about, stupid. Not now, as you have so... ungallantly referred to." she dropped her voice to a whisper, continuing, "to the intimacy of my body."

A broad grin came across Maureen's face, until both she

and Paul were infected with a fit of giggles, so much so that there was a great danger of her falling over in disarray. At last Maureen was free of the clothes and towel and stood resplendent in her navy blue one piece costume and to Paul's admiring eyes filling it nicely.

"Are you going to jump in? The tide's pretty high," said Paul grinning.

"I suppose so. It saves the slow torture of gradually entering the cold water down the steps," grimaced Maureen.

Paul grabbed her hand and shouted, "One, two, three, Jump!"

Maureen was obliged to jump with Paul; they both hit the water together and came up gasping with the shock of the coldness of it.

"Brr! Let's swim around the boats to get the circulation going," said Paul.

They both set off, Paul doing a lazy crawl and Maureen a sedate but competent breast stroke. Just under the horizon a small fishing boat was heading for the harbour mouth. Soon the fourteen-footer was moored up. Paul and Maureen could see an elderly man with grey hair and a much younger man who nimbly ran up the steps and hurried off up the hill. The old man watched him, scratching the back of his head and muttered something to himself. Then, seeing the young couple in the water, shouted out, "Hello there, young 'uns. You wouldn't like to earn a few shillings would 'ee?"

"How do you mean?" asked Maureen, being nearest the man, and treading water.

"My mate has had to rush off to the dentist. He's got acute tooth-ache, so he says. Too many sweets I reckon," he said grinning. "The point is, I could do with some help to off-load a catch of herrings and crate 'em up in ice."

Maureen, laughing, said, "We have never done anything like that before, but I suppose it doe's nae require any real skill."

She unconsciously emphasised her native dialect in contrast to the man's broad Devon brogue.

"None at all my 'ansome," said the old man, bending down with difficulty to talk to her. "You sound like a long way from 'ome. Scotland by the sound of 'ee."

"That's right," laughed Maureen.

The man asked, "How about it then?"

"Paul! This gentleman wants us to help him unload his fish. His partner has had to hurry off to the dentist," shouted Maureen.

"Right, well if you don't mind handling all those dead fish, I'm game," Paul shouted back.

Maureen was out of the water and up the steps first; Paul swam across. Maureen went over to where their kit was, and the old man who was watching said, "You can both change in the hut on the quay. I'll go and open it up for 'ee."

He hurried ahead and opened the large padlock on the heavy battered old door of the ramshackle old hut. Almost miraculously a cobwebby electric light bulb lit up the dingy recesses and the man showed Maureen where the crates were, plus the huge refrigerator which housed the crushed ice.

"I shall start off loading the fish from the boat while you two get changed, my 'ansomes."

"I'll be as quick as I can," smiled Maureen.

She waited until he had gone before she stripped off her costume quickly and dried herself, shivering in the cold interior. She looked up to see Paul standing in front of her grinning like a Cheshire cat.

"I bet I can think of more interesting things to do than crate fish," said Paul eyeing Maureen hungrily.

"We are going to be paid for this you silly boy!" said Maureen, putting her knickers on and turning her back on Paul. "Hurry up and change. The man will probably be back in a minute with a crate of fish. I had better go and help him as soon as I have finished dressing."

"Can't you wait for me?" complained Paul.

"I expect the poor chap will need a hand right away," said Maureen practically, buttoning up her blouse before putting on her skirt. She hurried out as Paul was hoisting his trousers up over his damp legs, in a hurry to leave this fish smelling cavern. The old man had filled several crates with fish and looked up at Maureen as she jumped into the boat.

"If you and your friend can carry the crates of fish into the hut I can carry on down here until all the catch is off the boat," he said, eyeing the pretty girl appreciatively.

Before long, all the herrings were in the hut and the old man showed them how the fish were sorted and graded, then how to spread the ice over them. About an hour and a quarter later, they all washed their hands in the small grubby sink.

The old man said, "I clean forgot to tell'ee my name. It's Sam, Sam Headon. I very much appreciates you helping me out like that. I would have had to wait a long time for my dinner if I had to sort all they fish on me own. Here's half a crown each, and you can have as many herrings as you can carry home."

"Thanks very much Mr Headon, but I don't think we can carry very many fish back on our bikes though," said Maureen, taking her half crown from Sam.

"I could carry some in my haversack that I usually pack inside my saddlebag," said Paul pocketing his halfcrown.

"I'll tell 'ee what, I got a couple of old frail baskets, I bin meanin' to chuck really, but they should manage till you get 'ome. A bit of rope tyin' 'em together and, Paul is it? He can carry 'em, dangle 'em across his shoulders, or over the crossbar I daresay. Mind they don't bang about against the wheel though. I don't want to be the cause of an accident and spoil your day out, do I?"

Sam was as good as his word and Paul and Maureen said goodbye, carrying a full raffia basket of fish each as they started to walk back along the little quayside and then up the steep cobbled hill.

Maureen looked back down into the harbour where the low afternoon sun picked out the mercurial shimmering sea. She sighed to herself and as they carried on up the tiring ascent, leavened by the old-fashioned quaintness of the setting. Occasionally a breeze would waft the perfume of a rose across to them as they listened to myriads of bees humming amongst the brightly coloured flowers, packed tightly in their miniature bowers.

Before they mounted their bikes to go home, they had one last look down into the harbour and the bay.

"Well, it's been a lovely day Paul, but I bet we shall both be tired by the time we get home. I know I shall at any rate, said Maureen wistfully.

"Perhaps it would be a good idea if we swapped bikes going home as mine has better gears then yours. I could lower the saddle to make it easier for you," said Paul with concern in his voice.

"No, that's kind of you Paul, but it would look silly with me on a boy's bike and you on a girl's. I will be all right so long as you don't go racing on ahead, which I know you won't, will you?"

Paul laughed and said, "I think I'll be struggling myself with all these fish around my neck. That's bound to slow me down, isn't it?"

Maureen looked at Paul as he was tying pieces of strong cord to make a sort of saddle to hang across his neck and shoulders as Sam had suggested.

"Is that going to be safe?" she asked, more to hide a fit of giggles than anything. "You are beginning to look more like a French onion seller by the minute," she teased.

"He who laughs last laughs longest," said Paul, jumping on the bike and pulling away.

They both pedalled slowly up the lane under the arbour of tall trees lining the hedgerows. When they joined up with the main road from Cornwall to Devon it was better surfaced, but a long journey ahead of them.

They arrived at Auntie's house very tired, especially Maureen. Auntie Florence did not know whether to scold Paul for wearing out her niece, or to praise him for his carriage of the basket of herrings: a valuable commodity as well as a favoured food. She hoped that there would be roes inside as most of the local people liked them as much as the rich folk liked caviar.

A local hawker used to travel the streets with a hand cart shouting, "Hake and cod, and your own delicious Clovelly herrings!" Served with mashed potatoes and peas, herrings were popular. The only draw back was the copious numbers of small bones, but they were dealt with easily enough by practised hands, with the inedible fish parts transferred to a spare plate in the middle of the table.

Auntie had packed her fish into the outdoor safe, a sturdy cupboard hanging on an exterior wall, using up all her salt in an effort to keep the fish 'sweet' as long as possible. Herrings were to be on the menu every day for the next week. Auntie racked her brains to use the fish in as many different recipes as she could muster. She borrowed a couple of recipe books from neighbours who were glad to receive a few herrings in return. She even made a rice dish with the fish, something she had only used before to make rice puddings with. She did not normally like curry, but as the last fish started to smell a little strong, she felt that the spicy flavour of the curry would mask anything that tasted slightly different.

Paul's mother viewed her basket of herring with mixed feelings. Then she remembered that a very good friend and benefactor of the church who lived close by and had a large refrigerator, so was able to store the fish using a modern appliance not yet available to most people

CHAPTER NINE

When Paul turned up on Auntie's doorstep the following morning, having allowed Maureen an hour's extra lie-in, Auntie made a point of opening the door to let him in.

"What are you two going to do today then?" she asked as Maureen looked at Paul shyly; they both kept silent momentarily.

"I haven't seen much of Maureen since you came a-courting her Master Paul," said Auntie unexpectedly, making Paul blush and Maureen giggle and fidget nervously. "I don't want you traipsing round the countryside today, even if it is going to be another sunny day. Maureen must rest today, otherwise she'll be worn out. That don't mean we can't do something mind. I thought the three of us could have a picnic over at Bad-Step. You know I don't travel too well on a bus, and in any case it's hanging around waiting for 'em. I don't like. I can't walk too far either," said Auntie, perking up at the thought of an excursion, which was, in effect, a few hundred yards from her house.

Paul was not really enamoured with the idea, especially as it was a place well used by everyone in the village, having a small stretch of sand, in an otherwise muddy location, when the tide was out.

"It will be nice to be together for the rest of the day Auntie. What shall we take for a picnic? Sandwiches?" asked Maureen, thinking more along the lines of Paul, but also knowing that it was only fair that she spend more time with her Auntie.

"It just so happens that I made pasties yesterday, and I was going to use them for our tea tonight, but that was before I knew you were going to bring back all they fish. So we can take pasties and cheese straws and jam tarts with us. Put the kettle on Maureen and I'll fill up that big Thermos flask."

"Oh lovely, Auntie, isn't that great Paul?" said Maureen,

winking at Paul. "Spiffing!" said Paul with deliberation, "Perhaps we can pick some cockles in the mud. Mind you, after all those herrings, a load of cockles are going to be a bit much I suppose."

Paul tried to keep a straight face as Maureen mocked him behind Auntie's back.

"Well, go on and make the tea then," snapped Auntie, knowing that something was afoot, but not quite sure what it was.

The three set off for Bad-Step as the sun shone down on Florence's straw hat. True to the youngster's expectations there were quite a lot of people on the little beach but they just managed to find a space above the high water mark. Florence had brought her knitting, so Paul and Maureen decided to have a swim before the tide went right out and was not suitable for swimming. As it was, Auntie was not too happy about them going into the water at all, but Maureen promised her that they would not go out of their depth. Auntie could not relax until the two youngsters came out of the water, teeth chattering but exhilarated by the strange Nordic craving for cold water torture.

As a small concession to the heat of the midday sun, Florence had taken off her woolly and rolled her stockings around her ankles. It would not have been seemly to have walked through the village with her legs bare. As soon as the swimmers were dry, Florence doled out the pasties and other treats as the sun continued to favour them.

With lunch consumed, Florence felt the need to cool down a little so, slipping off her stockings altogether, she went down to the water's edge for a paddle; she walked nearly to the bottom of the lifeboat slipway to reach the receding tide.

As soon as Florence's back was facing them, Paul rolled over on top of Maureen for a quick kiss and cuddle, keeping a wary eye out for Auntie. As soon as she had turned around to look up the beach he came away from Maureen, who could not help but allow her giggles to develop into guffaws, much to the amusement of other picnickers. Fortunately Florence was too far off to be aware of such 'shenanigans', as she would have called it.

When Auntie returned, Paul said, "We are going to pick cockles now that the tide is right. Would you like to come with us?"

"Oh, no. I'm not going out in all that mud. Besides, someone has to stay here and look after the bags and things. I've got my purse in the basket as well. We might have an ice cream on the way home. Well, that's if you're both good, we will!" said Florence, giving a little laugh.

Paul and Maureen sloped off, with Paul carrying one of the old frails that Sam had given them. The mud smelt disgusting when trodden on and they had difficulty moving out to the cockle beds. Several times they fell over, covering themselves in mud, although as they were in bathing costumes it did not matter. They carried on using their hands to search for the cockles, after locating the tell-tale air-bubble holes, until the frail was full and heavy.

Suddenly Paul said to Maureen, "Have you ever heard of mud wrestling?"

"No. What's the point of that then?"

"No real point I suppose. It's just good fun. Let's try it." With that, Paul put down the frail and grabbed Maureen, pulling her down in the mud. Maureen started screaming like a little child as Paul scraped up mud and plastered it all over her neck and shoulders.

"Why you beast!" said Maureen, feigning indignation, and scooping up a handful she slapped it against the side of Paul's face, rubbing it all over his hair and trying to spread it over the rest of his face. Soon there was not an inch of their bodies that was not caked in the sticky smelly 'goo'. They walked back to Auntie chortling and enduring the stares and amused comments of the folk around them.

Auntie was having a nap, the hot sun and full belly making her sleepy. Paul bent down and shook her gently until she slowly opened her eyes. "Excuse please Missy, but here in Africa the sun is very strong. Please be careful you do not get sunstroke."

Auntie's consciousness was returning as this black face seemed to be pressed right up against hers. She started, and sat bolt upright.

"My soul, who is it, for heaven's sake? Oh! It's you Paul! What a fright you gave me, and look at the state of both of you. Off with you and get yourselves clean of that horrible mud. Serves you right if you have to go a long way down the life-boat slip to get yourselves cleaned up in the water."

Auntie watched them scamper off, muttering to herself, although the creases around her eyes and a slight curl of the mouth denoted a half-smile of amusement.

As they walked home, the young couple were chattering away happily. Florence could see that her niece was happy with the parson's son, who seemed to have a mischievous sense of humour. She knew that her niece had a strong enough will of her own, and that she would not be likely to be influenced by something that she did not want to do. It was plain, however, that their young relationship had a bigger commitment than was usual for their ages. Florence also knew that Maureen was quite mature for her age both, emotionally and physically, and that she had the responsibility of looking after Maureen at a difficult time in a teenagers' life. On the other hand, Maureen was on holiday and she did not want to spoil her fun. Then fear gripped at her vitals as she remembered the real purpose of her visit to Bideford the day before – to the hospital – for tests to determine whether or not she had cancer.

Florence had been feeling rather poorly for some time now, but had kept it to herself. There was not much of a choice of people in whom she could confide. No husband or family living nearby. The only one really was the Baptist minister, but he was not a very charismatic person and seemed a bit cold to talk to on a personal level. It was funny really. Ten years before, during wartime, everyone had opened up their hearts and were not so prudish and secretive. Now things seemed harder and more hypocritical than they had been before the war.

Rationing, that had started during wartime, had nearly ended, but there was still a shortage of lots of things, and in any case money was in short supply for a widow like herself. In many ways it was a gloomy era, with the cold war at its zenith. The French had been thrown out of Vietnam- or Indo China, as everyone called it. The previous allies, Britain and the USA. had decided not to get involved at that time. The threat of the spread of Communism from the Soviet Union to the satellite states was quite real, although the Americans seemed to be more worried about the spread of Communism in their own homeland. Senator McCarthy was having a field day at home, much to the puzzlement of people in Britain and the rest of the world.

'Could there really be that many communists in the film industry?' Wondered Florence, walking along Irsha Street and passing the little local cinema, 'The Gaiety'. She did not like that man McCarthy, who was stirring things up. She preferred Billy Graham the Evangelist. She had heard him on the radio preaching. A fine man. A Baptist too. What a pity she could not open her heart to him – or someone like him. She sighed to herself as they arrived at her doorstep.

"I suppose you two will be off again tomorrow, as usual. Where is it going to be then?" Florence asked abruptly, startling the pair who had been in their own world.

Maureen looked shyly at Paul who reddened predictably and stammered, "I, I, I think it might be a good idea to cycle to Westward Ho! I heard on the radio that it is going to be quite windy on the north coast, so it might be a good idea for us to hire a surfboard and go surfing. We earned a bit of pocket money from the fisherman, didn't we?" said Paul triumphantly, looking across to a bemused Maureen.

"Surfing? My soul!" exclaimed Florence with the strange mixture of the West Country burr and the underlying Aberdeen lilt converging.

"Maureen's never done any surfing, have you Maureen?" said a worried Auntie as Maureen shook her head. "It's quite safe really. There's no undertow when the tide is coming in, and that's the only time that it's good for surfing. In any case, they won't hire out boards if it's going to be dangerous. The chap that hires out the boards is a good surfer himself; brings the surfers in with flags if it looks as if anything might be dangerous," said Paul, hoping that Florence would be convinced. "Hmm, well you make sure that you don't go into the water unless there's a lot of grown ups out there surfing, mind," said Auntie, frowning solemnly at Paul, who swallowed uncomfortably.

"No. We'll take good care Auntie," said Paul humbly, as Florence opened the door with a mortice key attached by cord to a piece of wood.

"I'll see you in the morning then," said a relieved Paul, moving up to the side of the doorway where Maureen was standing. As Auntie moved into the house, Paul gave Maureen a quick kiss on her cheek and they briefly said goodnight, though the night was young. Paul walked home cheerfully enough with the expectations of another good day with Maureen on the morrow.

CHAPTER TEN

The day dawned brightly enough, with high clouds being driven by strong winds. The humidity was replaced with a freshness that put energy into their leg muscles as they cycled along the narrow roads to Westward Ho!, their hair flapping in the breeze. Paul's saddlebag was crammed with home-made pasties swapped for herrings in a splendid barter arrangement.

"Wow! Look at the surf!" exclaimed Paul as they came in view of the breakers.

Maureen smiled, but felt a little nervous as she was more used to the swimming pool than the turbulent water in the bay. In due course, they turned off the roadway at the outskirts of Westward Ho! to cycle along a track that was used by the Marines on manoeuvres, when they used amphibious vehicles known as 'ducks'. A Bailey bridge had been built over the pebble ridge to give the 'ducks' a good entry into the sea. Paul got off his bike a short way off, to the left of the bridge, not too far from the slipway but reasonably private and quiet. He lay the bicycle against the back of the pebble ridge that rose up from the sweep of the burrows from the slipway to Greysands Point nearly two miles away. As Paul undid the straps of his saddlebag, Maureen removed her haversack from the basket fixed on the front of her bicycle.

"You are not expecting us to be in the water all day long, are you?" she asked anxiously.

"Oh no! Gracious me!" said Paul laughingly. "We would probably look like a couple of wrinkled prunes if we did, wouldn't we? Would you like to lie in the sun for a bit and rest?" said Paul gallantly, although he did have an ulterior, selfish motive in mind.

Maureen was not unaware of what might be in the offing but quietly agreed. Paul spread both their bathing-com-beach towels out on the sandy turf, side by side, near their bicycles.

"It's just as well we change into our swimming costumes right away, then we can get nice and brown. It's not so cold here as I thought it would be," said Maureen, pleasantly surprised.

"It's the pebble ridge acting as a windbreak. It will be pretty hot here by midday. That's probably the best time to be in the water. The tide may be a way out, but it will be coming in strong all the time, and will hopefully give us some good surfing," said Paul, looking forward to a sport which was usually out of range of his pocket money, the hire of the boards being raised to the level that holiday makers, from other parts of the country, could afford. Maureen picked up her towel and draped it round herself using a large safety pin to hold the towel together around her neck. Paul had his trunks on under his shorts, so he was quickly undressed and helping Maureen with her 'modesty', which she duly noted in an ironic manner.

"I think you can see more of me, holding up the towel, than if you were lying down," she said in a scolding tone.

"Ah! But I am protecting your modesty from strangers. I have already seen your naked body, haven't I?" he said cheekily.

"All right! All right! Keep your voice down. There are people only a short way off," said Maureen in a cross voice, but knowing that what Paul had said was perfectly true. Their relationship when together, could not go back from what it had become. They were now lovers, even if they could not fully consummate their relationship.

The towel, having done its job, returned to the turf and Maureen foraged inside her haversack. She went over to where Paul was lying on his towel and placed a small bottle of olive oil in his hand.

"We can spread some of this olive oil over our bodies to stop the sun from drying our skin, and also stop the salt from making us sore when we go into the water," she said, as Paul started to rub some oil over his arms, legs and torso.

"I thought you would be a gentleman and put some oil around my shoulders," said Maureen hands on hips and exasperation in her voice.

"Oh, sorry!" said Paul sheepishly, as he complied with Maureen's request.

"If we do each others backs, then we can do the rest ourselves," said Maureen pointedly, as Paul's hand started to stray until it received a sharp slap, which made enough noise to make neighbouring folk a short way off, turn their heads in the young couple's direction. Maureen could not help giggling and told Paul that it served him right. He had a red mark on the back of his hand and he worked the oil into the temporarily inflamed area.

Suitably greased all over, they lay down and let the sun relax the tensions in their bodies. Maureen had borrowed a scratched pair of sunglasses from Auntie and had put them on so that she could lie on her back. Paul tried putting a handkerchief over his eyes for protection, but tired of that option after a while and rolled over on his side to look at Maureen's youthful, rounded curves. He looked at her slim and now smooth and shiny legs and thighs. Suddenly the memory of the copulating woman at Greencliff with her mocking laugh and inviting sex, troubled and poisoned his thoughts. He put an arm around Maureen's slender waist enjoying the curve and then massaging a thigh.

"Careful now, people are watching," sang Maureen, mocking Paul, but not moving. Paul was beginning to regret choosing a spot out in the open, where everything they did, could be seen. He got bored quickly and after Maureen had turned over to even her tan a couple of times, she started to read a school textbook. It was the novel, *A Tale of Two Cities*, that she would be studying next term. Paul got up on his feet to walk around.

"Where are you going?" asked Maureen anxiously "Er, I have to go to the toilet. I can't stay too long in hot sun. I get burnt easily," said the fair skinned Paul, truthfully enough; though by the end of the holiday his skin would have a golden glow.

"Well, don't be long, or go wandering off somewhere. If you leave me here on my own for very long, some nice young fellow in a sports car might whisk me off somewhere," said Maureen, smiling now. "You had better take some pennies with you. Here! Take my purse, if you are going in just your trunks," said Maureen, throwing her small purse with a little loose change in it.

"Oh thanks. I'll settle up with you when I get back."

"I've counted what's there," sallied Maureen as Paul walked off.

He made his way to the seafront area where the public conveniences were, at the rear of the putting green. On his way he noticed a small funfair, mainly for children on holiday, with roundabouts and swing. a few stalls with a shooting range and darts to be thrown at playing cards.

As he was returning from the toilet he thought he would walk through the fun fair, uninspiring though it looked. It was more or less on his way back. Just a small detour to while away a few minutes. A steam organ was playing a lively tune to the accompaniment of cymbals and pipes. He noticed a gypsy caravan, brightly painted, and a sign stating that Madame Perspicacity, Clairvoyant, would tell people's fortunes for a small fee. Paul was naturally a little curious; fascinated more by the gypsy caravan, minus its horse, standing splendidly in front of him. He walked around to the front and saw a woman sitting on the step, with a crimson silk scarf on her head, a black velvety waistcoat over a wide necked low cut blouse and a long flouncy Flamenco-type skirt riding over black leather boots. Suddenly, he realised with a shock why her face looked so familiar. It was the same woman he had seen at Greencliff.

He was about to turn on his heel in embarrassment, when she noticed him and shouted, "Come along young sir. Come and have your fortune told. I like the look of you, so it will only be a very small charge."

Paul clenched his fist tightly around Maureen's tiny purse and stood there like a rabbit mesmerised by the headlights of a car. Slowly he turned and faced her.

"I don't think I have enough money on me," he said quietly, averting his eyes.

"Well, seeing that you are just a schoolboy, I shall only charge you sixpence. Come inside my dear," she said, grabbing his arm but showing no sign of recognition. They walked up the steps of the caravan and through the doorway to go inside. Paul trembling slightly with a sense of foreboding, but also harboured a strange sense of fascination that denied him the logic of flight, especially when she bolted the door from the inside.

Whatever the caravan had been used for previously, it was not now like the cosy interior one would imagine a traveller of the road to have. No signs of cosy artefacts like kettles, or strings of onions, or herbs. The caravan larger than traditional models seemed to be divided into two unequal parts by a pair of draped, heavy, maroon coloured velvet curtains hanging from wooden rings threaded on a horizontal metal rail. A small round table was in the middle of the room with a crystal ball on a stand in the centre of a heavy green velvet tablecloth. An ornately carved chair was near the curtain neatly upholstered on the seat and back. On the other side of the table another chair matched it perfectly. The main thing that struck Paul, however, were the mirrors. Large mirrors all around the walls and even on the ceiling, each set at a slightly different angle, some seeming to magnify the person's reflection, whilst others distorted. It was the same type of mirror that he had enjoyed looking in at previous fun fairs.

"Sit down my boy," the woman said, in the deep husky voice that heavy women-smokers have. The acrid smell of nicotine pervaded the caravan and would recall this moment on subsequent occasions when he was aware of stale tobacco. Paul sat down on the large chair, feeling vulnerable in his near nakedness.

The woman seemed to sense this as she sat down and asked, "You have been on the beach then?"

"Yes, my friend and I are going to do some surfing shortly," said Paul nervously, looking at his skinny reflection in the mirrors, and at the woman's fleshy cleavage looking down on him as he looked upwards.

"You like the mirrors, I see," she croaked, and leaned forward slightly to tuck the seat of her skirt neatly together with both hands and then sat back on her ample rump as she seemed to be tidying or re-arranging the front of the velvet red and black skirt. Paul had assumed that she was just getting herself comfortable and avoiding the creases that can easily arrive through carelessness, especially with pleats. He noticed a reflection from a mirror that had reflected the image from another mirror. It dawned on Paul that the mirrors had been set at a certain angle to cover a particular nominated image. The image that he was looking at could only have been possible if the chair that Madame Perspicacity was sitting in had been set back from the table, and would not have been visible if she was sitting close to the table; a fact that had puzzled Paul initially.

Paul's eyes were now drawn to this image, one that he was not aware of when looking at her across the table. The image revealed that the long skirt looped around a black belt and was designed with buttons down the front, now undone with the bottom of the skirt wide open and revealing sturdy but well proportioned stockinged legs and also the fact that Madame was not wearing any undergarments. She reached out to the end of the table and touched it with her long heavily lacquered fingernails, weaving her head and body as she looked inside the crystal ball. Paul's gaze was magnetised to the mirror image exaggerating every minor movement of the body.

"I see a young boy, and, ah yes, a young girl. They are very much in love, I think," said Madame in her low husky voice.

Paul gulped and wiped the perspiration from his upper lip and forehead with his fingertips, wiping them on the side of his bathing trunks.

Madame racked her brains to pick up little pieces of information – clues to the lifestyle of the client. There was precious little of this from the near-naked youth in front of her. This inspired her to a not unfamiliar recklessness that was now a part of her own lifestyle. After all, life was for living and if you could give others pleasure, then there ought to be some left for herself. He was a good-looking boy, she thought, even if he was quite thin. Better than a lot of her previous clients, some of whom were grossly overweight. He looked at her uneasily, a sensitive vulnerable virgin. She would enjoy this session, as a break from the predictable clichés that punters almost expected her to relate. They certainly did not want to pay good money to hear bad news.

The day was still fresh. She did not usually have a session this early in the day. In fact, most of her business was contracted in the evening. Some with young couples mooning over each other, or else the odd drunk whom she sent off home late in the evening and not really knowing what had gone on in any case. She was feeling fresh herself. She somehow felt girlish inside. This boy obviously was attracted by her sexuality. Something that was essential to ply her trade. Madame made the most of what she had. She did not have classic good looks, so she enhanced the attributes she had. Her generous mouth was made voluptuous with heavily applied crimson lipstick that matched her headscarf, sitting on top of her carefully dyed, long, black, curly locks. She looked into the crystal ball that picked and mixed the mirrored light as she weaved her head around in rotary movements.

"You are unsure of your future," she stated, guessing that most teenagers would be, if not the majority of the population.

"You are finding that the new responsibilities that are expected of you a great burden."

Although a fairly predictable statement for a teenager, she did not know how true this was in Paul's case, and as with the throw of a dice, the right number does come up sometimes.

Madame followed with, "You feel you should be allowed more control over your life."

This was something she knew every teenager wanted, even if it was not wanted by society as a whole. Her sympathies were with him, as she was a free spirit, although not a genuine Romany. She decided to take the bull by the horns and the dangerous legal term 'corrupting a minor' only added to her excitement. Slowly she got up from her seat, moving around the table to sit on it in front of the crystal ball and facing Paul. She sat silently for a while her legs spread unladylike and wide apart.

"Do you like what you see?" she croaked huskily.

Paul could not take his eyes from the offering, but felt he should answer her as he lifted his gaze in shame.

"You don't need to answer that question. I can see that you do," she said, pushing her rump forward whilst her hands took her weight as she left the table top to stand in front of Paul.

Paul had been mesmerised by the erotic combination of the fishnet stockings, visible over the top of her calf-length boots and linked across the fleshy white thighs by the universal fetish of black suspenders, and framing the central offering of a virtual Black Forest. Now the pupils of his eyes dilated even wider as Madame Perspicacity stooped before him, her cleavage almost in his face as her hands went to his sides.

"I think your little man is straining to get out, don't you, my son, so we had better set him free," she said pulling the top of his trunks down.

"Oh, it is a bit tight. I'd better be careful. I don't want you to have an injury now, do I ducks?"

Paul was still speechless as she felt for the elastic cord and the knot, which she deftly untied.

"Put your hands on the arms of the chair and lift your bum a moment," she demanded.

As if in a trance, Paul acquiesced and then he was naked, bar his canvas shoes. His manhood erect and throbbing. She gently stroked the underside of his shaft and said, "Quite a piece of equipment you have there my boy. I can see it needs protecting and lubricating though. Don't go away," she smiled, disappearing through the curtains and returning in seconds with something between the fingers of one hand and a jar of vaseline in the other. She placed the jar on the table while she brought the ivory coloured object towards Paul with two hands.

"You are going to get a real treat now. You are going to find out what that thing on the crossbar of your bike was all about," she said with a quick cackle. Then with a practised hand she unravelled the condom over his still erect member. Picking up the jar, she liberally applied the lubricant.

"I can see you are up for this my boy, but you are not saying much. I want you to do something for me now though. I want you to touch me gently, you know, inside, and also where you would like to feel, all right?" she almost pleaded, reverting to a less assertive mode, with an almost childlike tone in her voice as it rose several octaves as if to prove her femininity.

Paul again complied with her request tentatively, although losing some of his fear about her. The spell had been broken.

116

She was not the 'Wicked Witch of the West', as in the *Wizard of Oz*, after all. She had needs like himself, so he would help her if he could. He did not know what a nymphomaniac was, and she would not have admitted that she was one. At that moment, they were just two people with one need.

Madame now came around to the left of Paul's chair, her legs apart and her right arm across his broad shoulders, hoping that Paul was right handed. Paul was, in fact, mainly right handed and he slowly sent out searching fingers, tracing up over the rough surface of the nylon stocking and then onto the smooth surface of her inner thigh where the backs of his fingers encountered the taut elastic of the suspender. He let his fingers slip under the suspender enjoying the feel of the contrasting textures. He leaned forward in the chair so he could let his left hand go to the back of her thigh, under her skirt and resting on the opposite suspender. Now he felt better balanced to continue his explorations and moved his right hand up her inner thigh and allowed the tips of his fingers to explore her dense black tangle, cupping her mound and enjoying the bristly texture of her delta.

Madame was now the person who seemed in a trance as she stood at his side, her legs splayed and looking at the reflections in the mirrors. As his fingers felt for the parting she gasped a little, closing her eyes momentarily as the digits slid up under the folds, exploring the increasingly moist surfaces until they reached its zenith at the hooded secret.

Paul had learned quickly from Maureen's guidance and he now compared the old with the new, he rotated a finger, gently caressing the tender spot. They both grew excited as the organ swelled to its maximum growth and secreted its own fluids. Madame shuddered momentarily as she gasped again, putting her hands around the back of Paul's neck and bringing his face into her ample bosom. She thought to reward him for pleasuring her so well and adjusted her blouse and her brassiere so that her pendulous breasts cushioned Paul's face. He showed his appreciation by nibbling at the hard brown nipples inside their equally brown areola. She knew now that it was near the time of climax; she came in front of him and straddled him, easing herself down on his erect member.

"Brace yourself with your arms!" she commanded, and Paul grasped the chair arms as his pelvis sought hers.

She placed her hands on his shoulders as she thrust her groin and hips to ride him like a horse. Excitedly he felt under her skirt to try to get around the backs of her thighs to her buttocks, but could not reach. She was not finding it too comfortable this way, the angle of penetration not being quite right. She backed off just in time, realising that youths could not manage very long copulation without ejaculation. Madame turned around to face the table. She removed the crystal ball to the floor and threw the tablecloth off. Then she eased herself to sit on the edge of the table, her legs apart.

Paul was by now fully charged, and needed no encouragement as he quickly found the entrance to paradise. His hands searched under her skirts again until he found her buttocks and she stood up whilst he caressed them, sliding his hands under the suspender straps again, enjoying the warm relaxed feeling from his groin until he felt the need to surge forward, again and again. She could feel the urgency now and lay back on the table. His hands, deprived of rumps, found breasts instead. He clutched at them as he penetrated deeper and deeper, and then in his excitement and knowing that he might hurt her, he clasped her hips to draw himself to her, whilst she lay flat-backed on the table top, her breasts quivering with each thrust, her legs locked over his hips for support.

Paul could not help but see the many reflections in the mirrors and did not really need the stimulation from it, although it had the effect of making it a more surreal occasion. Madame, on the other hand, found looking up at the ceiling mirrors highly erotic and had used them for just such purposes as this on other occasions. She had never entertained one so young before, and rarely had she found anyone so gentle, although he was reaching an aggressive climax. If he was a virgin, he certainly had good instincts of how to treat a woman. It would soon all be over with; she strove to reach orgasm at the same time as him. She could now see he was near ejaculation and then, as a finale, she gripped the edge of the table with her fingers and put her legs on his shoulders, her short leather boots helping to grip him tightly.

After a few vigorous thrusts Paul grimaced as though in pain, gave a few long grunts and ended in along sigh. She watched it all in the overhead mirror and timed the occasion perfectly herself, with the benefit of years of practise. Allowing him a minute or two to collect himself, she hung on to him with her legs until she sat up brought her legs down over the table edge and gently massaged his shoulders until he looked sheepishly at her, still not knowing what to say.

Disentangling herself from him, she brought out a box of large tissues and removed the condom, allowing him to cleanse himself in the sink behind the curtain. Having followed him inside the little room she even dried him off with a towel. She was being motherly she told herself, as she saw how he had reverted to the shy awkward teenager.

"Was it your first time then?" she asked, with genuine curiosity. He looked up at her with the realisation that he was indeed not a virgin any longer. The exaltation he felt emboldened him to say with a smile, "You should know. You are the one who knows the future and what I was before I came here." She smiled at him, the way a mother humours her young child.

"So, now you feel like a man, right?" she asked, with humour in her eyes, slumping down on the little bed in the corner.

"Right!" He affirmed awkwardly. He suddenly realised that Maureen would be waiting for him down by the sea, wondering what had happened to him. He told her about his girl friend.

"I think you had better tell her the truth, don't you?" she said abruptly.

"The truth?" repeated Paul with horror.

"Yes! That you have been helping an old lady to... find her way," she said simply.

"Find her way?" Paul echoed her words again.

"You can tell her that you came across an old lady who had lost her way, and you helped her find it," she said, laying her head back against the pillow. Paul's face changed from a worried frown to a smile.

"Maybe that's not a bad idea," he said grinning.

"I think you had better be going along back to her now then, don't you?" Madame said wearily.

"Oh, er, yes, I suppose I had. Um, How much do I owe you?" he asked with dread.

"How much? You have only got a few coppers belonging to your girl friend; you better make sure that you pick her purse up, hadn't you? No! I shan't charge you anything or it will give the game away, won't it?"

"Well, thanks very much. It – was – quite an experience. I can't believe it's not a dream," he said frowning.

"It is a bloody dream, my son. I'm just a figment of your imagination," she said abruptly, letting out a cackle similar to the one that froze his heart at Greencliff a couple of days ago.

He thought it time to go, so he made it through the gap in the curtain. He picked up his swimming trunks from the floor, put them back on, picked up Maureen's purse, and made for the door, pulling the bolt back. He turned around to face where she was behind the curtain.

"Bye then!" he shouted. He waited for a reply, but none came.

Opening the door he squinted into the bright sunshine and then slammed the door shut and walked away. Madame lay on the bed with tears streaming down her face, making her mascara and face powder run into multi-coloured rivulets, like a Jackson Pollack stick painting.

Paul was in a quandary as he hurried along to re-join Maureen. Various emotions wheeled around in his head. One thing made his stomach sick: his betrayal of trust with Maureen. He knew he could not tell her what had happened; he could hardly believe what had happened. It was a bit like a bolt of lightning striking out of the sky to hit the only person around for hundreds of miles. Why had it happened to him? He had not encouraged it to happen. He should have turned tail as soon as he had recognised the woman.

It had been some experience though. Paul thought that none of his school friends would be able to boast of anything similar. He would never tell any of them what had happened, but would listen to any boasting of theirs and give a secretive smile, and it would remain a secret. Paul was as exhilarated as any youth would be after his first sexual intercourse. He would rather it had been with Maureen, but that was another matter. There was something not right about the difference of ages. He wondered if it had been a criminal act, technically, and was vaguely aware of underage sex but did not know the details.

He remembered a youth, only about three or four years older than himself, who had married a Spanish woman about forty years of age, who was old enough to be his mother. In fact she had a daughter who went to the Catholic School in Bideford. Paul quite fancied her and they once shared a seat on the school bus one morning, but she was so shy that he could not make conversation. She did not mix well with other girls on a social level either, Paul knew, or he would have made a friendship with her the same as he did with other local girls: mainly on speaking terms, with the occasional kiss, cuddle, and grope. The apparently miss-matched couple had created a bit of local scandal and eventually moved to a large town. Paul wondered how the daughter would get on with a step- father that was just a few years older than herself.

There was no more time to be thinking about the past. Paul mulled over in his mind what he was going to say to Maureen. Madame's story about helping an old lady was quite plausible if he could only work out the details.

That's it! He would say he came across an old lady wandering around, looking lost, muttering to herself and generally looking distressed. Being brought up in a Christian home, it was naturally his duty to go to her assistance. On asking where she lived, she told him that she was from the Catholic Old People's Home up the hill. He had walked her slowly back, whereupon the nuns were full of thanks for returning her.

It was with great relief that he had sorted the story out just before he approached Maureen, who was still in the same place when he arrived back and looking very indignant as soon as she saw him.

"Where the Dickens have you been then?" she hissed suspiciously.

"Hang on. Wait a moment. I'll tell you if you keep calm," he said, pretending to be cross. He then realised that he was not very good at lying. He could not remember ever telling a big lie before.

"Well?" Maureen snapped impatiently.

Paul recounted the tale he had rehearsed in his mind and waited for her reaction with bated breath.

"You don't look as if you have been out in the sun for over an hour. Only your face is red," she said suspiciously, smelling a rat.

"Well, I have been inside the old folks home for about half an hour. Honestly! You do your best to help other people and you get told off for it," said Paul, trying to sound convincing; hoping his guilt would come over as anger.

"Oh, and by the way, because my skin is fair, I do not tan as easy as you, that's also why I go red," he added, flopping down to the turf and scowling. Maureen stared at him for a while, then weakened a little, but still did not show it as she retorted

"I hope you haven't spent all my money in the Penny Arcade on those catch penny machines," she barked.

"No I haven't," he snapped back and threw her purse over to her. Maureen convinced herself that he was telling the truth, even if there was something sly about his manner. Paul had always been a little odd in his mannerisms and she had put it down to his innate shyness which, she mused, did not stop him being pushy in a certain direction where she was concerned.

"Are we going surfing before lunch or after?" she said, changing the subject.

Paul breathed a secret sigh of relief as he realised she had believed his lies; a cloud of guilt smothered his heart just the same.

"Mm. I wonder what the time is? Do you think it's noon yet? They say you shouldn't go in the water with a full stomach, so I suppose we ought to go surfing first," said Paul, enjoying getting back to normality He felt even happier when Maureen waved something at him.

"What's that then?" he asked curiously.

"Can't you see. It's a watch. It's Uncle Duncan's watch.

122

Auntie said I could use it, so there would not be any excuse for being late home. It's nearly a quarter-to twelve," she said, squinting at it through her sunglasses.

"If we go for an hour's surfing, that should be just right to get back for lunch. All right?" said Paul, with his usual enthusiasm for planning interesting things.

"I suppose we had better start packing up then. Shall we take everything with us?" asked Maureen, not so good at organising things herself.

"Oh yes. I think that's best. Well, everything but the bikes. When we've hired the surfboards, we can put our kit at the bottom of the pebble ridge on the sea-side so we can keep our eye on it while we are in the water," Paul said matter-of-factly.

"You think of everything don't you, smartly pants?" she teased.

"Yes, I think that they should make me a school prefect, don't you?" he said laughing.

"That'll be the day!" said Maureen, smiling as she picked up her basket.

They both walked off with Paul carrying his unstrapped saddlebag under his arm and Maureen with her haversack. A short walk over the pebble ridge and across the beach brought them up the slipway, to weave amongst the folk in deck chairs and arrive at the small kiosk that hired-out the surfboards.

A bronzed, Nordic-looking young man with piercing blue eyes, wearing a pair of tan shorts above sturdy legs, was standing outside. Paul recognised him and asked to hire a couple of boards for an hour, getting the money out of his white shorts pocket that he had put on over his swimming trunks for the express purpose. The man took the money, holding an amount for a deposit, and put it into a deep leather pouch strapped around his shoulder.

"Keep between the flags, if they get changed to red, come straight in. If the numbers on your boards correspond with a bat being flashed by someone at the edge of the water, it means you have gone over the hour. If you leave it much later to come out of the water you will not get your full deposit back. Right?" said the young man smiling. They both nodded and took the boards.

They moved down the slipway again carefully as the man went into the kiosk to pick up his binoculars to scan the surf.

Walking along the beach Paul noticed a respectable looking elderly couple sitting on deck-chairs and asked them if they minded looking after their belongings. The couple agreed and after some friendly conversation the intrepid pair made their way down to the surf, which was over halfway up the beach and coming in fast. They decided to get under the water as quickly as possible and minimize the shock of the comparatively cold water. Predictable screams from Maureen and grunts from Paul brought them out into deep enough water to catch a wave.

"You have got to lie on the board as far up as you can get, so we had better practise that a minute I think," said Paul wisely.

Maureen found that difficult without the impetus of a wave's natural buoyancy, so they practised hurling themselves on the swell to catch a wave. After about a dozen waves Maureen was doing quite well. So well, that Paul had to improve his technique, otherwise she might be better than him, and he was enough of a traditionalist to be annoyed by a female being better at a sport than a male: something ingrained in the male psyche, in any case. The hour soon passed with exhilarating pleasure, as the marine plywood body-boards with the upwardly curved ends plied their way right up the beach.

Paul and Maureen gradually moved back out into deeper water, although never getting deeper than they could comfortably stand in. The cold started to seep into Paul's bones first as he did not have the same amount of natural fat that females have. He had thoroughly enjoyed the challenge and was pleased to see that Maureen had as well, especially bearing in mind his recent erotic experiences, largely forgotten during the surfing, until he realised that surfing had an erotic symbolism of its own. There was, even in those early days of surfing, a cult of young men who were married to the surfboard and organised their lives around surfing, following it around the world. Paul could imagine surfing as a sexual experience, riding a board on top of a huge Pacific wave as being an orgasmic experience. However, he was not too upset when he noticed their board numbers being displayed on bats held aloft.

"Time to go in now I am afraid!" he shouted to Maureen, who was turning around to go back to gather another wave. He noticed the disappointment on her face, and knew that the occasion had been a great success. They slowly waded back to the slipway. Paul acknowledged the numbers being held up by holding his board up in one hand and waving with the other.

"We shall have to do that again, I can see," said Paul putting his free arm around her waist. They left the surf behind and the boards at the kiosk, regaining their deposits.

"I certainly hope so," said Maureen, sighing happily.

They made their way back to their belongings, Maureen thanking the couple for looking after them.

"We've been watching you," said the white-haired gentleman, although most of his hair was obscured by a neat straw hat. His goatee beard matched the whiteness of his hair.

"I think you really enjoyed yourselves, didn't you?" said his wife smiling.

"It's the first time I've been surfing," said Maureen with some pride.

"Really? How extraordinary. – You looked like a professional to me," said the man, correcting himself in case his abbreviation caused unintentional offence.

"You seem to be a natural born surfer," he remarked, and as Maureen beamed modestly, thanking him, turned to Paul, "Was it the first time you have been surfing then young man?"

"Er, no, actually. I don't do a lot though. I've not got enough pocket money to hire surf boards very often, I'm afraid," said Paul, a bit deflated.

"Hm. Do you live locally then, you two?" asked the man, his curiosity encouraged by the attractive young couple.

"Well I do. Maureen, my friend, is on her holiday," said Paul, hoping that the elderly couple would go back to their books.

"Did I denote a Scottish accent in your voice?" asked the gentleman, looking at Maureen.

"Yes. I'm from Aberdeen. I'm staying with my Auntie at Appledore. That's where I met Paul."

"Oh! How romantic. So you two have not known each other

very long then?" asked the lady.

"No. Not very long at all really," said Maureen shyly.

"Extraordinary," reflected the old man. "We are here on holiday to do a bit of golfing. Well, we are not as good at golfing as you are with surfing, but we enjoy it and it helps keep us fit, doesn't it my dear," said the old man to his wife as they smiled at each other.

"We could each do with a caddie now though. May has a trolley with wheels, although one of them looks a bit dodgy, and the wheels of my trolley fell off a long time ago," he said laughing. "We shall have to get new trollies of course. I don't suppose you could help us out and be our caddies once or twice, could you? Of course we would pay you. You would have plenty of money to go surfing then wouldn't you?"

Paul and Maureen looked at each other. What had been an awkward, boring conversation to Paul had been transformed by the word 'money'.

"I tell you what. We are staying at the hotel next to the golf course. Oh, here's my card. I'm George, by the way," he said, handing the card over to Paul.

"You don't have to make any commitment now, but if you call in at the hotel and produce that card after nine in the morning, someone will bring you to us. How's that? Not out?" said George, laughing heartily.

Both Paul and Maureen were taken with the friendliness of the couple now, so Paul said, "That's a very kind offer, Maureen and I will certainly consider it, won't we Maureen?" asked Paul.

Maureen smiled and said, "Yes. Especially if we can do you a favour. That would be nice."

"Yes, well, you can help us out and then do some surfing after, can't you. I tell you what, we'll see if you are as good at golf as you are at surfing. You can have a round with us if you like. There's no time limit and we shan't be very competitive. We'll be afraid that you will show us up, I should imagine. How's that then?" said George, laughing again.

"That's very kind of you indeed," said Maureen. "I'm sure that we will take you up on your kind offer," she said courteously.

"Yes, thanks again. We have to get back to our bicycles near the other side of the Bailey bridge, so we will leave you to your reading," said Paul, picking up his saddlebag.

They both strode off, after waving goodbye, and clambered over the Bailey bridge. They reached their bicycles and made camp so that they could eat their packed lunch.

"I'm just about ready for this now," said Paul after Maureen handed him a pastie.

"Me too. Good old Auntie Flo."

"Well? What do you think of George and May's offer then?" enquired Maureen.

"George and May? Oh yes. That could come in handy I suppose," said Paul vaguely.

"Anyone for golf?" she parodied.

"I shouldn't have thought that you would have been interested in playing, anyway," he said scathingly.

"Oh really! I don't suppose you thought I could be interested in surfing either," said Maureen, bristling with anger.

"I was glad that you did like surfing. Why shouldn't I be," said Paul, not wanting to upset her.

"Well, wouldn't it be nice to help the old folk anyway?" queried Maureen.

"They are not short of a bob or two, you know," said Paul, pulling George's card out of the pocket of his trunks.

"Here, look at this. George Fulton. Chartered Surveyor. Hey! He's got the room number on the back."

"Well, if you are not interested, we can always go cockle picking again I suppose," said Maureen, with a twinkle in her eyes.

"I'll give you cockles my girl," said Paul, putting his pastie down and rolling over to Maureen, to tickle her sides.

"Huh! I don't want your cockles, or your mussels come to that. They'll have to grow a bit in any case," she said, and screamed with laughter again as Paul tickled her harder than before. Her attractive nubile, body stirred him to kiss her on the mouth, long and tenderly, as she accepted his token of love.

"Ugh! Kissing after eating pasties is not the most romantic of things, is it?" she said, screwing her face up and bringing Paul back to earth with a bump.

He contented himself with the memories of his earlier erotic encounter, although this had had more to do with basic instincts than anything to do with love. Would he still love Maureen when she was as old as Madame Perspicacity? He decided he would. Maureen was much more beautiful, wholesome and clever. He also thought she could be a lot sexier too, if she wanted to. She would be going away shortly though. How would he cope without her? He shuddered, and tried to put it out of his mind.

"Are you alright?" she asked. "You've gone very quiet."

"Oh, I'm OK, sweetheart," said Paul. doing an impersonation.

"Who's that supposed to be then?" quizzed Maureen.

"James Cagney. Why, wasn't it obvious?" he said, tongue in cheek.

He did his best to remember Cagney's stock in trade remarks such as his 'Dirty rat' phrase, and the way he grimaced his teeth. They were consumed with convulsed laughter for a while, doing various impressions, poorly. They finished their lunch and lay in the sun all the afternoon, going in the water briefly to cool down a couple of times. They used up a lot of the olive oil to counter the salt and also stop the skin from drying out. In the end they had to cover up to stop themselves from burning, especially Paul, with his fairer skin.

"Sunday tomorrow. If I come over for us to go to the Baptist Church in the morning, do you think you will be able to come to the Youth Fellowship in our Church in the evening?" asked Paul, hopefully.

"You will have to sit in the same pew as Auntie and behave yourself," said Maureen grinning.

"I think I can manage that," he said.

Paul lay there content to be with Maureen, but also thinking back to the earlier experiences of the morning. Why did the woman dismiss him so abruptly after encouraging him, so blatantly, to have sex? What was it that repelled him and at the same time attracted him? It was a sort of morbid attraction that people have for poisonous snakes he fancied. You loath them for being venomous and dangerous, but are fascinated by their evil beauty and menace. Perhaps she was not so evil. She obviously liked the body functions that were ultimately responsible for giving life. Sexual intercourse was really the most natural of functions, wasn't it? People had sexual urges whether they were married or not. Paul thought that maybe she had lost a partner and could not find someone she could stay with. She still needed someone to be with and have sex with. He needed someone to have sex with and he could not be married, due to his age. Was it so wrong that they had come together? It had felt so right – except for the guilt. He had betrayed his sweetheart. His lover in everything except what he had with that woman. Would he become less of a good person because of that relationship? What about her? What sort of a woman did it make her?

Back in the caravan, in reality a trailer made to look like a real gypsy wagon, Constance Spiegelhalter, Connie to her friends, alias Madame Perspicacity, lay back on her divan, sipping whisky. She knew she should be parading herself outside the caravan, occasionally pirouetting to the Spanish gypsy music she played on a wind-up gramophone she left on the top step, trying to hustle a customer inside. Saturday afternoon was one of the best times for business. All sorts of people were around then, young and old. Connie did not like old men, smelling with stale beer on their breath, and their nasty groping hands, even if their money was good. Perhaps that was why she fancied the young boy. She had never entertained a boy as young as him before, she mused. She had recognised him as soon as she saw Paul, with his vulnerable good looks. Madame Perspicacity must be more careful in future. She was probably breaking the law, though she had not taken any money from him, had she. A nice, clean, sweet smelling boy. She wished she had given birth to a boy like that. She thought of her own youth at the turn of the century, in the East End of London: the poverty and squalor.

Her parents had been Jewish immigrants who had tried to make good, but were not strong enough to make it. Memories stirred of her mother singing Yiddish lullabies to her. She got her love of music from her mother. Over the years she did not admit to being Jewish, as there was still a strong anti-Semitic element in Britain, the champion of democracy. Connie had become Madame Perspicacity, a name given her by a grateful patron, who appreciated her extra professional tuition. When she was old enough, and both her parents were dead, she decided she had had enough of London, with its ugliness and grime, and would travel the country. Carrying her suitcase, she thumbed lifts; if the gentleman driver was going to somewhere that sounded interesting, she would go all the way to his destination. If he was single and reasonably attractive she sometimes stayed with the host and, metaphorically went all the way. She decided that she was amoral; initially through necessity, although there were only a few occasions which were regretted. After the first occasion, during which she was beaten up, she became very wary and acquired, through a friend, a First World War German officer's Luger pistol with ammunition: loot smuggled back to Britain by some 'Tommy' as a souvenir. This weapon gave her confidence and security, kept within easy reach. It was even now in the drawer of the table that supported the crystal ball. She had used it to threaten nasty customers on more than one occasion, and felt she would have used it if they had made a grab for the gun. The look on her face had been enough to convince the troublemakers that she meant business, and they left, hurling verbal abuses to cover their indignity

Connie now looked at the small washstand in the corner where the boy had freshened up she thought of him again. There was definitely something attractive about a young, virgin boy. Was that unusual for a woman of her age? She was not the type to be a housewife, pottering around the home and garden, settling down. Perhaps there was Romany in her family way back. She enjoyed the challenge of new faces and places. The cottage and chintz would have to wait There was still excitement to be had from life. Like riding pillion on that sailor's motorbike with no drawers on. She enjoyed shocking people. She never wanted to be predictable. She also enjoyed being intimate with new acquaintances, although it never seemed to be enough really, but she could not put her finger on the reason why. What should she do if the boy came back? He was sexually proficient, if inexperienced. Should she send him on his way if he turned up frustrated and obsessed by what she had already given him? Should she gently tutor him in the ways of making love? The idea gave her a tingly feeling. She reached for the whisky glass and downed it greedily.

CHAPTER ELEVEN

Sunday morning came and the Baxters were all at the Congregational Church, except for Paul who was down the road at the Baptist Church with Maureen and Auntie Florence. The service was the time-tried sandwich used over the decades and centuries: a hymn, a prayer, a hymn, a prayer, a hymn, the sermon, a hymn and benediction. Paul was dreading the service to come. When it did he fidgeted in his seat as the Minister, an aged Welshman, ranted on about the sins of the flesh, drawing attention to something Paul could not do anything about in church. Or could he?

He looked sideways at Maureen mischievously, but Maureen pretended not to notice. He dropped a leaflet on the floor and leaned forward to pick it up, with the hand nearest to Maureen. As he brought his hand up, clutching the leaflet, he brought it under her long, Sunday best dress, hitching the folds up onto the seat. Maureen could feel that her skirt was not hanging down any more on Paul's side and could feel a slight draught on her right thigh. She then felt something warmer touching her thigh, as clammy fingers slid under the loose folds of her dress on the seat and started to caress the side of her hip. Maureen knew that she could not do anything, or make a fuss, or commotion, so she pretended that nothing had happened; Paul's fingers grew bolder. She gave Paul a sidelong steely, glance that should have given Paul the message. She was really worried that Auntie Florence would see what was going on, even if the latter was foraging through the text in her Bible, and would not be able to see too much with her reading glasses on. Maureen knew she was well protected from the preacher's gaze upon her lower body by the high set pews. These had been designed in the previous century for privacy, when it was necessary for the congregation to relieve themselves during long sermons, having a pot put by for the purpose. Maureen had her thighs clamped together but as this did not seem to deter, but only agitate, she deemed the best solution was to part her legs slightly. Indeed, as Paul was able to rest his hand in her crotch only his busy fingers betrayed a slight external movement of her dress.

A gentle rhythm applied, by now more practised fingers, made the pupils of Maureen's eyes dilate as she became more aware of her imminent climax, controlling her breathing quietly. She put out her right hand to close over the hard area of Paul's groin and caressed him through his trousers. Within a short space of time there were two pairs of moist underwear and two persons who were more relaxed now than before they had come inside the church. The rest of the sermon was a blur to the young couple, who held hands discreetly in their fairly private box.

After the service on the way home, Auntie Florence turned to Paul and said with a glint in her eye, "That was some sermon wasn't it Paul?"

"Er... yes. I don't think I will ever forget that one, Auntie," said Paul, truthfully.

"Well, I thought you were both quiet, so you must have taken it in," said Auntie, smiling, ambiguously it seemed to a puzzled Paul. As Paul was invited to share lunch at their house, Paul thought he would balance things up by inviting Maureen to his home for tea, before going on to Youth Fellowship together in the evening.

As fog had begun to drift in from the sea again, Auntie Florence had got the Monopoly board out for the three of them to play in the afternoon. Florence also got the wind-up gramophone out of the cupboard and played some old favourite '78' records. She forgot her worries and sang along to the songs of the 'roaring twenties', as the young couple stoically, and in Paul's case, grimly, acceded to Auntie's whims. As the occasional mournful groans of the foghorn sounded Paul was reminded of the last occasion he heard it, while lying with Maureen upstairs in her bedroom.

Tea with Maureen and his parents earned him a scolding from his mother, who although she always tried to make Sunday tea a bit special, had not been warned in advance to get extra provisions for a guest. She was used to Barry coming to tea, but a young lady was a different matter. The logic being that a female would notice the finer points in life, and would appreciate the bone china and extra little preparations necessary for the occasion.

The one thing that they always had in the summertime for Sunday tea, was scones, jam and double clotted cream. Double because the milk had a cream factor of fifty per cent to start with. After the milk had been scalded, and the cream left to settle, to the remaining milky liquid was added a few drops of rennet to make a junket, spiced up with grated nutmeg. Ruth had already noticed that Maureen was a nice girl, well mannered and well spoken, healthy and attractive. She was not surprised that her son was besotted, if not in love, with his new companion. She was worried now that the holidays would soon come to an end and Maureen would not be around.

She somehow sensed that her son would be devastated; she shared some of his sensitivities, having passed them on to him. She was unsure of how to help them, and hoped that they would settle for love letters when the parting came.

Reverend Stephen Baxter had never met Maureen to talk to. He had seen the couple from a distance and stopped in his tracks when he realised that the pretty girl, talking and laughing with his younger son, was obviously more than a passing fancy in a mutually close relationship. He had been coming out of the doorway of the local tobacconist after purchasing some Old Shag pipe tobacco. He had watched them going away from where he stood. He realised later, after Ruth had told him about the new girl friend, that they would end up apart. He was more concerned about his son's educational prospects. He knew he had made a mistake in forcing the issue of the grammar school, but it was too late now and the boy must make the best of it. It was up to him to see that he did. Sitting at the teatable, with his dog collar on ready for the evening service, he was not surprised at his son's obsession with this charismatic and sensuous young woman. It surprised him that his son, sometimes painfully shy and lacking in confidence, could attract such a poised unselfconscious beauty. The estimation of his son's character went up a notch or two. After he had said grace, and passed the scones over to Maureen, he made a mental note to try to be more understanding about the problems of youth. It was still an age when teenagers were assumed to be young adults, who should conform to the same dress sense, appreciate the same music, art and literature as adults. Anything else would be pampering, and a stumbling block to the full participation in adult responsibilities.

"I understand you are not so against school as my son, Maureen. Is that right?" asked the minister, trying to break the awkward silence.

Maureen looked quickly across to Paul, who was frowning and also pursing his lips in a slight pout, a typical mannerism of his, and then said, "Er, that's right. I'm happy enough at school, but I'm also happy enough to be on holiday. Everybody's different I suppose," she smiled shyly.

"Yes, of course. That's only natural. All work and no play makes Jack or Jill, a dull boy or girl," said Paul's father smiling. Paul's mother could feel the tension building up in her son, so she tried to change the subject.

"How's your Auntie Florence, Maureen?"

"Oh, I'm a little bit worried about her. Sometimes she doesn't look well at all, but she won't tell me anything when I ask," said Maureen sadly.

Ruth's mouth dropped at this unexpected statement, after the casual enquiry, and had expected Maureen to affirm that all was well. She thought about this while everyone was cutting open their scones and spreading jam and cream on them.

Addressing Maureen, she said, "Does your Auntie have any friends of her own age she can confide in?"

"I don't think so. She seems to think that people avoid her because she was not born around here. Even some of the people we mix with at church," said Maureen, openly, and surprising Stephen with her frankness.

"Oh, surely not! That's terrible if it's true. Perhaps I ought to have a word with your minister, to see what he can do about it," he said, now quite concerned.

"I think a woman's touch might be more appropriate here, don't you think, my dear?" interjected Ruth with her feminine intuition.

"Ah, yes. Perhaps you're right. What about you then, my dear? Perhaps you are the right person to have a word with Florence? What do you think ladies?" asked the minister looking at both Ruth and Maureen.

Paul sat silently, yet with a reserved dread about his mother having intimate discussions with his girl friend's guardian, even if it was not ostensibly to be about him.

"How do you feel about that Maureen? Do you think that your aunt would talk to me?" Ruth asked.

"Hmm. It's a bit tricky isn't it? I'm worried that Auntie Florence will be cross with me for telling you. She is quite a proud sort of person, and she might not want to... sort of... change sides over this, if you see what I mean?" said Maureen sensibly.

Ruth nodded and thought for a moment until she said, "We are going to have a Woman's Day of Prayer shortly. Perhaps I could call in on her and ask if she would like to come. We are holding it in our church this time, but it is a United Church effort, so every denomination is welcome."

"That sounds like a good idea," beamed Maureen, relieved to get that worry off her mind.

The conversation then turned to more mundane matters until it was time to get ready for evening fellowship for young and old. Paul and Maureen headed for their fellowship at the Congregational Sunday Schoolroom.

As Paul and Maureen arrived that evening there was an argument going on in the vestry office between the two married couples who ran the youth fellowship. Voices were raised and then one couple stormed out banging the outside door behind them. The other couple were heard muttering to themselves and then came out into the big room where all the young people were gathered. The couple looked very ill at ease.

"I'm afraid that there has been a difference of opinion about what we were going to do this evening. Richard and Felicity wanted everyone to take a Bible out with them and do Bible study, either up at the Lookout or down on the quay – seeing as it is a nice evening. However, Vanessa and I thought that it would be too distracting to follow a theme of Bible study outdoors; also the fog might come back again. We er, fell out about it. Now, the thing is, we could do with a couple of young people to help out with the younger ones here. Let me see now... aah yes! Paul and Maureen, isn't it? You are a couple, aren't you? Perhaps you would like to help out after we have had a few Sankey hymns and prayers?" said Ben hopefully. Paul and Maureen coloured up bashfully. Ben said, "We have got a couple of leaflets for guidelines, so it should not be too difficult. The main thing is to keep them in order and not running about the place. Perhaps if one of you concentrated on that whilst the other reads out the Bible passages and then asks questions about it. The older ones will stay with Vanessa and myself in the big room. The vestry will be better to keep the young ones contained, I think," said Ben, handing out leaflets.

Maureen and Paul looked at each other anxiously, suffering a fit of nervous giggles. Then everyone found their places, before putting their hearts and souls into the hymns and prayers. After the prayers had finished there was a general commotion as the youngsters left for the vestry.

"I suppose I had better keep order whilst you sort the readings out," said Paul, copping out.

Maureen would have none of this, "We'll split it between us, all right?" she hissed. Looking at the leaflet and the readings, she whispered, "Mind you, I think this is all about you – the 'prodigal son'. You are the one that looks as if he is going to do a bunk and fritter away his inheritance."

"Huh! What inheritance? Fat chance for that," he whispered, grinning.

Paul helped the youngsters to find their places in the Bible and then got them to read a verse each, in turn, helping them out with difficult words. The youngest, a girl aged seven, was really too young for youth fellowship, but her single mother had brought her round for a couple of hours anyway. Local gossip had it that the child's 'uncle' used to call at her house of a Sunday evening. The restless child had ended up sitting on Maureen's lap sucking her thumb, laying her head back against Maureen's breast. Paul looked at them and felt a strange feeling, momentarily wondering what it might be like to be a parent. Then it was time to ask the simple questions that were on the leaflets: the names and deeds of the people in the story and, to sum it all up, there were view points about the morality of forgiveness.

Maureen came into her own here as she construed her own interpretation of the love of Christ, intriguing Paul as much as the young children. Children were still asking questions when the older youths came through the doorway, hinting that the teaching session was coming to a close. Ben strode through the doorway looking a bit anxious until he saw the relaxed looks on the faces of everyone, bar the telltale flushes of tension on the faces of Maureen and Paul.

"How did it go then?" Ben asked, smiling.

"Oh, not too bad. They have been behaving themselves very well really," said Maureen, relieved that it had not been as bad as she had thought it might be.

Paul had mixed feelings. His stomach had sunk when they were left with the fait accompli of taking the others for Bible study, as Paul did not consider himself a worthy student. The fact that Maureen was good with children contrasted with his own lack of self-esteem.

"Maureen's been a very good teacher," was all Paul could say, with a lame grin lopsided on his mouth.

"Excellent," beamed Ben enthusiastically.

"It's a pity you are not here all the time to help us out," he added.

Maureen affirmed this remark mentally and with moist sad eyes replied, "That's very kind of you Ben, but I am here on holiday you know."

"I know, I know, my dear. Thank you for helping us in this emergency. I really appreciate both of you helping us out. I shall convey my appreciation to your Father, Paul," said Ben, still beaming.

Bibles were stacked away in the bookshelves and everyone made their way out to meet the few parents of the younger ones who were waiting to collect them. The fog had cleared and now the sun's rays warmed Paul and Maureen as they walked around the church to go down Meeting Street, with the view of the river in the distance.

"You are good with children, Maureen. I couldn't have managed them on my own," said Paul, looking across at her.

"Well, girls are naturally better with children aren't they?"

"I suppose so. I was terrified they were going to run riot in there," said Paul ruefully.

"Ah! You have got to be firm with them and stop them from going too far. Especially the boys," she said knowingly, giving a little chuckle.

Paul smiled and gave her hand a squeeze as he looked across to Instow; the low evening sun reflecting an orange glow on the houses and the sea walls. There were quite a few people of all ages promenading slowly along the quayside, enjoying the cool of the evening

"We can get the ferry over to Instow in the morning. The tide should be just about right," said Paul, looking forward to another day with Maureen.

"Oh really, Master Paul? Just what have you got in mind to do all day in Instow?" said Maureen squinting shyly at Paul.

"I expect we'll find something to do. There are some nice sand dunes to lie in and relax," he said casually.

"Huh! Relax? With you? You must be joking! If I relaxed with you I should no longer be a virgin.

"The words had come out of her mouth before she realised it and with horror, she looked around with her hand over her mouth, to see if anyone had heard her. Fortunately no one was in hearing distance and they both giggled like the school children they were; young people at the crossroads of life with the major responsibilities still ahead of them. They leaned over the top of the high wall opposite the parish church and cemetery as the sun's rays got weaker as it slid down the back of Staddon Hill; the remains of an ancient hill fort buried in vegetation, its memories long forgotten.

"See you in the morning, OK? Usual packed lunch?" queried Paul, giving Maureen a quick peck on the cheek.

"We'll see what the weather is like in the morning, then," said Maureen, vaguely, to warn Paul against taking her for granted. They parted cheerfully enough, with both of them looking back to wave briefly before Maureen vanished out of sight, walking along Irsha Street.

CHAPTER TWELVE

The weather continued to be kind the following morning as they met up at Auntie's house and made their way along the quayside. There was a crude banner tied up to the railings near the slipway, entreating visitors, and local people on holiday, to a trip in a boat to Croyde Bay.

"That's an idea isn't it? Fancy a trip? They don't do trips too often to Croyde," said Paul eagerly.

"That's a long way in a boat to Croyde isn't it? I expect it will be expensive," said Maureen, worriedly.

"Its' a half-a-crown return young 'uns. We are just waiting to fill the boat, to make it worth our while, and then we will be off. It's a good bargain trip, this one," said a cocky young bronzed fellow in T-shirt and navy shorts.

"How much money have you got on you?" asked Paul, looking at Maureen.

"I've only got two shillings with me," she said mournfully.

"That's all right. I've got enough to cover both of us, if you hand over your florin," said Paul, and made up the five shillings necessary for the trip.

He made a mental note that he had paid the same for the ring that he now noticed on Maureen's finger, the same finger for engagement rings to sparkle from. The ring must have been a bargain, he thought quickly as they clambered over the side of the boat and sat down as the boat bobbed up and down waiting to be filled. Paul's mind was still thinking about engagement rings and more to the point. the committal of engagement. He liked the idea of it, but knew there was no point in thinking about this at the moment. However, it would be more of a reason to meet again, which would soon be the most urgent problem so far as he was concerned.

He leaned over closer to whisper in Maureen's ear, "You are wearing our ring on your engagement finger, so don't you

141

think we should be engaged?" he said bashfully.

Maureen giggled until the hangdog look on Paul's face betrayed his seriousness.

"You mustn't be silly about this, now, Paul. We can't possibly think about marrying at our age, now can we?" she whispered back to him.

Paul shrugged back at her and said quietly, "We couldn't marry for a while, but it would be a proper... commitment of our love, wouldn't it?"

"Let's just enjoy the day, shall we my love," said Maureen, squeezing Paul's hand.

Paul felt a tender feeling of hopelessness as tears came into his eyes and had to turn away, before he broke up.

The two boatmen agreed that they had a full enough load and so the younger fellow pushed the boat off the side of the slipway. The older man gunned the diesel motor to a bark, until steadying down to a lumbering chug after the younger boatman had jumped across into the stern. It was high tide now, the only safe way of getting through the narrow channel of Bideford Bar and docking at Croyde.

Maureen was exhilarated by the trip and enjoyed the slight choppiness that a westerly breeze had brought to the water. She looked across to Instow and the boats in the harbour, mostly the mast tops, bobbing as if they had a slight touch of St. Vitu's dance. Paul had made a good choice she thought, even if it was an expensive one by their standards. She realised that they needed to make the most of it in the few days remaining.

"Perhaps we will have to take up that elderly couple's offer of caddying for them, if we are going to have any pocket money tomorrow," she ventured to Paul.

"Hm, Perhaps you're right. Is that fixed for tomorrow then?" asked Paul as Maureen smiled and nodded the affirmative. This gladdened his heart, ensuring another day in her company on the morrow.

Maureen tried to pick out her Auntie's house and the small bedroom window that looked out onto the sea. The one she had looked out of in her nakedness, that foggy day that Florence had gone to town. The day that she had realised that she was a sensual woman.

Maureen had enjoyed Paul standing behind her as they listened to the foghorn in the gloom, his hands caressing her breasts. She pointed it out to Paul, but did not share her memory with him audibly, but wondered if he was thinking the same. Paul, however, was interested in looking the other way, across to Crow Point. A spit of low lying sands from where the salmon-fishing boats spread their nets hoping for a profitable catch. He speculated whether that would be a suitable place to spend a lazy day in the sun, but decided the lack of toilet facilities and the fact that it would be too dangerous to swim there, ruled it out.

Soon they were heading for the parting of the wall of surf and chugging along the deep-water channel of the Bar before turning around to starboard to follow a parallel course to Braunton Burrows and Saunton Sands, in front of them. They could see the amphibious 'ducks' out on manoeuvres from their nearby base at Fremington, an Amphibious Warfare Centre, that was not so warlike now that it allowed the general public in to view on certain days. They were getting a better view of Baggy Point, the ultimate headland viewed from the west, apart from Morte Point, which could only be viewed from Hartland Point, the massive headland farther to the south west.

Paul looked enviously and impatiently at the huge stretch of dunes and the beach in front of it, over three miles of it. A wilderness so private that it begged to be invaded by Maureen and himself, in a loving embrace. It was probably a very good place to be alone and moody, but perish that thought. He turned around to follow Maureen's gaze out to sea and found her pointing finger, as she said, "You can see Lundy Island quite clearly now." Paul nodded and smiled, seeing the excitement in her face, and was glad for her. He did not have the same love for the sea, although he was not a bad sailor in good conditions.

After what seemed an age, they rounded Saunton Downs at the head of Croyde Bay and gingerly gave a wide berth to the rocky shelf, before easing alongside the most suitable place for docking, which had a mooring buoy. Fenders had been lowered to cushion the surge of the tide against the rock shelf. Now the younger man made fast with a rope, to keep the boat tight against the rocks, before he jumped into the water to steady her. The passengers made their way to the bow where the boatman had jumped off and was now ready to help everyone onto the rock and then to the beach.

"You are gonna' have to be prepared to get your feet wet now my 'ansomes I'm afraid. But the most important thing I have to tell 'ee, is that you must be here by five o' clock. T'would be better to be early than late, 'cos we have to catch the tide right and after five I have to leave here again. So I am expecting you good people to be here in good time, or else you will have to get a bus back, and I couldn't tell 'ee when they run."

So with that chatty ultimatum, the passengers cheerfully disembarked with the usual Anglo-Saxon stoicism. The boat was then untied and made its way back to Appledore, where it alternated with the regular ferry boat that plied between Appledore and Instow the year round. Sometimes they would take trippers up the Taw and Torridge estuaries, to Barnstaple and Bideford respectively. When the tourists had gone home they fished for salmon, or anything else they could catch.

"Where are we heading then Paul?" asked Maureen, quietly.

"Oh, just a nice quiet spot on the beach. Later on we can walk through the village of Croyde and perhaps walk around the headland to Baggy Point. How's that?" he queried.

"Not out, I suppose," said Maureen, laughing and parodying their golfing friend.

"As usual you have got it all planned out," she teased him.

"It's a pity we can't surf here today. Even if they hire boards here, I haven't got enough for the deposit."

"Never mind. There's always tomorrow. I'm sure we can find other things to do," she said, still teasing him.

"Oh yes! A bit of sunbathing followed by a swim, followed by lunch. Is that about it?" he enquired.

"Yes, let's make our way over to a spot between those two lots of people over there," she said, pointing.

They made their way over to it and laid their towels out on the sand; Maureen got out the olive oil to spread over their

144

bodies. Paul had managed to get hold of some proper suntan lotion, as he found that his fair skin burnt easier than Maureen's. Maureen found that her skin was getting used to the sun, as long as she didn't over do it and covered up from time to time, there was no problem. They creamed each others backs before lying down on their towels.

"I hope I didn't alarm you too much, in Church yesterday morning," said Paul hesitantly.

"Yes, you know you damn well did," she replied scornfully.

"Yes, but you did enjoy it though. The excitement of doing something like that, with other people around I mean," he said huskily.

"I don't know about that. I couldn't stop you without letting everyone know something was going on. Especially Auntie Florence, sitting right next to me," said Maureen, getting up on her elbows to berate him.

"She couldn't see anything though could she?" continued Paul doggedly.

"Well I hope she didn't. I'd die if I thought she did," she replied with emphasis.

"Your Auntie is not such a bad stick, I think she has a soft heart really. She's not as sour as some of the folk around here."

"I don't know how to take that statement. I think you mean it as a compliment in relation to Auntie, but I should think we all get grumpy as we get older. The aches and pains, I suppose," said Maureen philosophically.

"I didn't know your Auntie Florence might be poorly. I hope she'll be all right," he said.

"I hope so too. She's a bit of a lifeline to me really… well, to both of us now," she said pointedly.

Paul didn't get the point however, and said, "What do you mean?"

"Well, if it wasn't for Auntie, I wouldn't be here now, would I?" she said bluntly, with tears forming in her eyes.

"Gosh! No!" said Paul, stunned by the stark realism of her statement. They lay there silently for a while until Paul said, "I've got to see you again you know, after you go back home." This made Maureen even more tearful, as she knew the difficulties involved.

"You might have to wait until next summer," she mumbled, her head bowed in her hands; the tears drifting through to soak into the towel.

"Is there plenty of work around Aberdeen?" asked Paul suddenly.

Maureen turned to face him her eyes red and her cheeks flushed.

"It's no good thinking like that Paul. You will have to wait till I come down next time. Maybe I can arrange to come down at Christmas, especially if Auntie is going to be poorly – but I do hope she isn't."

Maureen turned over again so that Paul could not see her weeping.

Paul, who had already noticed her obvious distress, wanted to comfort her in a tender way, so he cuddled up close to her back and put his arm around her to hug her, and said, "I'm sorry darling. It's just that I can't bear to be apart from you too long."

This statement only provoked another emotional surge, which racked through Maureen's slender body and made Paul feel miserable and frustrated. He had to change the mood, so he suggested they go for a swim. The shock of the cold water would make them forget the sadness and the present moment was the most important thing to them now and should not be wasted.

They enjoyed the exhilarating pounding of the surf and swam out beyond the white water to watch it curl and break. The comparative deep, calm, but gently surging power of the ocean, lifting them up and down on the swell. They were both, at this moment, prepared to take a chance that they would not catch a rip current, the strength of which would carry them out to sea. There was an unspoken pact between them that intimated that their drowning would solve the problem of their parting. That day however was destined to be a safe day for swimmers, and after an hour or so they were content to come ashore and eat their picnic lunch.

They were still subdued but determined to enjoy the day, although it was Maureen who tried to cheer Paul up by allowing him to kiss and fondle her, in spite of being in view of others on

146

the beach.

Paul was itching to get away to a more secluded spot so he said to Maureen, "Would you like to walk along the headland to Baggy Point, on the way back we could pop into Croyde village to look around?"

"Yes! That would be a good idea. We..." She was going to say that they would not be likely to have a chance of going there again, but she corrected herself, and instead said, "We might as well make the most of the day and have a good look around."

They hiked off, with the wind still mercifully fresh and invigorating, their rucksacks on their backs. Paul persuaded Maureen to walk up Middleborough Hill. As they left the track to cross the down land to join up with the cliff path, they stopped in a gully to rest. Paul knew that this was the best chance of the day for a bit of heavy petting, which was how they ended up, naked and throwing caution to the winds so far as being seen by anyone went. They were off the beaten track now and not likely to be encountered. They could, however, hear on the wind the distant cries of children playing.

Their passion became so strong that Paul tried to enter Maureen, who was now so stimulated that her body told her "Yes!" Until the gnawing moralities of her mind and, more particularly, the fear of pregnancy, stopped her from submitting. They had to be content to stimulate and caress each other to orgasm; a pleasurable enough event, but now that Paul had encountered full sexual intercourse he was not completely satisfied with second best, and vowed to purchase some sheaths.

They lay together naked on the grass with their arms around each other, silently for some time, before putting on their clothes and continuing on the walk to join up with the coastal path to Baggy Point. After rounding the small peninsula from Whiting Hole, they viewed the sweep of Morte Bay across to Morte Point and, in between, the long sweep of Woolacombe Sands with the houses of the village of Woolacombe just about visible, nestling at the foot of the steep combe. They cut across a pathway to bring them back to Croyde Bay before joining the road into the village. They did not have enough money to buy anything other than a couple of ice creams, but were content to browse along, like other tourists, giggling at some of the tacky things on display for people on holiday. Maureen was attracted to the jewellery counter displays until Paul grumpily complained, "We can't afford anything like that you know." Maureen made a mental note that Paul sounded more like a middle-aged husband than a teenage boyfriend and said, "It's all right. I've got this to keep me happy," and she brandished the dolphin ring in the air, smiling broadly.

Paul nodded gratefully and set about eyeing up the saucy postcards until he was dragged out of the shop by his ear.

"Ow! That hurts," he said, rubbing the inflamed appendage as they made their way back to the beach. Paul espied a portly, wealthy looking foreigner, probably American, with a bulging wallet sticking out of his back pocket and a cigar in his mouth, sporting a straw hat with a narrow brim, walking just ahead of him.

"Get ready to run after I've whipped the wallet out of his back pocket," hissed Paul into Maureen's ear. She looked sideways at him in fear and astonishment, until he started to laugh. She punched him in the ribs.

"I really thought that you meant that," she grinned at him.

"Well, I did for a moment," he admitted, although Maureen didn't believe him.

Paul strolled on, wondering if they could have got away with it by running back along the beach and hiding by the rocks until the boat came to take them home. He realised his intention to steal was motivated by his poverty and the fact that wealthy tourists did not have the same need for money as he did. If he had hundreds of pounds in his pocket he could take Maureen away somewhere and live with her. It was a tempting but purely escapist thought; he realised that they could only have done it if they were both very impulsive people and had done the deed on the spur of the moment, taking a gamble and not caring for the consequences.

Maybe that was it: he would have to take a gamble to win Maureen. He could meet up with her after she arrived back home in Scotland. Perhaps meet in secret. He required money to give him the independence he needed to be near her. He could not steal it however. Apart from the morality question, the chances of getting caught and the outcome for him and his family would have been horrendous. He could only get a job, any job, to make him enough money to be near her. Would that be what Maureen wanted though? He knew from his short relationship with her that she did not share his radical views. Perhaps he could win her around eventually. He felt he had to do something desperate to continue to see her. If only he felt more mature, more sure of himself, had more self-confidence. He walked along, brooding silently.

"You're very quiet, what are you thinking about?" she asked, concerned.

"Oh! I was just thinking about when you go home. How we can keep in touch," said Paul wearily.

"Well, we can write letters for a start. I told you that I would see if I could get down here for Christmas, but we have to face facts Paul," said Maureen, trying to be optimistic and putting on a brave face.

"Huh! The facts are probably stacked against us, like the odds of us seeing each other again soon," he said miserably.

"Oh, come on now. Like I said before, let's enjoy a day at a time. That's all we can do really, isn't it?" she said, squeezing his hand.

"I suppose you're right," he sighed.

They made camp nearby to where the boat would come for them then went in the water again for another swim. This time they did not go out so far, as the tide was further out but had turned, and they did not swim for so long. They came back to their towels to lie in the sun. As the return boatload of people began arriving, they packed their haversacks and explored the remaining rock pools that the tide had still to claim. They enjoyed the boat trip back; the two journeys being the furthest either of them had ever travelled by sea.

As Paul looked at the sand dunes of Braunton Burrows he was reminded of the golfing couple and the offer of caddying.

"So it's Westward Ho! again tomorrow?" he said to Maureen, thinking about a chance to make some money.

Maureen thought for a moment, pursed her lips, looked around at the vistas of sea and then, feigning indifference asked, "Will that be via Greencliff, or the short route?"

"I was thinking of the golfing couple actually," said Paul, grinning.

"Well, I should have to consult my diary of course," she continued to tease.

"May I take that as a yes?" he chuckled.

"I think you may," she said gracefully.

They docked at Appledore quay and made arrangements to meet up at Auntie Florence's house, to go out walking in the evening, ending up climbing over the gate at Lookout and lying down in the grass for a kiss and cuddle, listening to the surf pounding the Bar.

CHAPTER THIRTEEN

Paul and Maureen met up with George and May Fulton in the latter's hotel room the next morning. They felt ill at ease in the luxurious surroundings of the four star accommodation as they sat in the lounge while George and May changed into their golfing togs.

"It's really nice to see you two again. You are like a breath of fresh air to us geriatrics. Isn't that right May?"

"It certainly is my dear. They are like a couple of young playful puppies," said May, smiling and showing her large, even, white dentures.

"Yes. Young puppies. That's about it," said George, chuckling away.

Paul and Maureen smiled awkwardly and flushed with embarrassment. George sorted out the golf bags and they set off from the hotel and headed for the first tee past the Club-House.

"Now this is what we are going to do, all four of us are going to have a game. We shan't be scoring, so it doesn't matter if you miss the ball completely. You just take another swing at it until you hit it. I'd like you to keep a good eye out for where the ball lands, although I do have plenty of spare balls as we usually lose one or two in the rough," said George, trying to put the young couple at ease.

Predictably Paul and Maureen were struggling to get any sense of form to start with, but after a few holes settled down. After George had advised Paul to concentrate more on the accuracy of his swing than the amount of force needed to propel the ball to its ultimate destination, he seemed to improve. Maureen, on the other hand, had already been doing this and had not sliced the ball so much, although drives were a little pathetic by professional standards.

About halfway round, George brought out a hip flask of brandy and gave a tot to the young couple, which took their breath away but made everyone laugh. May turned down George's offer and brought out an orange to eat as they rested on the turf in the mid-morning sunshine. The brandy seemed to relax the play of the 'young puppies' and they were on a par with May, if trailing behind the seasoned practise of George.

George paid them generously for the caddying and also invited them for lunch in the Club House, which they accepted, more because they did not want to offend him than in pleased anticipation of a meal in pleasant surroundings. The Club House was rather quiet midday and busier in the evening. They were served smoked salmon as an entrée and then had steak and chips, as suggested by George, who knew the unsophisticated tastes of the young. George had ordered a bottle of red wine, which he encouraged Paul and Maureen to help finish off. May could only manage one glass. Paul was thirsty and was slurping the wine down quite hurriedly until May ordered some bottled water and coaxed Paul and Maureen to drink it, for fear of them becoming dehydrated, especially after being out in the hot sun.

Nevertheless, Paul had been given a second glass, much to the distress of May who scolded her husband. Paul didn't really like the vinegary flavour of the red wine, but enjoyed the heady effect it had on him and the excitement of 'living it up'. Maureen was struggling with her first glass, but did not want to seem ungrateful so swallowed it down, more as a dose of medicine than a tipple of some delightful beverage. After her glass was emptied she had started on a glass of water, to take away the taste of the wine, and was horrified when George refilled her glass, after May had excused herself to go to the ladies room. Maureen protested to no avail and decided to sip a small amount regularly, chasing it down with water afterwards. Although the alcohol was affecting their demeanour, it did not affect their appetites, and a fruit pudding with ice cream was also disposed of.

"Would you like to come back for a coffee before you go off on your bikes to do a bit a bit more surfing or whatever? Stay and have a bit of a chat with us before you whizz off and leave us old fogies to vegetate, eh?" pleaded George.

"Oh, I'm sure that they would rather be on their own now

dear. After all, they have been with us all morning now, haven't they," interjected May, a worried look on her face.

Maureen felt sorry for the old man, who was obviously short of company, and wanted someone different to talk to.

"I think coffee would be nice, wouldn't it Paul?" she asked the startled Paul, now a bit heady with the wine he had gulped down, having finished off what Maureen had left in her glass as well.

"Oh, er… yes. That would be nice," he lied, thinking that the fresh sea air might be a better option. He now followed behind the other three rather unsteadily as they made their way from the Club House. The golf bags seemed a lot heavier now than they had earlier in the morning, as they trudged over to the hotel. Paul and Maureen sat down in the lounge with George as May went out to make the coffee in the kitchenette.

"So you two will be parted soon then, when school holidays are finished?" George said bluntly.

"Yes, I'm afraid so. With Maureen so far away it will be difficult for us to see each other for a while," said Paul, sadly and more openly than he would have confided with a stranger, had he been a trifle more sober.

"How about you, young lady? Will you miss that young er, puppy, as my wife called you," George asked.

Maureen laughed and said, "I think he's a bit more than a puppy!"

"Oh? You don't mean he's a bit of a dog, do you?" George said, a strange look in his eyes.

Maureen frowned, a bit embarrassed, but said, "He's a bit of a handful, but he's a nice boy really. Well he should be. His father's a Congregational Minister," said Maureen smiling and looking over at Paul, sprawled in an armchair and grinning foolishly.

"I think the wine has gone to his head, and mine. We are not used to it, I suppose. Actually I didn't think they would be allowed to serve it to people our age," said Maureen innocently.

George coughed, put his hand up to his mouth and said, "Well, I suppose they are not really. That's my fault, I have to admit. I shouldn't spread it around that you had intoxicating liquor in there. You might get the staff into trouble. Don't want to do that, do we?" he said with a chuckle.

"You seem so grown up in some ways, I forgot you were underage," George said, looking directly into Maureen's soulful eyes.

"It was just a gesture of kindness, to show appreciation for your kindness in helping us out," he added.

Paul thought he should say something before he fell asleep in the cosy armchair.

"We appreciated your er, gesture," he slurred, his eyelids drooping, but he leant forward until he had delivered his short thank you offering and then slumped back in his chair.

At this point Maureen didn't know whether to smile at Paul's apparent intoxication, or to be concerned about getting him home. She was just coming around to the latter way of thinking when May brought the coffee in on a tray.

"Ah there we are!" said George gratefully, as if being saved by the bell.

May deposited the coffee pot, cups and saucers on a low table in the middle of the room, with a little bowl of brown sugar and a little jug of hot milk, then went out again to take the tray back to the kitchenette. Quick as a flash, George produced the hip flask from his pocket and poured generous measures into three of them.

"I can't make it Irish coffee so it will have to be Devonshire," he laughed wickedly.

Maureen gave him a puzzled look and sniffed at her coffee, quite liking the smell but was not sure that it was a good idea to put brandy in it. She sipped it cautiously.

"Oh, that tastes quite nice. That's good coffee too. We usually have Camp coffee."

"That's bloody chicory stuff, isn't it?" George enquired, tipsy enough himself not to moderate his language.

"Chicory chick. Cha la oh la...." sang Paul, his eyes closed.

"What did he say?" asked George of Maureen.

"I think it's a song he has heard on Radio Luxemburg. I think he needs to get out into the fresh air and…" Maureen's words trailed off as May came back into the room again.

154

George quickly gave her the cup without brandy in it, filling it with the hot milk. He then did the same with another cup handing it to Maureen. He was pouring some into Paul's cup when May said, "I think Paul needs to have some black coffee. He looks as if he's passed out," she hurried over to him and crouched down to shake him gently by his shoulders.

"Are you all right Paul?" she enquired anxiously. Paul's eyes opened wide with surprise.

"What is it? What's happened?" he asked, alarmed. Maureen who had been enjoying her coffee and nearly finished it, could not help giggling at the sight of him. May turned around to face George.

"You shouldn't have given the children wine, George. It's not right," she scolded.

"Children? They don't look like children to me. Young people, yes. Children, no," he said swaying slightly.

"Children should be seen, but not heard," said Paul, with a smile on his lips but his eyes still closed.

"Paul, wake up and drink the coffee," said May, unaware of the brandy in it and handing it to him as his eyes opened. She waited until he held the cup and saucer firmly in his fingers and then turned to her husband again.

"He needs a cold shower to sober himself up now," she said as Paul gulped the coffee down gratefully, enjoying the strange luxurious taste. May took his empty cup, in case he dropped it on the floor, and then smelled the brandy aroma for the first time, coming from Paul's breath.

"You have been giving him brandy, haven't you, you silly man," she said exasperatedly. Maureen then started giggling again, uncontrollably.

"I Suppose you gave Maureen brandy as well. You realise that you have given them the equivalent of two double brandies and about a quarter of a bottle of wine each. Lord bless me. These are children for God's sake," said May, getting herself in a state.

"Bless the little children, and send them to me," muttered Paul, his eyes closed again. Maureen burst out laughing. This induced May to action.

"Fill the bath up with water putting both taps on full. We don't want the water to be hot. We want to wake them up," ordered May to George.

"Are you ready for a shower then Paul," asked May, giving Paul another shake.

"Huh?" grunted Paul sleepily.

"Do you have a proper shower? I've only used a shower in the swimming baths after a swim," said Maureen, starting to sway a little now, as the effects of the last double brandy kicked in.

"Oh my Lord. Perhaps you had better use the shower Maureen, come to think of it. Paul doesn't look as if he can stand up at the moment. George! Give me a hand to take Paul into the bathroom." said May, and they lifted Paul onto his feet and guided him to the small bathroom, with a toilet and wash basin in it. George sat Paul down on the chair in the corner while he filled the bath with water.

May showed Maureen to the shower room, which also had a toilet and wash basin in it. Maureen marvelled at such luxuries as she eagerly stripped her clothes off to try the shower. Before she left May showed Maureen how to use the controls in the tiled cubicle, turning them on to tepidly warm so that she would not scald herself. Maureen eagerly plunged herself under the luxury of the cool water, making her body tingle all over with sensual pleasure.

May shouted to George who had nearly finished running the bath water.

"George! I'm going to have a lie down myself now. I feel exhausted after everything that has happened today. It would have been lovely if you hadn't overdone things," she said, going into their bedroom and slamming the door.

George made sure that Paul got in the bath all right and left him to bathe himself. He then remembered something.

Maureen was enjoying the shower and could have stayed in for another half-hour or so, but decided that she had better be ready for Paul when he had had his bath. Then they could go and rest up somewhere in the shade until they had sobered up properly. She pulled the shower curtain back and made towards

156

the towel; she saw in the large mirror ahead of her, the image of George standing there in the doorway with a large bath towel in his hands. She gasped as he came behind her, throwing the towel over her shoulders, looking at her mirror image as he said, "I'm sorry that you young lovers will be parted soon. If there is anything I can do to help you, please let me know. I might be able to– arrange something– you know?"

Maureen was no longer languid. She was wide awake, and the nausea she felt was nothing to do with the alcohol she had consumed.

"Er, thank you George," she said, wrapping the towel tightly around her body to cover it as best she could in the quickest time. She held the door open for George, saying, "I must get dressed now."

As George reluctantly sidled out of the doorway he said, "Don't forget to visit us again for another round of golf now." Maureen closed the door and locked it, while she dressed. When she was ready she tiptoed out of the shower room and along to the bathroom, opening the door quietly. Paul looked up and smiled at her, still drowsy, from the bathtub.

"Get out and get dressed. We have got to leave this place as soon as possible," Maureen said urgently.

Paul screwed his face up quizzically, "What's up?" he hissed.

"I'll tell you when we get outside. Now get out of the bath, and get dressed – quickly." she exclaimed, returning the hiss.

"I'll be waiting in the lounge," she said, leaving him to clamber over the side of the bath, reluctantly as he was enjoying the relaxing soak. He had sobered up considerably by now, but still had the pleasant euphoria that temporarily abides with the inebriated.

Maureen stepped into the lounge where George was seated in an armchair.

"I've been a naughty boy, haven't I," he said, scrutinising Maureen's face for her reactions. She looked at him uncomfortably not knowing what to say.

"Plying you young people with alcohol. How old are you Maureen?" he asked, genuinely curious.

"I'm nearly sixteen," she answered truthfully.

"Good gracious. I thought that you were a lot older than that. My wife seems to be a better judge of age than myself," said George coolly.

There was an awkward silence until Maureen said, "Thank you for the lunch, and the golf, and the use of your shower."

"Ah, yes, the shower. Did you enjoy it Maureen?" he asked. There was now a definite creepy emanation from George, thought Maureen.

"It was very – refreshing," she said, hoping that she would not be misconstrued.

"Don't forget my offer, of help. I may be an old man now, but I do remember what it is like to be young." He gave her a leering smile that convinced Maureen he was some sort of pervert. As she waited for Paul she decided to stall.

"Thank you again for your kind offer of help but I can't see how you could help us to see each other again. That is before the next school holidays, when it might be possible to come down this way again," she said, hoping that would call his bluff.

"Well now," he said, a look of triumph in his eyes, rubbing his goatee eagerly.

"I could always post you a return train ticket from your town to Bideford railway station. You'll have to give me your home address though," George said, his eyes glinting.

Maureen's jaw dropped with horror as she desperately tried to think of a polite way of refusing his offer.

"Oh! I couldn't possibly accept your kind offer. Em, I would be bound to get into trouble with my parents," she replied, knowing that was the truth.

"Oh come now, I'm sure young people nowadays do not tell their parents everything. Especially when it is a matter of the heart, so to speak," George said grinning in what was to Maureen a sinister way.

Maureen thought that she could hear Paul moving around in the bathroom and knew he would be entering the lounge in a very short while. She did not want him to know anything about George's offer until they had left the hotel. She now had to instigate a way of getting out of the hotel quickly, before George mentioned something that Paul might be eager to accept, not knowing that there might be a certain unhealthy ulterior motive behind it. She took a deep breath:

"I must think about your generous proposal, George, before I commit myself to anything. After all, I am only a young schoolgirl. I will talk this over with Paul and, if we decide to accept, we can always let you know. I don't want him to discuss it now, as he may not be properly sober yet. The main thing, however, is that we might not be able to repay our debt to you," said Maureen, relieved that she had kept her aplomb even if it had been quite a strain.

George had listened to her with increasing admiration, her cool reserve only excited his imagination. Whatever he was going to say remained unsaid, as Paul walked into the room grinning sheepishly.

"We have got to go somewhere cool for a rest, before we do anything else," said Maureen, before George could say anything. She picked up their haversacks, handing Paul his.

"Thank you for everything George. Say goodbye to May for us; we will see you again," said Maureen.

Paul grinned and said, "The same from me too."

"Goodbye and good luck," said George as he saw them to the door.

Maureen wondered if he had a premonition that he would never see them again. Once outside, and out of earshot, Paul turned towards Maureen.

"What's all this fuss about getting out of the hotel quickly?" he asked impatiently.

"That George is a pervert. He came into the shower room just as I was getting out of the shower. It…it was like he was waiting for me to come out," said Maureen heatedly.

"What! You mean he was just – ogling you?" he questioned with astonishment.

"Well, he did have a bath towel in his hands, but he could have left that on the towel rail couldn't he?" she reasoned.

"I don't see how that makes him a pervert. It might mean that he's a randy old gentleman, but not necessarily a pervert," replied Paul.

"There are other things, but I can't explain them all to you. Let's just say it's a woman's intuition."

"A woman's intuition?" echoed Paul. "You aren't even a woman anyhow."

"Oh yes, I am a woman right enough. That reminds me. A little visitor will be arriving very soon now."

"A little visitor?"

"Do you have to repeat everything I say word for word?" said Maureen, smiling as the recognition of what she had inferred made a deep furrowed frown across Paul's freckled forehead.

"Oh no!" he groaned, cursing himself for not acquiring a packet of contraceptives before it was too late. Maureen would be going back in a week's time. He might have been able to persuade her to go all the way if he had protection; but now – Maureen looked at him thinking her own thoughts. She knew she could not tell him George's offer, as she was sure that Paul would jump at it, and she would not be able to fully explain her fears.

"I wish we had a bottle of wine to get drunk on now," muttered Paul, as he slouched along miserably.

"Huh! That would only make you feel ill and you know it. Look! I know what we can do. We can have a quick swim and cycle towards home; before we go down the steep hill into Appledore we can turn off and go on up towards Lookout again. We can jump over the gate by the seat and have a kiss and cuddle in the long grass; like we did before. How's that?" asked Maureen, knowing, what Paul's response would be.

"Not out!" declared a jubilant Paul, bucking up and striding more purposeful now towards the beach. They had their swim, which quickly had the effect of sobering them up. Then they lay in the sun to warm up. Once they started to get hot Paul encouraged Maureen to head for home, the first time he had been in a hurry to be heading homewards since he had befriended Maureen.

As they were cycling along, Paul mused over the fact that the next few hours might be the last of the holiday in which they could be intimate with each other. A sobering thought, literally, although the fresh air and the exercise of cycling had already blown a lot of the cobwebs out of his brain cells. He wanted something special to remember later on, after Maureen had gone back. He needed a private place to take her, remote but easily accessible. He racked his brain but could not think of anywhere; then it came to him: a barn, with bales of hay to lie on. He knew the very place. Instead of going straight on at Diddywell and up Stony Lane, the shortest route, they could turn right at Diddywell and go up the steep hill to the crossroads at Marshford. Paul remembered the steep hill for two reasons, neither of them were romantic.

The first was when he had been given an old bicycle by the Sunday School Superintendent, when his family had first moved to Appledore. In his haste to try it out he had omitted to test the brakes. Coming down the hill, the steepest they had encountered for many a moon, the brakes did not answer, and a broadside into the hedge at the bottom, was occured and an undignified vault over the crossbar, into the brambles at the top, was the result. Fortunately, apart from a few scratches and bruises, no harm was done and it led to new brake-blocks being fitted to the machine.

On the second occasion a group of youngsters including, his brother and himself, had stopped to investigate an old, rotten elm tree, a victim of a lightning strike many years before. A boy had climbed up the decaying trunk to reach a hollow at the top which proved to have tawny owl eggs in the base of the hole. The parent had flown out to the other side of the lane and followed them up the hill, it's superior eyesight perceiving the four eggs coveted in the hands of the triumphant boy. Paul had been haunted by the vision of the unfortunate owl being mobbed by crows all the way up the hill. Now as Paul cycled along he was more interested in the barn in the field on the other side of the crossroads at the top of the hill. Paul slowed down to come alongside Maureen.

"I've an idea."

"What sort of an idea?" quizzed Maureen, furrowing her brow.

"I thought a barn might be a bit more private, for what we

had in mind."

"Is it very far?" Maureen wanted to know, and at least did not seem to be against the idea.

Paul explained, "It's on our way home really. The barn is in the next field to the football pitch."

"Well, they had better not be playing football today," quipped Maureen.

"Hardly likely," laughed Paul.

Eventually they came to the bottom of the hill and dismounted to walk up it. Paul did not mention the owl but told Maureen about his accident.

"I thought you knew a bit about bikes. You fixed Auntie's, didn't you?"

"Oh, it was a few years ago, and I suppose I was keen to try it out," said Paul ruefully.

They came to the crossroads and cycled ahead to join up with the road to the docklands, then turned off sharp-left for the road that eventually led down to Pitt Court, just across from Paul's house. Paul stopped at a gateway and looked over the gate to see that there was no one about, he opened it and let Maureen through.

"This is a bit naughty really. We're trespassing you know, Paul," said Maureen, looking across to the barn.

"We are not going to do any harm, now are we?" Paul rationalised.

They hid their bicycles in some brambles in the corner of the field and strode towards the barn. Paul knew how to get in as he had been there before. He rolled away a huge boulder from the base of the large double doors and then unsnapped a bolt to open a large battered door. As Paul moved inside quickly he beckoned Maureen to do the same. They both stood inside and looked around.

"That's where we head for!" said Paul, pointing at where a ladder leaned against a loft section with bales of hay and straw stacked neatly in piles. Paul led the way and climbed up the ladder. Maureen was looking up at him, so he said, "It's quite safe, come on up."

Maureen gingerly climbed up the ladder and reached the

top. Paul noticed that in one corner some bales had broken out of their twine and lay spread in a heap on the floor.

"Ah! Just right for what we have in mind," he said catching hold of Maureen's hand as she giggled nervously. They slumped down in the corner, their backs leaning against the cool stone walls of the structure.

"Well, here we are!" said Maureen, looking shyly at Paul as he sidled up to her and put his arms around her, leaning to kiss her.

They engaged in this for a while, their tongues entwining, whilst Paul deftly undid the buttons of Maureen's blouse with practiced ease. His fingers traced the outlines of her breasts, slightly fuller, like the outline of her belly, slightly distended at the outset of her menstrual cycle. Paul's hands went searching down her skirt to find her bare legs, then his fingers moved up underneath her skirt to the crotch of her panties. Maureen had closed her eyes now and spread her legs to allow Paul to continue unhindered. He caressed her inner thighs and then slid his fingers under the legs of the cotton pants, to feel for her pubic area. Maureen's breathing was coming faster; their cheeks glowed and their blood pumped and throbbed around their bodies. Paul stood up suddenly and removed his shirt as quickly as he could, kicked off his shoes, and then pulled off his trousers. Maureen looked across at Paul and removed her blouse and vest.

Paul was now naked and so he knelt in front of Maureen and pulled her skirt off and then her pants. He threw himself down on top of her kissing her from her mouth, down to her neck and below to her breasts. She made him be careful of her tender nipples. He traced his lips around her belly and then explored the length of her labia and the private places where only invited guests were allowed, soon to be banned during the curse of the monthly renewal. Then it was time to please him, so Maureen inverted herself over him and they supped off each other desperately, giving as much as they could to each other's needs before they parted. They lay quietly, arms around each other; a movement caught Maureen's eye.

"Look! There's something up there," she said, pointing up

at the roof beams. Paul's heart missed a beat until he realised what Maureen had seen.

"It's all right. It's only a barn owl."

"Oh, is it? I've never seen a barn owl before. I thought it was a ghost. It looks very white," she said excitedly, but less fearfully now.

"It doesn't have all pure white feathers, but it does look quite white, especially when it's flying," said Paul grinning.

"Do you think that's a male barn owl; or a female?" asked Maureen suddenly.

"Why? Does it matter? You call it a cock, not a male, by the way."

"Huh! That was what I was worried about. Him seeing us– making love."

"You're not serious? You can't be."

"I fooled you really though, didn't I?" giggled Maureen.

"You little madam you! You have always been a bit of a tease. It's about time I taught you a lesson,"

"Well I have been teaching you a lesson ever since I saw you," said Maureen, tongue in cheek, wondering if Paul would gather what she was really saying.

It gradually dawned on Paul and he knew, in his heart, that he was grateful. Nevertheless, it was still playtime and he struggled to pick Maureen up, then staggered over to where the bales were stacked. He lifted her onto a layer of bales as high as he could and rolled her over onto her front with her legs hanging down over the bales. Paul proceeded to slap her bare backside, which made Maureen squeal and protest. Paul then placed his hands over her buttocks and bit into them, nibbling around the cheeks, which had Maureen in a hysterical fit of laughter. Paul looked at her wonderful peachy orbs sadly and wondered when he would see them again. He lifted her down to his level with one hand under her belly and clasping her side, the other hand supporting her mound of Venus, settling her gently on the ground. She turned around to see the sadness in his eyes and put her arms around him.

"We have made the best of things, haven't we Paul?" Paul said nothing for the moment thinking about what had become unattainable.

"Yes, I suppose so. Not many people have everything."

"It's been good Paul. You mustn't be greedy," whispered Maureen. Paul squeezed her tightly and nodded silently, but he knew he could not have peace of mind with her gone.

CHAPTER FOURTEEN

When Paul arrived at Florence's house at the usual time next morning, Maureen informed him that she was going into Bideford with her Auntie to do a bit of shopping. She whispered to him that her little visitor had arrived, and that it might be a good idea if Paul called on his friend Barry, whom he had not seen much of, except in the evenings, for the past few weeks.

Auntie Florence had still not told anyone of her cancer fears, and the prayer meeting was not for a few days yet. On this particular morning she was going to send Maureen into the ladies' clothing store, the chemist, and also market place to purchase a few things. Then she could hurry up to the hospital for the results of her examination, under the pretext of going to visit a friend.

Paul found Barry at home, working on a balsawood model of an aeroplane. Barry was pleased to see Paul that morning. He had wanted to know all about Paul's relationship with Maureen; they had shared some comparisons about other girl friends that they had gone out with, in the past. This time, what Paul, felt was different. His relationship had become more intense and he knew that it would have to remain private between himself and Maureen.

Paul and Barry both cycled off to the burrows with model gliders whose wings could be slotted into a groove above the cockpit, making them easier to transport in their saddlebags.

The large, open, air space was ideal for gliders, or powered models for that matter, but only children from well-off families could afford the latter. Barry did not fair too badly as his father, being a skipper on a boat, made good money. They enjoyed the prospect of gliding. Barry made minor adjustments with little pieces of lead, to get the balance of the aircraft just right. He had also managed to purchase some fliers and rockets from a shop in Bideford. The proprietors, no doubt having an eye on enterprise, knew that schoolboys of a certain age, home on holiday, would be looking ahead to Guy Fawkes Day.

Barry had strapped the fliers to two primitive, balsawood, silhouette bodies, with a tail fin, thinner wings and tailplane to slot through grooves in the body. The other aeronautic delight, was a long V2 shaped fuselage with four small fins at the bottom end and four large fins swept downwards from the middle of the fuselage, like something from a Buck Rogers Space Odyssey. One half of the rocket was cut out of a single piece of a one-sixteenth of an inch-gauge balsawood, its matching partner was cut in half, to be stuck with strong glue, to make the whole aerodynamic shape. It was with a certain number of technical inaccuracies, to scale. The innovative design was then strengthened by four rockets glued to the intersection of the basal fins. The fuses were greased with paraffin wax, known as dubbing, and tied together with a piece of cotton to ensure that the rockets fired simultaneously when ignited. Paul was very impressed when Barry showed him what he had been doing, since Paul had deserted him for his new girl friend.

Barry preferred to have company when he tried out his new creations and it was also necessary to have another large bicycle saddlebag to keep the larger model separate. They duly loaded them onto their bicycles with the noses sticking out of one end of the saddlebags. They arrived out on the burrows with excited anticipation; they unpacked and looked for any damage caused in transit. Barry had brought a tube of quick-setting glue just in case.

Barry was keen to try out the rocket because of its exciting potential but he knew that the chances of it being an outright success were slim. They waited until they thought that the wind was reasonably settled then Barry lit the touch paper. It fizzed right away; Barry kept his fingers crossed and his heart thumped with the adrenalin of excitement. He hoped that the half-price rockets from last year's stock would not let him down. Suddenly one of the rockets fired, tilting the rocket over from its vertical angle, shortly followed by another firing. It took off quickly at an acute angle, spiralling low to the ground: it altered course when the third rocket fired and gained a bit of height, although still spiralling until the original rocket was spent, making it lose height. On the downward trajectory the remaining rocket decided it was now or never to justify its existence, but only manage to explode in a spectacular fashion throwing little bits of balsawood shrapnel to the winds

"Wow! At least it got airborne, Barry," said Paul, not unimpressed.

Barry was disappointed but realistic, "Well, yes. It was a bit of fun I suppose. I should like to have seen it go straight up in the air though."

"Never mind. Werner Von Braun had a lot of trouble with his rockets I believe, and I bet they cost a lot more than yours!" said Paul grinning, and they then both fell about laughing.

"It certainly put the fear of God into the bird population anyhow," said Barry, still seeing the funny side, as the gulls and peewits carried on protesting in the sky above them.

"Let's try the fliers and see how they behave," said Barry, picking one up and examining it. He then handed it to Paul

"Hold it out at arm's length and I'll light the touch-paper. As soon as it fizzes throw it straight, but slightly downwards, so that it doesn't stall," said Barry as Paul looked at him dubiously.

"All right, I can see that you are a bit worried about this. I tell you what, I'll hold it whilst you light the touch-paper, then if this goes right, you can have a go with the other one," said Barry. Paul was relieved of anxiety on his own behalf, but not for Barry.

"Go on, light it," said Barry as Paul dithered with the matches.

The match lit the touch-paper of the single flier; as it sparked off, Barry threw it hard and dipped slightly as the little plane, with its less powerful motor than the rocket, went into a gliding flight until, at the end of its initial manoeuvre, the propellant really got under way and powered it along into a gentle arc. A few seconds later it hit the turf, bouncing a few times before cartwheeling to a stop. They ran over to it and examined the damaged model, shrieking and hooting with delight that it had, indeed, flown nearly a hundred yards.

"I could give the other model a little more lift and see if it

168

goes a bit further," said Barry as they returned to their starting places.

Barry adjusted the wing flaps – incisions in the thin balsa wood sections taped over for flexibility. The tail-plane's flaps were also altered to give more lift. Barry gave the other model a dry run, with its gliding power only, similar to the tests he had previously done in his own garden, to satisfy himself that it would reach a longer trajectory.

"Your turn now," he suggested to Paul.

Paul was a little apprehensive about holding on to the model after the flier's touch paper was lit. However, he copied Barry's method of launch and the model lurched away to climb steadily, as predicted, until the powder seemed exhausted and it stalled slightly as it's nose dropped, flattening out and gliding fairly evenly until it was only a couple of feet above the ground. The last section of powder was used up in a sudden surge of power, sending it skyward again. Paul and Barry hooted with delight, chasing after it until it came to a textbook glide stop, without any damage. For the finale Barry assembled the wide wings into the slots of his fabric-covered glider. He had more patience than Paul and would sit for hours delicately cutting and gluing little matchstick-like struts to his models of an evening. Now it was time to see if this new model was going to be a successful glider. Barry hoped there was enough lift in the air. The thermal currents would prove if his optimism was well founded.

After a couple of tries the model did catch an upward thermal, keeping it in the air for several minutes. They took it in turns to send it up and thoroughly enjoyed their time on the burrows.

"I don't know what I'm going to do when Maureen goes home," said Paul sharing with Barry his sadness of the forthcoming parting. Barry was sympathetic but could not really believe that a girl could be that special.

"There's always plenty of girls around and they usually get fed up with boys after a while anyway. If you have enjoyed Maureen's company during the holiday, shouldn't you be thinking yourself lucky?"

As they cycled home Barry reminded Paul, "The TV documentary 'War at Sea' is on this evening, and you are welcome to come and see it."

Paul usually enjoyed the programme, and the TV that his own parents could not afford, but he had planned in his own mind that he was going to see Maureen after tea.

When Paul called at Florence's house, Maureen came outside looking pale and distraught.

"Let's walk along to the quay and sit down on a seat there as I've something to tell you," she said simply, walking ahead of him as he followed along in a puzzled manner. She parried his questions with the answer that she would tell him soon enough. They found an empty seat and Maureen turned around to him.

"It's bad news about Auntie Florence. She got her results of tests that were carried out shortly after I arrived here on holiday. It seems that she has a form of cancer," she informed him solemnly.

"Cancer? Oh God, how awful. I had no idea," he said, genuinely shocked.

"I did not think that Auntie was going to be that poorly," said Maureen, tears starting to form.

"How is Auntie Florence taking it?" Paul asked.

"She's resting in her bedroom at the moment, but she must be shattered I imagine."

"I've heard that they can cure a lot of people with radiation treatment nowadays," said Paul hopefully.

"Yes, Auntie is going to Bideford in a few days for that particular treatment. The poor soul, she didn't want to tell me about her illness but I forced it out of her. Maybe I should have let her keep it a secret. Do you think it would be worse for her – everyone knowing about it?" asked Maureen, breaking into wracking sobs. Paul put his arm around her not caring if anyone was looking.

"I think it's best that she can confide in someone. I could tell my parents, but nobody else needs to know. They would be very discreet about it. Do you think that Auntie would mind if they told the Baptist Minister?" he asked quietly.

"I'll find out from Auntie Florence," she mumbled wiping

her eyes and nose with a handkerchief.

"Will I see you tomorrow?" he asked.

"Well, I suppose we ought to try to carry on as normally as possible. We could all catch the bus to Westward Ho! and have a day there. We have a bit of pocket money from George and May. I'd sooner spend that money than have it hanging around my person," she said abruptly.

Paul was loathe to spend his money on bus fares, but knew this suggestion was a sensible one in the circumstances.

"We'll go back and ask her, shall we? Then we can prepare for the morning. You know, times of buses and things," said Paul, his practical side coming to the fore again.

"Yes, why not? It's better to tackle things head on I suppose," said Maureen, getting up from the seat.

They walked back along the quay and Paul sat in the living room while Maureen went upstairs to see Florence, who was propped up on the bed reading a copy of *Woman's Own* magazine.

"How are you feeling now, Auntie?"

"Oh, a…bit deflated is the word I think. The wind has definitely gone out of my sails at the moment. I'll be right as rain before long though I expect," she said, putting on a brave face.

"Do you think you would be up to a trip to Westward Ho! tomorrow? Take a packed lunch perhaps?" asked Maureen encouragingly.

"It's a bit of a palaver going to Westward Ho! Usually you have to get a connection at Northam because there isn't a bus running all the way. I find Westward Ho! Windy, and always crowded when you go into somewhere for a cup of tea or something. Why don't we go over to Instow on the ferry? I prefer a short boat trip to a bus ride any day. Besides, they have got a nice cafe over there and the toilets aren't very far away if you are sitting on the beach. That's something you should be aware of too my girl," she said nodding her head towards Maureen pointedly.

Maureen smiled and was grateful that Florence was not going to give up without a fight.

"Well, that's fine. Instow it is tomorrow then. Is it all right if Paul comes too?"

"Well I'm sure that you two lovebirds could not be parted for too long. Mind you, it's only about a week before you go back. You two are not going to see much of each other then are you?" Maureen's head drooped at the reality of the statement and she remained quiet.

"Touchy subject that one, ain't it? I did warn you though didn't I? Mind you, they do say 'tis better to have loved and lost, than never to have loved at all. Although I'm sure that there will be other times when you will be able to meet but you are both very young and you shouldn't get too serious at your age, should you?" said Florence. Maureen stood there quiet and sad, thinking that Auntie should be saying this to Paul, rather than to her.

"Well don't just stand there saying nothing my girl. Go downstairs and tell the boyfriend that we are going on the ferryboat to Instow tomorrow," said Florence gruffly, but her heart was heavy for her niece. Maureen smiled and ran downstairs. How Florence wished she owned the cottage that she lived in instead of paying rent for it, out of her small pension. There would be precious little to leave to Maureen when she did pass on.

Maureen informed Paul of Auntie's decision.

"Well that's good news, in the circumstances. We can have our trip that we postponed to go to Croyde," he said, ginning.

"In the circumstances, I think you ought to be on your best behaviour, with Auntie sitting next to you," said Maureen giggling.

"I was rather hoping that you might be sitting next to me," quipped Paul, relieved that Maureen had found her sense of humour.

They both listened to Radio Luxembourg, leaving the door open at Florence's request so that she could hear the music from upstairs. They sat on the sofa talking, kissing and cuddling, but without the passion of previous occasions. In any case, Florence could come down the stairs at any time.

CHAPTER FIFTEEN

The following morning was bright enough with a fair amount of cloud. Just right for Florence, who did not like it very hot. She got into the ferryboat, with her straw hat tied with a long leather bootlace, resting on her back, not her head, lest it should be blown by the wind into the river. Maureen was glad that her Auntie seemed like her old self again and was enjoying the boat trip. Both Maureen and Florence cupped the water with one hand as the little ferry boat chugged across the Torridge, aiming slightly into the oncoming tide to compensate for its surge.

Soon the high walls of the little harbour of Instow loomed above them and they disembarked. Paul jumped off at an early moment so that he could be waiting to steady Auntie Florence as she crossed onto the steep steps leading up to the top of the harbour wall. He was anxious to start the day off right, and get a good atmosphere going, if they were to be sharing each other's company for a long time. Florence was of an independent spirit and at first was not keen to be helped by a minor, as she saw it, until she saw the earnest and almost pleading look on Paul's face.

"Thank you," she said gracefully as she accepted the hand. They all walked up the steps and along the harbour wall with their basket, bags, and ex-army haversack, which Paul proudly carried on his back. Turning to the left they walked a short way along the seafront road until they passed down the slipway onto the beach. Paul looked longingly across to the right, where the sand dunes were, but knew that they would not be appropriate now, with Auntie in tow. He sighed to himself but made Florence laugh by getting between her and Maureen and linking his arms up with one of theirs. Somehow it seemed quite natural on that day, but the significance of the gesture was not lost on Maureen, and she had to stifle the tears that were forming in her eyes and threatening to flood out. They did not go far; Florence, mindful of the cafe and the conveniences which were situated close to the harbour, decided to camp against the sea wall, so that she could sit up against it.

There were no deckchairs available, unlike Westward Ho! where there were always hundreds in the summer season. Old towels were placed on the sand and Florence sat down with her back resting against the wall and got out a library book. Paul could see it was a novel and wondered if there was any romance in it. It was funny, he thought, how his parents generation, even when they were quite old, or even very old, seemed to go for romantic books and films. Surely they must be too old for that sort of thing?

Maureen had brought one of her school books along and Paul's heart sank as he realised that he had had the best of times for this holiday and it would now be over too soon with both of them going back to school. Maureen had noticed that Paul was restless and asked him, "Have you not brought anything to read then, Paul?"

"Er, no. I think I might have a swim as the tide is high now. It's the safest time to swim anyhow," he said, not really wanting to swim on his own, but guessing that Maureen would not be able to.

"Be careful then. Don't try to swim to Appledore and back," quipped Maureen, smiling.

Florence looked up from her book, frowning, and turned to Maureen, "Perhaps you had better stay with him to the edge of the water and see he does not go out too far," she said in a worried tone.

"Perhaps you're right. Anyway, I could have a little paddle."

With that, she stripped off her sandals as Paul stripped down to his bathing trunks. They made their way down to the water. Aware that now Maureen would be watching his every move, he thought he would engage in his own form of pair bonding, so he turned back from the cold shallows and circling her. He started to splash her with his feet. Of course this produced howls and squeaks of protests from Maureen standing there in her new navy shorts and white blouse, just purchased while Auntie was in the hospital. By the time Paul had started to use his hands to cup the water up over her, she had decided to fight back with water, but got the worst of it, getting a pretty good drenching up over her shorts and quite a few splashes up over her blouse. Paul stopped splashing as he was dismayed to notice that the wet blouse did not reveal anything more feminine than reinforced lines of support.

"Are you wearing a bra?" he asked, puzzled.

"Auntie gave me the money to get one yesterday. She thinks I'm a big girl now. Well, big enough to wear a bra," she laughed shyly.

"She's going to kill me for getting sea water all over my new clothes, and you of course. Well especially you. You are the one that got me wet, aren't you?"

Paul looked at her for a while, the tide slapping and caressing their feet. He said quietly, "I wish that I could lay you down here in the water and make love to you, just at this moment."

Maureen faced him as they gazed at each other steadily until she said, without visible emotion, "With Auntie Florence and other people watching?"

"They should know how I feel about you," he said simply.

"What about me, then. How should I feel?"

"You should be proud that I love you enough to do it," he said, not able to stop a twitch in his mouth that was a prelude to a smile, and Maureen knew it.

"I think you are an arrogant... bastard!" she said, punching him hard on the shoulder but regretting the use of the word 'bastard' even though it was in fun.

Paul grabbed her arms then put his arms around her and kissed her forcibly on the mouth. It was only a short struggle that stopped Maureen from kissing him back; she realised that Auntie Florence was looking at them both.

"Auntie is looking right this way you fool," she said, putting all the blame on him.

"I think Auntie Florence knows more or less what we do when we are together now, doesn't she?" he said

"I hope she doesn't know everything," she said, pulling

away from him and giggling.

"You had better cool down and have a swim," she said smiling.

Paul looked at her until he too smiled and then waded out into deeper water. Then throwing himself face down into it he pulled himself along with a vigorous crawl to offset the shock of the cold water. He came up gasping for air and turned over on his back to look back at Maureen, standing legs wide apart, her hands on her hips. Paul knew now, more than ever that he loved her, and could not bear the thought of being apart from her. He turned around and looked across to Appledore where he lived, and had to go on living – without her. Paul then looked across to the mouth of the estuary with the Bar in the distance. He felt like swimming on and on until he drowned; then the problem would be solved for him. Not for the others though. Maureen would be devastated. Also his mother and father, brother and sister. He turned around. She was still there, waving. She was waving him to come in. He hesitated for some time, now enjoying the water as his body got used to it, until he swam back to within shouting distance.

"I shouldn't swim out too far, Auntie is getting worried," Maureen shouted.

"All right, I'm coming in now anyway," he said, missing Maureen's presence in the water. They both walked back to Florence who scolded them for getting Maureen's clothes wet with seawater.

"You will have to wash those clothes now mind, Maureen. As soon as we get back they will need a good rinse and put out on the line to dry." she said to Maureen, but looking disapprovingly at Paul, who felt the need to say.

"It's my fault Auntie, I'm afraid I was the one that started the splashing."

"I'm very well aware of that young man, and also other things you were so brazen as to carry on with other people looking on. I was young myself once…but… there was a time and a place for everything," she said triumphantly, as Paul and Maureen looked sheepishly at each other.

"I'm sorry Auntie, but you know how fond of Maureen I

176

am," Paul apologised.

"Yes I, well, like I said, a time and a place for everything."

Florence wanted to say a whole lot more. She wanted to tell Paul that their romance had to be short lived. She wanted to tell him that he should be concentrating on other things, such as his schoolwork, when the holiday was over. She knew that the young couple would miss each other terribly and how painful growing up could be.

Florence looked at Paul, now drying himself off with the towel and chattering away to Maureen, who was lying down looking up at him her eyes sparkling and content. If only she was a fairy godmother and could snap her fingers and transport the three of them to a tropical island. Where would she fit in, though? She did not like too much sun in any case, she realised, smiling to herself.

Florence enjoyed the day as cloud continually masked the heat of the sun but Paul and Maureen sighed every time the sun was blocked. They had both acquired a decent tan by now. Paul a reddish, coppery glow, intermingled with freckles; Maureen's skin definitely deeply tanned brown.

They had their usual picnic lunch of sandwiches and Thermos tea. Florence took them up to the cafe for tea around four o'clock. Paul bought Florence a tea towel as a thank you present, and also as a peace offering, with the last of the money he had in his pocket. They all sensed that this might be the last outing that they might take together – for various reasons.

The final couple of days of the holiday were spent in a subdued manner, cycling and walking. The good weather was beginning to break up, matching their moods. On their last evening together Paul and Maureen went to the cinema, just up the road from Auntie's house, holding hands and cuddling in the dark, only seeing the film through a blur of tears.

CHAPTER SIXTEEN

The day Paul and Maureen had been dreading finally arrived. Florence had arranged for a taxi to take Maureen to the station at Bideford. Paul asked Florence if it would be all right to see Maureen off at the station. As Florence suffered from car sickness, she was quite happy to let Paul escort her niece.

They all knew that it was going to be a long train journey, changing at many different stations before Maureen arrived at Aberdeen. Florence also knew that the parting was going to be a very traumatic, emotional experience for the three of them, again for different reasons. Maureen kissed her Auntie Florrie goodbye and the taxi pulled away slowly. Maureen waved back at Florence with desperate resignation until she was out of sight.

Paul clenched Maureen's hand tightly all the way to the station. There were tears in both pairs of eyes and they were too emotional to say more than a few mundane words about the train journey. The driver noticed in his mirror how upset they looked, and decided that an attempt at cheerful banter would not be appreciated.

They waited on Bideford station in a subdued silence until the train rounded the bend after its short journey from Torrington. Paul's heart was pounding as he picked up Maureen's suitcase. The train screeched to a halt, releasing a loud hiss of steam. Paul yanked the brass door handle open and lifted the heavy suitcase inside the compartment. He found a suitable seat by the window and heaved the case up onto the luggage rack. After a few words of encouragement and advice from Maureen Paul got off the train; they stood facing each other through the open window of the door. Paul leaned forward and put his hands through to pull Maureen towards him. They kissed, despairingly more than passionately, until the guard blew his whistle. The little engine made up steam and chuffed into life. The carriages groaned as the wheels started to move. Maureen pulled away and Paul stepped backwards. Tears were flowing freely from both of them. Paul started to walk along with the moving train saying, "I'll send you a letter in a few days. We must keep in touch."

"I'll write back as soon as I get your letter, Paul," said Maureen, sobbing fitfully.

"I love you Maureen!" shouted Paul, as the train gathered speed, throwing up a column of smoke and steam.

"I love you too, Paul!" shouted Maureen, leaning out of the window, waving madly.

Paul waved back until the train disappeared around the bend, slumped down on a bench and wept for a long, long time. A stiff breeze made a soft whistling noise as it filtered between telegraph wires overhead. It seemed to Paul the loneliest place in the world.

Paul was left feeling desolate, knowing that he had lost something very precious. His mother was very concerned for him. Paul had to start a new term at school, which was crucial for his education. Ruth knew that Paul was already struggling with his schoolwork.

It did not help when his elder brother, Graham, teased Paul about his relationship with Maureen. There was a nasty fight and their father had to intervene. Stephen was more angry with Graham for showing a lack of sensitivity towards Paul, knowing how upset he was. However, he thought he had to tell Paul that no matter how upset he might feel, it was still his duty to return to his education and remember his priorities.

Paul and Maureen exchanged letters frequently to start with, although Paul felt inadequate to describe exactly how he felt. Miserable would have been the main thing, and that was something that could not give any comfort to Maureen.

The depression that had left Paul after he had met Maureen returned and gave both his parents cause for concern. Ruth found it ironic that both her husband and son seemed to drift off into another world, though for different reasons. The mournful classical music that Stephen played also reflected Paul's mood. Paul became listless, not showing interest in anything, especially schoolwork.

Then came a bombshell. Reverend Baxter received news from the Baptist minister that Florence had died of cancer at the end of November that year. Paul was ashamed of himself for feeling more remorse over the fact that it was now going to be more difficult, if not impossible, to meet Maureen during future school holidays, than remorse of Florence's death itself. Maureen's family would be coming to Appledore for the funeral, so it would be a chance to see her again briefly.

Paul felt awkward confronting Maureen's parents. Her mother seemed a good sort, but her father was a typical dour Scotsman: not giving away much in the form of conversation and seemingly irritated by this young southerner who had the audacity to court his daughter.

Maureen's family had started their journey the previous evening, travelling all night, and had arrived the day before the funeral. They were now staying at Florence's house in Irsha Street, the coffin being at the Chapel of Rest near the churchyard

Maureen had slipped up to Paul's house to let him and his family know that they had arrived. They had talked privately in the lounge. They embraced each other in the same way as at their parting on the station a couple of months ago; and weeping in their desolation and worries of how they would meet in the future. Paul wanted to take Maureen up to the Lookout and have a passionate session on the seat. Maureen refused on the grounds that it was too cold an evening for what he had in mind. She knew that it would only leave them feeling more frustrated if she gave in, the cold not being the main problem. Maureen encouraged Paul to get his mother to make them a cup of tea and all have a cosy chat.

Stephen Baxter turned off his radio and came out of his study to greet Maureen, offering his condolences. Ruth Baxter was also consoling, telling Maureen that she had kept in touch with Florence after their get together at the prayer meeting. She had seen quite a bit of Florence after the meeting, and had visited her when she was admitted to hospital. She was going to the funeral the following morning to pay her respects and told Maureen that Paul would have the day off school so that he could be there, sitting in the church.

"Mum and Dad and I, are going to stay overnight again at Auntie's house as Mum and Dad want to clear up Auntie's estate. Not that there is anything worth very much. It's just the usual things. The details you know?" said Maureen sadly.

"If there is anything outstanding that your parents cannot finish tomorrow, I am sure that the Baptist Minister and I would be only too glad to be of good service, my dear," said Stephen, trying to be practical in his ministerial role.

"That's very kind of you Reverend Baxter. I shall certainly tell my parents about that. Dad will want to be getting home and back to work as soon as possible, I'm sure, and it's such a long and awkward journey as you know," said Maureen, knowing that her father did not want to stay in this place any longer than he had to.

"Fine. That's settled then," said Stephen. He took his tea into his study where he continued on his typewriter, as Chopin tinkled its way out of the radio and bounced cheerfully around the room.

"Do you think Maureen could come down to stay here during the Christmas holidays, now that Auntie Florence has gone?" said Paul to his mother impulsively, not knowing what else to say, and with that important question clearly at the forefront of his mind.

"Well, I shall have to talk to your father about that, won't I now," said Ruth, suddenly put under pressure, which was partly what Paul had in mind.

"Besides, we don't have that much room for guests, now do we?" she said, hoping to forego any further complications and disappointments.

"There's that small box room. Graham and I could sleep in that room and Maureen could sleep in our room," said Paul desperately, knowing that he had to take his chances when he could. Ruth was getting embarrassed now, even though she sympathised with her son.

"I said we would have to talk about it, Paul," she said, taking Maureen's cup and filling it up again to alter the flow of thought and pent up emotion.

"I don't know if my parents would let me come down again at Christmas, Paul. Its cost my dad quite a bit in train fares to come down for the funeral. He won't be in any mood to cough up again for me to come down here for a holiday you know." said Maureen practically, but hoping that it would not be so.

"We might be able to get around that, some way, if it's only the money," Paul said optimistically.

"It may not be only the money Paul. As I said, we shall have to wait and see. You must be patient," said his mother, getting a little exasperated.

Paul became quiet after that and said little until he escorted Maureen down the hill to rejoin her parents. He was still scheming in his mind, but grateful just to be with her when he had thought that he might never see her again. They parted at Auntie's house, knowing that they would see each other in the morning.

The funeral was a quiet affair, on a cold Friday morning. Most of Florence's relatives lived in Scotland and only Maureen and her parent's represented the family, the rest put off by the difficult, long journey. There were a lot of local people from the Baptist Church, who always turned up for funerals and weddings as a sign of duty. But sometimes it was through curiosity, to try to learn something about their neighbours and friends that may have remained a secret for the years that they had known them. Refreshments had been laid on in the Baptist schoolroom Any awkward questions were soon rebuffed by the dour Scotsman. A reference to the close companionship of their daughter and the Congregational Minister's son was hastily abandoned, after a growl of dismissal and the showing of teeth. Mrs Baxter was doing her nervous best to smooth things along and comforting Maureen's mother, who was still upset by her sister's death. Ruth was trying to explain the intensity of their offspring's relationship in a sensitive way, without Maureen's father hearing; sensing that he might not be so understanding about it.

Paul and Maureen found the little kitchen the best place to hide and offered to help pour out tea and wash up the dirty crockery. They made plans to meet the following morning when, with Paul's parent's help, they would work out arrangements for

Auntie's memorial headstone. Maureen's parents could get on with the other things, such as informing the Registrar and disposal of Auntie's belongings. Paul's mother knew of someone trustworthy who might buy the furniture, but could not promise that it would amount to a great deal of money. She suggested that an auction in the house might be a good option for anything that was not likely to be taken away for a reasonable price. Maureen's father warmed to this canny approach and after that the two got on famously, to the relief of the others, so that when Paul and Maureen went off in the afternoon with the instructions regarding style and price of a headstone, no suspicions surfaced. A previous phone call from Paul's father to the stonemason enabled them to have a prompt appointment which left the young couple time to themselves for the rest of the afternoon.

Maureen's parents were out collecting any money owing from the Post Office Savings Account, and also tying up things with the landlord of the property in Irsha Street. Florence had made out her will before she departed, leaving everything to her sister and niece. Maureen was left the princely sum of ten pounds, providing all the bills from her estate had been paid. She was also given Auntie's jewellery and a few other treasures. Florence had known that this way her niece could have what she wanted her to have, and not what Maureen's father wanted her to have.

When he found out about the ten pounds, he demanded to know what it would be spent on. This put paid to the possibility of her catching a train down to Bideford during the Christmas holidays. Her father could not spend the money, so it would have to be saved in a bank. Maureen let Paul into Auntie's house, where they started sorting out drawers and putting things into boxes. After they had made a good start, to show that they had been working on the packing and sorting, they lay on Auntie's double bed for a kiss and a cuddle.

Not knowing when her parents would be coming back was a bit of a dampener to Maureen's sensuous nature. She thought that the best thing in the circumstances was to quench Paul's fires from the start. Remembering their last time together in the same room, earlier in the summer, Maureen thought that something similar would do the trick, only this time she would not be removing all her clothing and neither would he. Paul and Maureen lay on the bed for about half an hour in a loving embrace, the last time, maybe – forever. They then carried on boxing up Florence's possessions until stopping for lunch. Maureen made a cup of tea and used up a tin of baked beans from the pantry spread on some buttered toast.

Maureen's parents came back about an hour after they had recommenced packing up, giving them plenty of time to compose themselves. The family had to be ready for a taxi that would be take them to Bideford station in a couple of hour's time. Florence's two suitcases were used to put all the valuables and documents in. Paul was given a list of the things that they had not been able to settle in the short time before they had to return. Maureen's father had to concede grudgingly that Paul and his parents had been very helpful in what they had done for them. He was encouraged no doubt by his wife, who was taken by Paul's polite, boyish charm and good looks. This may have had the effect of jealousy on a later occasion, however, causing friction in the family.

When it was time to go, Maureen's Dad made no bones about a quick peck on the cheek by this parson's son to his daughter. A few grunts from him, and loud cheerio's from Maureen and her mother, left Paul flat and deflated again. He wandered into the empty house, with it's special memories – for him, for Maureen and Florence.

Mrs Baxter was really worried about her younger son. Paul's depression had returned again, even deeper than before, not surprising in the circumstances. She went to her doctor to get some advice. He recommended that Paul get himself involved in at least one vigorous sport, and 'Work it out of his system.' Ruth knew that this would not solve the problem and, due to the dearth of psychiatric counsellors, did not know what to do for the best. Her husband took the same tack as before and encouraged his son to get stuck into his studies. In fact he forbade Paul to go out when exams were in the offing. Paul had got to the stage when he did not care much what happened and was content to sit with school books – any book, leaving it open on his lap and staring into space. Perhaps it was his imagination, or his memories, that saved his sanity. He re-lived his time with Maureen in his own mind and fantasised about what he might have done, and what he might do in the future.

For hours he would just sit there. His mother, more discerning than her husband, realised that he was living in his own world and, for the moment at any rate, it might be the only way he could cope. She had a genuine fear that he would end up in a mental institution and the thought that he might be rubbing shoulders with permanently handicapped people horrified her. It was not so much the social stigma that condemned people with any psychiatric problem that worried her, but the fact that Paul might really go insane if he felt trapped inside a place with people he could not converse with.

Then Ruth thought that he might run away. He could end up anywhere – if he did not take his own life in the mean time. Ruth did the only thing she thought was any good at that time – she prayed. She prayed in the morning, in the afternoon, and in the evening. God must answer her prayers.

Paul continued to write letters to Maureen once a week. The daily letter writing had not lasted long. It seemed silly writing the same thing over, and over again, without having any news to relate. In his first letters he was able to tell Maureen and the family that he had been able to complete the necessary condensing of Florence's belongings into items of sale with the antique dealer his mother knew.

Then the other furniture had been sold at an auction. The proceeds did not amount to a great deal of money in that austere period of the fifties. Paul's mother had helped him quite a bit, with his father helping to shift a bit of furniture and peruse through some books. He also bagged a bookcase and paid the reserve price that the antique dealer had put on it. Ruth paid a generous amount into Florence's estate for the purchase of her linen and other things that she thought that Maureen or her mother might want to reclaim one day.

Paul duly recounted all these items to Maureen in his letters and also the fact that they had cleaned the place up nicely and handed the keys back to the landlord, once all the property was empty of furniture, bar a couple of things that the landlord was happy to keep. Maureen was aware that the main chance of her staying somewhere in Appledore was now gone; especially as it seemed that both of Paul's parents, particularly his father, did not really want her to stay at their house, even if she could get away and travel down. Maureen did not blame them for that, in the circumstances. Her only hope would have been to use the small amount of money that Florence had left her to take a train down, but Maureen knew this was not possible now. However, like Ruth, Maureen decided to pray, that some day they would be reunited. Until that time she would have to adjust to the parting and get on with her life.

In one of Paul's letters to Maureen, he wrote:

My Darling Maureen, I miss you so much. I feel I cannot bear to be apart from you forever. If you cannot come to visit me in my home town, maybe I can come to visit you in Aberdeen. It might be possible to see you during the Christmas holidays. That would really make my Christmas, and I hope yours too. The biggest problem is that I haven't got any money for the train fare. I think it is unlikely that my parents would encourage our meeting again. (My father is the main problem.) If I could earn some money doing part-time work, like gardening or potato picking or something like that, between now and next summer holidays, I could save enough for the fare and accommodation at the YMCA How does that sound? I love you so much and miss you. I am always thinking of our times together. I miss the feel of your lovely body close to mine and all those delicious kisses and the intimacies we have shared. If I cannot be with you at this moment, please write soon. Ever yours, Paul.

Maureen felt very emotional after reading Paul's letter, and cried for hours in the privacy of her own room. In her distress she had not hidden the letter well enough and her father found it and read it. She wrote back to Paul:

My Darling Paul, I also miss you very much and would love to see you again. There may be a problem if you came here though. My father would be dead against it as well. In fact he would be likely to get violent with you, or me, or both of us, if he found that you were here in Aberdeen. I could have kept it secret, but unfortunately my father found your letter to me and read it, which made him very angry and violent. We all suffered. It will be best if you mail your letters for me to a girl friend of mine, who will pass them onto me. Otherwise if father sees a letter with your postmark on it he will destroy it. If you come to Aberdeen I would have to meet you in secret, for an hour or two at a time, so that my father did not get suspicious about my whereabouts. We would have to meet in cinemas or somewhere like a park, but there would always be the chance that a friend or relative would see me with you and let it get back to my father. It's a pity I have no more relations near you where I could stay. In the circumstances, I cannot see that it is practical for you to try and see me here, or for me to see you down there. My only suggestion is that you forget about me. No doubt you will be able to find a new girl friend, the same as you did before me. I shall still answer your letters to me, care of the address at the bottom of my letter. I will always love you and remember you, Maureen.

Paul was very distressed after reading Maureen's letter and wept bitterly. Eventually his mother found out what it was all about and tried to comfort him, but could not offer any practical suggestion for their future reunion, except that he, like her, should pray for a solution.

CHAPTER SEVENTEEN

Christmas came and went. The most miserable one that ever was, so far as Paul was concerned. He now spent a considerable amount of time alone and on his bicycle. He did not see so much of Barry now that the latter was more concerned about his own education. They were no longer in the same form, as Paul had been downgraded. Barry had his own girlfriend and they were seeing a lot of each other. Also, Paul's state of withdrawal unnerved Barry, who was used to a brighter fun-loving friend, who could get up to mischief with the best of them.

Time passed, and Easter Holidays came along. Paul had frantically tried to arrange a rendezvous with Maureen, with no success. Paul had worked as many hours as he could to earn pocket money on local farms and through odd jobs for friends, to pay for the necessary fares to enable him to meet Maureen again.

Early one morning he cycled to Westward Ho! and approaching the beach slipway he heard the sort of music usually associated with funfairs; the sound of the steam percussion organ and cymbals, piping and crashing intermittently. When this music was resting, the strains of Johnnie Ray's record of 'Cry' came through the airwaves, reflecting with irony his own sentiments. It seemed a strange combination of sounds but it brought back the memories of the gypsy caravan and Madame Perspicacity, that had been situated in that particular compound the previous summer.

He carried on to the slipway and looked out to sea with the breakers in the distance, a long way off. He thought of the wonderful days with Maureen across the couple of miles of sand and surf at Greysands Point.

It was too much to bear, and he turned around to the direction of the music, doing a circular cycle tour to bring him inside the funfair precincts.

As he drew near to the steam organ he looked across to

where the gypsy caravan used to be and, turning a corner – there it was. Perhaps more to the point, there she was, sitting on the steps smoking a cigarette.

He had already dismounted from his bicycle in the narrow confines of the fair; and so he manoeuvred the handlebars of the bicycle in a wide circle to turn away from her.

"Hello my love! Haven't seen you for ages. Where you been then, eh?" rasped the deep, throaty commanding voice of Connie.

"Oh hello! I was…just looking for somewhere to park my bike," said Paul, lying and confused, but saying the most practical thing he could muster.

"Wedge it inside the metal chassis behind the towbar there. The bike I mean!" she said, pointing at the triangular frame and cackling with glee.

"Come inside and have a chat then, OK?" she pressed, helping Paul to park his bike, throwing her half smoked cigarette onto the ground and extinguishing it with her foot. She went back up the steps and opened the door. Paul hesitated at the bottom.

"Come on, my love," she said encouragingly, coming down the steps to guide him up by his arm.

She bolted the door behind them and went over to sit in her usual place behind the crystal globe.

"Sit dahn then my son!" she commanded forcefully.

Paul did as he was told, inured by the feudal practises of his ancestors to obey an order without question.

"Nah then! What you been up to since I last saw yer then, eh?" she demanded to know.

"Well… er…"

"What's the matter? Cat got your tongue, eh? I suppose you are missing that girl friend now, eh?" she bullied, expecting an answer this time.

Paul sat there his head bowed but nodding. A feeling of emotion came over him and his shoulders heaved and trembled.

"Here! You're all upset now aren't you? You come to see Auntie Connie to make you forget your problems then? There's me thinking you might have been round to see me before. I

189

might have been able to save you a lot of heartache my son."

Paul shuddered, knowing full well what she meant.

"My…Maureen…I don't think I'll ever be able to see her again," he sobbed, tears streaming down his cheeks and on to his grey flannel trousers.

"My! My! We are upset, aren't we?" said Connie, adjusting the same flamenco-type skirt that she had also worn the last time Paul had been here, in the same manner.

His head still bowed, she unbuttoned her low-necked blouse and unsnapped her brassiere at the front. This was a continental creation she found handy to encourage her male punters to part with some of their hard-earned money. Paul's head jolted upright as he found Madame's generous rump in his lap and a large, erect, brown nipple rubbing against his cheek.

"There you are ducks. You suck on one of these for comfort," Connie said, feeling in a motherly mood.

As his lips brushed the tempting appendages he acquiesced, but his eyes did not miss the fact that a bunched up skirt meant bare thighs with no garments between them. He brought his hands up from his side to support the mammary offerings.

Connie enjoyed his suckling and nibbling; his tears' wetness gave her the fantasy that was a crying suckling babe – something she would never know in reality. This boy though could give her comfort in other ways.

It was her turn to tremble as one hand supported and caressed her breasts, whilst the other hand found its way from her knees, along the tops of her stockings to the bare thighs; exploring and rubbing against the smooth and rough textures until the fingers found the black forest, but could not enter as her legs were drawn across.

"Don't you usually wear knickers then?" asked Paul, thinking it might be some sort of eccentric gypsy fashion.

"Never, my handsome!" said Connie, lapsing into the local vernacular as a special concession. She laughed her coarse cackle and then suddenly stood up. Deftly she removed Paul's trousers and underpants. Paul was in a dreamlike state of unreality, though a willing partner in this erotic game. Connie could see he was up for it so she said, "You can continue what

190

you was doing before, now that there's more room."

She stood in front of him, her legs tantalisingly wide apart, with her hands on his shoulders for support, her breasts quivering slightly in front of him.

Paul could not disappoint her. She would not allow it. With his left hand curved around the back of her right thigh, his right hand continued its explorations as before, but now unimpeded, and eventually found the 'incumbent tenant', which he duly invited out. His left hand then massaged her generous rump which, like her ample breasts, quivered slightly when touched. Tracing around to her girdle, his fingers enjoyed the elastic tightness and especially the suspender straps. The feeling in the tips of his fingers tingled with the sensation of something only enjoyed once before with her, when it led to his first real penetrative experience.

His practiced fingers were helped by his partner's natural lubrication as she enjoyed his searching fingers exploring every nook and cranny, finally staying with her most sensitive spot, which he massaged gently but thoroughly. Even in her final convulsions she vowed to pleasure his throbbing manhood, temptingly looking up at her.

She knelt in front of him and seized his stem with her right hand and then let her mouth enclose the head using her tongue to caress around the ridge of the enflamed and engorged item. She measured the length of the shaft with her lips, lubricating it with saliva until it slid up and down the whole length, Paul viewing the reflections of her profile in the mirrors.

He soon exploded into her mouth, which instead of bothering her, she slowly withdrew, swallowing, and then suckled it again, tenderly as it twitched slightly.

Paul marvelled at the sensations that had just been experienced, leaving him exhilarated and spent for the moment, but wondering what Connie would be wanting now.

"You enjoyed that my son, didn't you?" Connie said, still kneeling in front of him with her hand holding his member, only semi-hard now that the urgency had gone.

"You've got to do the same for me now, all right?" she pleaded, backing off from him and going to the heavy curtain which she pulled aside and walked through.

He sat there still, listening to the sound of water being poured into a bowl. He waited, wondering if he should make a break for it. He could easily put his clothes back on quickly and take off. She could not stop him. That would be a bit cruel though, and he would never again sample her exotic wares. He would run away feeling guilty and be left with frustration; the depression would only return to drain his spiritual being. Then she called to him.

"Come in here then, young Paul. That's what you said your name was. Is that right?"

"Er, yes. I'm coming," he said, walking through the doorway to see her naked on the bed, except for her girdle and stockings.

"I didn't take everything off, 'cos I know you like these," she said, snapping a suspender strap and then laughing in her usual manner.

"Come here then, and take your shirt off. You look silly with that on and no trousers."

Paul took his shirt off, feeling a little foolish.

"I don't care if you're a bit skinny. After all, I'm no beauty queen am I? But we are enjoying the different…charms we both have. All right?" she said, beckoning him to join her on the small bed.

"Oh! There's not much room here for two," said Connie as Paul tried to lay beside her; he could only succeed if he was laying on his side. Connie turned on her side to look him in the eyes.

"There's not too much room for cuddling up. I may as well get on with it I suppose," and with that, she inverted herself to him, straddling over him.

"Your old fella is not the same as he was. He needs reviving a bit doesn't he?" she said, fondling his penis and testicles. Paul gazed at her inverted sex framed by the smooth white thighs which showed the underlying blue veins in random criss-cross patterns. He touched them gently making Connie quiver slightly and then, as he was nearly an arms length from her delta and as he still had his head on the pillow, he let his

192

fingers explore her girdle. The fascination, or the fetish, of the stockings and suspenders, originated by his parents generation, led him to run his fingers around and across the nylon material, hard and scaly like the skin of a fish.

These delights muted the stark ravenous mouth of her sex, open and voraciously predatory with drooping lips.

"You'll have to move further down the bed if you are going to do the business proper, won't you?" she croaked, trying to leer at him, upside down. Paul eased himself down and Connie barked,

"Bring the pillows down to raise your head up will you?"

Paul acceded to this request and noticed that his head was now close to her pink open flesh with many folds and wrinkles. He explored with his tongue and the slackness of her belly, although tightened by the girdle, quivered, and she rewarded him by suckling his now erect penis.

He searched for the clitoris and found it under its little cowl. He continued licking and sucking, in little gentle bites, until Connie gasped and then went limp, her pink lips paler and shining with a translucent dampness.

"Wow! That was lovely. Now as a special reward, you can do what you want to me," she said unselfishly.

Paul knew that he wanted penetration, but as she had not moved from her inverted position. He moved up slightly and away from the close vicinity of her sex and played with her buttocks, that were beginning to show a slight flaccidness. There was enough looseness for his teeth to nip her and nibble without hurting as it would have done had they been firm and solid.

"Are you enjoying that," cackled Connie.

"Yes," said Paul sticking his hands up underneath the corselette to get better purchase and drawing up the cheeks at the same time with his thumbs. He then bit and nibbled till she squirmed and laughed.

"You little devil you," she said, moving her position until she knelt at the edge of the bed.

"I thought you might want to try me from this position with your feet on the floor. I'll have to go and get things ready though," she said, jumping off the bed and going to the little bedside cabinet. She threw the jar of vaseline, and a sheath, down on the bed and then pulled the sheath down over Paul's shaft and lubricated it with the vaseline.

"Get up then. I'm sure you can manage just one more time."

Paul got up from the bed as Connie positioned herself for rear entry. Paul was not used to this and did not realise that this mating position would fit so comfortably and so easily.

"Go on. Feel for, it you silly sausage," said Connie, and then laughed raucously.

Paul eyed the raised haunches with the open sex hungrily as he edged forwards, his penis in one hand and the other on Connie's waist to steady himself.

He nuzzled the head of his member into the parted lips using the lubrication on the sheath to make an entry, his fingers pointing the way and parting the lips further. He moved his pelvis forward and felt the delicious feeling of the suction inside her

"Keep using your fingers, ducks," said Connie, excited now.

Paul was surprised that there was enough room for these continued manoeuvres, and mentioned it to her.

"There's room for both sets of fingers my son, if you like. Go on try it. I'll let you know if it starts hurting." she pleaded.

As usual Paul was very curious to learn the different sexual techniques and caresses, especially now that he had the opportunity. Leaving the end of his member inside the warm and comforting womb, he brought both sets of fingers to the bush massaging it, until he felt for her twin set of parted lips.

He found he could carry on massaging these and also move fingers over the top of his shaft to tickle the smallest but most sensitive part of her erogenous zones.

Connie seemed to enjoy this immensely and gave him verbal encouragement, until he became so excited himself that his previous gentle surgings of exploratory thrusts from his doubty member, became a surge of uncontrollable passion. He now brought his fingers out from her and used them to support himself on the curve of her waist. So clamped, they drew her to him, tightly and urgently, as his piston surged as fast as its transmission allowed. He gasped at the end with a loud sigh, which was echoed by her own murmurs of approval, encouraging him to keep it up until spent. He could only hug her with his hands clasped under her breasts with his face against the exotic smoothness of her Levantine spine, kissing as far as he could reach, without moving his position, in gratitude. She let him stay like that for a few moments, catching his reflection in the mirror over the basin in the corner. Then, as his manhood reverted to normal size and he came out, she picked up the slippery sheath and cleaned him dry.

Paul stood there foolishly again, not knowing what to say, until he mumbled,

"That was very nice. I enjoyed that."

"I know very well you did my son, but I enjoyed it as well," said Connie, going up to him and embracing him.

"You are doing very well as a lover. You're learning fast. You make me feel good, any way. You are gentle in the way you are careful not to hurt me. I like that. Maybe you would like to come back and visit me sometimes. I'll be gone in ten days time though. Moving on, to somewhere near Exeter," Connie said as he started putting his clothes back on.

"I'll be coming back again in the summer for a few weeks and I shall be staying at my friend's little place in Westward Ho! That's where I go in the evenings, and when I am finished here for the day. You'll like her I expect, although she's quite a handful in more ways than one," said Connie, giving her inevitable cackle.

"I shall miss you when you're gone," mumbled Paul, his head still drooping to avoid eye contact.

Connie was not offended by it and knew that he was shy and awkward at his age, but not too awkward that he could not manage what seemed to come naturally to him.

"Yes, I expect you will miss me, my young cock sparrow. Anyway, I'll give you my friend Barbara's address and if I am not here, you can go and see her to find out when I am likely to be coming back to Westward Ho! If the caravan's here and I am not, leave a message in note form and pop it through the letter box." said Connie, who had a box with a padlock screwed on the other side of the letterbox. This was so that she did not have prying eyes looking through the post she received.

"I'll give you Barbara's address now," she said scrawling on a piece of scrap paper.

"There you are," she said as Paul scrutinised the address.

"You know more or less where it is now then?"

Paul nodded and went to put his clothes on. She watched him silently for a while.

"You don't have a telephone at home I suppose?"

"You weren't thinking of phoning me at home, were you?" he asked anxiously, pulling on his shirt.

"Why not then? Am I not good enough for you then?" she enquired, pretending to be hurt.

"Don't worry, I shan't let on that I'm your fancy woman. I'll say that I'm one of your school friend's mother, and let's see…" she paused, trying to think up an excuse.

"Ah yes, I'll say that it's your friend Billy's birthday and I'm inviting you around for his party, or something. Hey! I've just christened your 'member of parliament' Billy, a good name eh?" another joyous cackle escaped her lips

Paul was lost for a moment until it dawned on him what she meant. He managed a weak smile, and agreed to write his parents' phone number on a piece of paper, but with many misgivings. It was only the thought of what she could give him that made the risk worthwhile; the worst thing that could happen was that what was between him and Connie would get to Maureen somehow. He was beyond caring too much about himself, although there was a certain amount of dread that his father would pick up the phone if Connie called him. He would be more likely to be suspicious, but Paul hoped that Connie would just ring off if things became complicated.

"So are you going to come around again? Tomorrow morning perhaps? It's always better if I know that you are coming. That is unless you want to give me some sort of surprise. A special treat maybe?"

She laughed and enjoyed his shy confusion. He knew he wanted her – or that which she gave him. Another part of him was terrified that she became besotted with him and it becomes common knowledge to all and sundry. People would be talking about him and his parents just like the local folk talked about the Spanish woman and her young lover.

"Tomorrow morning, about ten o'clock?" he asked. She nodded in the affirmative.

"You had better be off in case somebody outside gets wind of what's going on between you and me. We don't want to make anything obvious, do we? It might be a good idea if you brought something like a newspaper, something to show that you was a family friend who used to pop in with something from your mum. I could be your auntie. That's it! Is that OK?" she asked brightly.

"Yes, that sounds like a good idea," said Paul. He realised the need for an excuse, and saw the logic of the need for subterfuge, even though it was against his nature, as was the telling of lies. He had been brought up in a stricter moral code than most youngsters would have been even in the beginning of the second half of the twentieth century.

"I'll be off now then. See you tomorrow, hopefully Connie," he said, smiling shyly.

"Give us a kiss then nephew Paul," she demanded, and going towards him quickly, she seized his shoulders and gave him a long, lingering kiss on his mouth, which he kept firmly clamped.

"Go on then, you young scamp," she said patting, his bottom lovingly.

Paul went forwards to the curtain, pulling it aside. Connie went ahead of him to unbolt the door. She looked outside furtively and as no one was hanging around, she let him get to the bottom of the steps before she waved goodbye and shouted,

"Tell your mum I'll see her tomorrow."

Paul looked back nodded and grinned as she gave an obvious wink, which he thought may not have been appropriate if anyone else had seen.

Paul continued to see Connie a few times before she moved off with the rest of the fairground to their new pitch

CHAPTER EIGHTEEN

Paul was introduced to Barbara one Saturday morning. He soon found that she was as free spirited as Connie, who had told Paul some things about Barbara so that he knew what to expect. He now knew that she divorced from a brute of a husband and worked part time, cleaning out caravans and chalets on the site underneath the steep cliffside of Kipling Tor. She also helped-out at the bar and did other jobs that were going in the holiday season.

He turned up at Barbara's terraced cottage after breakfast on a cloudy Saturday morning in June. Paul parked his bicycle against the wall of the house. He was nervous and did not know how to introduce himself.

"Hello…I'm…Connie's friend Paul. Are you Barbara?" he anguished, his cheeks flushed bright red as Barbara opened the door.

"Oh, hello Paul." said the tall large-boned woman looking well-fleshed-out under a bathrobe she was wearing.

"Connie has told me all about you. You had better come in," she said, looking to her right and left to see if there was anyone else around, before closing the door.

"I'm afraid I am a bit behind this morning. I was working late at the bar in the clubhouse last night and by the time everything had been cleared up, it was going on for midnight. I was just running the water for a bath," she said, looking him over, and pushing her long blonde hair, now untidy, back from her blue-grey eyes. I was going to suggest you wait in the living room while I finish my bath, but I know what you have really come to see me about, don't I now?" she said, giving him a pinch on his already red cheek.

Paul flinched and grinned foolishly.

"Oh, I shouldn't have done that now should I? Never mind, come and cool those burning cheeks in here," she said, unbelting her flannelette robe and flinging it over the balustrade knob at the bottom of the stairs.

She then looked back to a wide-eyed, slack-mouthed Paul, who could not believe his eyes.

Barbara approached him and putting her hands behind his neck drew his face into her ample bosom, lifting her heavy breasts to cushion his burning cheeks.

"There now. Does that feel better then, my dear," said Barbara in a motherly fashion, trying to put him at his ease right away.

"Yes, that's very nice," said Paul truthfully, allowing his lips to rub over her pink nipples.

"You little rascal. I can see Connie was right about you. Come on up to the bathroom, I've got to turn the hot water off anyhow."

Paul followed Barbara's naked and ample form up the stairs, appreciating in particular the wide hips and large buttocks, quivering as she walked up each step.

They walked into the small bathroom and Barbara bent over the bath to turn the cold water tap on and the hot water off. She looked back to see him stare at her and noticed the bulge in his trousers.

"I hope you are liking what you see," she said turning around and smiling at him.

Then she sat on the edge of the bath in a demure pose that she knew would really only excite him.

"I won't tease you any more. Get your clothes off and have a bath with me, all right?" she said, starting to help him unbutton his shirt.

He kicked off his gym shoes and pulled down his trousers and underpants self-consciously, as quickly as he could. His heart was thumping but his hormones urged him on.

Barbara bent down over the bath again to stop the tap as the water level was high enough now for two people to fit into it.

Paul could not resist sliding his hand up the outside of her leg and then over her hip, then, gently up her belly to cup a heavy breast.

"Well, you know what you want all right. Let's have a good

soak first though," she said climbing into the bath and gently easing down into the not too hot water.

"You can try sitting in front of me to save banging your head on the taps, if you like," said Barbara as Paul gingerly found his position in front of her, laying his head between her breasts, resting his feet up between the taps as he ran short of space.

Barbara put her arms around him to support the weight of him crushing her breasts awkwardly, although there was not a great deal of weight to Paul.

"Any news about seeing your girlfriend again then?" Barbara asked.

"No," he said almost sullenly, "I don't know if I will ever see her again now," he said his voice breaking.

"Come on, let's get you washed," said Barbara soaping the flannel and washing his back, chest and arms.

"Stand up and I'll wash the rest of you," she said, and Paul stood up his back towards her,

She washed his legs and feet as he hung on to the taps for support, then washed his haunches.

"You'd better turn around now," she said. He complied, his excitement showing. She soaped and cleansed his genitals thoroughly.

"You can bathe me now, starting from my neck, but you had better sit down facing me."

Paul sat down keeping his legs inside hers but leaving both knees bent. As he wetted her flannel he noticed the dark delta under the soapy water.

He started on her neck and then her breasts, washing gently and not hurriedly. He knelt to wash her belly steadying himself by placing a hand on her plump waist, alternating hands as he washed both hips. She then turned over so that he could wash her buttocks and thighs, working upwards towards her opened sex.

He worked his middle finger under the flannel's soapy lubrication to cleanse and explore the different apertures, making her giggle like a young girl being tickled –which in her guileless way she resembled.

She lifted her legs individually for her feet to be washed, and then lay back to soak and rinse herself but, slipping on the change over position, coming back down into the water with a loud splash.

"Ooh...oh...oh!" she screamed, but more in merriment than fear, as the tidal wave swept over the top of the bath and on to the cold linoleum flooring.

She hopped out, quickly considering her bulk, and used an old towel to mop up the bathwater. When she was done she fixed a shower contraption onto the taps.

"That's what Connie bought for the house. Now I can try it out on you to rinse you off."

Barbara pulled the plunger out and tested the water coming out of the shower head until it was right. She sprayed Paul all over, paying particular attention to his genitals which amused both of them.

When she was finished she told him to get out so that she could rinse herself. Paul watched her while he was drying himself off with a bath towel.

"Let's go and have a cuddle up on the bed. I've got to go to work later on, but I don't have any particular time to get there this morning. I get so much for cleaning a caravan out, so I get a lump sum at the end of the week. Not much, but at least I have the chance of earning more money the more work I do," said Barbara opening the bedroom door.

A breeze was blowing the curtains at the side of the window. Barbara quickly went over to the window, pulling the curtains across but leaving a small enough aperture for a couple of fingers to slide the bottom sash down closed. Then with the curtains pulled across to give privacy, she flicked back the covers and top sheet of the bed and jumped on the double mattress, patting the space beside her. The bed was large with a highcarved headboard and a low, carved footboard. Paul lay beside her as she turned to face him.

"How long was it before you summoned up the courage to come here Paul?"

Barbara smiled at him in her youthful innocent way, although she was thirty-eight years old, more than twice as old

201

as Paul.

"I thought about it a few times after Connie moved away. But then I thought…that you might not want to be bothered with me, although I suppose that Connie wouldn't have given me your address if she thought that. I tried your door once but you were out, so today I thought I'd try again," he said sheepishly.

"Oh yes? What's the matter with the girls your age then?" she said teasing.

Paul just shrugged, looking embarrassed.

"Well you wouldn't be lying naked on a bed with one I suppose," she said brazenly laughing.

Paul thought it best to say nothing, and just smiled, shyly but contentedly.

"Well come on then! Are you going to woo me or are you expecting me to woo you. You can kiss me if you want to," she said, noticing that he was aroused and had been eyeing her hungrily.

He came on top of her and she allowed him to put his legs between hers so that his genitals lay on top of hers. He was too self-conscious to look her straight in the eyes to begin with and kissed her cheek before he moved around to her lips.

Barbara, on the other hand, was eager to inspect this new person in her life, even though it might be for a fleeting moment of time. She had come to the conclusion that it was best to take an opportunity when it arose, especially if it was low risk to her health or her state of mind. She felt that this young boy was of no physical risk to her. He was not going to be violent with her on the contrary, she now knew that he was of a sensitive nature. She knew from Connie that he was capable of satisfying her needs. He was not likely to be of much use to her financially, although he might be able to do a few jobs around the house, like gardening, decorating and such, He was fit, agile, and strong, even though he was wiry. The last thing she needed was a sixteen-stone brute, like her previous husband. She could enjoy Paul the same as Connie had. They would do him no harm. They would not give him any disease, or encourage him to smoke or drink.

Paul was now kissing her on the mouth, after nuzzling the

lobe of her ear, then the nape of her neck. He was losing his innate shyness and his tension had disappeared. Barbara relaxed her mouth and he moved his lips around hers, kissing every inch of it. When he moved his tongue inside her mouth she responded by twirling her own tongue around his, while he played with her long hair sprawled back on her pillow, stroking it from her forehead, down on to her shoulders.

He moved down to her breasts, lifting them one at a time with his hand and using his pursed lips to trace over them, nibbling at the pointed nipples that no longer pointed upwards but rejoiced in their wholesome fullness.

She ran her fingers gently up and down his back, also his sides, and felt his perky bottom clenching the cheeks. This however seemed to encourage him to move down the bed and nuzzle in her belly, his tongue licking around her belly button, which tickled, and made her laugh aloud. Then as if to stop her laughing he moved further down, to her dark bush which shone perversely golden when a beam of light flashed through a gap in the curtains. The wind was blowing through the small aperture between the top window sash and the window frame.

She lifted her knees to allow his head to rest in her open crotch. He was content to run his hand over her furry mound and then part her lips with his fingers. Paul's previous experience led him onto the use of his tongue, which generated an immediate response from Barbara. As he locked onto the target her moans and sighs got louder; clamping her hands around the back of his head she willed him on to the climax.

She lay back exhausted as Paul lay his head back against one inner thigh. Paul's curiosity about the female genitalia and his observation noted that they were all slightly different like, male genitals were.

He traced his middle finger around her slippery lips as she twitched involuntarily.

"That was good. I suppose I have got to do something for you now. Connie has told me what you like, but I have a feeling that you are willing to try anything."

"Huh! I don't really know that much about sex. We are not taught anything about it in school or at home. My mum just hints about it, in warnings," said Paul from his cosy, near womb resting-place.

"Your mum warns you about what you get up to with girls friends?" said Barbara, content to lie still with Paul's head between her thighs.

"It's…mainly…since I've got to know Maureen. She knows I am particularly fond of Maureen," said Paul, getting worried now that he had shared something private about her. This was nothing he need worry about really, but he had a feeling that Barbara would ask him more about her than he wanted to tell.

"Your mother seems to think you know enough about sex to get you, or more particularly some poor girl, into trouble," said Barbara, giving a little smile that he could not see.

"She knows my brother and I are interested in girls, especially since she found one of those *Spick and Span* magazines, of women in their underwear, that my brother had hidden underneath his bed."

Barbara let out an earthy laugh which made Paul smile.

"Did she tell him off then?" asked Barbara chuckling.

"Oh, mum just told him not to waste his pocket money, and if she found any more of them she would stop the pocket money."

"Oh dear. He wasn't too pleased about that then?"

"No. He's scrounging a look from somebody else's now I suppose," said Paul tittering.

"I bet you all like looking at those magazines though?"

"Most boys my age, and above, like looking at them when they get the chance. Shirley Anne Fields is my favourite."

"Does she wear those stockings and suspenders and all those frilly bits and pieces then that you like?"

"I suppose Connie told you that."

"Yes, of course she did. She tells me just about everything. She's a good friend though. Do anything for me, especially when I am in need. She probably thought I needed you to buck me up. Perhaps she was right. Do women in uniform, or women in authority, turn you on, or get you excited?" she asked unexpectedly.

"Not really – oh, except one person."

"Who's that then?"

"She's an English teacher at our school. Sometimes when she gives us set work to do, she puts her legs up on the desk to read a book, and her skirt rides back to show off her stockings and suspenders. She's got good legs too, although she is not particularly good looking."

"What are my legs like then?"

"Oh, they're fine," said Paul, rubbing his hand along them gently as far as he could reach without moving.

"Are you all right down there? I hope you are not taking photographs of me or something. I might end up in those magazines you boys read."

Paul laughed and said, "I like you Barbara. You're fun."

"Do you like me more than Connie then?" she teased.

"You're different than Connie. A bit more feminine I suppose. Both of you like a bit of fun though don't you?"

"Yeah! Well it's a grim place nowadays without a bit of fun. They reckon we won the war but lost the peace don't they? I work all hours and then all the overtime is deducted from my pay for income tax. There's no justice in this world. Never mind. You're all right down there. You don't care, you don't have to earn a living yet. Hang on! I've just remembered something."

Barbara disentangled her legs from around Paul's head and shot off out of the bedroom, leaving Paul feeling cold and forlorn like a newly born infant.

He could hear her rummaging around, in what sounded like a wardrobe, in the next room. About ten minutes later a stick appeared waving in the doorway, then a teacher's black mortarboard was waved, complete with a black tassel hanging down. A cloaked hand then spread its pleats up into the air for observation, and darted back. A plump, stockinged leg then became visible until the whole of the leg, up to the suspenders, and the rest of the outfit Barbara was wearing, appeared the otherside of the doorway.

Barbara's entry was that of a variety-show actress. She stood there, a black mortarboard atop her long blonde hair. She had on an unbuttoned white blouse, hanging over a short black pleated skirt which was cut above the length of her stocking tops and suspenders. The teachers black pleated cape and black high-heeled shoes completed the picture as she posed, her arms outstretched as were her legs, with a long thin cane in her right hand.

Paul was sitting bolt upright in bed clapping.

"I wish I had a camera now with flash equipment," said Paul, grinning with appreciation.

"I'm the only one who is going to do the flashing today, my boy," said Barbara, threatening him with the stick.

"Oh, I wish my English teacher was as glamorous as you Barbara," said Paul truthfully.

Barbara came over to where Paul was sitting and clambered in beside him. She put her arm around his shoulder and Paul put his arm around her waist.

"You liked it eh?" said Barbara, basking in her triumph.

"You bet," answered Paul.

"It belongs to Connie really. It's part of her carnival costumes and things she wears to parties, especially when she goes up to London. They go a bit wild up there sometimes. I thought you would like the schoolteacher pose. The short skirt can be used to make a St Trinians schoolgirl. All the rage in London after the new film *The Belles of St. Trinians*. I expect you have heard of that one."

"Yes, I saw it in Bideford. It was smashing. I could fancy you as one of the older St Trinian schoolgirls," he said, sliding his free hand over to rest on an exposed thigh.

Barbara still had the switch in her hand and used it to slap the hand that violated her thigh.

Paul recoiled instinctively, as Barbara's laughter goaded him into action. He took the switch out of her hand and, wrestling with her, threw her face down on the bed and then pulled her mini skirt up from her buttocks and gently slapped her with the switch.

She squealed like an excited schoolgirl but did not now attempt to get up; Paul rightly deduced that this form of play excited her. He started to hit her harder and noticed that angry red welts were appearing across her buttocks. He paused, not wanting to hurt her any more.

"It's…all right…I deserve it," she said, getting down from the bed to lean against its side, her head resting on an arm, her eyes closed and her legs splayed with her high heels dug into the carpet to keep her in position.

"What do you mean, you deserved it?" enquired Paul in disbelief.

"I murdered my baby," she said starkly.

"You what?" said Paul in horror.

"It was when I was about your age, I got friendly with a boy – I got pregnant –. My mother knew Connie in the East End of London. Connie knew some woman that would give me an abortion, to save all the palaver and all the neighbourhood knowing all about it. Well, it all seemed to go off all right. It was very painful at the time, but I was grateful to be rid of the problem. I didn't think any more about it until I married my dear departed."

"He wanted children and when I didn't conceive he wanted to know why. He went ahead to have tests to see if it was his fault. When the doctors decided there was nothing wrong with his sperm, I had to be examined properly. They found out I was damaged inside and would never have a baby."

Barbara's sobs added to the tears that had formed in her eyes as soon as she recalled the memory. Paul lay on the bed facing her, his hand on her shoulder.

"It's not your fault, you did what you felt was best at the time. You're not a murderer. They would only have taken your child away. You probably would never have seen it again," said Paul, who had heard of a similar case.

"Perhaps you're right. Anyway I did take a life. I was responsible. So I am a murderer."

"What did your husband say then, when he found out?" asked Paul, deciding it was best to ignore her last statement.

"He wanted to know all the ins and outs – if you'll pardon the pun. Not intended actually. I had to tell him. It was the honest thing to do. He would have found out sooner or later. He was furious, and that's when he started to beat me. I knew it was over then, between him and me. We got divorced eventually. He's still around here somewhere, driving his lorry," said Barbara, looking up and staring at the window, almost as if she could hear his vehicle driving by.

"When did you come down to this area, if you lived in London previously?"

"Oh! Well it was not long after I lost the child. Connie felt a bit protective towards me as she was a lot older, sort of like a big sister I suppose. Anyway, she was getting fed up with London. It was a pretty grimy sort of miserable place to live in those days, what with the smog and poverty. It's better to be poor in the country than the city, I can tell you. You could live off the land up to a point in the country. There was always work on a farm even if the wages were poor. So long as you had a clean bed to sleep in and food on the table, you felt secure."

"Connie made a trip to this area, by chance really, and thought it would be a good place for me to start up a life for myself. It was going all right until my marriage breakup," said Barbara sighing.

"So you never married again or, perhaps more to the point, you never wanted to get married again," said Paul sympathetically.

"Well the trouble is, if I get pally with a bloke and I know he's going to get around to ask me to marry him, I have to tell him that I can't have a child, or it would be unfair to him. That's been the situation all along. That's why I am more like Connie with my social life. Just out for a laugh and a giggle, only I don't want to go travelling around the country all the time like her."

Barbara sighed again and then remembered what they were supposed to be doing on the bed.

"Well, if you are not going to beat me anymore, what are you going to do?"

"I would like to make love to you, but tenderly, not hurting you. Just the same as I would like to make love to … my Maureen," he said, tears coming to his eyes.

She turned around to face him, and saw the hurt.

"Oh, you poor thing. Mind you, she was right not letting you do it at her age. She could have easily ended up like me.

You would have hated yourself then wouldn't you? Even if she had had the baby, they would have taken it away; you couldn't have married and supported her very well could you?"

"I…I…I think I would have done. Somehow," he protested, but knew that it would have been difficult.

"We could have had intercourse if I had got hold of condoms."

"They are not a 100 per cent reliable, especially if you are not used to them. You'd be surprised how many people come unstuck," Barbara squealed. "I didn't mean that as a pun neither," she said, putting a hand over her mouth and then laughing.

"Well come on then, treat me tenderly," she said, unbuttoning her St Trinians mini-skirt.

"Oh that's better, that's a bit too tight for me," she giggled, throwing it on the floor along with the cape, blouse and mortarboard, the latter having fallen off.

Paul now started to caress her again; she kicked off her high heels and lay beside him. He familiarised himself with her lips and breasts and started to get excited again as his fingers traced over her thighs and suspenders. He played with her labia, tracing her contours up to the tenderest spot.

"Oh! Before we do the business right? I have got condoms handy. I don't need one myself, but fellas should be particular, as well as girls. It's so easy to spread disease, apart from anything else, you know. So if you feel happier using one, it's all right with me," said Barbara, knowing that she did not have to worry about disease from Paul.

Paul preferred to try the natural way. It would be the first time for him, and he might not get the chance again for a long time.

"If you don't mind, I would sooner make love to you without one," he said.

"Well, it's a smoother ride as they say, without one. It's better for me and I think I can trust you not to infect me with anything. Just one thing though," she said, getting up off the bed and dashing into the bathroom. She came back with a towel and spread it on the end of the bed, sat on it, more or less in the same place as before, and retrieving her high heel she said,

"We'll stay like this if you like, 'cos my heels will grip the carpet and it will be a better purchase for you with your feet on the floor."

Paul restarted his foreplay, as Barbara congratulated herself on making her seduction last. She was relaxed in this boy's company not having to worry about complications that arose with men of her own age or older. Paul did not want to claim her, or expect her to be available to him whenever he desired. He was just grateful for her company and, what was more, he didn't feel the need to prove himself all the time. He knew he was experimenting and learning all the time. Sex was a wonderful mystery for his whole being and she hoped she would not spoil it for him.

Paul was now back to the crucial point, of the unenforceable code of conduct, that gave the passport to paradise for women. Barbara squirmed with delight and made appreciative sighs. As his fingers tantalised her clitoris, another finger, with the aid of a thumb, caressed a nipple; his mouth continued to kiss and gently bite her wherever he could reach.

He's doing this instinctively, she thought, and knew that nobody, not even Connie, would have taught him how to make love like he did.

Paul now judged it time to insert his shaft, using his fingers as a vanguard to point the way. He started a gentle rhythm, his hands around her waist, supported by her hands around his back, her spiky heels pegged into the carpet. His pelvic thrusts were gaining momentum as her vaginal muscles contracted to devour the invading beast. Her legs lifted to wrap around his hips, gripping him tightly to assist the compression of the invader. He forced harder and harder, time and time again, until her enveloping muscles seized on his member, locking it inside and drawing its life blood to its own.

Paul gave a groan and collapsed on top of Barbara, his face alongside hers, his elbows and arms just under hers allowing his head to rest on the top of her bosom.

His hands clasped her shoulders; his body and soul seemed

to have completed a harmony he had not felt before, surpassing his first penetration experience with Connie.

Barbara had experienced her first vaginal climax for a long, long time, and was content to lay there with him cradled in her arms and her wrist touching his cheek. She looked at him tenderly and, like Connie, felt motherly to him, yet could not deny his aggressive masculine love making that reminded her that she was also a sensual woman.

She had work to do this morning – but the hell with it. It could wait. She had done her bit last night, and had put up with the usual loud-mouthed banter from her male customers. She knew that a lot of them fancied her, but she could not fancy them, with their crude humour and crude ways. Not that she was a prude. They would never believe that she had just been made love to by a boy young enough to be her son. She could keep what was left of her dignity and remain in good humour with them, doing her job and leaving it at that. Though she did miss a man's company and wondered if she would ever meet a man again with whom she would want to settle down.

What would become of this young fellow, lying on top of her? She had a feeling he would want to come back. Well he would wouldn't he? Barbara smiled to herself as she remembered his wide-eyed surprise as she had entered the bedroom as a teacher, and how he wanted to take a photograph of her.

There was a thought: posing for photographs. Easier money than doing what she was doing now. She was too fat though. All the models were about the same size and looked stick-insect thin, as if they kept to a strict diet, if they ate anything wholesome at all. Barbara found that she could not get through the day unless she ate well enough to keep up her strength, she had always been a big girl – 'bonny' as her mother called it.

Paul started nuzzling into her breasts.

"I've got to get up and get ready for work in a minute. I'll make you a cup of tea and then you'll have to go. You can come and see me tomorrow morning though if you want to. If you get here about nine, you can bring some breakfast up to me in bed. I'll leave a note where everything is and what to do. I'll give you a front door key or, better still, hide it under the plant pot to the side of the front door. I don't want you to make any noise to alert the neighbours though. Bring your bike through the gate and leave it against the hedge.

"Come on get dressed now, and see me in the morning; nice clean and fresh, OK?" Barbara said, getting up and going into the bathroom.

"I've just remembered something. I bought you a little present. I'll pop it inside the door before I go," said Paul, reluctantly pulling his clothes on.

"Cheerio, and thanks for everything. See you tomorrow then," he spoke through the gap of the bathroom door and waited for her to say goodbye.

He brought the box of Cadbury's Milk Tray out of his saddlebag, wrapped in a brown paper bag, paid for out of his pocket money and laid it on the bottom tread of the stairs.

Barbara picked it up later and opened the box, to see the half-melted chocolates inside; she smiled to herself.

Paul did see her the following morning and for many weekends after. Then his father kept him home as his exams were imminent. He took his exams but his heart was not in it, the only writing he wanted to do was to write to Maureen, which he did keep up, just about every week, although there was not really all that much he could say that was new.

He concentrated on the pop music that he heard on Radio Luxembourg, either at Barry's home if he was free, or at home when his father was out. Les Paul and Mary Ford were his favourites, the revolutionary staccato notes of the electric guitar, pioneered by Les, were so fresh and exciting; liberating the spirits from the sentimental and insipid constraints of the popular music of the time with gems like *The World is Waiting for the Sunrise* and *How High the Moon?* Most of this new progressive music seemed to come from the USA.

A Cuban composer, Ernesto Lecuona, had written some fiery Spanish numbers in the thirties and forties which were resurrected, and sung with passion, by a sultry Caterina Valente in the mid-fifties. Her records, solid seventy-eight RPMs, sold very well. Paul very much appreciated the passionate statements of *Maleguena*, *Siboney* and the *Breeze and I*. Frankie Laine's lusty pleadings were also in favour, with the recent recording of *My Friend*, a religious composition, as was *I believe* and *Answer Me*.

Paul made copious notes as he listened to the music, so that he could refer to them when writing to Maureen.

One radio programme that did lift his spirits, was the *Goon Show*, which reflected his own anarchic outlook. The zany adventures of Eccles and Bluebottle, Neddy Seagoon and Colonel Bloodnok made him laugh and temporarily filled the void that was engulfing him.

One Saturday morning he turned up at Barbara's flat, let himself in as usual and called up the stairs.

"Hello! It's me, Paul."

He walked up the stairs, tapped on the bedroom door gently and opened it. He popped his head around the door and froze.

"Surprise, surprise!" came from both Barbara and Connie. They were sitting up in bed together with their naked bosoms showing above the bed covers.

"Come and give me a kiss then ducks," said Connie, holding her arms wide for an embrace.

Paul was rooted to the floor, momentarily in a state of shock.

"Come on! You've seen us both naked before even if you haven't seen us together. It's your lucky day my boy. Isn't it?" said Connie with her usual cackle.

Paul felt he had to go and do as she commanded or else flee down the stairs like a frightened rabbit. He approached Connie awkwardly and bashfully as she motioned him to sit on the bed next to her. As he did so she pulled him down by his shoulders to kiss him on his mouth.

This was easier said than done and, not making very good contact, Connie threw back the bedclothes, struggled out of the bed, jumped on top of Paul and kissed him as hard as she could.

"Connie, control yourself! You're embarrassing the poor boy. He doesn't know what's hit him," said Barbara, shaking her head and laughing in disbelief.

213

Paul's face had turned a beetroot red by now and he was indeed not sure how to react to this situation.

"Well are you staying to have a chat with us, or are you going 'ome my boy. My lovely 'ansome boy," said Connie, giving Paul a bear hug.

"Let's get your clothes off and then you can come and join us," she said, unbuttoning his shirt and then starting on his trousers.

"Let him do that himself, poor chap. He doesn't know whether he's coming or going when your all over him like that," protested Barbara.

"Oh! And I suppose you never touch this young gentleman then?" said Connie scornfully.

Paul found a short respite to take the rest of his clothes off himself, and wondered where he was going to lie. His mind was made up by Connie saying,

"Here you are my boy, set yourself down in here," and pushing Barbara over to make a space for him, he quickly crawled into it and sat between them, looking at them individually, but clearly perplexed.

"So how's things with you then Paul? No luck with your girlfriend I suppose?" asked Connie with a sympathetic lilt in her voice.

"No I'm afraid not. We write to each other every week, but that's about as far as it goes," he said, his head down and looking glum.

"Cheer up sunshine. You don't know when you are well off. In bed with two naked women, well practised at seducing young men like yourself," she chuckled again until Barbara scolded her.

"Leave him alone and let him compose himself. He has had a bit of a shock finding us both here, now haven't you Paul?"

Paul nodded quietly, with a nervous smile.

"I had better relax him a bit, while you give him a welcoming kiss; I have already done that, haven't I ducks?" said Connie who felt for Paul's masculine charms under the bed sheets.

Barbara moved closer to Paul, putting her hand between his

shoulder and neck, to draw his mouth to hers. She gave him a long, lingering kiss, using her tongue to seek his to prove that it was not platonic in nature.

Connie had thrown the covers off completely so that they had more room to manoeuvre. She positioned herself to get between Paul's legs and give him her special attention.

Paul continued kissing Barbara as his hands stroked her hair, her neck, her breasts and then her belly to her groin.

Connie felt that she was losing out, especially as Paul had not seen her for some time, and a flare of jealousy stabbed at her heart. She discontinued what she was doing – to Paul's disappointment – and inverted her body so that her sex would be within his reach. She delayed contact with his rigid member until he parted her dense black bush and probed the silky caverns beneath, gently, in a practised manner.

It was Barbara's turn to feel neglected as Connie's deliberations had distracted Paul's fondling of her. To make him more aware of her needs she now straddled him, her hands on the top, high curve of the wooden bed-head and supporting her weight she thrust her pelvis towards his face.

Paul clasped her buttocks and drew her near to himself, delivering some well-placed kisses that had Barbara gasping with pleasure. Paul's excitement reached a grand conclusion as Connie's expertise left him, for the moment sated, and relaxed. Not knowing what to do to please both women at the same time he carried on caressing them both gently at the same time.

"I was nearly there just now," Barbara complained to Paul.

"Well, I will have to finish the business for you, won't I dear," said Connie, as Paul watched in fascination as Barbara sat down in her previous position and the two women demonstrated their bisexual nature, Connie raised Barbara's buttocks on pillows. Barbara clasped her hands over the top of the wooden bed head raising herself up.

Paul felt shocked, but stimulated at the same time. He knew what lesbians were but he hadn't realised that there were women who would make love to both genders.

"Don't forget I haven't come yet, either," said Connie to Paul, breaking off from her love making with Barbara and

215

leaving her squirming with frustration.

Connie waved her haunches in the air to tempt Paul, patting the area of the bed just behind her. Paul crawled around to the bottom of the bed and, now aroused again, negotiated his position for a rear entry, in the narrow space now available.

As Connie continued before, Paul started his foreplay with Connie, sliding his hands up and down her open thighs and then entering his fingers into her proffered sex.

Sensing that she was ready for him, Paul carefully inserted his penis and then, with the erotic picture of both his sexual partners in view before him, and enjoying his part in it, he used the low bed board as a purchase for his feet as he clasped his hands around Connie's waist and drove himself into her. The harder he worked, the harder Connie worked on Barbara. Because it was his second experience of the day he was able to delay his ejaculation until he heard Barbara give a cry, and then Connie groaned as if she had been hanging on until Barbara had climaxed

The three of them collapsed after Paul gave an almighty heave forward, the bottom of his feet pushing hard against the bed board; his sperm shot like a bullet out of a gun onto the wall of Connie's womb.

Connie had previously taken precautions, not wanting to interfere with the spontaneous nature of the love play.

They lay exhausted but happy, all barriers gone, in harmony with each other in their primordial, sweaty stickiness.

After they had slumbered a while in the quiet stillness, Paul imagined himself in a surreal world of pleasure. Then Barbara stirred and went to the bathroom and started to fill up the bath.

Their bathing became more of a ritual, sometimes bathing before and after their lovemaking and using the same bathwater, with Connie in charge of the shower attachment, making sure that they all rinsed off properly, cackling away happily.

CHAPTER NINETEEN

While Paul waited for the results of his O-Level examination papers – although knowing that he was not going to pass anything – he was allowed more time to relax. His parents did not know where he was going, on his bicycle with his packed lunches in the saddlebag, and they did not ask too many questions. In fact, they presumed that because his attitude had changed favourably the same, as it had when Maureen was with him, that he had a new girl friend.

Paul was happy to go along with this deception knowing that his parents wanted him to get on with his life. He would not forget Maureen that easily though, even if he was revelling in his adventures with the two mature women.

Without them, he was sure that he would have run away from home and tried to reach Aberdeen, however brief, his encounters with Maureen might be, even if they would be unrequited as in the film *Brief Encounters* starring Trevor Howard and Celia Johnson. Just seeing Maureen again occasionally would have kept him sane.

Now, he had someone with whom he could relax, even indulge his wildest fantasies. Barbara even pandered to his whim by dressing up in the St Trinians schoolgirl uniform.

He was now content to bide his time until he started work, which he felt was not far away. He would then be able to save money for a trip to Aberdeen.

The results of Paul's O-Levels were posted to his house; he knew what to expect – that he had failed them – the official notification meant that he could leave school and find a job.

He continued his relationship, off and on, with Connie and Barbara. He marvelled at how their difference in ages only seemed to make their relationship more natural, in their own eyes, but they realised that others would not see it as such.

Looking back in later life as a mature adult, Paul asked

himself if he considered that Connie and Barbara were corrupt in any way, and how they might have corrupted him. By the standards of the times the law, in particular, would have been quick to condemn their actions.

Paul reasoned that the youthful backgrounds of Connie and Barbara had led them to feel abandoned by men and difficult for them to form natural loving relationships. They both snatched at the latter when opportunities arrived, but probably could not get the unselfish commitment that they gave to each other. He did not feel corrupted himself. They did not do anything different from that which couples in a loving relationship do, in modern times.

Paul reasoned that it was no longer expected for a wife to remain submissive in the marital bed while the husband did his duty to produce progeny. If it is was right in modern times to be more compassionate and allow the other partner to enjoy mature relationships, then it was not wrong in the past. What they did was in private, and as far as he was concerned had educated him to the needs of women. That was more natural than a couple living together in a sham of a marriage, where neither gave a fig for each other's needs. He knew that Connie and Barbara had lifted his depression and without them he might have been driven to suicide.

In one way Paul had wanted to punish his father, who had been the real instigator of condemning him to that hateful school in the first place.

He decided to try horticulture as a career, trying to make up for lost time, but ended up on a bulb farm as there was nothing else available locally.

National Service caught up with him a year later. He joined up as a soldier willingly enough, and was not too upset about the pointless things he was made to do; he thought that he had already done years of that.

After his two years were completed, mostly in the British Army of the Rhine, in Germany, he decided that he did not want to do a year or two at an Agricultural and Horticultural College at Bicton in Devon. This was part of the deal that started him off in horticulture – he had to do a years' practical work before getting a place in college. This was, presumably, to see if the prospective student was serious about a career. However, Paul had had enough of schooling and people ordering him around; and wanted to have space and time to think for himself.

His mother, who was always on his side in reality, saw an advert in the paper about workers for the National Trust. The starting pay was not good, but there was free accommodation in most areas, and outdoor work, which she knew Paul preferred. The idea appealed to Paul and he got fixed up in a job right away, starting in the Lake District.

He said his goodbyes to his family, and also to Barbara – Connie had moved on temporarily. Barbara had seen how the Army had put more flesh on him and had shed many a tear after he had gone.

By now he was used to travelling around and soon settled into the work, happier than he had ever been, except with Maureen.

Whilst he was in the Army his parents had moved to another church in another district, and Maureen had moved from her previous address, so the box number postal address became irrelevant. Neither of them now knew where the other was, even to send a Christmas card, which distressed both of them, until the grief gradually faded. They both now had regular jobs; both married in their twenties.

As normal life went on, they remembered each other at times but felt it was unlikely they would see each other again.

CHAPTER TWENTY

Paul was sitting down in his favourite armchair, watching the late news on TV, on a warm September evening. The usual depressing things about war, refugees and other tragedies were all too evident.

He was still pondering the plight of the unfortunate in his mind when the words 'Appledore shipyard' brought him back to focus, as the news passed on to a brighter note.

The good news was that Appledore Ship Builders were due to launch the largest container ship they had yet built; because of it's vast bulk and the comparatively shallow of water for the launching, it could not go ahead until the following day, when the tides would be more favourable, with help from the wind coming from the Atlantic.

The screen then switched to a weather forecast with a predominancy of sun symbols spreading over the map of Southern England including the West Country.

Paul had stopped registering the weather forecast and was now thinking of Appledore. He thought of his previous home there, and the bittersweet memories came flooding back, and uppermost in his mind was Maureen. He had a mental picture, passing through the barrier of time, going back about thirty years. There was Maureen in her white blouse and navy skirt smiling at him.

He thought of all the other things that had happened to him. The milestones of his life. Going off to do his National Service in the Army and his experiences in Germany. Starting work with the National Trust in the Lake District. His marriage and the birth of his two lovely daughters. Their happy family life which was brought to a tragic end when his wife had died recently after more then twenty years of marriage.

A sudden thought came into his mind. Why didn't he drive to Appledore. It was a Saturday evening. If he drove through the night he would be there in plenty of time for the launching, at high tide on Sunday.

Paul was suddenly wideawake. Previously he had been almost soporific, after a spaghetti bolognaise TV dinner with a part bottle of wine he had finished, not having anyone else there to help him out.

The adrenaline was starting to pump through Paul's veins now, and a film of sweat formed on his brow and over his upper lip. He knew it was going to be one of those sleepless nights for him anyway. Especially with the unusual warm humid weather. He opened the chest of drawers with clean shirts and underwear and started to throw some things in the holdall. Noticing a swimming costume in one corner of the drawer he threw that in with a couple of towels. He put some things in his toilet bag, locked the house and jumped in the car.

Paul arrived at Appledore at about four in the morning on Sunday. Instead of going down into the town, he decided he would stop the car in the area above the town known as Look Out. He left the car parked near the public bench with a tall street lamp next to it which, being on a right angled corner, lit up the roads running south and east.

On getting out of the car, Paul was transported back in time with all its evocative memories. For a moment he was filled with emotion, and he found it difficult to breath as his heart pounded and his head throbbed. He looked at the seat; it was on the same spot that he had courted Maureen, and other local girls before her. He looked up at the now modern light remembered the time he had tried to shoot out the bulb with smooth pebbles and a steel catapult, brought with him for that purpose, to make courtship a more private affair. It was funny how he could still remember the quaint little mirrors that somehow reflected the light downwards, under their bonnet shaped covering.

Paul smiled to himself, thinking that he never usually got involved in any vandalism. He went over to the nearby farm gate and, leaning on the top rail, looked across the field and out to where the bar continued it's rhythmic roar, as the breakers broke over the sand. The wind was coming in from the sea, bringing the sound with it. A fairly full moon picked out the white surf of the breakers all along the horizon.

He thought of Maureen, with him at a point in the distance, all those summers ago. The excitement and the tenderness he felt for Maureen returned; he was surprised that he still remembered that longing for fulfilment of their relationship during his youth.

He went back to the car and sat thinking, with the window wound right down, as he listened to the roar of the surf.

Paul awoke to the sound of birds singing and a cow lowing far away. It was broad daylight. He looked at his watch, seven thirty-two. Paul decided to get freshened up at the public toilets down on the quayside. He started the car up and drove slowly along the road that used to border the private grounds of The Holt, a big private house built by a wealthy merchant, who had named it Richmond House. Now it had been developed into flats and a housing estate, as well as the allotment grounds opposite.

Leaving the 'plantation' behind, he descended a steep hill and was soon approaching the church that his father, now long deceased, had preached in. He stopped the car outside and looked up at its decaying bleakness. The front of the church around the entrance had a cared for look, and its paint work kept up. There was not a resident minister to look after the place now, but lay preachers and visiting ministers kept the place going, with the help of a few loyal helpers.

Paul looked in the Sunday School yard and although it now looked as if no one came in there much, he remembered how they used to meet in the yard of a Sunday afternoon, before going inside for the different classes.

The very best things he could recall, were the 'socials'. Most of the games seemed to encourage an interchange between the sexes thought Paul, smiling to himself. He remembered the Sunday evening with Maureen when they had to take charge of a class. He remembered the young child sitting on her lap, and wondered if Maureen had become a mother now.

He also remembered, one social evening, dancing with a girl a few years his senior, so that his chin was just about in line with her bosom. Paul could remember a very soft fluffy cardigan she had worn, which brushed his cheeks, but he could not recall her name now. Was it Pauline? Perhaps not.

He sighed and got back into the car, coasted down the hill and came alongside the Baptist Church on the opposite side of the road. The first thing that came to his mind was the occasion of the 'erotic' sermon... He smiled to himself again and remembered Auntie's 'a time and a place for everything' phrase. If it was a sacrilegious offence, he hoped God had forgiven him for it. Making mistakes was part of growing up he reasoned.

Paul could now see the quay and the river quite clearly, with the boats bobbing up and down on the water. It was four hours until high tide though. He turned the car left and carried along into the car park at the end of the quay; once used by children when it had swings and roundabouts at the end. He used the facilities in the WC to freshen up, and then went for a walk down memory lane.

Walking 'out west' along Irsha Street, Paul noticed that the fronts of the houses were kept up well, as they were traditionally, except that he did not see one housewife scrubbing the doorstep before breakfast. Part of the traditional ritual thirty to forty years ago.

Paul came to the spot where he thought Auntie's house was. There was a ceramic plate stuck on the wall now with the words 'Pam's Place' on it. He remembered the last time he was inside it, the furniture and everyone else gone. Paul walked along with his memories, and came to the building, which was once the local cinema, the Gaiety, the only cinema for miles.

Halfway through the performances in the interval, when the management sold refreshments and ice creams, there was a musical item. A very pretty girl, probably in her late teens, in an evening dress of satin cloth, shiny and elegant, would sing songs from Cole Porter and Irving Berlin. Songs like *Night and Day* would be delivered with a fascinating innocence and mellowness. It was a gem of an idea, but Paul wondered how many people of the time appreciated it. Although the singer used a microphone, she had the backing of a grand piano, which was played by the manager, very proficiently and with flair.

Paul walked past the building wondering what it was used

for nowadays, but the strains of *Night and Day* were still humming in his brain.

The pub was still there, but the chip-shop was gone. The lifeboat-house was still there and the slipway, which bathers could use to enter the sea.

Paul walked back along the way he had come and decided to find somewhere for breakfast. Walking along Paul remembered the two sailing vessels that used to be moored there, when not at sea. *The Kathleen and May* and the *Irene* used to take cargoes of timber across to the Mumbles in Wales and bring back coal. He still had black and white photographs of them at home; prized, treasured possessions.

There was a café open, where Paul breakfasted. There were still a few hours to go before the launching. He did some more sightseeing and relived many half-forgotten memories, visiting the old haunts of his youth.

Paul felt an exhilaration and sadness. The saddest part being that he could not find anyone living here now that he had known then. He had heard that Barry was living in Exeter, but did not have his address. Nearly all the older ones were dead, and the people of his age had moved away to find work. There was a feeling of grief for things lost. A feeling of grief for lost places, or places changed so much that they were unrecognisable. A feeling of grief for lost friends. For folk who had cared for Paul's welfare and were now gone, so that he could not thank them.

Then there was the grief of his wife of twenty years, buried under the ground, and the loss of his future with her. This had been in the forefront of his thinking and his moods prior to coming back to this place. He had no doubt in his own mind that this had brought on the melancholy he was now feeling. There was another grief though, for the lost opportunities, especially where Maureen was concerned.

If only he had had a more mature outlook when he had lost Maureen. If only he could have gone after her to meet again. If only…

Then he would have been a man and not a boy, thought Paul, knowing in his heart that these things happen, yet the grief

224

was there just the same.

Was it love or infatuation he had felt for Maureen? Surely it could not have been love? He was only a boy.

He had felt he needed her, and cared about her. He was not mature enough to provide for her. He knew that. Why was he infatuated with her now? He hadn't a clue where she was, or even if she was alive.

He would have a drink and a pasty perhaps, and then it would be time to go to the shipyard for the launching. As soon as Paul had thought about a pint and a pasty, he remembered the pasties that Auntie had provided that first day he had met Maureen.

CHAPTER TWENTY ONE

Paul parked his car with the others alongside the high fencing of the shipyard, then walked inside the shipyard gates, which were normally closed to the public, to join the crowd of onlookers.

The greater proportion of the crowd were the ship building staff and local people of the town. There were a few holidaymakers; the people at the front were the directors and press.

Paul spoke to the fellow standing next to him in the crowd.

"There's quite a lot of people here this afternoon, I suppose a lot of them are on holiday."

"Are you here on holiday then?" asked the tall ginger-haired man.

"Well, sort of. I used to live here though. My father was the Congregational Minister here not long after the war ended," said Paul.

"Oh, hang on a minute, let's see if I can find Richard. He used to go to your father's church," said the helpful stranger to Paul.

He led the way through the crowd to a shorter fellow in his late sixties.

"Here Richard! Look! There's a fellow here you might know."

Richard turned around and gave Paul a good look.

Paul was smiling as he had already recognised the face, allowing for the passing of time.

He remembered Richard as a lay worker in his father's church. He was the same person that had the argument with the other leader, when Paul and Maureen helped out. Richard had probably worked in the dockyard for most of his life.

"Why, it's Paul, the Reverend Baxter's son. Gosh, I haven't seen you for some time. How are you?" said Richard, holding out his hand to Paul.

"I'm fine Richard, thank you," said Paul, his heart lifting now he had seen someone he recognised.

"How's your wife and family, Richard?" asked Paul.

"Well, a few aches and pains like the rest of us," said Richard. "Are you married now? I heard you were, years ago mind."

"I was until recently. She died, and I'm on my own again now," said Paul, his face changing from happy to a nervous sadness.

"Oh, I'm sorry boy," said Richard, gently patting Paul on the back.

"Here it's funny seeing you here today. I suppose you came down especially to see the launching. See about it on the telly did 'ee?"

"Yes, that's right. I had a sudden urge to visit the old place, the old home."

"Well I've got something interesting to tell you, boy. Something you might be very pleased to hear," said Richard, all smiles now.

"Oh what's that now?" said Paul not having the faintest idea what Richard might have to tell him that could possibly relate to him.

"Do you remember that girl you got friendly with, who had an aunt that lived out west? She came here on holiday years ago when you was a boy. I remember your parents getting a bit worried, they thought you was getting a bit serious on her. Here, are you all right? Your face has gone white as a sheet."

"I'm all right, honestly. Go on Richard. "

"Well it's a funny thing, but she's on holiday down here! My missus seen her in church last Sunday morning. She used to come to church with you a few times didn't she?"

Paul nodded, desperately trying to hold back the tears and emotion that were building up inside him.

"I wouldn't be surprised if she's here in the crowd somewhere," said Richard. "She was a fine girl as I remember. Well you know that, don't 'ee boy," said Richard in his usual broad vernacular, giving Paul a wink.

"Well, this is a coincidence, Maureen being here at the

same time as myself. Of course I would love to see her again. I wonder where she is staying?" said Paul. He was still in a state of shock and not revealing his true feelings, of tremendous optimism, that had now replaced his previous gloom.

"I can't tell 'ee that, I'm afraid boy, but I expect you could soon find out. Tisn't that big a place 'ere is it?"

Paul smiled and said, "No, I expect I'll find Maureen."

Paul continued talking to Richard and was interested to hear the local news and ask questions about all the people he remembered.

In a close community news does the rounds, and Paul thought that his own presence here would be recorded with a certain amount of interest by the depleted few who would remember him.

The time came for the *Saxon Warrior* to be released into the river. The traditional bottle of champagne was shattered over the bow of the ship, and the giant, by Appledore standards, slowly slid down the slipway by her chains into the full tide of the river. As she settled easily in the water, great cheers went up from the workmen who had built her. A great moment for them to see the fruits of their labour nearly ready to earn its own living in the world.

Paul thought how times had changed from the days he remembered, when the riveters were joining the steel plates together with their endless hammering noise. Sometimes from early in the morning until well into the evening.

As soon as it became obvious that the party was over, Paul said to Richard, "I think I had better make my way now Richard. I'm not sure that I might be blocking someone else's car. Everybody will be wanting to get out at the same time in a moment."

"That's all right my handsome, I'm going to talk to some of my old work-mates for a bit anyhow. I don't get much chance to talk to some of them now I'm retired," said Richard, his eyes registering a little sadness, for the days did not have the same purpose and meaning as they had done a decade or two ago.

Paul and Richard shook hands and said goodbye, exchanging addresses. Paul made a mental note to remember a

Christmas card for Richard and his wife, Felicity.

What Paul did not tell Richard was that he wanted to hurry back to where he might be able to watch all those making for the exit and their cars.

Paul noticed that someone had already left a parking space near the entrance gate so he moved his car up to the front where he could see everyone coming out. He hoped that none would think it odd or take any notice of him. He could always say he was moving his car nearer for an elderly relative so they wouldn't have to walk too far, an excuse ready in his mind.

He sat in the car and scrutinised all the folk coming out. Would she be there? Would Maureen be in that crowd somewhere? Paul knew there was now a good chance, that she was.

As people filed through the gateway, some gave Paul a curious glance, and Paul pretended he was writing in a notebook. Perhaps they might think that he was a reporter.

By now many scores of people had gone by and Paul was beginning to feel disappointed, when he saw a woman approaching on her own.

CHAPTER TWENTY TWO

She was wearing a blue and white-floral patterned dress, navy high-heeled shoes, and carried a navy blue handbag. The dark sunglasses made a blur of her face from a distance. As she came nearer Paul could see she had an attractive, slim figure, although it became apparent that she was not a young woman – thankfully, as far as Paul was concerned. She wore no hat and there was something familiar about those short, black, curly locks.

Paul got out of the car and walked towards the woman. She was looking towards Paul now, and as their eyes met Paul said,

"It is you isn't it Maureen?"

The woman stopped. A look of surprise on her face as she studied Paul. There was an endless silence that made Paul so tense he thought he might faint. Then her face broke out into a smile, so sweet to Paul, that he thought he might faint with exhilaration as she said the one word,

"Paul?"

Paul, not usually a demonstrative fellow, put his arms around Maureen and gave her the biggest hug he had given anyone for a long time. Then realising that people passing by were staring, with an amused look on their faces, Paul stopped, and releasing Maureen said,

"I'm sorry Maureen, I got carried away."

Maureen looked at him with a twinkle in her eyes as she said, "I think I can remember that line somewhere!"

Paul blushed with embarrassment, but also pleasure, as he grabbed her hand and said, "Oh it is good to see you Maureen. There are so many things for us to talk about. It…it's such a long time ago, but so wonderful to be together again. We've got to go somewhere quiet to talk. Is that OK?" he asked anxiously.

"I daren't say no, had I," teased Maureen.

"I saw an old friend here this afternoon and he remembered

you. He said he thought you were here on your own, but if you are here with someone else I would understand."

Maureen's expression changed to one of sadness as she said, "No, I am here on my own. It's a long story really. I'll tell you about it later on. Are you here on your own then Paul?"

"Yes, my wife died a couple of years ago, and I haven't found anyone else yet."

"Oh, I'm sorry to hear that, – about your wife."

"We had been married over twenty years when she went," Paul said, his eyes moistening a little.

Maureen squeezed his hand slightly.

"I got married when I was young. Too young I suppose. I was stupid enough to marry someone like my father, who used to hit me about a bit. I've met several men since, but I'm afraid I couldn't stick with any of them."

"Well, I'm sorry about that too. You deserve better than that," said Paul looking longingly into Maureen's eyes through her dark glasses.

"Now where shall we go, somewhere a bit more… private," said Maureen, with that mischievous smile that Paul remembered.

"Where are you staying, Maureen?"

"Oh, the Seagate on the corner of the quay. Do you remember it?"

"Yes, that's fine. Look why don't we drive over there; I can buy you a drink perhaps."

"Why not," said Maureen, a teasing glance coming out of the corner of her eyes, as she blinked her long black eyelashes.

They drove the short distance slowly, along the narrow road, and parked the car in the hotel car park; Maureen having walked over to the shipyard.

"Have you been back here before, since you used to live here?" asked Maureen as they crossed the road to enter the hotel. Paul was glad that she had removed her sunglasses.

"Not very often, about three times that's all. And you?"

"Once since Auntie died. Just after I broke up with my husband, nearly ten years ago."

They both entered the bar. Paul paid for drinks which he

brought over to where Maureen was sitting.

"This is quite a coincidence, seeing you here now. I heard about the launching on TV, but you probably booked a holiday in advance. Did you know anything about the launching?" Paul asked.

"It's a long story really. I was talking to a friend of mine about holidays. Well – she was talking to me about it actually, wondering where to go, in the UK for a change, on a short break, and I mentioned here. So she and her husband came down here, had a nice time and found out that they were building a big boat in the yard, that they would be launching in a few days time. They were so impressed with the area that it made me feel quite nostalgic for the place, and I came down as soon as I could fit in a temp in the office. I'm here for another week. How about you?"

Paul's mind raced as he thought of the possibility of being with Maureen for a week, but he knew he would have to speak the truth. He took a long swig at his pint of beer and said, smiling, "I only came down here on a whim, expecting just to be here for the day, but seeing you has altered things I must say."

"I'm flattered, I must admit," said Maureen, smiling in her teasing way again.

"But you must have some work to go back to, surely?" queried Maureen, changing into a serious mood.

"Well I'm my own boss really. I can always make a few phone calls and stay on a bit longer."

Paul knew there was no way he was going home whilst Maureen was here.

"Do you have any plans for tomorrow, Maureen?" said Paul, looking at the creases around Maureen's eyes that the sunglasses had hidden; the light make-up could not hide the passing of time.

"I was thinking of exploring Braunton and Croyde tomorrow; I have been everywhere on this side of the water around here, including a trip on the ferry to Instow," said Maureen, brightly enough, but hoping that Paul might say something exciting.

"What's it been like going around on your own?" asked

Paul.

Maureen lowered her eyes and said, "Well, I've got used to it now. Sometimes it's a change – from being with someone who only thinks about himself."

"I suppose I used to be selfish when I was with you, and so immature," said Paul holding onto Maureen's hand.

"I remember you were immature in some ways, but in other ways you were quite forward for a boy of your age," giggled Maureen.

Paul smiled, happily remembering those times.

"Why don't we go down memory lane tomorrow, just to lay the old ghosts," said Paul.

"What do you mean – 'lay the old ghosts'? I'm not sure I like the sound of that," said Maureen frowning.

Paul was sure she was teasing his unintentional double entendre.

"Well it's hard for me to explain really, but when I was having a quick look around the area this morning, on my own, all the memories came flooding back, like ghosts to haunt me, and filled me with a sort of grief for the things I had lost," said Paul sombrely. "You know, like the time that is now lost, and the opportunities lost, as well as all the friends who died or just moved on somewhere, like us."

"Yes, I know what you mean," said Maureen, as tears started to form in her eyes, thinking about her Auntie Florence.

Paul squeezed her hand saying, "Well if we visit some of those places again, as we did all that time ago, then we can sort of make up for being apart."

"I've got to hand it to you Paul, you're still a very persuasive man with a boyish look on your face," said Maureen smiling.

"Why don't we walk up through the copse to Bideford and get the bus back to Appledore, or else a taxi if the bus is not due for a while," said Paul eagerly, getting the feeling of the place back in his bones, as well as the thought of being with Maureen, and the romantic possibilities.

"You mean the track by the river and past King Alfred's Cave?" enquired Maureen.

233

"Yes, that's it, it's a lovely walk if the weather's right. I've got a couple of flasks in my car. Perhaps we can get them filled before we set out in the morning, and take some sandwiches or something for a picnic," said Paul, warming to the subject.

"How about a couple of pasties?" said Maureen teasing again.

"You haven't forgotten Auntie's pasties then?" said Paul grinning.

"How could I ever?" laughed Maureen.

"We'll see what we can get in the morning, unless we do a bit of shopping now, this afternoon. Oh, I forgot, it's Sunday. There won't be anywhere open for that sort of thing I suppose," said Paul disappointed, as he always liked to make an early start to go anywhere special.

"Oh dear, what a calamity," said Maureen with laughter in her eyes.

Paul smiled and said, "Well the shops will be open at nine in the morning, we can get something on the way."

"Aye, aye, Captain," said Maureen giggling.

"You can tease me all you like, and it won't worry me. I'm so glad to see you Maureen."

Maureen looked at Paul steadily, then said, "I'm pleased to see you Paul. It doesn't seem that long since we parted now, just sitting here like this and talking."

Paul nodded his head; he was filled with emotion, the tears welling up in his eyes. After a pause, he struggled to say,

"I missed you so much when you left, Maureen."

"I know. I missed you too. But we were very young you know," said Maureen, tears starting to tumble down her cheeks now.

"'They tried to tell us we're too young, as the song goes," said Paul, trying to lighten the emotional tension.

"You've got it," said Maureen smiling, through her tears.

"Well this won't do. I'm afraid I've turned the reunion into a morbid affair. It should be a joyous, happy occasion, shouldn't it?" said Paul smiling weakly.

"It is Paul. It really is wonderful to be together again," said Maureen, putting her hand out to clasp Paul's.

"What shall we do now? I feel I want to go outside and walk a bit right now. How about it, Maureen?"

"Yes why not? I'll just go upstairs and change into something more comfortable for walking. I won't be long."

Paul watched Maureen's feminine curves swerve around the table and disappear from sight. He sighed happily and went into the Gents to freshen up. He splashed water over his face and noticed how his beard was starting to look unsightly. He thought he was looking a little less haunted, now he had seen Maureen. Yes, perhaps haunted was a good word. Laying the ghosts? An odd phrase he thought, chuckling to himself. He entered the bar again and sat down to finish his drink. The presence of Maureen had made him forget to drink. Now he gulped it down, so that he would be ready to go walking with Maureen down memory lane.

CHAPTER TWENTY THREE

Maureen quickly changed into a pair of light, tan slacks and sandals with a tight-fitting striped T-shirt.

'Well, I've kept my figure pretty trim so I had just as well take advantage of it,' she thought, eyeing herself in the mirror. 'If you've got it, flaunt it. That's what I say,' she thought, smiling to herself, and then sadness came over her as she wished she had stretch marks and a big stomach from having children.

She ran down the stairs to where Paul was waiting.

Paul had finished his drink quickly and was now starting to feel the effects of the alcohol, as he was not an inveterate social drinker.

Maureen had already finished her gin and tonic, so she said, "OK Paul? Shall we go?"

"Aye, aye Cap'n," said Paul grinning.

"Oh. So you're getting your own back are you?" said Maureen smiling, as she stepped outside.

"Shall we walk along Irsha Street?" said Paul, feeling bold with the drink, and clasping Maureen's hand as they walked along.

Maureen did not mind, although she felt a little awkward. 'Why is it so much harder to feel romantic, and natural, when you have lost your youth?' she wondered. On reflection she changed her opinion. 'Hey, I'm not too old yet. There's life in this girl yet.'

Paul retraced the steps of his jaunt earlier that morning when he had been on his own. How different it was now that he was with Maureen. As they came towards Pam's Place, Paul said, "Isn't this Auntie's house?"

Maureen looked at the number and said, "Yes that's right. I wonder who lives there now."

"Oh, some yuppie type has got it for a summer hideaway place, I expect," said Paul cynically.

"Oh that's horrid. I hope it's being lived in by local people," said Maureen frowning.

"Do you want me to knock on the door and see if anyone's in?" asked Paul.

"No. It would spoil it if what you said was true. I'll pretend, or assume, that local people are living in there," said Maureen.

"You always were a romantic, Maureen," said Paul, squeezing her hand

"I don't know about that. A romantic? Do you know, I can't really remember. Well I wasn't really old enough to be romantic, now was I?" said Maureen, looking across at Paul.

"Well, you were a bit more mature than me, but perhaps you're right. Romantic, in one sense, comes with the maturity of age. Romance in the other sense, now that's different," said Paul, looking at Maureen to see how she would react.

"How do you mean?" said Maureen startled.

"Well, making love in the old fashioned way, or courting as we used to say," said Paul walking along slowly.

"What about it?" said Maureen, making Paul do all the explaining.

"What I was trying to say is, no matter how young you are, you can feel something special for a person."

"Isn't it more to do with hormones and things at that age?" said Maureen uncomfortably.

"Of course, that is a major part of it. But I think I wanted to know you as a person as well as… a mate, or a sexual object if you like."

"Are you sure Paul?" said Maureen, giving Paul a half smile, then pouting her lips.

"When I first saw you, and went out with you, I suppose I was thinking of you as a sexual object; well I mean I wanted to know you sexually that is. What about you?"

Maureen paused, thinking. She had to admit that she must have been like any normal young girl and wanting to experience things, but afraid.

"It's a bit different for a girl. Well it was then. We were supposed to play hard to get," said Maureen evasively.

"But did you want to know me… sexually?"

Maureen laughed with embarrassment. "For a parson's son you ask the most awkward questions."

"Whisper in my ear. Yes or no," said Paul grinning.

Maureen stopped and whispered into Paul's ear. "Well you got to know me sexually up to a point, didn't you?"

Paul whispered back, "Which point was that?"

Maureen felt a fit of giggles, and stopped by the old cinema.

"I was afraid Paul. I think we both were, weren't we?"

Paul smiled wryly and said, "Yes you're right. I suppose a good thing in one way, that we were."

"Do you mean for moral reasons?"

"Partly. It wouldn't have looked very good if the parson's son got a girl pregnant would it? I didn't have any money to get contraceptives and I didn't have the nerve to ask for them, well, until it was too late," said Paul with a wry grin.

"You poor boy," said Maureen.

"You poor girl," parried Paul, smiling.

"This is the old cinema, do you remember it?" said Maureen shyly, trying to change the subject.

"Yes of course. I remember sitting beside you in here, the night before we parted," said Paul smugly.

"Can you remember the film then?" asked Maureen sharply, teasing again.

"I can remember it yes. It was *The Blue Lamp*, with Dirk Bogarde," said Paul triumphantly.

"Bravo!" said Maureen laughing.

"I loved to cuddle up against you in the dark," said Paul.

"I always worried what you were doing with your hands," said Maureen shyly.

"Oh, I thought I was keeping you warm."

"I didn't feel cold in there, I can tell you that," said Maureen her dark eyebrows raised.

They walked through the street silently for a while until Paul said, "I hope I'm not embarrassing you, or disturbing you in any way, Maureen."

"Well it's a bit awkward baring your soul, so to speak, to someone I haven't seen for so long. Although in another way, if we part in a day or two, and go back to where we came from, it will all be forgotten, won't it?" said Maureen with a hint of sadness.

"I hope it won't be like that Maureen. As I said before, I thought our relationship was a bit special even when we were so young. It can be again you know. Do you want it to be?"

"I don't know."

"Are you still afraid?"

"Perhaps."

"I can't let you go this time Maureen. Not without you saying that you never want to see me again."

"That's a bit dramatic isn't it?"

"To be honest, I can't bear to leave this place without you now. But I'll settle for a parting if we can see each other again soon."

They were walking up to the lifeboat house and slipway now.

"Can you honestly say you love me, when we haven't seen each other for about thirty years?" asked Maureen, concern and worry showing in her eyes.

Paul looked across to where Greysands Point, Burrows and sanddunes beckoned in the distance; the distant roar of the surf breaking beyond the sand bar.

"I can honestly say that I never stopped loving you Maureen."

Maureen turned to look Paul straight in the eyes.

"Oh, Paul," she said, tears streaming down her face.

Paul went over to Maureen and embraced her as she sobbed quietly. He kissed her on the cheek and apologised for his rough beard.

"You look like a pop star," Maureen said.

"The ones with the designer stubble?" asked Paul.

"Yes. That's right," said Maureen trying to smile.

"If only I had their money," said Paul. "We must have a swim where we went the day I met you."

"Have you a cossie?"

"Yes, I packed one just in case. Mind you we didn't need one before, did we?"

Maureen smiled nervously, looking at the tourists and not wanting them to hear anything.

"Shall we go back and have some tea?" asked Paul.

"Yes, that sounds like a good idea," said Maureen, and they walked slowly back the way they had come.

When they got back to the hotel, Paul treated Maureen and himself to a Devonshire cream tea.

"There's something you've forgotten isn't there Paul?" said Maureen suddenly.

"What's that then?"

"You haven't arranged anywhere to stay the night yet, have you?" said Maureen, looking at him over the top of a jam and cream scone.

"Oh Lord! No I haven't, and it's a busy time of year, I wonder if they'll have a room here?"

"They seem to be pretty busy but you can but try," said Maureen, wondering on the possible outcome if there were no vacancies anywhere in the town.

"We'll finish our tea and then I'll make some enquiries," said Paul, licking cream off his fingers.

"I didn't get much sleep last night, so I ought to sleep well tonight even if I stretch out in the back of the car," said Paul, cutting into another scone.

"Why didn't you sleep properly then?" asked Maureen.

"Well I got down here in the early hours of the morning and parked at Lookout, you know, where we used to sit on the bench there and listen to the breakers on the sandbar."

"Oh, yes, I remember it well," said Maureen, a mischievous smile in her eyes.

"Well I could always do the same again, I suppose," said Paul with another wry smile.

"Not with me you won't," said Maureen laughing.

They finished their cream tea and Paul looked at his watch,

"Coming up to six o' clock now. Usually I would be getting ready to go to church."

"You still go to Church then?"

"Yes. I've found it a great help – when my wife died, I mean."

240

"I go occasionally but not regularly. I've got some good friends who are regular church goers and I usually go with them," said Maureen.

"Is there anything you would like to do this evening, or anything you have planned Maureen?"

"No, nothing special. What about you?"

"What about taking the car onto the Burrows and seeing how far we can get to the sand dunes and the sea," said Paul, his eyes lighting up.

"Well, if it gets too cold and breezy, we could always go on to Westward Ho! I suppose."

"That's the spirit," beamed Paul. "Shall we take our bathing costumes just in case we fancy a swim?" said Paul hopefully.

"I don't know. Do you think it will be warm enough? I haven't been in the sea yet," said Maureen, unsure of herself.

"Well, just put your towel and cossie in a bag, just in case," said Paul helpfully. "I've got to find out if there is a room for me. Why don't you go up to your room and freshen up whilst I enquire about a room, Maureen?"

"OK Mr, Bossy Boots," said Maureen, "Good luck "she added turning round and smiling.

Paul enquired at the bar to see if there were any vacancies.

"We've only got a double at the moment sir," said a young girl polishing glass.

"I'll take it," said Paul, knowing that he might have a job trying to find anything better. Paul was given a key.

"Could you tell me the room number my friend is in please? I would like to let her know where I am. Then I can shower and shave."

"Certainly sir, it's room four, just along the passageway from yours."

"Thank you," said Paul.

He quickly walked upstairs, belying his years, to tap on Maureen's door.

"Who is it?" said a muffled voice from somewhere within.

"It's me Paul. I've got the room along the corridor, number seven," said Paul, straining to hear what Maureen was doing.

The door opened slightly to reveal Maureen's head but nothing else.

She strained her head around the door to see if anyone else was with Paul, and then said.

"Come on in a moment, Paul then."

As Paul entered the room Maureen clicked the lock on the door and turned round to him.

"Well, what do you think?"

Paul looked at Maureen standing there in a modest blue and white one-piece bathing suit.

"Wow! Great! You look terrific," said Paul admiringly, taking in Maureen's curves: a little rounder than when he first knew her, but still feminine and firm.

"Well, I thought I had better put this on if there was a chance of going swimming. It's a bit of a bind changing on a beach," said Maureen being practical.

"If we went to the spot where we first met, there shouldn't be anyone near to see anything," said Paul, going nearer to Maureen, putting his hands around her waist and resting on her hips.

"Hadn't you better be getting your stuff up from the car, and scraping that beard off your face, Paul? Maybe a cold shower would be a good idea," giggled Maureen.

"Point taken," said Paul giving Maureen a kiss on the cheek.

"Now what am I going to do while I'm waiting for you?" said Maureen frowning.

"Perhaps you had better have a cold shower then," said Paul hurrying out of the room as Maureen picked up a pillow to throw at him.

Eventually Paul tapped on Maureen's door and Maureen let him in.

"About time too. I've read half of my holiday-reading book waiting for you," said Maureen, teasing.

"I ought to look and smell a bit fresher now, shall we go?" said Paul smiling.

"Aye, aye Cap'n Paul," said Maureen saluting smartly.

They walked down to Paul's car carrying their grips and set

off on the road to the Burrows. Soon they were on the road they had cycled on, when they went on their picnic, at their first meeting.

They looked out across the estuary and the bar, then ahead to the Burrows. They reached the cross roads and turned right to go down the lane, where the magpies used to build their incredible domed nests in the impenetrable hawthorn trees with long spikes.

At the end of the lane, there was a gate, the same as before but strangely looking bigger now. Maureen got out and opened the gate to let Paul drive through. They went on over the little hump-backed bridge and noticed that the road went over the top of the reclaimed land, protected by huge boulders at the base of the low cliffs.

Paul headed towards the point and they both noticed how the golf course had expanded outwards, encroaching on the sand dunes and altering the previous routes for public access.

"Well this makes for a quick trip to the point," said Paul, stopping the car in a parking area, near a compound for recycling waste.

"It's not the same though is it?" said Maureen, slamming the car door.

Paul brought both grips out of the boot.

"No it's not the same. Nothing stays the same I suppose. Not even us."

"You don't seem that much different to me," said Maureen. "A bit beefier I suppose. Like me."

"What about inside. How much have we changed inside?" said Paul, clasping Maureen's hand.

"Quite a lot really, I suppose. We don't look out at the world through teenagers eyes do we?"

"No. We're no longer imprisoned by fear and uncertainty are we Maureen?"

"What do you mean?"

"We are old enough to have mature friendships now, if we want to," said Paul, striding across the sandy turf towards the point.

"You mean there's nothing to stop us?"

"Well I hope there isn't Maureen, is there?"

"We can always be friends, but you are implying our relationship should be as lovers aren't you?"

"Until today I thought I had lost that chance forever. Now I've found you again, I must know how much you feel for me," said Paul earnestly.

"Let's not rush things Paul. I imagine you had a happy marriage until your wife's death. I did not. It's a bit too early to talk about that sort of commitment. I still like you Paul, and I think you are fun to be with. I know you are a caring person, but you have got to give me a little time."

"I'm sorry. Perhaps I am rushing things. I'm just worried that I shall leave this place and never see you again this time."

"Oh, come on, Paul." said Maureen laughing. "You are getting quite morbid, let's change the subject. Race you over the dunes and the pebble ridge."

Maureen took off, her grip banging against her legs. Paul ran after her and noticed how the dunes had changed. There was only a small area of marram grass, reaching just a few yards back from the pebble ridge. No sand pits at all. He caught up with Maureen who was struggling to cross the pebbles.

"I think you need a hand again," he said.

"I think I'll do better on my own actually," said Maureen breathlessly.

"Did you notice, the sand pits seemed to have been reclaimed?" said Paul.

"Why? Were you hoping for a déjà vu scene? Were you hoping to throw me down in the sand and ravage me?" said Maureen, as she cleared the pebbles and looked back at Paul. Paul came quickly to her side.

"No. I wouldn't have ravaged you, but I may have kissed you like this."

Paul dropped his holdall, put his arm around Maureen gently, and then kissed her on the lips. He cupped his hands around the back of her neck and her hair, letting his lips caress hers. A warm feeling swept through him as he felt Maureen kissing him back.

"We had better have our swim now, to cool down a bit!"

244

said Maureen shakily.

Paul did not want to stop, but as he saw Maureen stripping off her clothing he started to do the same.

"I bet it will be cold," said Maureen, as they walked hand in hand towards the surf.

The cold hit them as soon as they put their toes in the water.

"Come on, let's get in quickly. It's better that way," said Paul, pulling a reluctant screaming Maureen towards the surf that came relentlessly to meet them.

"In we go!" shouted Paul as he grabbed Maureen around the waist and pushed forward into the surf.

They both came up again, shaking the water out of their eyes, splashing around in the deeper water and letting the swell lift them up and down like corks.

Maureen pointed to some big fish jumping out of the water just on the horizon.

"What are they Paul?"

"Oh, they will be porpoises I expect. They will stay out in the deep water."

"They could be sharks. I'm going in. I'm starting to get cold now."

"They won't be sharks. I've never heard of anyone being attacked by sharks in these waters."

"Race you back to our kit, Paul," said Maureen wading out of the water.

Paul followed dutifully and they came to the pebble ridge.

"We had better get dried right away, or else we shall get cold," said Maureen, getting her giant beach towel out of her grip.

"Need a hand?" said Paul grinning.

"No thanks," replied Maureen, discreetly turning her back on Paul as she started to change.

When they had both dressed, Maureen said, "I could do with a hot drink now."

"Yes, it's quite a bit cooler coming out of the water at this time of day. We'll start heading back to the hotel."

Maureen felt Paul's hand clasping hers and thought to herself, 'Paul feels very strongly about me that much is obvious.

Do I feel the same way about him? It's difficult to pick up something that was left all those years ago. It's as if he is sweeping me off my feet again. Can this work out? We must both have changed so much anyhow. He's so…intense and overpowering. He was always a bit like that. Going ahead and taking things for granted, without really finding out if that's what I wanted to do. I don't think I could live with anyone like that. He might turn out to be just like the others I have known. He won't settle for anything platonic whilst I am here for a few days. What am I going to do?'

The main thing that worried Maureen, because of what had happened in her life, was that she needed to feel in control and not have anyone else taking over. That was how things had gone wrong in the past.

While these thoughts were going through her head, she looked at Paul, who was so obviously content to be with her again. A panic started to seize her but she tried not to show it.

Then Paul said something that made her wonder, for a moment, if he had read her mind.

"I'm sorry if I have been a bit pushy about things. I haven't given you much time to think about whether you want to be with me or not. Perhaps I have been a little selfish," said Paul quietly.

"Perhaps pushy, but not really selfish. Don't forget, if I didn't want to be with you, I wouldn't be here now would I?"

"I'm glad you feel like that Maureen," said Paul, kissing her on the cheek, just before they got in the car.

Paul was in a state of euphoria as they drove back to the hotel.

Maureen was just beginning to feel warm again after her swim in the cold sea. She was wondering how the evening would go. What would Paul suggest to do?

"Do you think it would be a good idea to have dinner at Westward Ho! and try and find somewhere to watch the sun go down?"

"I think you are psychic," said Maureen.

"What do you mean?"

"I was just wondering about the rest of the evening. What we were going to do. We haven't showered, to get the salt off ourselves yet," said Maureen.

"Perhaps we could get dinner sent up to my room. I'm paying enough seeing there's only me in a double room."

"So it's back to the hotel then," he said, and they took the same road back.

Maureen's mind was in a turmoil. Could they really expect to turn the clock back all those years. They were just children then. All right – young people, but innocent by today's standards. She was not innocent now, even by today's standards. A broken marriage and countless affairs. She wouldn't know how to settle down again. If he turned out to be bossy, as she thought he might, being so opinionated about everything, what could she do?

She didn't fancy being trapped in another unhappy marriage, especially if she ended up being in England with him but without the friends and family that she was used to in Aberdeen. Perhaps it would be better if she faded out of his life, like she had before.

They pulled into the Seagate car park and went up the staircase to their rooms,

"I've got an idea. Why don't I get a bottle of your favourite tipple from the bar and then you join me for a little celebration drink in my room?" said Paul eagerly.

"That sounds like a good idea. A bottle of Vermouth would be nice. They should have some," said Maureen, giving Paul a nervous smile.

"Right ho. If they haven't got that, I'll get the nearest to it. See you in a bit," he said, coming back from the staircase to go to the bar, with a spring in his step.

Maureen hurried up the staircase, unlocked the door and went straight for her suitcase. She crammed everything inside, just as it came out of the wardrobe and drawers. She furtively opened the door and peeped out with the full suitcase in her hand.

She tiptoed up to Paul's room and listened. She heard the sound of glasses tinkling and the sound of a liquid being poured from a bottle. Quietly, she moved towards the staircase and went down as quickly as she could with the heavy weight. The manager was in the bar and she asked to settle up her bill.

He was very surprised and asked, "Is everything all right?"

"Yes. I'm afraid I have to get home. Something has cropped up," said Maureen shakily.

"I'm sorry to hear that madam," the manager totalled up and gave her the bill.

She gave him her credit card, signed the slip and he gave her the receipt. She hurried out of the door to her car.

Paul thought that Maureen was a long time in her room, so he went along and tapped on her door. There was no answer so he opened it and went inside. He saw the wardrobe doors open wide revealing the bare interior. From there his gaze went to the chest of drawers and he saw that they also had been emptied. His mouth went dry and he felt his throat constrict. Now panic was welling up inside him. He dashed outside and down the stairs, two at a time, through the lobby and out into the car park, to see Maureen's car just pulling away in the growing darkness.

He sprinted to his own car, feeling for the key in his trousers pocket. Inside the car he gunned the motor into life and took off with a screech of tyres. Maureen's headlights showed the way as she accelerated along the quayside road.

Paul flashed his headlights several times but to no avail. Maureen continued to accelerate along Marine Parade, and now Paul was in a quandary. He knew that if he was not careful there would be a terrible accident. He let Maureen start up the hill, then decided on a course of action.

He turned left by the Richmond dry dock, brakes squealing, and traversed the narrow lane to the side of the docklands. People came out of their doors to see if there was someone being chased by the police. Paul hared past the gates of the shipyard, where both he and Maureen had been only hours before. He gained speed and had the advantage that if there was anything coming in the opposite direction, their headlights would give him good warning. He came to a screeching halt as he joined the main road.

He was given hope when the headlights of a speeding car approached him. Gambling that it was Maureen, he manoeuvred his car to straddle the highway.

Maureen had taken the hill too fast and stalled the car a short way up. She had seen Paul turn off, in her mirror. By a quirk of fate she saw that she had stopped opposite his old home. She was blinded by tears now; as she restarted the car and pulled away, burning rubber. She quickly got the car up into a screaming second gear and tried to make up the lost ground. At the top of the hill she changed into third gear, the tyres squealing around the wide bend, and then another one. She changed into fourth gear as the road straightened out and increased her speed. Suddenly her lights picked up a car slewed right across the highway. She took her foot off the accelerator and started to brake frantically.

Paul opened his car door and ran towards the other car to verify that it was indeed Maureen. She was sitting with her head bowed. He opened the door, and said with anguish,

"Maureen! My darling Maureen! What have I done to you?" Paul sprawled over her in an awkward embrace. "Why did you have to run away from me, when I have only just found you after all these years?" He collapsed, sobbing uncontrollably, his face against hers.

"I...I...I'm so sorry Paul. It's just...that I'm frightened," she sobbed.

"Frightened? What do you mean?"

"I'm frightened that it just wouldn't work out," she mumbled almost incoherently.

"You have got to give it a try, my darling. Will you, for my sake? If it doesn't work out, that won't be so bad as if you had never given it a try, now would it?"

"I suppose not," she whispered, her tears still streaming down her cheeks making gentle tapping sounds as they hit the dashboard in the quiet of the evening.

Then there was the sound of a motor in the distance and the presence of an even stronger headlight.

"I'm going to drive back to the hotel. I'm going to trust you to follow on in your own time. I don't know what I'll do if you don't. I can only beg you not to leave me tonight," he said, sobbing again. He heard the sound of someone getting out of their car.

"Is everything OK?" asked a worried looking, middle aged man to Paul, as Paul straightened up to face him.

"Yes, yes. It's a private matter. Nobody's hurt though."

"Oh! Good. Well I'll wait whilst you move your car – you are blocking the highway you know," said the man, pointedly.

"Ah, yes. I'm sorry. I shan't be a minute," said Paul, going back to his car and moving it to the side of the road to let the man drive past. Then Paul went back to Maureen.

"Are you OK?"

"Yes! Just a bit shaken. Just leave me a moment. I'll follow on in a minute. You go on," she said, miserably.

"Right! I'll see you back at the hotel," said Paul, trying to sound convincing, but unsure of the reality of his statement.

He drove off, his knuckles as white with tension as his face, drained by the uncertainty of the next few minutes. He looked at the reflection in his mirror as he drove out of sight of her; maybe this would be the last time in his life.

CHAPTER TWENTY FOUR

He went up to his room, exhausted, and feeling sick to his stomach. He sat on the edge of his double bed wishing that she was with him. He looked at the bottle of Vermouth on a bedside table that was staring at him ironically. He got up and picked up the glass of Vermouth he had poured earlier. He downed it, decided he did not like the taste, but started to drink the other. Sipping it this time as his head had started to bang and his legs were feeling unsteady. He wanted to feel unconscious and forget the anguish he felt, but knew he could not sleep for a while now, until all the tension had gone.

He stripped off all his clothes and turned the shower on in the cubicle. He was spreading shower gel over his feet when there was a sharp sliding sound, which made Paul's heart miss a beat.

The shower curtains parted and Maureen stood, directly in front of him, completely naked.

"Maureen! My darling!" gasped Paul.

"Come on, move over. There's plenty of room for me to shower as well. Why should I wait for you to finish? Don't you stand there gawping, do something," said Maureen trying to sound cross.

Paul was mesmerised by the sight of Maureen's nakedness. Then he reached out with both hands to draw her to himself. He hugged her tightly and began to kiss her passionately. He was aware of her full breasts against his chest as the water poured down on the pair of them. Paul ran his hands gently up and down her back, and over her hips and buttocks.

Maureen felt weak at the knees, and started to whimper softly, her tears mingling with the water.

Paul kissed her neck and his hands massaged her breasts, gently teasing at the nipples. His fingers gently explored inside her, as she caressed his manhood.

251

Their lovemaking was vigorous and passionate, each yielding to the other's needs. Their bodies supporting each other, and pulsing to the core of their beings, the ultimate climax was reached.

Paul, his voice heavy with passion, pleaded with her.

"Maureen, I love you. Never leave me again, will you?"

Maureen put her finger over his mouth.

"Shush. Just hold me tight," she said gently, knowing now that all pretence was over; they could give themselves to each other without holding back. That was what love should be all about. Total commitment to each other. There was no need to pretend any longer, she had better just enjoy it.

Maureen kissed Paul's neck and then gently on his lips.

"So you love me then do you, lover boy?"

"I think you know that by now Maureen."

"Well hurry up and finish your shower. Then can you put the kettle on," she said laughing.

"Right ho," said Paul, lathering himself over with a soapy sponge and starting to tease Maureen's breasts with it.

"I'll do that if you don't mind. Now hurry up. We have got to order dinner yet. That's another job for you to do. Also I have to book my room again."

"I was hoping we could just lie down and cuddle up on the bed together," said Paul, caressing Maureen's face with his hands.

"Well, get to the kettle first. In the movies lovers have a cigarette after making love. I'll settle for a strong cup of tea," she said, slapping Paul's bare bottom. "Go on."

Paul got out of the cubicle and quickly dried himself. Then he put the kettle on and made the tea. He went back into the shower alcove and said, "I've got a towel for you."

"Oh good. I've finished now. That was lovely," said Maureen, sliding the curtains back and stepping out.

"I'll give you a hand to dry yourself," said Paul, wrapping the towel around Maureen.

"You get the tea, lover boy."

"Aye, aye cap'n, ma'am," said Paul, putting his broadest West Country accent to the test.

Maureen gave Paul another hefty slap on his bare buttocks as she giggled again.

Paul brought the tea over to the bedside table, and lay down naked on the bed.

"Hurry up, I'm getting lonely," said Paul.

"Don't be so impatient. I won't be long, I'm trying to comb my hair. To make myself nice for you, don't you know?"

"You look lovely to me just as you were in the shower," said Paul dreamily.

A moment later she sashayed her way over to Paul as he lay on the bed watching her.

"My! You are pleased to see me," she giggled.

As Maureen came up to Paul he pulled her on top of him.

"You always were a tease, all those years ago," he said smiling at her.

"No I wasn't, I was an innocent little girl. It was just you and your dirty mind," she said, putting her finger in her mouth and trying to look innocent as a maiden.

"Well I'm glad your not an innocent little girl any longer," said Paul.

"That's horrid, and you ought to have known better, being a parson's son, seducing me like you did," said Maureen continuing the play-acting.

"Are you sure it wasn't the other way around?" said Paul chuckling.

"Well really. No wonder young girls fall by the wayside," said Maureen, unable to stop herself giggling.

Paul took a long gulp of tea and said, "Let's just snuggle up and enjoy being together. I no longer care what's going on in the world. I just want to be here with you."

"We had better finish our tea before it get's cold," said Maureen, climbing over Paul to get to her cup.

Paul ran his hands over her breasts and thighs as she stretched away from him.

Maureen shivered slightly as his gentle touch excited her. She sipped her tea, as his hands explored her breasts. "You always were a rover, weren't you Paul?"

"A rover?"

"You always had roving hands."

"Didn't you like it then?"

"A gentleman is not supposed to ask that of a lady you know."

"Go on, tell me. Did you like it?"

"Well, you were a bit clumsy in those days, weren't you?"

"Yes, I suppose I was. Well, you've got to learn somewhere."

"I don't know if I like the sound of that."

"Why?"

"It sounds as if you were just practising on me."

"Oh, I did know a few girls before I met you, you know."

"Oh, did you now? You shouldn't have been so clumsy then."

"Come and lie down for a while, and forgive me," said Paul, giving Maureen a quick peck on her lips.

"I don't know if I will," said Maureen straddling Paul, grabbing his wrists, then bearing down on him.

Paul felt the need for Maureen stir within him, and Maureen almost involuntarily responded to him. Their urgency already sated, they made love in a more leisurely fashion. As Maureen released her grip on his wrists he held her, kissing and caressing her all the while. She eventually slumped down beside him exhausted.

"Now look what you've done to me. We'll need another shower now," she moaned.

"Just relax my darling and enjoy the moment," said Paul, putting his arms around her.

"I thought I had lost you again, you know," said Paul quietly.

There was a pause until Maureen said, "I was undecided until I could see that you would risk everything for me…maybe even your life." She sobbed silently, "I knew I could not leave you, then I knew that I did not want to leave you. It was as if…a veil had been lifted off me. The guilt of a broken marriage and… other things…fell away. I knew I needed you as much as you needed me. I could see it would be stupid not to give things a second chance. Sitting there in the car alone, I suddenly remembered how I felt at our parting all those years ago. Now we had a chance to…really consummate those feelings and I had not the courage, nor the common sense, to grasp the challenge with both hands."

Paul gave her another hug and said, "I'm so glad you changed your mind. I don't know what I would have done if you had not come back. I just know I would have been devastated – maybe more than the first time we parted."

Tears had formed in his eyes at the painful memory.

Maureen felt them as they met her cheek, and leaned back to wipe them gently with her fingers.

"It's all behind us now, my love," she whispered.

They lay quiet for a while until Paul said, "Are you still hungry?"

"Well, I'm not exactly ravenous. What time is it?"

"It's just gone nine," said Paul, looking at his watch.

"It's a bit late to have dinner brought up here now, we had better dress and go down for something. We can have a drink or two as well," said Maureen getting up.

"Well I suppose so, I don't want to leave this little room now somehow," said Paul sadly.

"Come on silly. There will be other times you know," said Maureen smiling.

Paul embraced Maureen in a bear hug, "Do you know how happy I am?"

"Oh I think I can guess. You're like the cat who got the cream," she said, still smiling.

"No, that's you," he said, teasing her for a change.

She slapped him hard on his buttocks again.

"You are taking liberties young man."

"But aren't you glad?" said Paul kissing her neck.

"This won't do. I'm going to wash all that sweat off me and get ready for dinner," said Maureen, stepping into the shower again.

"It's going to be from one extreme to the other for me. I have spent a greater part of the day unwashed and unshaven. Now I've bathed in salt water and will have showered twice in the space of a couple of hours," said Paul.

"Are you boasting or what?" shouted Maureen. "Hey! Are we going to dress up for dinner?" she added.

"No. I really didn't come prepared for any sort of nightlife. Just wear what you've got in here."

"OK. You can come in the shower now, I've finished," said Maureen stepping out.

Paul stepped under the showerhead and let the hot water and shower gel cleanse him.

When they were both ready to go down, Paul said, "Do you want a drink at the bar first, or just sit down at a table and have a drink there, while waiting for the meal."

"Oh, it would be nice to be quiet tonight. Let's find a table on our own and just relax," said Maureen looking tired but happy.

They went downstairs and into the dinning room. Some of the things on the menu were finished, but they both settled for Beef stroganoff. Maureen had a gin and tonic and Paul thought he would have a brandy and ginger ale.

"No beer tonight then?" said Maureen.

"I usually have a brandy and ginger ale when I am flying out on my holidays somewhere. I feel as if I'm flying tonight somehow," said Paul smiling across at Maureen.

"Steady now," said Maureen sipping her drink and looking at Paul enigmatically over the top of her glass.

"I feel like as if I've been flying ever since I met you again," said Paul, reaching out and clasping her hand.

"Are you sure you don't say that to all the girls?" said Maureen, squeezing Paul's hand.

"I think you are enough for me to handle," said Paul.

Their meal arrived and Paul ordered the wine suggested by the waiter. They finished one bottle and started another. By the time the pudding had been consumed both Maureen and Paul were pretty inebriated. Paul tipped the waiter more generously than he would have done if he had been sober.

As they left the dining room, but before going up stairs, Maureen had the slightly embarrassing task of rebooking her room with the hotel clerk, but no comments were passed. They went up stairs and Paul was sober enough to say to Maureen,

"Will you sleep in my room tonight darling?"

"Do you snore, Paul?"

"Only when I'm on my back."

"Well, you're not lying on top of me all night," she whispered.

"Spoil sport."

They reached the landing, Maureen saying, "I'll just get my things from the car and take them to my room. See you in a while.

Paul entered his room and went to clean his teeth. He looked up at the reflection in the mirror. Was it all a dream? How could he feel so happy? The door clicked open and Maureen's face appeared as she came to look at his reflection.

"Hi, handsome!" she said her eyelids droopy with the wine.

"Hi, gorgeous!" said Paul, drying his mouth on a towel, and giving Maureen a kiss on her cheek.

By now Maureen had lost all her inhibitions, but she still felt the need to control the situation. Something inside her psyche would not let her be dominated by men any more. She had had enough of that from her previous experiences. As well as this, she felt the need to be loved, and she thought Paul might be the man to fulfil her needs and fill that place. Maureen threw herself on the bed, kicking off her shoes. Paul looked down at her and smiled.

"Gosh, I feel so relaxed. Do you think it was a good idea ordering that second bottle of wine?" said Maureen, letting her eyes close for a moment.

"Not if you are going to sleep my darling," said Paul, kneeling down beside the bed and stroking the nape of her neck with the tips of his fingers, exploring her cheek, her lips, and the lobes of her ears.

Maureen left her eyes closed but then said, "Do you remember the socials we used to have in your Sunday School hall?"

"Oh yes. That's where I learned to like kissing girls, before I met you," said Paul sighing.

"What's that big sigh for?"

"Oh, I don't know. I was just thinking how painful growing

257

up was. All that yearning and wanting fulfilment, but unable, through social pressures, to do just that."

"That's a bit deep for this time of night. Especially after a couple bottles of wine."

"One bottle of wine, you had the other one," said Paul, lying down beside Maureen.

Maureen felt for Paul's wrist and slapped it.

"What's all this about social pressures anyhow?"

"Well, I expect your mum warned you about the opposite sex more than my mum did me."

"Oh that."

"Well, it was a big thing in those days wasn't it? I expect you can remember the odd girl who got herself into 'trouble', and what a scandal that caused, can't you?"

"Ye…es, I suppose so."

"That's what I mean. The dire consequences of un-adulterated lust," said Paul, tongue in cheek.

"What about adulterated lust then?"

"We have never had that, I'm glad to say," said Paul putting his arm around Maureen's waist.

"I have never taken another man's wife, and I hope I never will."

"Shouldn't you say, 'I know I never will'?" queried Maureen.

"It's all very well to say these things, but we can never be sure about the future."

"Well, that's a fine thing. You mean if you and I got married, I could not guarantee that you might not come running home one night and tell me that you had been having it off with someone?"

"You're teasing me Maureen. You always were a tease," said Paul, kissing her cheek and the back of her neck.

"It's no good you sucking up to me now, you two-timer," said Maureen, her eyes still closed, but enjoying the attention just the same.

"I don't think I would make a good adulterer any way. How can you hide those sort of things from some one you love?" he said.

"A lot of people don't bother nowadays."

"That's horrible. There's no point in being together then, is there?" said Paul.

"I don't think so, but maybe I'm not typical," said Maureen raising an eyebrow.

"I still think there are a lot of people like us. Well, a majority of people like us, who remain faithful to their partners."

"You think so?"

"Yes. We may not be perfect, but we have certain standards we try to keep up."

"You speak for yourself, when you talk about not being perfect, OK," she teased.

"Technically we've committed fornication together, you know that?"

Maureen's eyes opened and she said, "No, I don't like that word, fornication."

"No, I don't either, but it's supposed to be the case, when two unmarried people make love."

"I like to think that when two people make love, they are already married in the eyes of God."

"That's a beautiful way of putting it my love," said Paul, giving Maureen a hug.

"Going back to what I was saying before we got side-tracked," said Paul.

"What was that? I've forgotten."

"Er, about a girl getting herself into trouble."

"Oh that again."

"Yes. Well I was thinking how society makes it difficult for people of all ages to have meaningful relationships without feeling guilt."

"I don't feel guilty about anything."

"I don't, when I'm with you. Even if it has only been a few hours. I was just wondering what some of my Christian friends would think, if they knew I was..."

"A randy fornicator, you mean?" said Maureen giggling, but keeping her eyes closed.

"I suppose so," said Paul sighing. "I feel I don't want to deceive anyone, but yet I can't be truly honest about everything."

"Who is truly honest about everything? You are not supposed to be baring your soul all the time are you?" said Maureen quickly. "Do you think your friends are truly honest about everything? Even pastors themselves. They are not likely to get up in the pulpit and confess that they looked at a pretty girl walking down the street and committed adultery in the eyes of God, are they? Some of them have done a damn sight worse than that, haven't they? You only have to read the papers to find that out," said Maureen, now a bit worked up by the wine.

"That's true. As I said before, no one is perfect, but we shouldn't judge others," said Paul, trying to calm Maureen down a bit.

"Sometimes you have to grab at a chance when it comes," said Maureen, still petulant.

"Are you referring to me or somebody else? Something that happened in the past?"

"Someone else, in the past, you arrogant so and so," said Maureen, slapping Paul's wrist again.

"When my marriage was going down hill I met this man I fancied, and we had an affair. I don't want to talk about it much now, but it was exciting, and an opportunity I felt I couldn't miss at that time. I found out later that I didn't want to be with him forever, but life is like that sometimes. You win some, you lose some. That's it basically. Maybe I was unlucky."

"I'm sorry that things didn't work out for you, even if I am benefiting now, so to speak," said Paul quietly, snuggling up against Maureen and nibbling her ear.

"Are you still hungry or something?" Maureen teased.

"I'm hungry for love, I suppose."

"Well have you finished all that stuff about un-consummated love when we were young? You were talking about that when we first met. Are you obsessed by it or something?"

"I feel quite strongly that society sidestepped the issues in the past and still does today."

"How do you mean?"

"Well, in the past we were supposed to curb our sexual feelings because one of the consequences in those days would have been teenage pregnancies."

"Nowadays, the social services are encouraging birth control."

"It's a debatable issue though, isn't it. There are still a lot of people, especially the churches, that are against it."

"You are not telling me that you are against it are you, you hypocrite?" teased Maureen.

"It's a difficult subject that you cannot say yes or no to," said Paul seriously.

"Aren't you side stepping the issue?"

"What I was going to say is that I believe that young people should be committed to each other, until they find out if they are compatible or not. If they are going to have sexual relationships, and indulge in sex with many partners without a caring relationship, then they are asking for trouble, aren't they?"

"So you encourage teenagers to use birth control methods?"

"Yes, from a certain age."

"What age limits would you state?"

"I think it depends on how mature the young people are. The parents of children under sixteen should have some say as to whether they indulge in sex. It's not really practical to make laws to stop under-age children from having sex. So far as parents go it's always been a matter of trust between them and their children."

"Your parents wouldn't have liked you having intercourse with me when we were young would they?"

"No. Neither would your parents I imagine."

"My father would have killed me. Mother wouldn't have been very pleased either."

"I'm not so sure that times are any better. Sex is no longer a mystery for young people, but the times we live in put pressure on them to do things they sometimes don't want. Then it becomes something ugly. Perhaps that's one of the guiding factors. If intercourse is a beautiful experience with tenderness and love, then it's all right. If it's ugly, then it's wrong," said Paul simply.

"My, we are philosophical tonight. So you think you have answered my question about sidestepping the issue?" said Maureen, tongue in cheek.

"What do you think then?" said Paul, squeezing Maureen's

hand.

"You are saying that we, as a society, should encourage stable relationships between young people. Are not some parents worried that their children will get too serious with their partners?" Maureen asked.

"Yes, some are, no doubt. I think that they are mistaken to be worried about that, and ought to encourage any relationship if they think that the opposite partner is a good influence on their child. I suppose the trouble is that very often the parents are not very mature people themselves."

"Right, professor!" teased Maureen.

"Am I allowed off the platform now?" said Paul smugly.

"If I don't, you might bore the pants off me."

"Does that mean you want me to take your pants off another way?"

"No, it doesn't. I am going to play a variation on one of the games we used to play at the socials. Well, it's going to be a cross between two of the games we used to play actually," said Maureen, opening her eyes and getting up from the bed.

"Now then, I'm looking for something to blindfold you with. Ah yes, one of your handkerchiefs."

Maureen picked up the handkerchief and bound Paul's eyes, tying a tight knot at the back of his head.

"Right, you be patient a minute and sit still on the end of the bed."

Paul did as he was told in obedience to Maureen's wishes and felt somewhat excited at what she might do.

Maureen felt the intoxication wearing off and couldn't make up her mind whether she preferred to be sober or a little bit high. She saw a glass of Vermouth that had not been finished on the table and took a long draught from it, emptying it, before she tiptoed to the other side of the room. Then she stripped off all her clothes as quickly as she could. She tiptoed back to where Paul was patiently waiting.

"Now Paul, I want you to bow to the wittiest, kneel to the prettiest and kiss the one you love best."

Paul smiled, "I haven't heard that for about thirty years," he said.

Now it was Maureen's turn to wait patiently as Paul rose from the bed, his blindfold still in place.

Maureen stepped back apace as Paul dutifully bowed, and then put one knee on the floor. Maureen came closer to him.

Paul reached out with one hand to feel for her, and touched the back of her calf. He brought his other hand round to touch the other calf. His hands moved slowly upwards as he gently caressed the outside of Maureen's thighs.

He was going to say something but he decided not to break the spell. The smile that played about his open lips gradually left him; Maureen looked down on him, feeling the urgent need of him. Paul traced his fingers to the top of her hips and then clasping both hands firmly on her hips gently kissed the offering in front of him. Maureen shivered and put her hands gently around the back of Paul's head. Paul continued to worship Maureen's body and to satisfy her need.

After a while she whispered, "Sit down on the bed, Paul."

She helped him to lower himself backwards and then lifted his feet and pulled his shoes off throwing them on the floor.

Maureen then pulled his socks off, going next to un-button his shirt, pulled it away behind him, sleeves turning inside out. Finally she undid the buckle in his belt and unzipped the trousers. She pulled on the legs of the trousers until they slid off his rump and landed on the floor.

Maureen slid the underpants down Paul's legs, with his help, and he lay naked on the bed except for a blindfold. She then lay down beside him and gently massaged his body, attended his excitement with a long loving kiss. Her tongue seeking out the places that rejoiced in their expectations of erotic promise. Maureen straddled Paul and used her deeper passion to ride the heights of arousal that needed the final quenching of her love ardour.

When it was finished, she lay beside him and took off the blindfold.

He blinked and said, "I think I must have died and gone to heaven."

"You and me both," murmured Maureen, putting an arm across Paul's chest.

CHAPTER TWENTY FIVE

They slept soundly that night, until Paul was awakened by the cry of gulls. Momentarily he wondered where he was, being used to his own familiar bed. He rolled over and saw Maureen lying next to him, and a warm feeling flowed over him. He took in her naked body and caressed her breasts softly, to reassure himself that he was not dreaming or imagining things. She stirred faintly, but he did not waken her. He looked at his travelling clock and saw that it was nearly seven-thirty.

He got up quietly and looked out of the window. The weather looked pretty good. A few clouds, but no sign of rain. He showered and then started to shave.

"Hey! Paul! What are you doing?" cried Maureen from the bed.

"Hi, Maureen, how are you this morning?"

"I'm OK. Why are you up so early? I wondered what that hissing noise was when you were in the shower," she scolded.

"I'm sorry I woke you. I was trying to be quiet too. I'm just finishing shaving. Be there in a tick," said Paul, rinsing his face in cold water. Paul came out of the bathroom to find Maureen sitting up on the end of the bed.

"You haven't answered my question. Why are you up so early?"

"We have to be up early if we are going for our walk through the copse today, don't we?"

"Do you mean that you think the copse is more important to you than me?"

"We did plan to go for a little expedition yesterday, didn't we?"

"That was before…we got to know each other better," said Maureen with a hint of a sulk.

Paul came across to Maureen and lay down beside her on the bed.

"We have got plenty of time together, but we had just as well enjoy the sunshine while we can."

"Oh you are so maddening Paul, with your practicality!"

"We can always stop somewhere and have a snogging session, like we used to. Apart from that, I have got to make a couple of phone calls back home, to say that I shall be... uh, detained for a few days," said Paul smiling at Maureen.

"Is that detained at Her Majesty's pleasure?" giggled Maureen.

"Yes, I suppose so," laughed Paul.

"Right. We had better have an early breakfast and then we can pick up a pasty or something in the shops," he said.

"We might be a little early for breakfast. I don't think they start serving until eight," said Maureen trying to delay Paul.

"If it's too early, we can see if the shops are open, and do our bit of shopping before breakfast."

"There aren't so many shops about, as there used to be. I suppose a lot of people go to the out-of-town supermarkets," said Maureen, with a trace of sadness in her voice.

"Yes, times change. Some people say you should never go back to the old places, but I'm glad I did," said Paul, grinning at Maureen.

"You are soft soaping me again, young man, because you are trying to get me out of bed. It was only a few hours ago you wanted to get me into it. Huh, times change all right."

"I'll pop downstairs when I'm properly dressed and see if we can have an early breakfast, OK?" asked Paul, trying to hurry things along.

"All right, I can take a hint. I'm getting up now," said Maureen climbing out of bed.

"I'm supposed to be on holiday you know," she said, as he went around the bed to grab her and pull her close to him.

"I'm very glad you are on holiday my darling, and I hope we will spend a lot of holidays together. Maybe go abroad somewhere in the sun."

"You can make me warm, you know Paul. I think you are pleased to see me this morning," she teased.

"I shall be pleased to see you every morning, but we can't

spend a whole week in this room, can we?"

"Spoil sport," said Maureen, making her way to the shower.

Paul dressed quickly and shot down the stairs. He rang the bell and a young girl came into the foyer.

"Do you think it would be possible to have breakfast for two in about half an hour please?"

"Certainly sir. I can start laying the table now for you, if you like. You can have cereal, and I shall bring in a pot of tea as soon as it is ready," said the young girl helpfully.

"That's very good of you. I was wondering if there are any shops handy to get pasties or sandwiches to take away for a picnic?" said Paul.

"I could make some sandwiches for you if you like, sir. How about cheese salad, or egg salad? I could do ham or tuna salad?" said the young girl, her large expressive brown eyes seeming to move around in her plump round face.

"Well that is really kind of you. Could we have one of each, four in all, and put it on the bill?"

"Certainly sir. I'll do them whilst you're having breakfast."

Paul thought it a stroke of luck. Problem solved right away. Maureen was still in the shower when Paul entered the room again.

"We can start breakfast when you're ready, and guess what? The young girl is going to make up some sandwiches for us to take," said Paul, pleased with himself.

"That sounds great," said Maureen, the shower livening her up and leaving her tingling.

She came out into the room and Paul wondered at the lost years as he looked into her face, matured by time but still girlish and feminine. Her short, dark, curly hair swept back, still damp, and shining in the light.

"So you're just waiting for me then?" she said.

"I'll start getting things together. You haven't got a haversack have you?"

"Yes, I have, in my room. Here's the key. It's in the top of the wardrobe."

"Great, I'll go in and get it," said Paul, catching the key and striding out again.

Maureen decided to put on a skirt and blouse, so she shouted to Paul. "Leave the door open Paul, I've got to get some clothes." Maureen wrapped a towel around herself and shot into the passage. She met Paul coming out of her room with the haversack.

"I won't be long," she said, giggling as she passed Paul.

Paul started to pack all the things that he thought they might need, carefully placing them in the haversack.

A few minutes later Maureen came into the room, wearing a white blouse and a pleated navy skirt. Paul looked at her; he felt an excitement within him that compared with the first time he had seen Maureen, with a basket in her hand, wearing similar clothes to that which she was wearing now.

She put a few things in the haversack, clipped up the straps and threw the haversack to Paul, who caught it neatly.

"Are you ready then?" said Maureen brightly.

"Yes, ready and willing," said Paul smiling.

"Ready and willing for what?" teased Maureen, as they left the room and went down the stairs.

They ate their breakfast quietly, looking at each other and marvelling that the passing of time had not diminished the intense feelings that they had originally felt for each other. Paul collected the sandwiches, a carton of orange juice, and two plastic cups from the kitchen, and they set off.

They walked along the quayside hand-in-hand, looking at the boats and across the water to Instow, which had not seemed to have changed. They walked past the dry docks with noises of hammering and metal cutting, but there was no longer the explosion of the riveters' pneumatic hammer, to sear the early morning's silence. When they came to the area that used to be a quarry, with the building known as Chanters Folly sitting precariously on the edge, they noticed that it was gone and the quarry was now used for storage purposes. Travelling towards the newer shipyard, where they had recently met, they skirted around the perimeter fence until they came out into fields, with a signpost stating directions. They noticed that the dyke, that stopped the river water from flooding into the meadowland, had been breached, turning the meadow into a salt marsh at high tide.

The tide had only recently turned and was low enough for them to clamber over the stepping stones, to clear them of the estuary mud and continue along the dyke path. They came across a property with it's own little beach, known as Boat-Hide. Here the path veered to the right, over the headland until, it came down in an inlet, with rotten hulks of wooden vessels, their working days spent now lodged in the mud.

Paul helped Maureen to step down onto the shingle, which gradually turned to mud, and guided her over stepping-stones until they came to the foot of the cliffside path. As they reached the top they came out of the wooded cliff path and saw a grassy bank on their right. This brought back memories of their teenage romance.

Paul felt a surge of emotion, and as the place was deserted he said, "Let's just sit here awhile," and moving off the main pathway walked up the grassy slope.

"Are you sure that's wise?" mocked Maureen, as she guessed what Paul was thinking

"It's too early for a picnic," she teased again, as they walked through the long grass.

"This looks like a nice spot," he said, pointing to the view of the river, and up to Bideford, where the irregular archways of the bridge were visible in the distance.

"A nice spot for what?" said Maureen trying to keep a straight face, but her lips twitched inadvertently, perceptible only to Paul, who was looking at her so closely, as his face came nearer to hers.

"A nice spot to make love to you," he said, kissing her on the mouth gently as his arms embraced her.

Maureen closed her eyes and imagined that she was a teenager again as their lips gently parted, with Paul's mouth slowly traversing around her lips full circle.

Paul gradually eased her blouse outside her skirt and ran his hands up her bare back to where her bra was clipped together. He quickly unclasped it and put his hands on the top straps, pulling them down off the shoulder. Putting his hands up the wide sleeves of her blouse he eased the straps off her elbows, over her wrist then, with one hand, gently tugged. The bra slithered over and out of the blouse sleeve.

Maureen murmured, "You've been practising, since you met me."

"You never used to wear a bra," he said.

"My mother thought I didn't need one."

"Well you did, and you didn't, if you know what I mean?"

"No I don't," said Maureen, her nipples starting to swell as Paul's fingers caressed her free breasts.

"You did need a bra for support, but you looked lovely without it," said Paul, pulling Maureen's skirt up and sliding her panties down.

"Look Paul, I haven't done this since we were young, outside in the open. There could be other people around," said Maureen nervously.

"I've never done it outside with anyone but you, but I'm finding it very exciting. There's not likely to be anyone who can see us, and they aren't going to see much if they do," said Paul grabbing Maureen's hand and pulling her down on the grass by him.

Maureen quickly slid the panties off her legs and slipped them into the side pocket of the haversack along with her bra.

"I wondered what those side pockets were for," laughed Paul.

Maureen came back to Paul, kneeling over him as he lay back in the grass, and pointed her finger at him in mock indignation.

"Look here Paul Baxter, you are taking a lot of things for granted, I must tell you."

"And I must tell you that you are looking lovely and that I want to kiss you again," said Paul, putting his arms around Maureen to bring her down to himself.

They kissed again, passionately this time. As Maureen straddled him, he caressed her breasts, and unzipping his flies, entered her; her skirt covered their nakedness. As their passions mounted, Paul rolled over on top of Maureen until they came to a climax. Paul kissed Maureen gently on her lips and on her closed eyelids and on the nape of her neck.

He lay beside her with an arm around her waist.

"It's almost like we've gone back in time, but with the bonus of being mature people, without the fears and uncertainties of youth," said Paul, slowly and softly.

"You're getting very philosophical again," said Maureen dreamily.

"I think philosophy is the spice of life," said Paul.

"Don't you mean variety is the spice of life," murmured Maureen.

"No, I'm a one woman man myself," said Paul, keeping a straight face.

"You trapped me into saying that you brute."

Maureen gave Paul a weak slap on his wrist. They were content to lay there in the warmth of the morning sun for a while, until Paul gave an audible sigh.

"What's that sigh for?" asked Maureen.

"I was thinking that we both live in different places so far apart, I don't want to go home without you," said Paul sadly.

"Why don't you come back with me? There's room in my flat for two. Well just about," said Maureen with optimism in her voice, but doubt in her mind that Paul would do that.

"Well, I've got to say that my work is where I live, but I know that is the same for you. I would be prepared to move to Scotland if that's what you really wanted though," said Paul, hoping that he could, in the clear light of another day, pack up everything he had got to know and accumulated; he would have to ditch most of it.

Maureen opened her eyes wide now and said, "Do you really mean that Paul?"

"Yes, if that was the only way I could be with you," he said, knowing in his heart it was the truth.

"What about your work and everything?" said Maureen, echoing his own thoughts. "What is your work now, and what did you tell them on the phone?" she asked.

Paul told her briefly what had happened to him after they had parted and that he was now living and working around Keswick in the Cumbrian Lakeside District, as a warden for the National Trust.

"There you are! I always said that was the sort of work you

were suited to, didn't I?" said Maureen triumphantly.

"That's right," he said grinning wryly. "And I have been quite happy doing it, even if the pay is nothing exciting. It is still worth a lot, to be doing the job you want to do. I suppose I could get work in Scotland if I tried hard enough," said Paul, outwardly confident, but not being able to imagine the totally different locality and lifestyle. "People are basically the same the world over," he said, trying to convince himself.

Maureen put her hand on Paul's,

"Maybe it would be better for me to uproot myself. You have got your daughters near you I expect. I haven't got any near relatives now. Let's not talk about all these things though, let's just enjoy these few days and take one day at a time, as the song goes," said Maureen sighing.

"Yes. You're right. Shall we move on to King Alfred's Cave then, my love?" said Paul, getting to his feet and pulling Maureen up.

"Oh you're a bully you are. I was enjoying lying there in the sunshine relaxing," complained Maureen.

Paul smiled and said, "Sorry if I'm a slave driver."

Then he picked up the haversack and slung it over his shoulders.

"Hang on a minute. I've got some thing rather important in the side pocket if you remember."

Maureen pulled out her bra and panties, then had to unbutton her blouse to put the brassiere on. Paul waited until Maureen had pulled her panties up.

"Right, we're all set then," said Paul striding out as if he was an explorer.

"You men. You're all the same. When you've had what you want, you desert us," moaned Maureen, struggling to catch up with Paul.

Paul looked back and held out his hand.

"I'm sorry. It was a bit awkward for two together back there, but now we are on a broader path we can hold hands again. Women enjoy touch more than men I suppose."

"So you don't then?" teased Maureen.

"Oh! You know I do. Perhaps more than most men though.

I don't know why."

"Do you think you are more sensitive than most men?"

"I don't know. There are some things I regret not doing before my wife died."

"Like what?"

"Little things. Maybe I should have told her I loved her more often than I did."

"It's easy to be critical in hindsight. Even of yourself."

"That's true. We all make mistakes. Sometimes we learn by them, and sometimes we don't," he said sadly.

"Did you have a happy marriage on the whole?"

"Yes. We had our ups and downs like most people, but we never seriously thought of breaking up. I should think that breaking up can be a worse form of bereavement than your partner dying."

"Yes, when your marriage breaks down, you know that your partner is still out there somewhere. There are all sorts of guilts and niggling doubts, and your mind seems to be unable to let go," said Maureen uneasily.

"Well, you have the same sort of feelings when someone dies. Death is more final, but there are still feelings of guilt and sorrow, even if you have happy memories," said Paul reflectively.

"Maybe you don't have the bitterness though."

"No, I don't think I have any bitterness. Although I suppose I wonder why she was taken before her time. But I'm not the only one in that respect am I?"

"No. It can't be easy though, when you lose someone you love, whether it's ten years or fifty years since you met."

"There are different ways of looking at it I suppose. If you lose a partner when comparatively young, you can find another, there's still time. If you lose a partner when you're old, then some people break their hearts and just fade away."

"My aren't we getting morbid. Let's change the subject."

"Not far to King Alfred's Cave now. Ah yes, there's the ancient oak that marks the path. We turn down there."

Paul pointed ahead and to his left. They left the main track to wend their way through the trees and shrubs, which grew up to the cliff edge and the little gully that led into the cave. The cave was little more than a cliff overhang now. Whether due to vandalism by youths hacking away with improvised tools, or just erosion, Paul could not be sure.

"Well, here it is, but it looks different somehow," said Paul disappointedly.

"It is only a cave, part of a legend, or a myth," said Maureen.

"You mean about where Alfred's men lay in wait for King Hubba the Dane and his Viking warriors? I'll have you know, young lady, that it is well documented that King Hubba the Dane was slain at Bloody Corner not far inland from here. The Vikings came up the river in their longboats and were defeated by Alfred's Saxon warriors."

"Well I think this cave is too small to take enough men to ambush a Viking war party," said Maureen petulantly.

"Don't you pout, young lady."

"Oh, I like the young lady bit!"

"You're as young as you feel, so they say," said Paul, giving Maureen a big kiss on her lips.

"I think I have lost a few years in the past day or two," smiled Maureen happily.

"Yes. I think I have too. I feel I have got something to live for again."

"Oh Paul, I've got something important to say."

"What's that my love?" said Paul, looking at Maureen in expectation.

"Do you think it's time to have our picnic?"

"You tease. You had me going again, didn't you?"

"Who me? Little old me?"

"Yes, this is as good a place as any."

They put their lightweight anoraks across the ledge overlooking the river and sat to eat their lunch. They watched the tide as it surged upstream to Bideford. Little wading birds hurried to get their pickings in the mud, before the tide covered their fare and they had to huddle together in groups, for comfort and safety, above the tide line of drifted seaweed and flotsom.

Paul was still on a high and wolfed his sandwiches down

with relish. He had not been so happy for years and felt that he had been rejuvenated. His confidence had been restored and his outlook on life completely altered. He felt he could work things out for the future now. What he felt was much the same as when he had met Maureen all those years ago. Paul saw a heron standing motionless on a mud flat at the edge of the water. 'I'm like that heron, optimistic', he thought, as he compared the heron's confidence that his patience would be rewarded with a tasty morsel, with his own future, and the promise of a new partnership.

Maureen felt content to be there. It was good to be with someone who needed her, and cared for her. She thought she knew Paul well enough to trust him, and that he meant what he said about being together. He had not mentioned that magic word yet, 'marriage'. Although she could hardly expect him to do that in the short space of time they had now been together. Surely this was not just infatuation? A sort of fantasy, just a dream he was reliving. That thought sent a shiver down her spine. What if after a few days, he just thought that he had sampled enough of a middle-aged woman, and when he returned home, would send her a note saying that there were complications and it would be better if they cooled off for a while. She knew she could not bear another let down in her life. She also felt that she would never get a chance like this again. Maureen put her arm around Paul's waist and said, "A penny for your thoughts, Paul."

Paul cuddled her back, and kissed her cheek and said, "I reckon I'm the happiest man between Appledore and Bideford."

"Huh! There are not many men on this route between Appledore and Bideford that I've seen," she said in her now customary teasing manner.

"Perhaps it's a good job there aren't. I wouldn't want to lose you to some charmer or other."

"What other?"

"There might be somebody stalking these woods, with intent to kidnap some young woman and keep her in a room somewhere and have his willing way."

"Isn't that just about what you did with me?"

Paul laughed huskily and said, "You always enjoyed a bit of fun and a joke, but you have a really sharp sense of humour now."

Maureen smiled, but thought that she had needed to see the funny side of life for a long, long, time.

Paul's face became serious as he said, "I'd really like you to come and join me at my house when you can settle things in Scotland. I could make some enquiries about a vacancy for secretarial work, if you let me know some details."

Music to my ears thought Maureen as she realised that Paul was travelling along her thought patterns for the future.

"Would it be all right to move in after a short space of time?" she asked.

"Why not? I'll try to get tidied up, and maybe do some decorating. There's plenty of rooms you know. Ah! I know what you're thinking, the fact we are not man and wife. Would you like me to marry you before you move in?"

Maureen stopped eating and swallowed the last bite, nearly choking on it.

"Are you proposing to me?" she spluttered, and then had a short fit of coughing.

"Well, yes. I'm sorry I haven't made it seem very romantic. I suppose it's because things have happened so quickly that I haven't had the right opportunity up to now. Will you marry me Maureen?"

Maureen looked at Paul, who had stopped eating now, but looked awkward with a half-eaten sandwich in his hand.

"You had better finish that sandwich off while I make up my mind," said Maureen smiling. Paul did as he was told.

"Well?" he said trying to sound confident.

"That's what you really want then, marriage?"

"Yes. I think it's what I wanted the first time I saw you again, but I couldn't very well say so, could I, Maureen?"

"Perhaps not. You don't want to think it over for a while. To weigh up the pros and cons so to speak?"

"No, not really, do you? I don't want to rush you into anything. Maybe I'm not being fair to you."

"I was just wondering where we would be married."

"But you haven't said you will marry me," said Paul, getting slightly exasperated now.

"If I say yes, do you promise me you won't run off with a teenager, because you found out that I wasn't a teenager anymore?" Maureen looked at Paul with a serious expression on her face. Paul could not be sure whether she really meant it or not.

"I promise," he said simply.

"Then I will marry you," said Maureen softly.

"Oh my darling," said Paul. He brought Maureen into his arms, and they hugged each other as tears started to flow on both sides.

"Hell, I'm feeling dry, shedding all those tears. I'm thirsty now. Let's break out the orange juice and celebrate," said Paul, getting out the carton of orange juice and two paper cups.

"I feel like I have washed away all my pain and sorrow in those tears. Here's to a new tomorrow, Paul," said Maureen, touching her paper cup against Paul's.

"To a new tomorrow," echoed Paul.

They linked through each other's arms as they raised the cups to their mouths in unison, and both started to giggle when they found it difficult to drink that way.

"You never answered my question you know, Paul."

"What question?"

"About where we would get married."

Paul sipped his orange juice thoughtfully and said, "Why don't we get married down here? We could probably arrange a Register Office marriage in Bideford, and then have a proper church wedding anytime when it was convenient!"

"Your family are going to be pretty surprised to know that you are getting married. Do they know that you are down here?" asked Maureen.

"I rang Sarah, my eldest daughter, and told her I was staying here a few days as I had met an old friend, but I didn't tell her any details. No more than the reason I came down here, which was the truth."

"You didn't say you were with a mystery woman then?"

"Nope. Of course I shall tell them everything, well not

everything, later on, but I think it would be nice to have a surprise for them, and my friends. They don't look on me as being an exciting person."

"They don't know you as I know you then."

"No, they wouldn't though would they?" smiled Paul.

"A Register Office wedding eh? Maybe it makes sense, and if you make a respectable woman out of me, that part will be behind us. No need for either of us to feel embarrassed about living in sin."

"That's right. Well, my daughters were brought up conventionally, as you can imagine. I think they would find it embarrassing if we did live in sin."

"They are going to be really taken aback when you tell them."

"Yes, it's going to be difficult for them to understand. I shall tell them the truth of the matter."

"What's that then?"

"That I met you, an old friend…"

"Watch it with that 'old friend' business, I'm not that old."

"…and how we picked up where we left off."

"I think they are going to find that hard to believe."

"Maybe you're right. I will have to tell them the true facts. Anything else would make matters worse."

"How are they going to take me as their new mother?"

"They are pretty mature in outlook. I don't think there will be any problems. We have to live our own lives. They must appreciate that."

"Won't they feel upset if we don't tell them we are married until after the Register Office ceremony?"

"Well I hope not, if we are going to have a Church wedding later on. I thought it would be a bit awkward for them to come down here at such short notice. They would feel pressurised to make the effort. I think it is better for all of us if we go ahead and get married first, tell them later."

"Well your ears are going to be buzzing before long. Everyone is going to be talking about you – and me. I'm forgetting me. I can imagine your daughters getting together and talking about us though."

"Yes," said Paul giving a little laugh, and imagining the same scene in his mind. "They'll get used to it," he said.

"What about your friends. What are they going to say?" asked Paul, feeling guilty that he had been more concerned about his own family and friends.

"I think they will be very pleased for me. They know I have had some bad luck, though they will be surprised," she smiled.

"That settles it then. A Register Office wedding, followed by a church wedding. Right, come on! We might be able to catch the Registrar. You never know, he might be able to marry us on the spot."

"You have got to be joking young man. Hang on, I want another drink. All this talk about weddings has made me nervous," said Maureen reaching for the orange juice and her cup.

"We could do with something stronger than orange juice. Did I see you pack my little flask of brandy?" asked Paul hopefully.

"Now you're talking," said Maureen, suddenly remembering and pulling out the flask from the side pocket.

She poured the brandy into the paper cups, "A toast to the blushing bride."

"The blushing bride," echoed Paul, laughing.

They packed their things back into the haversack and made their way back onto the main path. Soon the wooded part of the walk was behind them and they passed into the inhabited area, with secluded cottages. The path broadened out into a road and they were able to walk hand in hand in the sunshine. They passed close to a dried up pond where Paul remembered taking black and white photos of ducks swimming, now the mud lay baking in the dry, late summer heat.

There were a lot of new properties, some still being worked on. The road led to the embankment and past the park. They continued on towards the quay proper.

Paul, pointing to the pavement separating the main road from the road adjacent to the river, said, "I remember catching the school bus to go home, from the pavement opposite the boats there."

"Look Paul, there's a boat getting ready to sail by the look of it. I wonder where it is going?" said Maureen, watching some tourists on board. They were lining the rails looking at the crewman by a capstan.

As they walked alongside the boat, *MS Oldenburg*, they could see that it was going to Lundy Island. Smoke was coming out of the funnel as the sound of the engine idled away, in preparation for the imminent departure.

"Oh Paul, how about us having a trip to Lundy?"

"Well, we will have to be quick about this. They are just about ready to sail," said Paul, noticing a couple of crewmen approaching the gangway.

"Is there a chance we could join you on this trip?" Paul asked one of the men, who looked at Paul, startled.

"Why yes. We were just about to take up the gangway, but if you hurry we'll hang on while you see the man in the little office there," he said pointing.

"Thanks," said Paul as he grabbed Maureen's hand. "Come on, we'll get our tickets."

The fellow in the kiosk looked up from his desk as Paul said, "We'd like two return tickets to Lundy please."

"We are not coming back to Bideford tonight, sir. We are staying overnight on the Island on this particular trip. You will need to pay in advance for overnight accommodation. Here's the list of prices," he said handing a brochure to Paul.

Paul looked quickly through the brochure with Maureen at his side, and then turned to her.

"What do you think Maureen?"

"Why not?" shrugged Maureen.

"We didn't really come prepared for this, but we would like to do the trip, so I'll pay for everything," said Paul reaching for his 'plastic' money.

"Well you won't need too much, everything is provided for," said the salesman cheerfully, and showed Paul the list of available accommodation with the photos to match.

Paul quickly settled up and they dashed across to the ship and up the gangway. The crewmen grinned good naturally at the unexpected delay. Paul and Maureen found places at the rear of the boat.

"I'm afraid all the best seats have been taken already," said Paul, shrugging his shoulders.

"Oh, I don't mind. We've got a seat, and there will be a chance to get in the bar if it gets a little chilly. The sea should be pretty calm. So it's goodbye Bideford and hello Lundy," said Maureen, spreading her arms as if to embrace the Island and nearly pushing a young fellow off his seat. Maureen apologised, laughing, as the mooring ropes were untethered and the ship set sail.

Paul pointed to some of the places they had passed on the way up to Bideford. They looked for the cave and thought they recognised a recess in the top of the cliff. The vessel chugged steadily downstream against the tide, and soon they were passing the huge sheds of Appledore Ship Builders with the *Saxon Warrior* moored up awaiting trials and finishing touches. The dockyard seemed strangely silent as if in salute to the ferryboat passing by. Looking in the other direction, across to Instow, memories stirred in Paul of the father and son plying their ferryboat. The old man with his mahogany coloured, hewn face, the huge jaw and slit for a mouth, prised apart with a pipe. His brilliant blue eyes squinting against the sun and his white and navy cap on the back of his white-haired head. Paul imagined the son to be exactly the same now, forty years on. He hoped so anyhow. It was comforting to be able to rely on some things remaining the same, but they rarely did.

Maureen followed Paul's gaze and said, "Remember when we got the ferryboat across to Instow, with Auntie a couple of days before I had to go home, Paul?"

"I remember," said Paul smiling ruefully. "I couldn't bear to think you would be going away without me."

Maureen put her arms around Paul's shoulder and snuggled against him.

"I'm sorry I didn't keep up the correspondence. I wrote much later but you must have moved, like I did. You've got a funny look on your face now. What are you thinking about Paul?"

"It's a strange thing, but I have just remembered something my mother said, shortly after you went away. We saw a pair of swans flying up the river and one veered off, leaving the other one, presumably it's mate, and flew around in a strange circular detour before rejoining it's mate up river. My mother then said, "Those swans remind me of you and Maureen. Perhaps you will see each other again one day."

"I didn't really believe her at the time, but it looks like she was right after all."

Paul smiled, although Maureen could see the tears forming in his eyes.

"A pair of swans? Hm., swans represent something; regal, haughty and grand don't they? I see us more like…why of course!" Maureen paused as she held up her left hand and looked at the ring on her finger. Paul's face lit up with surprised recognition.

"It's the ring with the two dolphins entwined on it. The ring I bought for you in Clovelly. You've still got it. That's great," he said beaming.

Maureen smiled delightedly in the same cheeky way that Paul remembered from the time they first met.

"You mean you see us as a pair of dolphins?" he said, laughing.

"Yes. Well, we were never graceful like swans, but we were more…" She paused, then lowered her voice so that the people around them would not hear, "playful – if you know what I mean."

Then Maureen had an embarrassed fit of giggles that entreated Paul to clasp the hand with the ring, squeezing the fingers.

"Yes. We were always more playful as I remember," he murmured, kissing her cheek tenderly.

"After all, swans mate for life, don't they? We didn't have the chance to do that," said Maureen, with a look of sadness and hurt in the moist brown eyes, that made Paul gasp involuntarily.

"No my love. Perhaps we can make up for lost time though. There should be plenty of time to – swim together – and play like the dolphins."

He smiled to himself with a warm feeling of optimism as he looked forward to the future.

"How come you never noticed the ring on my finger then?" asked Maureen, scolding Paul in a tease, as she had done in the past: to change the mood of either of them when they became morose because of their circumstances.

"You don't wear it all the time do you? I think I would have noticed it before if you had," said Paul defensively.

"No, I put it on this morning, as it happens. When we parted I wore it until my mother saw it; she made me put it away somewhere safe, as she knew my father would have done something nasty about it. It's a funny thing, but when I decided to come here to Appledore, I remembered the ring and, I don't know why, I decided to bring it; I didn't expect to see you down here. Although I must admit I did think about you when I was preparing for the journey. I suppose that's why I popped the ring in my purse. I only wear the ring when I am on my own. It something I associated with you, Paul, I couldn't wear it when I was with anyone else."

Paul squeezed Maureen's hand as she used the other hand to point to the bar ahead. The surf was pounding on the sand-spit as their vessel searched for the deep-water channel to take them out into the Bristol Channel proper, and Lundy. They were looking back at Appledore and the sweep of sand and dunes around to Westward Ho! – with those memories so bittersweet, with the yearning for fulfilment of body and soul. Paul looked over to the starboard side and could see Crow Point and Braunton Sands not too far off now, with Croyde Bay at the far end before Baggy Point. He remembered their excursion there, and the sadness attached to the occasion.

He was about to mention this to Maureen when she said, "Look Paul, we're going through the bar now. Isn't it exciting? Gosh! Remember the last time?"

The roar of the surf seemed powerfully exhilarating as the boat passed through the narrow gap in the middle.

"I've just thought of a canny idea," laughed Maureen. "Why don't we ask the captain of this ship to marry us?"